Lynsay Sands

What She Wants

AVON
An Imprint of HarperCollinsPublishers

AVON BOOKS
An Imprint of HarperCollins*Publishers*
10 East 53rd Street
New York, New York 10022-5299

Copyright © 2002 by Lynsay Sands
ISBN 978-0-06-202028-4
www.avonromance.com

First Avon Books mass market printing: May 2011

Avon Trademark Reg. U.S. Pat. Off. and in Other Countries, Marca Registrada, Hecho en U.S.A.
HarperCollins® is a registered trademark of HarperCollins Publishers.

Printed in the U.S.A.

10 9 8 7 6 5 4 3 2 1

For Helen and Mackenzie,
two of the sweetest Southern ladies I know.

Prologue

Her passage through the woods set the leaves atremble. Her childish laughter rang through the trees and the wind blew her hair out behind her in a golden stream. The sun covered her with kisses and the rain-damp earth squelched up between her toes, embracing her with each step.

Willa loved to run barefoot after a rain. However, if Eada or Papa found out about this, she knew there would be trouble. It was worth the risk.

She broke into a clearing and abruptly paused. Her laughter faded at once, the happiness slipping from her face. Something was wrong. It was so silent. Too silent. The birds had stopped singing and were motionless in the trees. Even the bugs had stopped buzzing. And she couldn't hear Luvena running in front of her anymore.

Her brow creased with worry as she peered slowly around the clearing.

"Luv?" she whispered, taking a tentative step forward. "Luv?"

A quiet rustle drew her head around. Something dropped from the small cliff near where she had entered the clearing. Cloth—golden as the sunlight—fluttered through the air like a chick tumbling from its nest. The bundle landed with an ominous thud.

Willa swallowed nervously. Her gaze slid slowly over the bright pile of gilded material on the ground. It was the gown Lord Sedgewick had brought back from London for her. The one Luvena had been so eager to wear.

Then she spied the small, motionless legs, in their fine new hose, peeking out from beneath the skirts. One of the soft slippers was missing. A hand lay half-curled in supplication amidst the material of the gown. Shiny red-gold tresses lay limp in the grass. Luvena's pale face was turned away, her head at an odd angle.

These images assaulted Willa one after the other like the threads of a tapestry that had yet to be created. By the time her brain had woven them together and understood their meaning, she had been screaming for several moments.

Chapter One

The door flew open, slamming into the cottage
with what would have been a crash if it had been
made of stronger material. Hugh had been about
to dismount, but paused to run a wary eye over
the old woman now watching him from the open
door.

Eada. She was very old, age bowing her shoulders and gnarling her hands and fingers. Her hair
was a long coarse cape of white around a face
puckered and wrinkled by the passage of years.
Only her cobalt eyes still held any hint of snapping youth. They also held a knowledge that was
unnerving.

*She can look into your eyes and see your soul, pick
out every flaw you possess, along with every grace. She
can read your future in the dregs of the wine you drink
and read your past in the lines on your face.*

Hugh had been told all of this and, still, a jolt
went through him as he looked into the eyes of

the old witch. He felt a shock run through his entire body, as if she truly were looking right into him. As if she could see all the way down to his presently curling toes. She held Hugh in thrall for a moment with just her eyes, then turned to walk into the hovel. She left the door open— undoubtedly an invitation for him to follow.

Hugh relaxed once she was out of sight, then glanced at the mounted man beside him: Lucan D'Amanieu, his friend and confidant for years. Hugh had rather hoped his companion would soothe the foolish superstitions suddenly rising within him. The old childhood beliefs in witches and haunts were all rattling to life in his suddenly fancy-filled mind, and he'd been counting on Lucan to arch one amused eyebrow and make some derisive comment that would put everything back into perspective. Unfortunately, it appeared his sensible friend was feeling rather fanciful himself today. Rather than soothe him, Lucan appeared nervous, himself.

"Think you she knows?" he asked.

Hugh gave a start at the question. It hadn't occurred to him that she might. He considered the possibility now, his gaze fixed on the hovel. "Nay," he said at last. "How could she?"

"Aye," Lucan agreed with less confidence as they dismounted. "How could she?"

The old woman was fussing over the fire when they entered the shack. It gave the two men an opportunity to survey their surroundings.

In contrast with the filthy and delapidated state of the outside of the cottage, the inside was clean and quite homey. Flowers sat in a wooden bowl in the center of a rough-hewn table at one end of the room, while a narrow cot was pressed up against the wall opposite. A fire was built into the wall across from the door, and it was here the woman stood stoking the flames. Once satisfied, she moved back to the table and collapsed upon one of the three chairs, then waved Hugh and Lucan to the others.

After a barely noticeable hesitation, Hugh took the seat opposite the woman, placing his back to the door. Lucan took the seat adjacent to her, leaving him a clear view of the door, should anyone enter. They then waited expectantly for the woman to ask their reason for coming. Instead, she took the wine flask from the center of the table and poured two mugs full. Ignoring Lucan, she pushed one to Hugh, then lifted the other to her mouth.

For want of anything better to do, Hugh drank. He was immediately sorry. The wine was bitter, scraping across his tongue. Doing his best not to show his distaste, he set the almost full tankard back on the table's worn surface. Hugh returned his gaze to the witch, still expecting questions regarding his presence, or at least his identity. The crone merely eyed him over the lip of her own mug, waiting. When the silence had grown long and tense, he finally spoke, "I am Hugh Dulonget."

"The fifth earl of Hillcrest."

He gave a start as she finished the introduction for him. "You know of my uncle's—?"

"Dead. Heart."

"I beg your pardon?" He stared at her nonplused.

"I said he's dead. His heart gave out on him," she repeated impatiently. "Ye'll succeed to his title and holdings."

"Aye. I am his nephew. His only heir."

"The only one, hmm?" Her tone was dry and had him shifting uncomfortably.

"Well . . . aye," he lied, squirming under her all-knowing gaze. He said, "Nay. Uncle Richard left a bequest for—"

"A bequest?" She seemed to look right through him.

Hugh picked up the wine, drinking from it almost desperately despite its bitter taste. Slamming the tankard down once it was empty, he straightened his shoulders and scowled. "Of course, you shall continue to receive coin for her care."

"Her?"

"The girl. This Willa person my uncle was so concerned with." He did not bother to hide his distaste for the matter.

"Coin for her care, hmm?"

Hugh swallowed and felt his discomfort increase. Her steady stare was disconcerting. He could almost believe that she *was* looking into his soul. If so, he suspected the flaws to be found were many. He doubted if there were many graces to be seen at the moment. After all, he was lying through his teeth.

"Do ye not mean she'll be well cared for once she marries you?"

Hugh went still. He could feel the blood rush

into his face with reawakened rage. That same rage had consumed him on first hearing this news from his uncle's solicitor. He'd inherited it all. The earldom, the money, the servants and estates ... as well as his uncle's bastard daughter to wed. In effect, he'd been willed a wife. Nothing more than a village bastard, raised by an old crone who had once served in the castle. It was one of the most asinine situations Hugh had ever imagined himself being forced into. He, a lord, the son of a great knight, and now the heir to an earldom, to marry some village brat! Not even a titled lady, but a *bastard* village brat with no more training than how to milk cows or whatever it was they trained village brats to do. Impossible. Inconceivable. But true. Now, as he had that morning, he felt his body cramp with fury. His hands clenched on the tabletop, aching to fit themselves around the crone's throat. That was when he heard the singing. It was a woman's voice, high and clear and as sweet as a tankard of meade on the hottest afternoon.

Everything seemed to slow; his anger, his thoughts, his very heartbeat all stilled in anticipation, even the room around him became motionless. Lucan and the hag sat unmoving. A fly he had absently noticed buzzing around his tankard landed on its lip and remained there as if listening to the voice as it drew nearer.

The door behind him opened, bathing the dim interior of the cottage in afternoon light, then something moved to block that light. The singing abruptly halted.

"Oh! We have guests."

Hugh heard Lucan's gasp. Wondering over it, he turned inexorably toward the source of the lovely voice. He felt his jaw slacken in shock.

An angel. Surely, that was what she was. Only an angel would glow golden, Hugh thought as he stared at the radiant outline of the female form. Then she stepped away from the door. She moved to the old woman's side and he saw that the golden glow had merely been the sunlight reflecting off her hair. And what a glory that was! Full, thick strands of pure gold.

Nay, not pure gold, he decided. Those tresses were brighter than gold and there were strands of red shot through them. Her hair was woven sunlight set afire. It blazed down over her shoulders and trailed past her hips to her knees. Hugh had never before beheld such a vision and was sure he never would again. At first, he was so transfixed by the sight, he noticed neither her face nor figure as she bent to press an affectionate kiss on the cheek of the old hag. Then she straightened. Her limpid gray eyes turned to him and his attention shifted, taking in their pale color and bold expression. His gaze dropped to the smile on her luscious lips and he found himself swallowing.

"You must be my betrothed."

Those words stopped Hugh cold. His admiration of her beauty became instead a grim perusal of the plain and patched gown she wore. The garment hung on her like a sack. She looked like a village girl, a pretty village girl perhaps, but a village girl just the same whereas he was a lord, above being bound to a simple female of such uncertain parentage. Marrying her was out of the question, though she would make a fetching mistress.

"Gold is gold whether buried deep in the mud or adorning a king's crown," the crone said.

Hugh frowned at the comment, annoyed at the suggestion that she'd known what he was thinking. He was even more annoyed at the meaning of her words, since he was positive they didn't apply here.

When he remained silent, the witch tilted her head to the side, considering him. She then reached up to clasp the hand at her shoulder, drawing the girl's attention. "We will need more garlic, child. For the trip."

Nodding, the chit collected a basket and left the cottage without making a sound.

"Ye'll marry her." It was a simple statement of fact.

Hugh turned sharply on the witch, but froze, eyes widening when he saw that she now held his empty mug. She was squinting at the dregs that had been left behind when he'd finished the drink. That knowledge sent a frisson of something akin to fear arcing up his spine. This woman was said to see the future in those dregs. In these uncertain times, Hugh did not think he wished to know what was yet to be. But whether he wished it or not, the woman read on.

"Ye'll marry her for yer people, but she'll quickly come to claim yer heart."

He sneered at this possibility, but the woman paid him little heed as she continued to stare into the tankard. "The future holds much joy, happiness and children aplenty . . . if ye solve the riddle."

"What riddle?" Lucan asked breathlessly and Hugh sneered at his being taking in by this trickery. When the woman merely raised dark eyes to stare at the other knight, he shifted and asked, "Well then, what if he does not solve the riddle?"

"Death awaits."

Hugh saw the conviction in her eyes and swallowed nervously. Then she sat back and waved an impatient hand. "Begone. I am weary and your presence annoys me."

The two men were more than happy to comply. They removed themselves from the dim cottage, and stepped out into the sunlight with relief.

"Well?" Lucan queried as they returned to their mounts.

Grim-faced, Hugh waited until he was back atop his mount to ask, "Well what?"

"Do you return on the morrow for her or no?"

"He'll return."

Head snapping around, Hugh glared at the old woman for eavesdropping, then angrily tugged on his reins, drawing his horse around before spurring him into a canter that left Lucan scrambling to mount and catch up to him.

Hugh had to slow down once he hit the trees; there was no true path to or from this cottage, which had made finding it an adventure. His decreased speed allowed Lucan to catch up to him. The moment he did, he again asked whether Hugh would marry the girl.

Hugh scowled at the question. His visit with

Lord Wynekyn and the solicitor had been short. Once he had heard the bit about his being expected to marry some by-blow named Willa, he had worked himself into a fine temper. After bellowing and stomping about a bit, he had headed for Hillcrest. Hugh had no desire to marry the girl. But he wasn't sure how he could get himself out of it. The way the solicitor had phrased it, he *had* to marry her in order to gain his inheritance. "I do not wish it, but fear I may have no choice if I want Hillcrest."

"Surely you cannot be denied Hillcrest," Lucan argued. " 'Tis yours by law of primogeniture. You are next in line. Whether you marry the girl or not, Hillcrest cannot be refused you."

Hugh perked up at this comment. "Aye. You are right."

"Aye. So what will you do with her?" Lucan asked and Hugh's posture deflated, along with his mood. "I do not know."

They were both silent, then Hugh said slowly, "I suppose I really have to see to her future. She *is* a relative after all."

"Aye," Lucan murmured. Then, when Hugh did not continue, he suggested tentatively, "Perhaps you could arrange a marriage for her. See her settled."

Hugh pondered that briefly, then gave a slow nod. "Aye. That might be just the thing. She may even have a fondness for someone of her own class."

"Aye. She may."

Relaxing a little, Hugh set his mind to accomplishing the task. He would have to work around the old woman, that was obvious. If the hag got wind of his idea, she would most likely put an end to it right quick and make trouble for him. He supposed that wouldn't be his responsibility. After all, the only thing he could do was *try* to see to the girl's future well-being. If the old woman wouldn't accept anything from him but marriage . . . well, she was going to be disappointed. It was just a shame if she made things harder on the girl than need be.

The melodious voice—high, clear, and angelic—came to him again moments later. Cocking his head, he turned it by degrees until he could tell from which direction the song came, and then he headed his horse toward it. Hugh came upon a clearing to find the sound sweet in the air, but no sign of the girl from whose lips it came.

Perplexed, he scanned the area more carefully. He spied her half-hidden in a crush of weeds. Rather than search out the garlic the old lady had sent her after, the girl lay in a tangle of weeds and flowers. She made dandelion chains as she sang. Hugh urged his horse forward, almost sorry when her song died mid-word and she sat up abruptly.

"She sent you for garlic. Is this how you obey your guardian?" Hugh asked. When she merely stared up at him in blank confusion, he shifted impatiently. "Answer me!"

"She has no need of garlic, my lord. I collected that yesterday."

"Mayhap she needed more. Why else did she ask you to fetch it?"

"She merely wished to speak to you alone."

Hugh accepted that news in silence. His gaze moved around the clearing and he began to frown. "'Tis not wise to wander about alone. You could be set upon. Then what would you do?"

"Wolfy and Fen would keep me safe."

His eyebrows rose, but he did not question her.

She tilted her head in a listening attitude before collecting her empty basket and getting to her feet. "I must return. She will want me now that you have left."

"Wait." Leaning down, Hugh caught her arm, then released her as if stung when she turned back in question. Shaking his head at his own reaction to her, he held his hand out. "I will take you back."

Willa did not hesitate, but promptly placed her fingers in his. For one moment, Hugh wondered at her placing her trust in him so easily. Then he reasoned that as far as she knew, he was her betrothed. Of course, she would trust him. The issue resolved in his mind, he lifted her up and settled her on the saddle before him, then adjusted his hold on the reins. Hugh turned the horse in a slow circle back the way he had come, aware that Lucan was following a discreet distance behind on his own mount.

"Who are Wilf and Fin?" he asked.

"Wolfy and Fen," she corrected, then added, "friends." The girl wiggled about a bit on the saddle in search of a more comfortable seat.

Hugh gritted his teeth against his body's natural

reaction as she rubbed against him, but continued determinedly with his questions. "Would you ever consider marrying either of them?"

That brought her head swinging around, her lovely golden tresses brushing across his face. Much to his chagrin, a burble of laughter burst from her lips. "Nay! My lord, that would be *quite* impossible."

Her sincere amusement at the idea brought a scowl to Hugh's face as she turned to face front. Unfortunately, though she turned away, her hair remained plastered across his face, caught in the stubble on his cheeks. He jerked his head backward to dislodge the soft tendrils, then considered his next question. While he was still curious about the Wolfy and Fen she had mentioned, Hugh was more concerned about resolving this situation in such a way that he would not have to marry her, yet would not have to feel guilty either.

"Is there anyone who holds a special place in your affections?" he asked at last.

"Of course."

Hugh went still, his hands tightening on the reins as hope rose at those easily confessed words. He hadn't expected to be so lucky. But if she held a *tendre* for someone, all he need do was to arrange for her to marry the fellow. He would then settle some money on the couple and his troubles would be over.

"Eada is like a mother to me," she said, bursting his bubble. "She is a wonderful woman. Very special."

Hugh rolled his eyes at that, finding it hard to

see anything special or wonderful about the hag.
But, in any case, the girl obviously hadn't understood his question. It seemed he would have to be
more specific. He should have expected that, of
course. She was an uneducated peasant, no doubt
simple-minded.

Willa shifted about on the saddle before him,
then gave her head a shake that sent several strands
of golden hair up to catch again on his unshaven
cheeks. Scrubbing one hand down his face as if
removing cobwebs caught there, Hugh thought
with some irritation that he should have taken the
time to bathe and shave before seeking out the
hag's cottage. He hadn't been in the mood for such
niceties at the time, however. After learning the
particulars of his inheritance, he had made the
two-day ride to Hillcrest with Lucan as company.
He had stopped at Hillcrest just long enough to
look around, ask a few questions, and get direc-
tions on where to find this Willa who had been left
to him. It was then that he had heard about the
hag, Eada. His uncle's men and servants had been
eager to warn him of her witchy ways, but less
happy to part with news of the girl the creature
was said to guard. From what he had seen, the de-
scriptions of the crone had been right on the mark,
he thought, recalling her spooky air.

Shaking the memory of her out of his head, he
turned his attention to the matter at hand. "I fear
you misunderstood me when I asked if there was
anyone who held a special place in your affections," he told her. "What I meant was, is there
any particular *man* for whom you have feelings?"

The question had her swiveling to peer at him and Hugh found himself once more with a face full of the soft golden strands. Those strands clung lovingly, forcing him to again remove them. They were driving him mad. It wasn't just the tickling sensation they caused, but the scent, as well. Her hair smelled like sunshine and lemons. Hugh had never before felt any attraction to the scent of lemons and sunshine, but coming from her head, the combination seemed delicious. Almost as delicious as the feel of her backside rubbing against his groin with every step his mount took. Why had he offered to give her a ride back to the cottage, he wondered with disgust. He had thought it a good opportunity to speak with her away from the hag, but he was finding her nearness terribly distracting at a time when he needed his wits about him.

"I am sorry, my lord. I misunderstood." She turned further to give him a contrite glance. The girl was, apparently, wholly unaware of the fact that the movement pressed her breasts against his chest and arm, and her butt firmly against his now growing manhood.

Hugh let his breath out in resignation. He had been semi-hard since he had first settled her on the saddle. Now he could have been a flag-bearer.

"Aye. Well," he said gruffly, wondering if she could feel what she was doing to him. "So . . . is there any particular man you have feelings for?"

Much to his relief, she shifted to face front again, easing his discomfort somewhat. Unfortunately, her answer wasn't quite as pleasing.

"Of course, my lord. You."

"Me?" Hugh's upper body went as stiff as his lower. "Surely you jest, girl? You have just met me. How could you claim an affection for me?"

"How could I not?" From the face she turned to him, he guessed that she was surprised by the very question. He puzzled over her answer even as he shifted behind her, vainly trying to put a little space between them. He wished with all his heart that she would simply sit still.

"You are to be my husband," she reasoned as if it were the simplest of concepts and one he should comprehend without need of explanation. " 'Tis my duty to love you. Papa explained this when he informed me of our betrothal when I was fifteen."

Hugh pulled his thoughts from his much-abused lower regions and gaped at her. "When you were fifteen?"

"Aye." She nodded. "Papa told me when he made his will. He felt 'twas best to inform me that he had made some plans in that regard, and to tell me a bit about you so that I would get used to the idea and understand my duty."

"I see," Hugh said shortly. "And I suppose 'twas not important for me to know of these plans? What if I had married in the meantime?"

Much to his relief, she shrugged and turned forward again. "I presume he would have arranged for me to marry someone else."

Hugh snorted. His uncle would have found it difficult to convince any other nobleman to marry the girl. No doubt his uncle had hoped Hugh would be so grateful to inherit Hillcrest and its estates that he would marry her out of gratitude. The old man had presumed too much.

Hugh, like most men of his station, had been pledged to a lady of equal standing while still in his infancy. It was just his bad luck that his own betrothed had died ere reaching marriageable age, else he would have been wed long ago. It was equally unfortunate that while she had died too young to have married him, she had also died after bad fortune had struck and his father had squandered what little wealth his family had possessed in his search for more. Those circumstances had made it difficult to arrange a second betrothal. Fate had changed matters, however. Hugh was now wealthier than he had ever hoped to be. He could not wait to be pursued by all those women who had let him know that his "circumstances" left him good for little more than stud service. Hugh would enjoy returning the insults they had thoughtlessly dished out over the years. He would turn them down, one and all, explaining that they were not virginal enough, as he was in a position to know firsthand.

The woman before him shifted again and Hugh sighed softly. She was a beautiful little bundle. Her smell was intoxicating, and the way she kept squirming against him was giving him ideas he just shouldn't have when he did not plan on marrying her. Hugh almost wished she were a lady. He would have married her then. He would have draped her in silks and jewels to accent her glowing beauty, then paraded her at court to flaunt her before all those lords and ladies who had sneered at him over the years. He allowed this fantasy to fill his mind: Escorting her to the table to dine with the king before all of court, presenting her to him, dancing with her, sharing his wine goblet with her, hand-feeding her luscious bits of succulent food. Then he would escort her back to their room where he would strip off all the jewelry and silk, lay her on the bed and proceed to nibble and lick his way from her delicate toes to her—

"Are all saddles this lumpy, my lord?" The question drew Hugh from his daydream to the realization that she was shifting again in an effort to find some comfort. "There appears to be some great hard thing poking me just here."

He felt something brush his thigh and glanced down. She was reaching between them, trying to find what was poking her. Hugh snatched at her hand with alarm and held it firmly.

"Er . . . saddles are not made for two," he said in a voice that came out entirely too husky. Realizing that they were nearing the clearing where the cottage was nestled and that he had yet to finish this conversation to his satisfaction, Hugh drew his horse to a halt.

"What are you doing?" Willa asked him with surprise when he dismounted.

"As you find the saddle uncomfortable, I thought we might walk the last little distance," he prevaricated. A glance over his shoulder showed that Lucan had paused a good distance back. He was waiting patiently.

"Oh." Smiling uncertainly, Willa allowed him to help her to the ground.

Hugh dallied about the job of tying his mount to a tree as he tried to think how to proceed with this discussion. He had never been much of a conversationalist. Battle had always been his game. There was not much need for eloquence on the field of war. Unfortunately, none of his battle skills would help here. Lacking in diplomacy as he was, Hugh decided he would have to rely on blunt honesty. He gave up fiddling with his horse's reins and turned to face her. "Is there no one you can think of whom you would desire to marry?"

"I am marrying you . . . am I not?"

Hugh avoided her now uncertain gaze. "Though my uncle wished that to be so, I fear 'tis not the best of ideas."

"You do not want me?" He could not resist glancing at her then, but immediately wished he had not. She resembled nothing more than a wounded puppy. Feeling guilt assault him, he quickly looked away again.

" 'Tis not that I do not want you," he began with discomfort, and nearly rolled his eyes. Wasn't that the truth? He did want her. Hell, he was still hard as a staff as he stood there. He just didn't want her to be his wife.

"Nay. You do not want me," she said unhappily and took a step back from him, looking suddenly pale and miserable.

It was amazing how yellow her face could look under all that golden glory, he thought guiltily. Hugh had never been one to bear up well under culpability. Feeling guilty made him extremely uncomfortable and unhappy and generally roused his anger, as it did now. This was none of his fault. He'd never even heard of the woman until two days ago. His uncle was the one who had gone about making promises he could not possibly keep. Which was probably why the bastard had up and died, leaving the problem in his lap, Hugh decided bitterly.

Frustration and anger churning within him, he scowled at the girl. "My uncle never should have told you that I would marry you without first speaking to me."

She didn't look any happier or more understanding after his comment. He straightened with determination. "It simply would not do. I am an earl now, while you are a simple village basta—" Hugh paused abruptly as he realized how he was insulting her, but it was too late. She'd already blanched and turned to flee. Hugh stopped her with a hand on her arm.

" 'Twas not well done of me. I apologize, but I'll not marry you. We simply would not suit. I will see to your future though. A dower and a match. I—"

"That will not be necessary. You need not trouble yourself so. I need nothing from you, my lord. Nothing at all." She turned to race out of the woods.

Hugh stood gaping after her. The girl's lack of gratitude took him aback. True, he was not marrying her himself, but it was no small thing he offered by promising a dower and a match. Yet she'd refused outright and there had been a hint of fire in that proud refusal. It seemed the cuddly kitten had claws, after all. Though she hadn't said a single hurtful thing, Hugh still felt he bore the sting of those claws on his conscience, if nowhere else. He simply could not allow her to refuse his aid. Her pride would have to be set aside. A woman without protection was terribly vulnerable and though he refused to marry her, he felt he owed it to his uncle to at least see that no harm befell her.

Hugh took a step forward, intending to follow her and pursue the matter, only to halt abruptly as the door to the cottage flew open and the hag appeared. She allowed the girl to rush past her, then took up a position in the center of the door frame, arms folded, body stiff, and glaring eyes fixed on Hugh. He had the distinct impression that she was ripping him to shreds in her mind. Then she jerked her head up in a dismissing gesture and whirled to stomp into the cottage. She pulled the door closed with a bang.

Chapter Two

"Well. That went well," Hugh muttered to himself with derision. Shaking his head, he turned and moved back to mount his horse. It was only a matter of moments before he reached Lucan.

"That did not take long," the other man commented as they headed back toward the keep.

"Nay."

"She seemed to take it rather well," he added. When Hugh turned a glare on him, Lucan shrugged, amusement tugging at his lips. "Well, at least she did not burst into tears and hysterics."

"Aye," Hugh agreed on a sigh. "There is that."

They rode in silence for a moment, then Lucan commented, "I noticed back at the field that she speaks well for a village brat."

Hugh frowned at the other man's words. He hadn't noticed, but, in retrospect, he realized that she *had* spoken well. She had the pronunciation and diction of a lady. That bothered him briefly, but then he shrugged it away. "Even the lowest-born serving wench can speak well if trained to do so."

"Aye. But then who trained her?"

"Not the hag. That is certain." Hugh really had no desire to think about the girl and the mess he had just made of rejecting her. He had wanted to be diplomatic and gentle. There had been no need to hurt her feelings. But he had botched the job horribly. Calling her a bastard to her face had been the action of a loutish ass, he thought with disgust. Then, because it was not in his nature to agonize over things that could not be undone, he reminded himself that, badly done or not, it *was* done. No matter how gently offered, rejection was painful. He knew that well from his experiences over the years since his father had lost the family fortune. He was sorry to have visited that pain on Willa, but the fault for it really lay with his diabolical dead uncle.

"The old bastard."

"What was that?" Lucan asked.

"Nothing. Let us hie back to Hillcrest ere the men drink all the ale."

"What does it say?" Willa asked unhappily. She paused to peer over Eada's shoulder. The woman who had been a mother to her for as long as she could recall had pressed a mug of wine on her the moment Willa had finished telling of Dulonget's rejection. Now, she sat reading the dregs at the bottom of the cup with concentration. Willa leaned closer to peer at the bits of sediment in the bottom of the mug, but could not make anything of the random shapes they seemed to form. She didn't understand how Eada could. But she did. And the old woman had always been right. Until now.

Eada had said that Willa would marry Hugh Dulonget and come to love him. She had said that they would have many children and much happiness. It now appeared that would not be the case. Not if he had any say in the matter.

Eada set the cup on the table with a shrug. "Same as ever. You shall marry the earl as the old earl wished."

Willa mulled over this revelation, trying to sort it out. She was quite sure that Hugh Dulonget truly had no intention of marrying her and could think of nothing that might change his mind. "Is it possible that Hugh may die and another become earl and marry me? Perhaps 'tis another I will love and—"

"Dulonget is the earl you will marry. The nodcock," Eada added under her breath. Willa heard the insult, but let it pass without comment. She was not feeling very charitable toward the man at the moment either. Despite her duty, she was finding it terribly difficult to love the arrogant lout. How dare he think her beneath him! As her betrothed it was as much his duty to love her as it was hers to love him. Yet he arrived here with his strong warrior's body and deep silky voice and announced that she was beneath him.

The clicking of Eada's tongue drew Willa from her thoughts. The old woman was examining the dregs of wine again. "Nay. He will not die. At least, not ere the wedding."

Willa stilled at this news. "What does that mean? He will die after we are wed? But you said—"

"There are forces at work here. Some possibilities are only now making themselves known," Eada explained calmly. "He'll marry ye, but how long he lives afterward depends on you."

"Me?"

"Aye. On whether ye give in immediately when he returns to announce his decision to marry ye, or whether ye wait."

"Wait? For what?"

"Ye must wait for him to crawl to ye on his belly."

Willa's eyes widened incredulously at this news. "Never. He shall never crawl on his belly to me or anyone else. He has too much pride."

"He'll crawl," Eada announced firmly. "And ye must not accept him to husband until he does, else ye'll lose him ere the next full moon."

"Ah, my lord. You are back."

Hugh halted in the keep doorway, eyes widening as he took in the tall, thin form of Lord Wynekyn, his uncle's friend and nearest neighbor. Realizing that he was standing there looking as taken aback as he felt, he forced himself to move again. Nodding politely in greeting to the man, he walked toward the table and the pitcher of ale waiting there. "A drink, Lord Wynekyn?"

"Aye, fine, that would do me well. Your servant offered me some when I first arrived, but I decided to await your return."

Nodding, Hugh began to pour three mugs of ale. "Your servant mentioned that you had gone to the cottage. How did you find Willa? She was pale and thin when last I saw her, but then she was suffering from shock and grief over the loss of your uncle."

Dark ale splashed onto the scarred surface of the wooden table as those words struck Hugh. Cursing his own clumsiness, he poured the last drink, then straightened slowly and turned to hold it out to Wynekyn.

"You know the girl?" he asked carefully as Lucan stepped forward to take the drink Hugh now pushed along the table in his direction.

"Oh, aye." Wynekyn smiled with gentle fondness. "I have known Lady Willa since her birth."

"I see." Hugh pursed his lips, wondering how to inform the proper old man he had no intention of marrying the chit. Wynekyn wouldn't approve, of course. After all, it had been the earl's dying wish. Hugh was still considering this when Lucan, who apparently had been paying more attention to Wynekyn's words than himself, murmured, "You refer to her as *Lady* Willa?"

"Aye. Did you not know she was of nobility?" Wynekyn appeared startled at the possibility.

"Nay. I thought—" Hugh's gaze slid to Lucan.

"Surely, you did not think your uncle would marry you to a village brat?" When Hugh flushed guiltily, Lord Wynekyn shook his head. "You should have known better." He frowned at them both briefly, then shrugged his irritation away and set his drink down as he asked, "I take it all is well and you have no objection to marrying her?"

Hugh trained his gaze on his ale as he set it down. "What if I did?"

"Well—" The man looked as affronted as if it were his own daughter Hugh would dare to refuse. "Well then, you would inherit the title and this castle by right of primogeniture, but Lady Willa and the wealth would go to another. That would be . . . Now, let me think . . ." Pausing, he lifted a finger to his chin, tilted his head upward and pondered the matter, wholly oblivious to Hugh's horror.

He would gain the title and estate but not the funds to run it? Dear God! Feeling dizzy, Hugh dropped weakly onto the bench. That was like giving a penniless man a horse, but no food to feed it. It was autumn; the crops had already been taken to market; the monies gained from them. He'd learned that on his arrival this morning, along with the fact that his uncle had fallen ill ere buying those extra provisions the castle inhabitants would need to keep body and soul together through the winter. Hugh hadn't been concerned at the time, thinking that he could tend to the matter soon enough. But that was when he'd thought the fat coffers in the storeroom were his. If he did not marry Willa, they were not.

Dear God! No wonder she'd rebuffed his offer of a dowry and claimed she needed nothing from him. She really did not. But he needed her, he realized faintly, then glanced up when Wynekyn gave an exclamation of success. "Ah, ha! I believe 'twould be your cousin, Jollivet."

"Speak of the devil!"

All three men turned at that high cheerful voice. A slim young man now stood in the great hall entrance. Shrugging under the weight of their surprised eyes, he grinned, then raised his hands to pose palms upward and finished, "And he shall surely appear."

"Speak of the devil indeed," Hugh grumbled.

"Ta ra, cuz." Jollivet breezed into the great hall, smiling widely at them all. "Heard the ghastly news about Uncle dear and flew here on my charger to present my suitably sad, solemn and sober demeanor." Pausing before them, he waved his arms expansively and struck another pose. "Ta da. Here I am."

"Sober indeed." Lucan hid a laugh behind his mug as he gulped some more of the ale.

Hugh grunted his agreement, then addressed his cousin. "Sit down, Jollivet, or better yet, go outside and chase the stable boy about. We are discussing business here."

"So I heard," he rejoined cheerfully. He poured himself a mug of ale, then moved to sit on the trestle table bench, annoyingly close to his irritated cousin. Ignoring the warrior's immediate scowl, he asked, "So? Why was my name being bandied about?"

"I was just telling Hugh—" Wynekyn began, only to be rudely interrupted.

"We were just discussing who should be invited to my wedding," Hugh lied, ignoring Wynekyn's sharp glance. He had no intention of letting his cousin ever sniff out the fact that there was a possibility of his marrying money. The man was a fop, purchasing clothes and jewels he could not afford to impress those at court. Were he to learn that marrying Willa would gain him riches beyond his wildest dreams, he would charm the gown right off her to see it done. And recalling her wounded expression earlier that day, Hugh suspected that Willa would be susceptible to such charm just now. In fact, there was a distinct possibility that she might refuse to marry him. Though he hadn't realized that his uncle had settled his wealth on the girl, she obviously had. She would know there were any number of lords who would overlook her questionable birth for her dowry. Her looks would not hurt, either.

"Wedding?" Jollivet looked stunned. "Who would marry you?"

"Lady Willa," Wynekyn answered.

"Lady none-of-your-concern," Hugh snapped at the same time, but Jollivet ignored him yet again.

"Lady Willa of what?"

"I am not at liberty to divulge that," Wynekyn said.

"Well, surely—" Jollivet began on a laugh, but Wynekyn shook his head firmly.

" 'Tis for her safety," the old man said solemnly.

Hugh left off frowning at his cousin and turned his glare on the older man instead. " 'Tis not safe for us to know even her name? If I am to marry the woman, surely I have a right to know her name?"

"Whether I agree with you on that count matters little, my lord, since I myself do not know her full name . . . And I am her godfather."

Jollivet gave a titter of laughter at that. "You do not know her full name? But you are her godfather. How perfectly delicious."

Hugh spared a moment to grimace his displeasure at his cousin, then asked Wynekyn, "Why would you agree to be her godfather when you did not even know her name?"

Wynekyn smiled. "You have met the girl. The first time I saw her she was just a babe. She was lovely as a princess even then. Big gray-blue eyes and little wisps of that glorious blond hair. Richard showed her off to me. He was as proud as a father, and probably not unlike yourself, I assumed she was his. When he lifted her up and turned her for me to see her, I vow she smiled right at me. When I put my finger out, she clutched it in one of her wee hands and gave a little chuckle." He shook his head slightly. "She stole my heart right then."

"You agreed to be her godfather because she clutched your finger and chuckled?" Jollivet gave a giggle and Wynekyn frowned at him.

"Nay. Hillcrest did not ask me to stand as her godfather until much later. After . . . *the incident*," he said.

"The incident?" Hugh asked.

"Aye. Your uncle was living at Claymorgan then. He had done so since he and your father had their falling out. Willa was about ten at the time. I was a regular visitor to Claymorgan and had become quite fond of the child. But that time I ran into

Richard at court and we rode back together. Since Claymorgan was on the way to my own estate, I stopped to rest a night or two ere continuing on home, but when we arrived we found the castle in an uproar. Richard had a cook whose daughter was about the same age as Willa, and the two were friends. They were missing. They had sneaked out of the castle—they were not allowed to play outside of the keep, you see. Anyway, they had apparently gone out to play. Their absence was discovered and half of Richard's guards were out seeking them. The other half were searching every corner of the castle itself."

"I take it they were found, all was well, and that was when my uncle asked you to be her godfather?" Jollivet guessed.

When he shook his head sadly, Hugh scowled. "Well, they must have been found, Wynekyn. Willa is here."

"Oh, aye. They found them," the older man agreed. "But all was not well. Eada had barely finished telling us they were missing when the men returned. The first man through the gates was cradling a dead girl in his arms and at first we thought it was Willa. I thought Richard would have an apoplexy when he saw them ride through the gates, but then as they drew closer we saw that 'twasn't Willa, 'twas the cook's daughter. Willa was huddled up against the second rider, silent and pale. I thought her dead, too, at first until they reached us and I saw that she was shivering madly."

"What had happened to the cook's daughter?" Hugh asked curiously.

"Her neck was broken," he announced bluntly. Wynekyn allowed a moment for his words to sink in before continuing. "According to Willa, they were playing chase. Cook's daughter, Luvena, was a good distance ahead. Willa chased after her into a clearing just as the lass fell from above. She thought the girl must have tried to climb a small cliff to hide from her and fallen. Willa was terribly distraught. Luvena was like a sister to her."

A brief silence filled the room; then Wynekyn went on, "'Twas shortly after that incident that Richard asked me to be Willa's godfather. I had always assumed, like yourself, that she was simply a bastard child of his, but he set me straight on the matter. He assured me that she was neither a bastard nor his own. She had been placed into his keeping, willed to him in effect, which was why he named her Willa. And he had vowed to protect her with his very life. He loved her as his own. Of course, I could not refuse. She was such a charming little thing, all curly golden hair and enchanting smiles."

A soft chuckle slipped from his lips. "It seemed every time I came to visit her here, she was chasing about with Wolfy and Fen, charging after the birds." He sighed, his eyes gone soft with memory; then he frowned. "She never played with other children, however. She never made friends with another child again. I—"

"Just a minute," Hugh interrupted. "When did Uncle Richard and Willa move here from Claymorgan?"

"Oh, dear. I am sorry. I forgot to tell you that

part, did I not?" Wynekyn clucked and shook his head with mild self-disgust. "After the murder, he decided Willa would be safer here and—"

"Murder?" Jollivet cried shrilly. "What murder?"

Wynekyn was growing impatient with the constant interruptions. "I am sure I told you that. The cook's daughter."

"The cook's daughter? Murdered?" Hugh questioned. When Wynekyn nodded, he protested, "But you said she broke her neck in a fall."

"Aye. Well, that was what we assumed at first. But though the girl's neck was broken, we decided 'twas not from a fall. There were bruises on the child's arm as if she'd been grabbed roughly. There were also marks at the base of her neck, and red marks on her chin as if someone had grabbed her face and jerked it to the side and up. Richard thought, and I had to concur, that someone had broken her neck deliberately."

"Why would someone have killed the cook's daughter?" Lucan asked with confusion.

"He would have thought Luvena was Willa," Wynekyn explained patiently. "Cook's daughter was a fair-haired child and she and Willa had traded gowns that day. The mistake would have been an easy one to make." He shrugged. "At any rate, 'twas Luvena's death that persuaded Richard Willa was no longer safe at Claymorgan."

"Safe from what?" Jollivet asked with fascination. "Whom did he think was trying to harm Willa?"

Wynekyn shook his head. "I do not know. He

never explained that to me. He only said that 'twas a very powerful man and that she was at terrible risk." Wynekyn grew silent, his expression thoughtful then he glanced at them. "Richard took great pains to keep her safe. He had Willa and Eada smuggled out of Claymorgan in the dead of night and brought to the cottage here at Hillcrest. Three of his most trusted and skilled warriors were sent with them. Alsneta, the cook, was brought here to the castle. Everyone but the men who had found the girls was told that Willa had died and that Richard could not bear to remain at Claymorgan with the memories of the child he'd loved as a daughter. The men themselves were sworn to secrecy. Fortunately, the ones who found Willa that day were Richard's most trustworthy soldiers."

Standing, he paced a few steps before adding, "Richard did not just place Willa in the most remote part of this estate. Once he had moved here himself, he not only refused to allow her entrance to the castle, he would not even allow himself to visit her for the first five years." He shook his head, his bewilderment showing. "She missed him terribly, of course, but still their separation was harder on him, I think. He adored the child. He wrote her letters every day. For five years that was the only contact the two had with each other. Letters and small gifts to her from him, and messages and small gifts she sent back. Your uncle also grilled the messenger every night on his return. I witnessed this on several such occasions. Richard would ask what Willa was doing, how her health was, how she had played that day, every word she had said." He smiled faintly at the memory. "I was questioned myself every time I stopped to visit on my way here. He was quite upset about her refusal to make any more friends. That troubled him greatly, but he . . . we . . . none of us had any idea how to make her feel safe to have friends again."

"You mentioned that before," Lucan said. "Why did she refuse to have friends after Luvena?"

"We never understood why, ourselves, until Eada explained it. Willa apparently overheard Richard and me talking about the child's death and our suspicion that she'd been murdered. After that, she refused to have playmates again lest someone else be accidentally killed in her place."

Hugh muttered something unpleasant under his breath and Wynekyn nodded.

"Aye. It made a lonely childhood for her, I think. She allowed only the old witch, her guards, Richard and myself close to her. Her only playmates were the animals."

"So Wilf and Fin are the guards my uncle sent with her. What happened to the third one?"

Wynekyn glanced at Hugh in confusion. "What?"

"Wilf and Fin. They are her guards?"

"Oh." He gave a slight laugh. "You mean Wolfy and Fen. Nay. Baldulf is her guard."

"You said she had three guards," Jollivet pointed out.

"Aye. She did. Howel and Ilbert were also her guards. But Richard's steward died some five years after the move here. Howel was the only man he trusted to take over the position, and since nothing had happened in all those years to suggest that Willa was still in danger, he called Howel back to be his new steward here. That is also when he finally allowed himself to see Willa again, though their meetings were always clandestine."

"What happened to Ilbert?" Lucan asked when Wynekyn fell silent.

"He died a year ago." When that announcement brought sharp glances from all three men, he quickly added, " 'Twas of natural causes. He fell ill. A fever. That left just Baldulf to guard her. Richard debated sending another man down to replace Ilbert, but decided against it in the end. There seemed little need."

"So where is this Baldulf now?" Lucan asked.

"And who are Wilf and Fin?" Hugh asked irritably.

"Wolfy and Fen?" Wynekyn murmured, apparently deciding to answer Hugh's question first. "Are they still about? Goodness I would have thought they would have moved on ages ago."

"Who *are* they?" Hugh repeated.

"Wolves."

"Wolves!" all three men exclaimed at the same time, expressions horrified. Wynekyn grimaced slightly.

"Aye, I reacted much the same way myself when they first appeared. It seems Wolfy got caught in a snare . . . Or was it Fen? I cannot remember now. Oh well, no matter. One of the beasts got caught in

a hunter's snare. Willa found him halfway through
the job of biting his—or her—own foot off. She
somehow managed to get him undone and tended
his injury, then fed him or her and the mate.
Wolves mate for life, you understand, so she knew
the mate would not be far away. The injured one
was so weak, it could not travel for a bit and she
fed and tended the beast until it mended. After
that, the wolves stuck around. I guess even a wolf
knows a good thing when it comes across it, hmm?"

Hugh and Lucan exchanged a grimace at that.
Neither of them had recognized Willa for "a good
thing" as they should have. As even a wolf was
smart enough to do.

They were all silent for a moment, then Wynekyn cleared his throat, straightened his shoulders
and raised his eyebrows questioningly. "So, when
is the wedding to be?"

Hugh knew they were all waiting for his answer, but his thoughts were in a bit of a muddle.
He stood and began to pace. He would have liked
to have said right away. Unfortunately, he very
much feared that was not a likelihood. He suspected he would have to make some reparations
before Willa would agree to marry him, and he
didn't have any idea how long that would take.
Oh, how quickly the mighty had fallen. Two days
ago he was a poor knight. Then for a few glorious
days he had believed himself a rich earl.

And hadn't he strutted as arrogantly as any of
those women who had rejected him for his pov-
erty? he thought with self-disgust. Now he was a

poor earl and it did not seem any more glamorous than being a poor knight. In fact, it seemed worse to him at that moment. As a poor earl. . . . His gaze slid over the servants moving busily about. Dear God.

Chapter Three

"My lord?" Wynekyn prompted.

Clearing his throat, Hugh moved back to sit on the bench again. He picked up his ale to avoid meeting the older man's gaze. "A week or so should do."

"A week or so?" Wynekyn looked amazed. "But Richard wanted the deed done as soon as he died. He—"

"Nay. That is out of the question."

"Why?"

When Hugh sat silent, helpless to come up with an acceptable excuse without revealing his own blunder, Lucan smoothly intervened.

"Hillcrest has only just died. The poor girl is still grieving, as is Hugh himself. Surely 'tis not too much to allow two or three weeks to pass first? At the very least, it would allow them some time to prepare for the ceremony and the feast to follow."

"Ah." Much to Hugh's relief, Wynekyn looked

less appalled. "I had not thought of that. Perhaps a short delay would not be amiss," he allowed.

"Aye," Hugh murmured and looked down into his drink, pondering his situation as the conversation drifted around him. His immediate urge was to go speak to Willa now and attempt to repair the damage he'd done. However, he was thinking that allowing some time for her anger to ebb might be the better idea. How long would that take, he wondered. He was guessing two or three months might do it, but knew he didn't have that kind of time.

"What do you think, Hugh?"

Pulled from his thoughts, he glanced up blankly. "What?"

"Lord Wynekyn was just suggesting that perhaps Lady Willa and the hag ... er ... Eada," Lucan quickly corrected himself. "That perhaps we should move them up to the castle in the meantime."

Alarm immediately coursed through Hugh. With Willa here in the castle, both Wynekyn and Jollivet were sure to realize there was something wrong between them. He was reluctant to allow that. He would prefer the opportunity to ... well ... he supposed he would have to woo her now. He berated himself for the idiot he was. If he'd stayed to hear all the particulars of his uncle's will in the first place, instead of storming out and muddling things with his arrogant announcement that she was beneath him. ...

Odd how she suddenly wasn't beneath him anymore, he thought with self-derision. She was the same woman she'd been but hours ago and yet suddenly she was a suitable wife. And it wasn't just the wealth which she had and he needed, but also the fact that Wynekyn assured him she was a lady by birth. Odd the difference a word could make. The old hag's comment came to him then. *Gold is gold whether buried deep in the mud or adorning a king's crown.* Damn the witch! She'd been right, of course. Willa was a lady whether in a castle or a hovel, and he should have recognized that. As Lucan had pointed out, she spoke well. She also carried herself with the bearing and pride of a lady despite her sacklike clothes and bare feet. And, he realized now, she'd sat straight before him on his horse, moving with the animal with a natural grace rather than slapping about on his back like a sack of turnips. She'd been taught to ride, he was sure. But he'd missed all these signs and assumed she was a by-blow of his uncle. He was an idiot.

"Hugh?"

"What" he asked, his irritation at himself showing in his tone. Then, realizing that they were awaiting his response to the suggestion that Willa and the witch be brought to the castle, he frowned. "Nay. She'll not be brought to the castle. My uncle thought it unsafe. She remains where she is until the wedding."

Wynekyn pursed his lips thoughtfully over that, but he was shaking his head even as he did. "I do not know. The moment we start making preparations for the wedding, I believe she will be at risk. Would it not be easier to keep her safe here than in that hovel?"

"Uncle Richard thought not."

"Richard counted on the fact that everyone thought her dead. 'Tis why he sent her to live in the cottage with Eada, if you will recall."

Hugh shrugged impatiently, then distracted the man by asking, "Wynekyn, how can I marry the girl, when I do not know her name? The wedding contract must bear a name."

"Well, surely the girl knows her own name." Lucan peered at the older man in query.

"Nay. I do not think she does, and that is a problem, of course. Richard said that he would leave a letter explaining all on his death. But I have yet to find it."

" 'Tis missing?"

"Nay. Well, I hope not. I did look for it after his death, but there was very little time. I had to ride to court and inform the king, and. . . ." He shrugged. "I shall search again now that I am returned. I am sure it will show up."

Hugh noticed that he did not look as certain as his words suggested.

"In fact," the old man said, "I think I shall go take another look now. Perhaps you should ride back to the cottage and inform Willa that the wedding will take place in two weeks and ask her where she would prefer to stay. I really think that she might be safer here. I also think that the wedding would be better performed right away, but first we do need the letter from Richard, explaining all and giving her name."

Taking Hugh's dull silence for acquiescence, he left the three younger men alone and headed for the stairs to the upper level.

"Well." Lucan moved to sit on the trestle-table bench on Hugh's other side. "What do you intend to do now?"

Hugh grimaced at the question. "What indeed?"

"About what?" Jollivet asked, reminding them of his presence.

Hugh scowled at his cousin, then straightened as a thought occurred to him. "Jollivet, you spend a lot of time at court. You know what women like."

When Jollivet arched one eyebrow, Hugh scowled. "I said you know what women like, not that you cared about it or even liked women, themselves."

Jollivet gave a short burst of laughter. "You do insist on seeing me in the most unpleasant light." He shook his head. "Now why do you mention my courtly manners and knowledge of the fairer sex?"

Hugh hesitated, then began haltingly. "Well, imagine you had insulted a lady at court. Called her a . . . well . . . say a . . . bastard."

He paused as Jollivet gasped. "You did not?"

"I did not say I had. I said *you* had," Hugh snarled, flushing guiltily.

"I never would!" Jollivet said firmly.

"Well, say you had!"

"Nay, I could not."

"Dammit! Just say you *had*."

Jollivet tsk tsked impatiently. "Very well . . . but I never would," he added just as his cousin opened his mouth to speak again. Hugh paused then and the two had a small glaring war. Hugh was the first to give in.

"As I was saying," he got out between clenched teeth. "Say you *had*. How would you make reparations and win her hand in marriage?"

"Impossible."

"Impossible?"

"Aye. 'Tis impossible. She would never forgive you."

"Dammit!" Hugh bellowed, lunging to his feet. It was Lucan who touched his arm in a calming gesture and leaned past him to peer at a smirking Jollivet.

"But you could try, could you not?"

"Aye. But it would never work."

When Hugh tensed again, Lucan said, "Aye, but how would you try?"

Jollivet heaved a melodramatic sigh at the question and tipped his head to stare thoughtfully upward for a moment . . . several moments. Just when Hugh was sure he would lunge for the man's throat, the thoughtful look cleared. Jollivet brightened and thrust one finger up in a victorious gesture. "Ah ha!"

"Ah ha? Ah ha what?"

"Poetry," he said with satisfaction. "An ode to her beauty."

"Nay."

Jollivet scowled at Hugh's abrupt refusal. "Nay? You ask for my aid then nay-say my suggestions?"

"I do not write poetry. I was never tutored in it." He shuddered at the very thought of performing such a task.

Jollivet relented. "Nay. I suppose you would be

hopeless at poetry. You would probably say something like she was more lovely than your trustworthy steed."

"She is," Hugh said defensively. "What is wrong with that?"

"God's teeth," Jollivet breathed, then began thinking again.

The silence drew out. Hugh could almost feel the first of many gray hairs making its appearance on his head. He was so startled when Jollivet suddenly gave another exclamation, he nearly jumped in his seat.

"Ah ha!"

"Ah ha what?"

"Flowers."

"Flowers?" Hugh asked dubiously. It was fall. The only things still growing were weeds.

"Aye. Flowers. The finest you can find. And little gifts to immortalize—oh wait! This is perfect!"

"What is?" Hugh asked warily.

"Lord Cecil insulted Lady Petty at court by refusing to partner her in a dance when her father suggested it. Then, he found he needed her favor to sway the queen to a cause of his. Lady Petty is a good friend of the queen's, you see? Anyway, he painted a picture portraying her as Venus, the goddess of love. Cecil sent it to her with a letter claiming her beauty was such that he had feared making a fool of himself, hence his refusal. It worked beautifully, of course. She was quite undone by his passionate claims."

Hugh nodded his head slowly in understanding, then shook it. "I do not paint."

Jollivet threw up his hands in exasperation. "No poetry! No painting! What are you trained in?"

"I am a warrior," Hugh snarled. "I was trained in battle."

"Oh, brilliant," Jollivet said. "You can protect her. That is a useless skill."

Hugh had to agree that it was, indeed, useless in this instance.

The three of them sat in glum contemplation for several moments, then Lucan perked up. "Perhaps that is the answer."

"What?" The other two men asked.

"He can protect her."

"Protect her?" Jollivet asked dubiously.

"Of course I can protect her," Hugh said irritably. "How does that help me."

But Lucan ignored him, turning excited eyes to Jollivet. "We shall draft a letter, apologizing and stating that Hugh has seen the error of his ways. We shall present it to her and Hugh can sit outside the cottage on his destrier, sword in hand, guarding her to prove his devotion. Enough of that may soften her."

"Hmmm. Perhaps." Jollivet sounded doubtful.

"*Enough* of that?" Hugh queried, not looking too certain himself. "How long must I sit there?"

"Until she softens enough to come speak to you."

Hugh didn't bother to hide his alarm. He had little experience of women other than camp followers, but if Willa were anything like his mother, it would take until hell froze over for her to forgive his calling her a bastard and saying she was beneath him. On the other hand, it wasn't as if he had any better suggestions.

"An hour or two ought to do it," Lucan assured him. "Little enough trouble to regain the wealth to sustain this place and Claymorgan."

"What is he doing now?"

Eada straightened from peering through the cracked door and glanced around. "He's still sitting his steed . . . guarding ye."

"Guarding me from what? The rain?" Willa asked impatiently and quit her fretful pacing to peer at the woman. "Perhaps I should go tell him 'aye.' He shall catch his death sitting out there in the pouring rain."

Turning away before her wrinkled face could bloom into the amused smile threatening to eclipse it, Eada peeked out to where Hugh Dulonget sat his mount in the drizzling rain that had started shortly after his arrival that morning. Erect and stern-faced, he held a lance in one hand and a sword in the other, apparently prepared to battle the elements to prove his devotion. He appeared completely oblivious to the rain weeping on his hair, running down his face and dripping onto his armor-clad chest. Both he and his mount were unmoving and could have been a stone statue.

Eada was sure he must be cold, wet and miserable, yet he'd remained there since the break of dawn that morning. That was when a knock at the door had drawn them from their sleep. Eada had waved Willa away when she'd scrambled to answer it, and had gone to the door herself. She'd found herself confronting the same man who had accompanied Dulonget the day before. He'd not been alone. Lucan had been attended by a smaller, more colorful fellow who had tried to peer past her into the cottage. Scowling at him, Eada had done her best to block his view, then had turned her attention to Dulonget's friend. He'd started to pass a scroll to her, only to pause and ask if either she or "the girl" could read, or if he should read it to them.

Willa had suddenly appeared at her side, snatching the scroll from his surprised hand, saying, "Thank you, my lord. I am able to read."

Eada had closed the door on the men's startled faces. When Willa had read the scroll aloud, the vow to stand guard over her loveliness sounded almost poetic. For a moment, Eada had feared she intended to rush out and accept the offer. However, Willa had merely opened the door to peer out at the mounted man in the clearing.

Eada had barely glimpsed him before Willa closed the door and turned to ask, "You are sure he will die if I accept before he crawls?"

Eada had nodded, wondering if perhaps Willa's pride had not been pinched by Dulonget's refusal. She was normally the most sensitive of creatures, hating the thought of any man or beast suffering in the least. Despite her question, however, she had not seemed overly distressed by the sight of Dulonget sitting his steed in the pouring rain.

Dawn had been many long hours ago. Dusk was falling now and the man still kept his post. His demeanor was as staunch as it had first been, despite the fact that the rain had increased in violence with the passing of time. It now poured over him like a waterfall. There was no doubt in Eada's mind that he must be terribly uncomfortable, but none of that showed in his expression.

"Stupid man!" Willa snapped impatiently, moving toward the door. "He shall catch a chill and die from this."

"Perhaps," Eada agreed calmly. "But he'll surely die if ye go out there and accept him ere he crawls."

Willa paused with her hand on the door, then turned back in frustration. "Well, what if he does not crawl?"

"He'll crawl."

Willa scowled at her confident claim. "When?"

"When the time is right." Eada was not surprised by the flash of frustration on the girl's face. Nor was she surprised when it disappeared just as quickly as it had appeared and a calm facade covered the struggle taking place in her. Willa had learned young to control herself and her emotions. When a girl had everything taken away from her, she learned to control the only thing she could. Herself. And in her short life, Willa had lost everything there was to lose. Her mother. A father. Her friends. Her home. Even the man who had been like a father to her . . . twice; first during those years right after they had moved to the cottage, then most recently to death's icy grip.

On top of that, she'd lost her childhood far too early. The veil of innocence had been ripped away with Luvena's death, casting the responsibility for the very survival of others onto her slender childish shoulders. Willa had grown up aware that someone wanted her dead. She'd shunned the company of other children so as not to endanger anyone else. She had grown up in the company of adults . . . and her animals. Her upbringing had made her a mass of contradictions in some ways. She could be the most biddable of people one moment, and incredibly stubborn the next. She was sad and lonely due to her self-imposed solitary state, yet by nature full of optimism and a love of life. Willa was also wise beyond her years in some matters and terribly naive in others. She appeared soft, but was as hard and strong as the Toledo steel now so much in demand for swords. She was, in Eada's considered opinion, an amazing young woman. Worthy of a king. Certainly more than worthy of an earl, and Eada had no doubt that Dulonget would eventually come to see that. Oh, he was showing interest now, but she knew this sudden turn around was most likely due to his discovery that the will left her the wealth. In time, however, he would discover that her worth was more than that of a couple coffers of gold and jewels. The question was whether he would discover her value in time to save his life, or on the moment of his death, when it would be too late to do anything about it.

"I am to bed."

Eada felt herself relax at that abrupt announcement from her charge. It was early to go to bed, but it had been a long, dreary day, the rain trapping them inside the small airless cottage with only the immobile Dulonget outside to look at. She hoped the morrow brought sunshine and some relief from this nerve-wracking boredom, else she feared the soft-hearted girl might accept his offer ere it was safe to do so.

Blinking against the rain, Hugh turned his eyes miserably toward the cottage. A small sigh escaped him when he saw the flickering candlelight that had been spilling from the window blink out. This was absolutely the very worst idea that Lucan had ever had, he decided. And he himself had once again proven his stupidity by agreeing to it. It just went to show how dealing with the fairer sex rattled him, he thought. Hugh had never felt very comfortable around women. They were all so small and delicate. He tended to feel big and clumsy around them, like a colossal giant bumbling about in a tiny room filled with breakables.

Men were different. A man could thump another man on the back and he would laugh and thump you in return. Try that sort of affectionate greeting on a woman and she would most likely fall to her knees with a cry of pain. And women did not like to relax by exchanging war stories over a pitcher of ale. What was a man suppose to say to them? All they ever seemed interested in hearing was how lovely they looked, or what a pretty gown they wore.

Hugh tended to avoid women because of that. He felt like a tongue-tied fool around them, which raised his ire and made his speech short and harsh in their presence, as he had been when he'd come upon Willa singing in the field. He hadn't given a good hoot what she was doing or that she hadn't been collecting garlic as she'd been instructed, yet he'd snarled at her like an ogre. It was not the first time he'd allowed his discomfort around women to make him act an ass. That kind of reaction on his part was the reason he'd hired a bride-seeker to approach various ladies at court about the possibility of a marital alliance with him. Better to hire someone who would not drive them away with harsh tones and harsher words.

Unfortunately, the responses to his proposals had been upsetting, to say the least. Each one of the "biddable virgins" his man had approached had responded that while she found Hugh quite handsome and knew him to be a skilled warrior, an alliance of marriage was out of the question due to his impoverished circumstances. However, almost every single one of them had hinted that another, less proper association would not be out of the question. Hugh had accepted this news with an apparently unconcerned grunt, but inside he'd felt like something was shriveling up and dying. He knew it was to be expected, but having his value equated with his wealth and title, or lack thereof, had left him feeling like a warrior standing alone on a battlefield with an entire army lined up against him. He'd felt small and overwhelmed.

Thinking about that now as he sat his mount alone in the dark and rain, however, he supposed he had made a lucky escape from those ladies. What man wanted such a woman to wife? Her husband would be an unsuspecting cuckold before he ever married, with chicken or goat blood secretly spilled in the wedding bed to falsely prove the bride's purity.

Considering that, Hugh admitted that his brief determination to flaunt his newfound title and supposed wealth had been a rather petty and childish response to his hurt. He was now even more ashamed of his rejection of Willa. He'd treated her no better than those ladies had treated him. Which was why he still sat his mount, stiff and cold in the dark and pouring rain, he supposed. And why he would stay there through the night. It was a penance of sorts. One he felt he deserved. He just hoped it would soften Willa so that she would listen to the apology he owed her ... before the rain and chill killed him.

Chapter Four

The rain stopped just as dawn crept across the sky. Hugh was too wet and weary at that point to care. He'd actually begun to doze off in the saddle when the whistling caught his ear. Straightening in the saddle, he cocked his head, listening for the source of the cheerful sound. It was only then that he caught the accompanying clip clop of a horse. Hand moving to the sword resting at his side, he urged his mount to the center of the clearing, putting himself between the cottage and the man who now rode out of the woods.

Judging from the sudden alarm on the newcomer's face as he drew his horse to a halt on the edge of the clearing, Hugh's presence came as something of a shock to him. The stranger's appearance was no less of a surprise to Hugh. The man was older than he by a good twenty years, and though he was dressed as a peasant, there was no mistaking him for anything but a soldier. He was well-muscled

and his horse was definitely a quality beast. The
stranger's response was telling as well. After that
first moment of shock, the man's gaze slid over
Hugh, his weapons, his horse, then the peaceful
cottage behind him. He appeared to relax a bit,
but Hugh didn't miss the way the man's right
hand dropped to rest on one of several sacks that
hung from his saddle horn. Deciding the sack
looked long and slender enough to hide a sword,
Hugh decided to get the introductions over with
quickly.

"Baldulf?"

"Whom have I the pleasure of speaking to?"

Hugh didn't miss the fact that the man had
neatly avoided answering his query. It didn't really
matter; there had been a flash of surprise in his eyes
before he covered it. It was enough to tell Hugh he'd
guessed correctly.

"Hugh Dulonget, lord of Claymorgan and earl
of Hillcrest." Despite his cramped and complaining muscles, Hugh managed to sit a little straighter
in the saddle as he made that announcement. It
was the first time he'd used his new titles and he
almost winced at the pride evident in his own
voice as he claimed them.

The other man let his hand slide away from the
sack. He gave a nod in lieu of a bow as he road
forward until they were side by side. "Aye. I am
Baldulf. 'Tis an honor to meet you, my lord. Has
there been trouble?"

"You could say that," Hugh said dryly.

Panic promptly entered the soldier's expression
and he cursed volubly. "I knew I should not have

left, but Willa insisted she needed black cloth for proper mourning. Of course, there was not any in the village so I had to—was she harmed?" he interrupted himself to ask. "Your presence here tells me she still lives, but—"

"She is fine," Hugh assured him, realizing that his self-deprecating comment had alarmed the man unnecessarily. "I did not mean that any physical harm had befallen the girl."

Baldulf's eyebrows flew up at this news. "Then what harm has she come to?"

Hugh was reluctant to admit he had insulted the chit by calling her a bastard and refusing to marry her. However, he had no doubt the man would eventually hear the news from Eada, if not Willa herself. He decided it was best to get the matter over with himself.

"I fear when I first arrived, I was less than pleased to find myself willed a wife."

The man nodded sympathetically at this news. "I am sure that came as something of a surprise."

"Aye." He grimaced. "In my . . . er . . . surprise, I was perhaps less than diplomatic on first meeting Lady Willa." Hugh winced inwardly at his own understatement.

Baldulf was a sharp man. After eyeing him consideringly, he asked, "How much is less than diplomatic?"

"I called her a bastard and refused to marry her." The words tumbled out of his mouth like those of a boy at confession. Recognizing the ire rising in the other's man eyes, Hugh felt resignation fill him. Really, war was so much easier than this marriage and relationship business. "I have since apologized, of course."

"Well, I should hope so!" Baldulf's tone was rather disrespectful, not at all the proper manner for a knight to take with his new lord, but Hugh felt it behooved him to let the matter slide for the time being. He even allowed the man to glare at him for several moments before straightening and glaring back. Recalled to their positions, Baldulf let his eyes drop and glanced toward the cottage before clearing his throat and saying in much milder tones, "You appear to be soaked through, my lord. Have you been out here long?"

"Since yester morn."

"Ah." He nodded slowly. "If, as you claim, there has been no attack, might I ask why you have stood guard out here so long?"

That was something Hugh had asked himself several times through the long rainy day and night. "I am attempting to persuade Lady Willa to marry me."

Baldulf nodded, then asked in extremely respectful tones, "By sitting outside the cottage on your horse?"

"I am guarding her to show her my devotion," Hugh said stiffly. He felt foolish even saying the words. Seeing amusement fill the other man's face, he added, " 'Twas not my idea. My cousin and a friend of mine thought it might soften Willa's anger if I vowed to stand guard over her beauty until she accepted my—are you laughing?"

Baldulf covered his mouth with his hand and made coughing sounds, then thumped his chest as he shook his head. "Nay, my lord. I have a . . . er . . . something caught in my throat." He turned his head away, alternately coughing and snuffling.

Hugh harrumphed irritably and waited for the fit to pass. The moment the man regained control of himself and turned a solemn face back, he speared him with a glance. "Knowing her as well as you do, perhaps you could suggest a more useful approach?"

Humor promptly returned to the soldier's face, deepening the lines that time had etched on his harsh features. Hugh noticed that it wasn't very sympathetic amusement.

"Well now, that would be difficult to say, my lord. She is not like most ladies." His gaze shifted past Hugh, his voice becoming distracted. "You might try gifts. Little trinkets and such. My wife always enjoyed those. By your leave, my lord."

Much to Hugh's amazement, Baldulf urged his mount forward and was away around the side of the cottage without awaiting the leave he'd requested. Hugh glared after him in frustration, wondering if perhaps he did not have a commanding enough demeanor. First, the hag treated him as though she were the queen and he a common peasant. Now, one of his own new soldiers rode off ere he'd finished talking to him.

He'd had several questions for the man besides how to please Willa. Hugh had spent a good hour that first night after Wynekyn had explained things questioning the former guard, Howel. Unfortunately, the man who now served as seneschal at Hillcrest appeared to know no more than Wynekyn himself. Regarding some things, he knew even less. It was doubtful that Baldulf would know any more than Howel, but still—

He was still glaring at the spot where man and horse had disappeared when he heard Lucan and Jollivet approaching. Their words and laughter were audible several minutes before they actually broke into the clearing. They were obviously making no effort at stealth as they rode through the woods. Ignoring his stiff and sore bones, Hugh slicked back his still damp hair and sat up straight in the saddle. Grim-faced, he awaited their arrival. At that moment, he was torn between wanting to take his sword to the pair, and wanting to take his lance to them. Then again, taking his fists to them sounded attractive, too. They were, after all, the source of the misery he'd withstood all night and was still suffering.

"Good morn!" Lucan called as he broke from the trees on horseback.

He looked well-rested and damned cheerful, Hugh thought with disgust as his friend rode toward him. When he growled something in the way of a greeting, Lucan raised an eyebrow and quickly unfastened a bag from his saddle pommel.

"We brought you something with which to break your fast." He offered the bag with a winning smile.

Hugh's response was to grunt and snatch the bag like a hungry dog snapping up a bone. Even as he began to tug the bag open, he caught the glance his friend exchanged with Jollivet, who had urged his own horse to Hugh's other side. The two men flanked him.

"Actually, we did not expect you to still be here. It rained last night." Jollivet made the announcement as if that fact might have slipped Hugh's notice. Fortunately for his cousin, Hugh was too hungry to waste time knocking the idiot off his horse as instinct urged him to do. He satisfied himself with a stinging look and a dry, "I noticed," then continued rooting inside the bag.

Lucan winced. "Surely you did not stay out here in the rain? All night?"

"What else was I to do?" he snarled, pulling out a hunk of bread and a skin of ale. "You wrote in that damned letter of yours that I would remain here until she accepted my suit . . . or some such nonsense. I signed the damned thing. I am a man of my word."

Lucan grimaced at that. "Er . . . aye. Perhaps that was not the brightest of ideas. My apologies, Hugh. I take it she has yet to accept your suit?"

Hugh's baleful expression was answer enough as he chewed on the dry bread.

"Well, perhaps she shall relent after seeing that you have spent the entire night in the rain guarding her."

"She was not moved to relent after I spent all of yesterday in the rain. Why should a little darkness make a difference?" he growled, then took the ale-skin Lucan now handed him and lifted it to his mouth.

"Perhaps Jollivet and I can come up with something to convince her." He paused as Hugh nearly choked on the ale he was downing. Pulling the ale skin away from his mouth, he turned hot eyes on his friend.

"I shall thank you and Jollivet not to help me anymore."

Lucan bit his lip and glanced away. "Well, did you come up with anything on your own whilst sitting here last night?"

Hugh's expression was answer enough, but he said, "Nay. She has done no more than peek out the door at me. I assume she is still angry about my calling her a bastard. I suppose saying she was beneath me did not help either." He sighed. "If I could but figure out how best to apologize . . . what she would accept."

"Did you try flowers?" Jollivet piped up. "I did tell you that women are partial to them. They—"

"Perhaps," Lucan interrupted when Hugh started to growl deep in his throat at his cousin's suggestion, "perhaps someone who knew her better would know best how to please her."

Hugh gave up glaring at the younger man to nod his agreement with that suggestion. "I did consider that. In fact, I asked Baldulf for suggestions."

"Baldulf?" Lucan straightened with interest. "Has the missing guard returned then?"

"Aye. But moments ago. He left just before you rode up."

"Did he say where he had been?" Lucan asked as Hugh took another gulp of ale.

"I gather he was seeking black cloth for Willa to make a mourning gown."

"What did Baldulf suggest?" Jollivet asked curiously.

"He said she was unlike other women," he answered glumly. "He did say his own wife liked gifts and trinkets."

A small silence reigned as Hugh ate; then Lucan shifted, his gaze sliding to the cottage. "It occurs to me that perhaps the hag would have a suggestion or two that may be of more use."

Hugh's stomach roiled at the suggestion, but he considered the idea and found he could not argue it. The old woman *did* know Willa better than any of them. Which was unfortunate, really. He wasn't pleased at the idea of having to ask the witch for anything. She'd not seemed to think much of him from the beginning and would hardly feel any more charitable toward him now that he had dared to insult her baby chick.

He would have to approach her, he supposed, but managed to put the task off for a few moments by asking, "How went your inquiries yesterday?"

Hugh had agreed to this ridiculous suggestion of standing guard out of sheer desperation. But he'd not left his men idle while at the task. After his fruitless questioning of Howel, he'd told Lucan and Jollivet to go to the village and ask around. He'd also sent several men to Claymorgan to question the villagers, peasants and servants there about Willa's birth and Luvena's death. Someone must know something that would be of use.

"Not well," Lucan admitted apologetically. "'Twas a long time ago and 'twas not even here that most of the things we were asking about took place. Perhaps the men will have more luck at Claymorgan."

"The hag might know something useful," Jollivet suggested.

"Hmmm." Hugh grimaced. Then he heaved a sigh and handed his half-eaten food to Jollivet before dismounting. He had to question the woman sooner or later, and the prospect was ruining his appetite anyway. Perhaps if he got it over with he could finish his meal in peace.

A day and night in the rain and damp had made themselves known. Hugh barely restrained a groan as his legs, back and buttocks complained at the shift of position. His legs—which had first ached, then gone numb shortly after dusk the night before—nearly collapsed under his weight. He was forced to hold onto his saddle for several moments. Once he was sure he would not fall, Hugh turned and moved stiffly toward the cottage door.

The old witch opened the door almost before he knocked, making him suspect that she'd been spying on them and noted his approach. He refused to believe she had "seen" it in some unnatural, witchy way.

"What are you doing here?" she barked before Hugh could offer anything in the way of a polite greeting.

"I—"

"I thought that you had vowed to guard Willa until she accepted your suit?"

"Aye. I—"

"Well then, what the devil are you still doing here? You should be off guarding her."

"Off guarding her?" Hugh exclaimed. "Is she not here?"

"Nay. She left several minutes ago."

"What?" he thundered, then peered into the gloomy cottage behind her, unwilling to believe what she said. The chit had to be here. How could she have left without his seeing her? He was guarding her, for God's sake!

"Aye. Oh, she'll be alright," the hag continued, noting the alarm replacing his surprise. "Baldulf saw her go and followed. But, I must say, considering your vow, it does seem rather sloppy of you to be sitting here while she is traipsing about with Baldulf and those beasties of hers."

Cursing, Hugh whirled to make a run for his horse, his aches and pains forgotten.

" 'Tis fine, Baldulf. Better than fine." Willa rubbed her cheek against the soft black material he'd just presented to her. When she'd sent him in search of cloth for a mourning gown, Willa had fully expected Baldulf to bring back material of the same coarse quality she had worn for years in her guise as peasant. But the cloth she now held was the finest ebony silk, soft and shiny.

"It befits a lady to wear silk," the old man said gruffly as he took back the cloth. He wound it clumsily into a ball and stuffed it back in the sack hanging from his saddle. Willa winced at his cavalier treatment of the delicate cloth, but refrained from comment.

"You must honor Lord Hillcrest with the fine black gown of a lady," he announced firmly, once the material was stored safely away. They began to walk along the path again.

Willa smiled sadly, but merely nodded. She had been pleased when Eada had looked around from her position at the door to announce that Baldulf had returned. After dressing, Willa had looked out for herself and found him talking to Hugh. With the new lord's back to her while the two men spoke, it had been little trouble for her to slide outside, offer the older soldier a silent nod of greeting, and slip around the cottage into the woods. She'd known even as the forest swallowed her that Baldulf would follow. The only uncertainty in her mind had been whether he would bring Hugh with him. Willa had been grateful when he'd ridden up alone and dismounted to join her.

"He was asking me how to please you."

"Was he?"

"Aye. He wishes to soften your heart so you will marry him."

"What did you say?"

Baldulf shrugged. "That you were not like other women, but that my wife liked trinkets."

Willa smiled slightly at that, then said, "Eada says he must crawl to me on his stomach ere I relent and marry him, else he will die."

She glanced over to see the doubt on Baldulf's face as he said, "I have never known Eada to be wrong. Yet I do find it difficult to imagine Dulonget crawling for anyone. Or anything for that matter."

"Aye." Willa frowned. "He is too proud to crawl. But Eada says he will, and I must await that or see him dead ere the next full moon."

"Hmmm." He looked as troubled as she felt at this news.

They continued in silence until the path came out at the river's edge. Willa picked a comfortable spot and settled in the high grass. She began digging meat out of the basket she'd brought with her as Baldulf saw to his horse.

"For Wolfy and Fen?" he asked as he settled himself on a nearby rock. It was his usual spot when they came here, allowing him to survey the surrounding area and watch for possible attackers. Despite the intervening years without trouble, Baldulf had never given up his vigilance in guarding her. In fact, that vigilance had made it difficult for Eada and Willa to convince him to go in search of the mourning cloth they needed. They had managed to do so only after promising Willa would never stray far from the cottage, whether Wolfy and Fen were with her or not.

"What will you do about the beasties?" he asked as he watched her divide the meat into two separate piles.

Willa made a face at the question. It was one she had been asking herself repeatedly since Hillcrest's death. Wolves were pack animals who hunted as a group. Wolfy and Fen's pack had either abandoned them, or simply disbanded, when the male was injured. Only Fen had remained with her mate. Hunting alone, she could not bring down the larger animals, such as deer. She had been reduced to chasing down rabbits and other smaller creatures. Knowing that a lone wolf had trouble finding enough food for herself, let alone for an injured mate, Willa had started supplying meat for them. She had kept Wolfy in the cabin the first several nights, taking food out and leaving it at the edge of the clearing for his mate to find. At first she hadn't seen the animal. Willa had known she was there only by her baying in the evenings, Wolfy's weak attempts to respond, and the fact that the food was always gone in the morning.

Once Wolfy had recovered enough to show an aggressive desire to get out of the cabin, Willa had let him go. However, she'd continued to leave food at the edge of the woods. The two wolves had stuck around, accepting her offerings as Wolfy healed. Willa supposed she'd expected them to leave once the male was completely well again, but they had stayed. The pair had shown themselves to her more and more until one day she'd fallen asleep in this spot by the river and woke to find Wolfy lying not far away and Fen down at the river's edge, lapping up the cool water. The moment she had moved, both animals had slunk off into the woods. But they came around again and again, getting closer, staying longer, accepting her more and more until now they seemed to have adopted her.

As affectionate and doglike as they had become, Willa never made the mistake of forgetting that they were wild animals. And that was part of the problem. As Lady Hillcrest, she would have to move from the little cottage that had sheltered her for so long. But she could not take the wolves to the castle with her. Their very presence so close to so many strangers could endanger both themselves and the castle inhabitants. She could not risk that.

On the other hand, they had been part of her life for several years now, and had proven themselves to be as protective of her as she was of them. She supposed that they had adopted her into their pack. Willa was not at all certain that they might not follow her to the castle and attempt to establish a lair near by, where they might be in danger from hunters.

"You cannot take them with you," Baldulf said.

Despite the fact that Willa had been thinking the exact same thing, she scowled.

"Ah. I think perhaps I should take the cloth to Eada now and then see to settling my horse."

Willa glanced up in amazement at Baldulf as he stood and moved toward his mount. Other than this last necessary trip, the man never left her side unless she was safely inside the cottage. She could not believe that he would simply leave her there in the glen alone. It wasn't that she feared attack, but she did not know what to make of his odd behavior.

It was the way he gazed narrowly over her shoulder as he mounted that drew her own glance around. The sight of Dulonget riding swiftly up the path was not completely unexpected. Willa had known the man would eventually discover her absence and seek her out. After all, he was supposed to be "guarding her." Willa was just surprised at how quickly he had discovered her absence and set out in pursuit. And that was probably the reason behind the sudden alarm coursing through her veins, she assured herself. It had nothing to do with the fact that he might ask her to wed him, and she would be forced to say "nay" or see him die. Willa found it difficult to say nay most of the time. She did not like to hurt or disappoint people in general, but saying nay to Hugh . . . well, that was—

Alarming. Willa had been assured five years ago that Hugh Dulonget would become the next earl of Hillcrest and that she would be his lady wife. She had lived with that certainty about her like a cape protecting her from the wind. She had wrapped that truth around herself at night and slept cuddled in its warmth. She'd allowed it to color her dreams of the future and used it to shield her from nightmares. Over time he'd become her white knight. The man who would keep her safe from harm, give her children to hold to her breast and who, in turn, would clasp her to his own heart during those long dark nights when the wolves howled without end.

Perhaps she'd built him up too much in her mind. In her fantasies he'd been tall and strong with flowing blond hair, a silver suit of armor that reflected the sun, and a fine white charger. He was gallant and kind and gentle and—

The drumming of his mount's hooves pulled Willa from her thoughts and she focused on him clearly, the reality replacing the dream man. He'd removed his helmet at some point during the night and his hair now flowed around his head in

the breeze as he approached. It was not quite the
golden glory of her dreams. In fact, it was more a
dirty blond, almost more brown than blond, but
the sun picked up traces of pure gold in its depths
as his hair whipped about his face. As for the armor, Hugh's was more tarnished and dented than
that of her fantasies, but it did shine as the sun
struck it. And that face . . .

Willa's dream man had been faceless all these
years. She'd had no idea what he looked like. Now
she knew and was not displeased. It was perhaps
not a classically handsome face with aquiline features and flawless skin. This man had a rugged
face, his skin tanned from being so much out of
doors. His flesh bore several small scars from bat-
tles past. One creased his chin nearly dead-center,
looking more like a dimple than a scar. Another
split his right eyebrow, leaving a small, white,
hairless separation. A third graced his cheek, em-
phasizing his cheekbone. None of them was dis-
figuring, but together with his clear blue eyes,
slightly crooked nose and firm lips, they made up
an interesting face. A strong face full of character
that became almost beautiful when he smiled. His
face pleased her. As did the rest of him. As he'd
been in her dreams, he was tall and strong with
muscular arms and legs. He even rode a white
charger. Well, a mostly white charger. There was a
splotch of gray on its side, but the saddle all but
hid that from view.

All in all, Hugh Dulonget was the white knight
of her dreams. He was even, in her estimation,

kind and gentle. She was sure another man might have sent a servant to rid himself of an unwanted betrothed, but he'd come personally. He had even seemed truly pained to tell her that he did not wish to marry her. Of course, that had been before he'd learned that she was not the bastard child of a village woman, as he'd assumed, and that the coin had been left as her dower.

Were she the impractical sort, Willa might be wounded that his interest in her was spurred by the wealth he would gain when he married her. But she was not the impractical sort. Marriages were made in such a way. One partner brought wealth, the other title, and together they made up the whole of the estate. Such was the way of the world. And she was aware that while she'd had five years to become acquainted with the idea, her existence and the expectation that he would make her his bride had come as something of a shock to Hugh Dulonget. It was her task to see that he adjusted smoothly to this new future. And she wanted to perform her duty. That was the problem. She wanted to say "Aye" but could not until he crawled to her.

She glanced back at Baldulf, intending to stay him with a word. She was too late; he was already urging his horse into a canter. She would have to face Dulonget alone. And be strong. It was for his own good.

Her gaze slid over his body again as he rode, taking in the way the muscles of his legs flexed and bunched around the belly of his horse. Willa swallowed thickly. This was not a good idea. Truly, she should just avoid the man as much as possible until he crawled to her.

With that thought firmly in mind, she leapt to her feet.

Chapter Five

Willa was about to make a break for the woods when it struck her that such an action was most likely not behavior befitting a lady. That thought made her pause and the opportunity was lost. Realizing that Hugh was now too close for her to be able to evade him, she promptly turned back toward the river. She dropped to her seated position, forcing herself to appear relaxed as she awaited him. Appearances aside, however, Willa was not relaxed. She was as tense as Wolfy or Fen at the approach of strangers. She was painfully aware of the drum of his horse's hooves as he approached, the creak of leather as he dismounted, and the quiet sounds of his tying his mount to a nearby tree. Then there was a shuffling she could not identify. She gathered from the direction of the sounds that he was moving about in the area just beyond the tree where he'd tied his horse, but could not think what he would be doing. She was also reluctant to turn and look. As foolish as it might seem, she was afraid that one glimpse of her face might show him her lack of resolve, encouraging him to press his suit. It would be better if she ignored him entirely. Willa tensed as she heard the soft sound of his approach through the tall grass.

By a sheer effort of will, she managed not to start or shift nervously away when he settled on the grass beside her. They were both silent for a moment, Willa afraid to peer about at him, he apparently at a loss as to what to say to her. Then a rather sad fistful of flowers was suddenly shoved in front of her face. She blinked at the limp white blooms, then glanced at his face, but he wasn't looking at her. Hugh was staring fixedly at the river coursing by before them, his face flushed red with embarrassment.

"Er . . ." was all Willa could manage. For want of anything else to do, she took the pathetic little bouquet from his hand and stared at it. It explained what he'd been doing in the woods just now. He'd been plucking flowers for her.

"They are flowers," he announced. Apparently her lost expression made him think she didn't know what she held.

In actuality, they weren't really flowers. They were weeds, and half-dead weeds at that, but she wasn't going to say so. Besides, she supposed it was the thought that counted. And it had been a terribly sweet thought, she decided as she felt tears sting her eyes. No one had ever picked flowers for her before.

"They smelled good, so I thought I would pick you some," he added, his voice gruff. Willa ducked her head, aware that he was now peering at her.

"Jollivet said that women liked men to pick them flowers." He was beginning to sound a bit defensive, she noticed, so she gave a quick nod of agreement in the hopes of reassuring him. She wasn't sure, but he seemed to relax a bit. At least his thigh and arm suddenly brushed against her as if he had released them from a stiff stance. Then she heard him heave out a breath.

"I am not good at courting," he confided. "I have spent more time in battle than at court."

Willa managed another nod and buried her face in the limp flowers, inhaling their odd fragrance with a wrinkled nose.

He continued, "Now Jollivet, he spends lots of time at court. No doubt he would know just what to say to please you . . . or at least what to say to please your guard, since he prefers men to women."

Willa glanced up sharply at that added thought. He was again staring out over the water, but now his nose was twitching slightly.

"What is that smell?" His gaze dropped suddenly and landed on the two piles of meat she'd set out. A perplexed expression covered his face, only to clear a moment later. "Oh. For those wolves of yours. I suppose—"

He sat up so abruptly that Willa stiffened in concern. Then he was suddenly on his feet and urging her up as well. "Come. I must see you back to the cottage."

"To the cottage?" Willa echoed in bewilderment as she found herself hurried to his horse. He tossed her up on the beast.

"Aye. There is something I must do and—" He paused, reins in hand, and frowned. "But I vowed to guard you until—" He shook his head. "Baldulf will take my place briefly, but I shall return to guard you the moment my task is finished," he assured her as if she might be concerned about that. Then he was up on the horse behind her and urging it back up the path to the cottage.

Willa spent the ride in a confused silence. She was as bewildered by his sudden excitement and urgency as she was by her body's reaction to being near him. She had the decidedly unsettling urge to melt into him. Every muscle in her body seemed to be aching to wilt into his embrace. It was only through stiff determination that she managed not to do so. Even worse was the slightly breathless response she was having to the sight of his hands clasped before her. They firmly gripped the reins, occasionally unintentionally brushing the undersides of her breasts as they rode. Each touch set up a maelstrom inside her. It was a great relief when they reached the clearing and he slid from the saddle to help her dismount. He did not leave her right away, but marched her to the cottage and pushed the door open.

Eada had the new black cloth spread out on the table. Baldulf was sharpening his sword by the fire. Both of them glanced up in surprise at their entrance. That surprise only deepened when Hugh urged Willa to take a seat at the table, ordered Baldulf to keep an eye on her, then turned and left as quickly as he'd entered.

The three of them stared after him curiously for a moment; then the patter of rain on the roof returned. As if it were a cue, Baldulf shrugged and went back to his sword sharpening. Eada bent to her measuring once more. Willa's gaze slid affectionately from one to the other; then she stood and went to help Eada with the gown.

They managed to measure and cut the cloth as the rain poured. Willa would have helped Eada sew, but she had long ago proven herself useless with a needle, so Eada waved her away. With nothing else to do, Willa began to pace. It was a relief to all of them when the rain stopped and Baldulf suggested that he accompany her on a walk. Willa donned a cape, fetched some more meat for Wolfy and Fen, and moved to wait by the door. Baldulf's joints always pained him when it rained and so he was slower than normal. She watched him wince as he tried to pull on his boots, then frowned and glanced outside, immensely relieved when she spotted Hugh riding back into the clearing.

"Never mind, Baldulf," she said as she watched Hugh's friend Lucan approach and hail him. "Hugh is back and as he has pledged to guard me, there is no need for you to trouble with it."

" 'Twould have been no trouble," the older man lied through his teeth, but that was answer enough for Willa. He was content to stay by the fire in the hope that it would warm his old bones and ease his suffering. She flashed him a smile, then opened the door and slipped outside.

Pausing in the center of the clearing, Hugh turned his horse and waited a tad impatiently for Lucan to reach him. He had spent the last two hours traipsing through the rain, then crawling through the mud in search of the prize presently hanging in a sack from his saddle. He was eager to see if it pleased Willa.

"What news?" he asked as soon as Lucan had reined in facing him. "Surely the men are not returned from Claymorgan yet?"

"Nay." Lucan shook his head. "I do not expect them until later this evening at the earliest. If they should return before that I would wonder whether they had time to make the inquiries they were sent to ask."

Hugh nodded in agreement and arched an eyebrow. "Then what brings you out here now?"

Lucan promptly unhooked a sack from his saddle and held it out. "I was restless so I brought you more food. You did not finish your meal this morn."

"My thanks, friend." Hugh accepted the sack and opened it eagerly. He hadn't realized it until just that moment, but he was famished. The scent of roasted meat wafted out and nearly sent him into a swoon.

"You also did not have the chance to ask the hag what might please Willa this morning," Lucan went on as Hugh began to gnaw on a chicken leg. "So I did."

Hugh stopped chewing, and glanced up. "Did you?"

"Aye." Lucan looked rather pleased with himself. "And she suggested that the best way to please Willa is to please those she loves. I thought she meant herself at first, but she said no, the wolves. I think she is underestimating her own place in Willa's affections. The girl seems to bear great love for the woman and doing something nice for the old hag would, no doubt, please her well. But so would doing something for the wolves, I think. Why are you smiling?"

Hugh shook his head, but his smile widened even as he did. "Because that also occurred to me while I was sitting with Willa by the river."

"What did?"

"That doing something nice for her wolves would please her. And I have that something nice right here." He happily patted the sack hanging from his own pommel, then bit off another chunk of meat, chewing it with true enjoyment.

"What—?" Lucan began, only to pause. His gaze narrowed and his mouth turned down in a frown as something beyond Hugh's shoulder caught his attention. "Uh . . . you had best . . ."

Following his pointing finger, Hugh peered toward the cottage just in time to see Willa disappear into the woods behind it. Alone. Cursing, he shoved yet another unfinished meal at Lucan and grabbed up his reins to go after her.

Willa was aware that Lucan had seen her and would no doubt alert Hugh. She fully expected him to come after her. She even wanted him to. She didn't wish Baldulf or Eada to worry. But she also didn't wish to spend any more time with Hugh at the moment. She found his presence disquieting, to say the least. To avoid his unsettling company, she broke into a run the moment she hit the woods, then shimmied up the first likely looking tree. Willa just managed to settle herself in its upper branches before Hugh rode past under her. She watched him go, knowing that he would search high and low for her ere thinking to revisit the cottage to see if she had returned. By her guess she had perhaps half an hour or so to relax ere she would have to go back to prevent his alarming Eada and Baldulf.

Willa waited several moments after Dulonget was out of sight before scrambling back down to the forest floor. She then struck out to the side, making a new path through the trees. She knew she had succeeded in throwing Hugh off her trail when Wolfy and Fen suddenly slunk from the woods to join her. The two wolves might have formed an attachment to her, but they were not friendly toward other human beings. They would not have joined her if anyone but Baldulf were nearby. Not that they were ever far away. They simply tended to melt into the surrounding underbrush and wait until they felt comfortable approaching. Even Eada's presence was enough to send them skulking into the trees.

Smiling at the beasts, she ruffled the fur on Wolfy's head, then scratched behind Fen's ear as she walked along. The animals brushed up against her legs in return, almost as if petting her back with their bodies.

Despite this more roundabout and difficult new path, it wasn't long before they came out at the edge of the river. Willa walked alongside it until she reached the spot where she had earlier left the meat for Wolfy and Fen. As she had expected, the meat was gone. She praised the animals, then retrieved the small cloth-covered bit of meat she had stuffed in her pocket before leaving the cottage. She divided it equally, then set it out for the two bright-eyed beasts and retreated to the rock Baldulf had sat on earlier.

Wolfy and Fen waited patiently until she was settled, then approached the meat she had brought them. Willa hadn't brought much this time. Just a snack really, and it was gone swiftly. Once they had finished eating, both animals settled on their stomachs to lick their paws clean.

Willa watched them, a soft smile curving her lips, then leaned back on her hands and let her head loll backward. The breeze was dancing across her body and blowing her hair gently about. It was soothing and she felt the stress of the last two days dropping away. Then, the drum of hooves made her stiffen. She straightened to glance around a bit wildly as Hugh broke from the trees and trotted toward her.

The fact that neither Wolfy nor Fen—who both had much keener hearing than she—had given a warning of his approach mystified her. Up until now they had only accepted Eada and Baldulf. Her confusion deepened when she realized that not only had they not warned her of Hugh's approach, but they had slunk off, leaving her alone.

"There you are."

"Aye. Here I am." She got warily to her feet as he dismounted. Willa wasn't at all sure how he would react to her deliberately running off. He did appear to have something of a temper and she suspected he would not care for her disobeying him. He hadn't actually ordered her not to leave the cottage unattended, but it had been implied.

However, Hugh didn't appear to be angry when he removed the sack from his saddle pommel and turned to approach her. In fact, she thought he looked rather pleased with himself.

"Where are Wolfy and Fen?"

Willa blinked. That question was the last one she'd expected of him and it took her a moment to find the correct response.

"Well, they . . . er . . . they were here a minute ago. No doubt they are still around." She glanced toward the woods rather vaguely, then turned back to eye him suspiciously. "Why?"

He grinned. "Because I brought them a gift."

"A gift?" Curiosity drew Willa forward to peer into the sack he opened for her. At first, all she could make out was a bundle of soft looking gray brown fur. Then, as her eyes adjusted to the dim interior of the sack, she could distinguish features such as long ears and whiskers. "A rabbit?"

"Aye."

She glanced up to see his pleased grin and then, unexpectedly touched at his thoughtfulness, looked down into the sack again. "That was very kind of you, my lord. I—'Tis alive!"

He nodded eagerly. "Aye. And I cannot tell you what a difficult feat that was. I have hunted before, but never with the object of bringing the animal back alive."

"But—" She stared at him in horror. "Why alive?"

He seemed surprised at the question. "Why, because Wolfy and Fen will enjoy the hunt. It was seeing the meat you had set out for them that gave me the idea. No doubt they have missed the thrill of the hunt."

Willa shook her head. "Pray, excuse me, my lord. Are you saying that you intend for them to hunt this poor animal?"

Finally appearing to recognize that she was not pleased with this gift, Hugh frowned. " 'Tis what wolves do. They hunt. They chase and hunt and bring their prey to ground."

"When necessary, aye," Willa agreed. "But I feed them. I—"

"Aye. But this is their nature." He shook the bag slightly and it began to move as the rabbit kicked about inside. "They are probably missing the thrill of the chase."

She frowned at that and did wonder briefly if she were not somehow hampering Wolfy and Fen by removing their need to hunt. She'd begun feeding them out of necessity, but had continued because . . . well, she supposed she'd been treating them as pets when she knew they were not. Which had caused a bit of a problem now that she would be moving to the castle and, in effect, abandoning them. Then the rabbit began kicking desperately inside the sack and her gaze was drawn down to it. The animal's nose was twitching frantically, its eyes almost rolling in its head as it kicked futilely against the cloth around it.

Hampering Wolfy and Fen or not, Willa could not watch them rend this poor little creature to pieces. Bringing them raw meat that Baldulf had butchered somewhere out behind the stable was one thing. Watching them tear apart a living rabbit was quite another.

"Call Wolfy and Fen," Hugh suggested and Willa sucked in a breath of air.

"Nay!" she cried. Then Willa impulsively snatched the sack from a startled Hugh and made a run for the woods.

She heard his surprised shout, then a curse and knew he would be after her on horseback in a moment, but she wasn't concerned. Willa knew the woods around here intimately. It was a simple matter to lose him.

The arrival of Wolfy and Fen on either side of her once again assured Willa that she'd lost Hugh. It also presented a new problem. She could hardly let the rabbit go with them about. After a brief hesitation, she turned her steps toward the cottage and wound her way swiftly back home. She made sure to come out behind the stable rather than the cottage itself, in case Hugh was already watching for her there.

Much to Willa's relief, Wolfy and Fen were not overly concerned with the sack she carried, or its contents. They were content to drop back and let her slip out of the woods on her own. Willa made straight for the stable. Sliding inside, she left the door open so she could see what she was doing. She'd just let the rabbit loose in a small pen when someone stepped into the doorway, blocking the light.

Willa wasn't at all surprised to turn and find Hugh glaring at her.

"You—" he began, then paused abruptly as his eyes adjusted to the dimmer interior and he had a clearer view of his surroundings. The stable was actually larger than the cottage itself. The first half was taken up with four stalls, two on either side of the building. Three of them held horses: Willa's, Baldulf's and a third horse that was used when they needed to take the cart. The fourth and final stall had no gate to keep a horse in. It held a chair, a pallet and Baldulf's personal effects. Willa saw surprise cross Hugh's face as he spied this. It was followed quickly by respect as he recognized the depth of the old soldier's loyalty.

Willa found herself almost relieved when his gaze moved on to the second half of the stables. This was where the cart should have been housed, but what space there had been for that was now taken up with several small cages and pens, leaving the cart to sit out in the elements.

Willa watched his gaze move over the pens and cages, saw his eyes narrow as he caught sight of a falcon that sat eyeing him with disdain.

"That falcon is missing a wing," he observed. When Willa remained silent, he moved further into the stable. He looked more closely into some of the other cages. "And this thrush has only one foot."

He turned slowly, his gaze moving over animal after animal. Willa glanced around with him, seeing what he saw. A building full of animals. Some were missing body parts vital to their survival in the wild. Those she kept, knowing that they would not have a chance otherwise. But there were other animals in the process of recovering from injuries or merely sickly and in need of tending. Those she would set free as soon as they were able to fend for themselves.

Her gaze slid back to Hugh and she saw dawning horror on his face. She supposed he was concluding that presenting her with a rabbit for her wolves to tear apart had been the worst possible way to please her.

"You were doing better with your flowers, my lord," she said softly and his gaze shot to her.

Hugh stared at her helplessly for a moment. Then he growled in frustration, grasped her arms and drew her forward to press his lips to hers. For one moment, surprise made Willa go still in his arms. It was long enough for him to brush his lips firmly over hers, then slip his tongue out to urge hers open. In the next moment, she was breathing in his breath. The smell and taste of him overwhelmed her. The caress of his tongue ignited something inside her she had never experienced. It was as if she were suddenly burning up from the inside out, as if a fever were raging through her body.

Willa should have wished to get away from that

fever, but instead the opposite was true. She found herself aching to experience more of it, to get as close to it as she could. She began to press against him, almost squirming in an effort to climb inside his skin. When Willa felt his hand slide down toward her chest, she thought he was about to urge her away from him. She moaned in protest. But he didn't push her away; instead that hand closed warm over her breast. She moaned again, this time with undeniable pleasure. The fever coursing through her seemed to coalesce there with tingling excitement added to the heat.

Hugh's lips released hers suddenly and shifted to her throat. She heard him groan her name against the soft skin and her body made a response she was unable to articulate in any way except to grind her lower body against his codpiece. That brought a rather startling, but wholly satisfying, response from Hugh. The kiss, which had already been rather passionate, became almost violent and he suddenly rushed her backward until he had her pressed up against the wall. Pressing one knee between hers, he held her in place and leaned back to begin jerking rather desperately at his chain mail.

Willa watched him in bewilderment until he gave up the effort with a growl and grabbed her by the upper arms. Almost rough in his excitement, he dragged her against his chest for another fast and furious kiss. Willa was breathless and nearly brainless when he ended it . . . until he growled, "Marry me."

The words pierced her pleasure, bringing her

crashing back to earth with a thud. Ducking her head, she tried to clear her poor, woolly mind. He destroyed her efforts by simply covering her breast with his hand again and squeezing encouragingly. Willa stared at the sun-darkened hand covering the mound and found it difficult to breathe.

"I—" She gasped as he released her and suddenly jerked the neckline of her peasant dress down. For one moment, her breast was vulnerable to the open air, her hardened nipple appearing unusually dark against her pale flesh. Then his hand covered it again, and this time the slightly rough skin of his callused hand was actually against her bare flesh. Willa closed her eyes against the erotic sight and tipped her head back. She panted softly as he caressed her.

"Marry me." This time the words were a whisper against her skin as his lips replaced his hand. He began to suckle her flesh, tugging her nipple as if he were a babe at his mother's teat. Willa's response was not maternal. Crying out, she arched into him, then cried out again in protest when he stopped and straightened.

"Do not stop," she pleaded, catching his face in her hands and trying to tug him back down. He resisted, waiting until he had her attention before repeating, "Marry me."

Willa went still in his arms.

"Marry me, so that I can do this to you again and again." He shook her slightly. "Marry me."

She stared at him, her mind in an uproar. One part of her wanted to scream, "Aye. Now. This minute." Anything to keep this unbearable pleasure

from ending. To experience it over and over again
through the long years ahead with the sanctity of
marriage to make it sweeter. But that was the trick.
If Eada were correct, it would not be over and over
again through the long years ahead. If she agreed
to marry him before he crawled to her on his belly,
he would die within a month.

"Willa?"

He gave her a gentle shake, drawing her gaze
back to his and she bit her lip briefly, then murmured, "I do not suppose you feel like crawling
around on the ground, do you?"

"What?"

He looked utterly confused by the question and
she took advantage of his muddled state to slip out
from between him and the wall. Without a word,
Willa turned and hurried from the building.

Chapter Six

Hugh shifted on his saddle, trying to find a comfortable position. That seemed to be more and more of an impossibility of late. Earlier in the day, he had noticed a certain tenderness on his behind and had briefly wondered if it might be a saddle sore; he had just as quickly shrugged the idea away. Hugh had spent countless hours in the saddle over the years and though he'd suffered the complaint a time or two as a green lad, his hide had toughened with time. It was highly unlikely that he would experience it now. Still, there was definitely a tender spot on his seat. There was also nothing he could do about it at the moment, so he merely shifted again in a futile effort to ease his discomfort and set his mind to other things.

The rain was the first thing that came to mind. That was probably because it was presently pouring over him in a steady drizzle. Which, he supposed, was better than the deluge that had been tormenting him throughout most of the last two days. Tipping his head back, he surveyed the night sky, wondering if the rain would ever end. Blinking raindrops away, he looked over the large dark clouds at the lighter, starless background. Dawn was coming. By his estimation, it would crest the horizon within the hour.

Another wasted day and night had passed. Thank God, he thought wearily. But then he realized that another was sure to follow and straightened in the saddle with a sigh followed by a sniffle. Stiffening, he sniffed experimentally and almost groaned at the wet sound his nose made. Damn! Now he was catching a cold. Was there no end to the misery he must suffer to win this woman?

Willa. The name played through his head and a picture of her lovely face suddenly rose before him. The more time he spent with her, the more beautiful he found her. That was an oddity. Usually, Hugh found his attraction waning as he got to know a woman. But not with her. She grew more glorious with every passing moment. Even her stubbornness had become somehow attractive, a challenge to overcome. And it was sheer stubbornness that now made her refuse him, he assured himself. He'd felt her passion when he had kissed her. She'd melted against him, opening for him like a rose to the sun's first touch. He had felt her quiver beneath his caress and heard her moan a plea for more. Willa had responded to him. She wanted him. And still she had refused to call an end to this game and marry him. Hugh didn't understand why. But then, he'd never claimed to understand women and their reasoning.

A growl from the black shadows on his left made him peer into the bushes. Hugh could not see the source of the sound, but the growl could not have come from anything but Willa's pet wolves.

Oh, this is grand, he thought unhappily. Her wolves will attack me, I will kill them in self-defense, and she will never speak to me again.

Willa awoke with a start and found herself staring into stygian blackness. She lay still for a moment, wondering at the source of the anxiety that was creeping over her. Then she realized the night was completely silent. Unnaturally so. There was no snuffling or scuffling or calls of nocturnal animals. There was not even the patter of rain on the roof anymore; it had stopped again.

She strained to see through the dark. The fire was out. Judging by the damp chill that had stolen into the small hovel, it had died hours before. Shivering, she bundled under the fur on her pallet and wondered what had awoken her. A growl sounded somewhere outside and she stiffened. Willa knew instinctively that it wasn't the first time she'd heard it. That was probably the sound that had drawn her from sleep.

"What was that?"

Willa sat up as Eada's hissed question pierced the silence. "I think 'tis—"

Her explanation died abruptly as a cacophony

of sounds erupted outside. Growls, shouting, and a horse whinnying and stomping had both women scrambling out of their beds. Willa reached the door first and exploded out of the cottage. She hadn't even formed a full idea of what might be happening outside. What she found shocked her into stillness just outside the door.

After the inky blackness inside, the chaos taking place in the moonlit clearing was startlingly clear. Hugh Dulonget was off his horse. Shouting and cursing loudly, he was in the midst of a sword battle with another man. Wolfy and Fen circled the fighting pair, growling and nipping at whatever bits of the stranger they could reach.

Just as Willa pursed her lips to whistle the animals to her side, Hugh stumbled backward over one of the circling beasts. He tumbled to the ground, his mail jangling loudly. The moonlight glinted off the stranger's sword as he raised it, then Wolfy and Fen lunged almost as one. Both wolves went for the face and neck, the only unarmored portions of the man. The melee was over as quickly as it had begun. The intruder went down under the attack with a gurgle of sound that ended as he hit the ground.

"Wolfy! Fen!" Willa ran forward, tried to stop when she reached them, and lost her footing in the mud. She ended on her knees at the attacker's side. She was between the still-snarling and gnashing Wolfy, who now stood on his chest, teeth buried deep in the man's neck, and Fen who stood on the ground and appeared to have gone for the face. A sob breaking from her throat, Willa grabbed at the scruff of first one, then the other of the wolves. She knew it was a dangerous move. Even domesticated dogs sometimes turned on a master in the midst of blood lust. These were no domesticated animals and they had no master. But neither animal turned on her. Both calmed almost at once, their growls and snarls turning to rumbles in their throats as they allowed her to tug them away from their quarry. It was too late, however. The man was dead, his blood pooling around his throat and shoulders on the already damp ground. Wolfy and Fen had done their jobs well.

Turning away from the gory sight, she sought out Hugh. He had taken a bad tumble. Hampered by his heavy mail armor, he was only now rolling to his stomach in the mud. He got to his hands and knees and paused to shake his head as if dizzy. Then his concerned gaze found Willa and he crawled through the mud to her side.

"Are you well?"

Willa stared at him. His voice was thick and his breathing hampered. Hugh was obviously developing a cold. He was also bleeding from the head. Releasing the wolves, she shifted to face him on her knees and took his head in her hands. She turned him so that she could peer at the source of the blood trailing down his face. "You are hurt. You must have hit your head when you fell."

"'Tis nothing," he said gruffly, shaking off her hold so that he could turn his head to peer at the prone man beside them. "Who is he?"

"I do not know. Should I?"

Scowling, Hugh edged closer to the dead man.

He examined him briefly, apparently looking for some identifying feature.

"Do you know him?" she asked, forcing herself to look at the man's ruined face. It would be difficult for anyone to recognize him.

"Nay." Apparently finding nothing helpful to identify the man, Hugh settled back on his haunches. "I do not think I have ever seen him before."

They both stared at his waxen features in the moonlight, then she asked, "What happened? Did he attack you?"

"Aye. Right after the rain finally stopped. There were a few minutes of silence, then I heard one of those beasts of yours growl. I thought he was growling at me, but I presume he was warning me, for in the next moment this fellow—" he nodded toward the man on the ground—"rushed out of the trees. He ran straight at me, sword raised. I barely managed to get off of my horse in time to counter the first blow."

Hugh rubbed his forehead fretfully. He shifted to get to his feet, only to stumble back to his knees with a startled curse when Willa caught his hand and tugged him off balance. "What are you doing?"

"You should not be getting up just yet. You should rest and regain your strength," Willa said firmly. She tugged at him again and he tumbled forward in the mud, his head dropping face-first into her lap. "Head wounds are tricky. You should rest until Eada has seen the wound and checked your eyes."

"Checked my eyes for what?" His impatience was evident, despite the fact that his voice was muffled against her upper leg.

"I am not sure," Willa admitted. She turned his head so that his face pressed against her stomach and carefully examined the wound at the side of his temple. "But she can generally tell the depth of damage done by looking into the eyes. You took an awful knock."

"I am fine," he repeated, but made no effort to remove his head from her lap. Instead, he shifted onto his back and peered up at her. It was only when he glimpsed her concerned features that it occurred to him he might use this situation to his advantage. The written apology had not worked, nor the vow to guard her, nor his pathetic attempts at pleasing her with limp flowers and a live rabbit. Even the passion he'd brought to life in her in the stable had not persuaded her to agree to marry him. However, perhaps the events of this night and the concern he now saw in her face would do the trick. Hugh should have been ashamed to stoop to such manipulations, but with two castles and all of their attendant servants and soldiers depending on him, he had no time for such petty considerations.

That thought spurring him on, Hugh suddenly lifted one hand to his injured head. He squeezed his eyes closed and moaned as if in pain. Then he peeked at her from between two fingers. The alarm now filling Willa's face was quite encouraging.

"You *are* badly injured!" she cried and bent

closer. Her hair drifted around their faces, a curtain between them and the world.

Hugh produced what he hoped was the brave smile of a man on death's door and let his hand fall feebly away. "Nay. I am fine." He was rather proud of the breathless, almost trembling quality he had managed to infuse into his voice. Never having needed the skill before, he'd not realized what a masterful thespian he was.

Willa certainly seemed convinced. Looking fearful, she straightened and peered desperately toward the cottage. Her voice anxious, she fretted, "Where is Eada? She will know what to do. I should fetch her."

"Nay!" Hugh winced at the sharp strength in his tone, but the last thing he wanted was for Eada to interrupt his best chance at convincing the chit to marry him. "Nay," he repeated, his voice gentler this time. "Prithee, my lady. Do not leave me to die here alone in the mud."

"Oh, Hugh," she breathed in horror. Her arms tightened around him in a protective gesture. "You must not say such things. You will not die. Eada said—"

"Hush." He pressed a finger to her lips. "Do not fret so. 'Tis an honor to die for one as beautiful as you. 'Tis my penance for treating you so shabbily on our first meeting. I have no excuse for my behavior except that Uncle Richard's death came as a shock to me. The madness of grief must have made me behave so."

Now that was inspired, he thought. Perfect! His words had moved her, he could tell. She bent closer, her expression soft as she brushed her fingers lightly over his cheek and breathed, "Oh, poor Hugh."

He blinked his eyelashes several times, trying for the sweetly innocent look women had used on him over the years. It didn't have the desired effect. Instead of melting further, she frowned slightly and straightened the smallest bit away from him. "Have you something in your eye?"

"Nay." He caught at her hair to draw her back and debated what to do. In the end, he decided to push forward. " 'Tis nothing but—"

"But?" she prompted gently.

"I would wish to ask—Nay, beg. I would beg during these last moments of my life that you forgive me my unchivalrous gaff. Pray, say you forgive me."

"Of course, my lord," Willa assured him. "But I promise you, you are not dying. Eada would have seen—"

"She is not all-seeing," Hugh interrupted impatiently, then forced his temper away and managed a pious smile before raising his hand to let it drop across his face in a forlorn gesture. "Alas, no one can see the future. Had I but been able to foresee what the future held, mayhap this night would never have been. Mayhap we would even now be married and cuddled warm and safe in our marriage bed."

He peeked between two fingers again to see how she would react and was gratified by the distress he saw on her face. He let his hand slide away and offered yet another brave smile. "Never fear. I am not afraid to die. Now I shall sleep the long sleep, and at least be able to dream that we were married. Unless. . . ."

Willa leaned closer. "Unless?"

He tried for an expression of longing. "Would that you could find it in your heart to grant a dying man's wish and agree to be my wife."

"Ye're laying it on rather thick, aren't ye?"

Willa lifted her head abruptly, the curtain of her hair swinging away so that Hugh had a perfect view of both Eada and Baldulf standing over them. The pair stood with arms crossed, amusement obvious on their faces. It was Eada who had spoken, and with her usual disrespect. Hugh glared at the woman, wishing he could throttle her for interrupting what he was sure would have been Willa's acceptance.

"Oh, thank goodness you are here, Eada," Willa said. "Hugh has a head wound you must tend to at once."

"So I see." The old woman seemed not in the least impressed. "Well, let him stand up then and I shall tend it. I am too old to be kneeling in the mud in my nightshift."

"But—" Willa began, only to pause when Hugh sat up and began to struggle to his feet. It *was* a struggle. Not due to his head wound, however. Chain mail was not made for crawling around in the mud. Fortunately, Baldulf unbent enough to lend him a hand. The moment Hugh was on his feet, Willa leapt to her own and placed a hand on his arm as if to steady him. He was too busy mentally cursing his bad luck to appreciate it. One minute. One more minute and he would have had her agreeing to marry him.

"I shall have a look at his head while you dress," Eada told Willa pointedly. Her words drew Hugh's attention to the fact that the girl stood there in nothing but a thin cotton shift. A damp and muddy shift. Worn nearly see-through by many washings, it clung to her breasts and hips with loving affection. Damn! He really must have sustained some damage to the head to have missed that, he thought as Willa moved toward the cottage.

Hugh watched her go, wanting nothing more than to grab her up, toss her over his mount's back and ride off to the castle. Unfortunately, that would hardly convince her to marry him. Things would have been much easier if his uncle were still alive. As her guardian, Richard could have ordered her to marry him and the deed would be done. As it was, she had neither a name nor an identifiable father, so only King John could order such an event. Hugh thought briefly about going to court and asking the king to do just that, then pushed the notion aside. He could not leave her alone while he traveled to court. Tonight's events had made that clear. Even ten years after the "accident" that had killed young Luvena, someone wanted this woman dead.

Willa had reached the cottage. She opened the door, allowing candlelight to spill out and highlighting her scanty garb for him. He was enjoying the view immensely but Eada spoiled it by poking him in the stomach.

"Bend over so I can see yer head," the crone

ordered, unmoved by the glare he now turned on her. "And stop looking so morose. Ye got what ye wanted."

"Got what I wanted?" he echoed irritably even as he did as he was bid.

"Aye. She has agreed to marry ye."

"What?" Hugh straightened to stare at her with amazement.

"Did ye not hear her order Baldulf to start packing?" she asked with exasperation.

Actually, he hadn't. Hugh had some vague recollection of her saying something before turning to walk to the cottage, but he hadn't been paying attention. He'd been too busy ogling her in her shift.

"She ordered Baldulf to start packing so that we could move to the castle. She's marrying ye," Eada announced and poked him in the belly.

"I did wonder if that was what it meant," Baldulf said as Hugh automatically bent forward, submitting to the witch's prodding. "But why?"

"'Tis obvious," Hugh snapped, straightening to scowl at him. The guard was presently scratching his head in apparent bewilderment over what Willa could see in Hugh. His attitude was highly insulting. "She appreciates my saving her life this evening."

Baldulf look doubtful. "That knock to the head appears to be more serious than I thought, my lord. It has rattled your brain." Even as Hugh was stiffening over that announcement, the soldier continued, "First off, it seemed to me that 'twas Wolfy and Fen saving *your* sorry hide. Secondly, what makes you so quick to assume 'twas her life that was threatened? The fellow attacked you, not her."

Hugh heaved an impatient breath. "He only attacked me because I stood between him and the cottage."

"Uh-huh." Baldulf did not appear convinced. "And why, after all these years without incident, would someone suddenly make an attempt on her life again?"

"Perhaps he did not wish her to marry me. Perhaps she is no threat as a simple village lass, but becomes one as my wife."

"Hmmmm. The only problem with that suggestion is that she had not agreed to be your wife before the attack," Baldulf pointed out dryly. "Perhaps everyone thought her dead until you came along and drew attention her way with your pledge to guard her until she accepted your suit."

"Are you holding me responsible for this attack?" Hugh gaped at him.

"My lord, Eada, Willa and I have lived here for nigh on ten years. In that time, we have never once been attacked ... until now. This fact suggests to me that the attack was—"

"My fault? Hugh's mouth dropped open, then just hung there. He was flummoxed by the man's reasoning. He was also thinking, however, and it wasn't long before he made the reluctant admission, "Perhaps my presence did prompt the attack. However, I cannot help thinking it may have been for the best. Ere this we were uncertain as to whether her life was still in danger. Now we know 'tis and may strengthen our guard."

"Hmmm," Baldulf grunted as Eada poked Hugh to get him to bend to her level once more. Then the soldier asked the old woman, "Is it safe for her to marry him?"

"Safe?" Hugh straightened indignantly. "I would never harm a lady."

"There was never any question of that, my lord," Baldulf assured him, then explained, "Willa is a very forgiving girl. She would have married you yesterday, but for Eada's vision."

" 'Twasn't a vision," Eada corrected with a grin that struck Hugh as rather evil. "I read it in the dregs of his wine. She was not to marry him until he crawled to her on his belly, else he would die ere the next full moon."

Hugh snorted at the very thought of such an occurrence. It would be a cold day in hell before he would crawl to any woman.

"He crawled." Eada announced with satisfaction.

"I did not!" Hugh stood upright in surprise, only to bend forward once more with a grunt as the old witch poked him again.

"Aye. Ye did," she corrected in gleeful tones as she dabbed at his head. "I saw ye. Ye crawled through the mud to her side." Hugh now recalled that he had indeed crawled through the mud to get to Willa. Which meant that all that nonsense he'd spouted afterward about dying and last wishes had been unnecessary. So was sitting in the rain for two days and nights. Nothing he could have said or done would have convinced her to marry him because, thanks to the witch, she'd thought she was saving his life by refusing him.

He was muttering under his breath over that when it occurred to him that he'd crawled through the mud, and she'd now agreed to marry him. He had won. She was going to marry him and she, Baldulf and the witch were moving to the castle.

He was just starting to grin at this realization when the old crone smiled at him wickedly and said, "I knew ye'd crawl. I'm never wrong."

"Ah, hell," he muttered, wondering for the first time if he shouldn't just give up the money and the title and flee for his life right now.

Chapter Seven

"Hugh."

A tap on Hugh's shoulder startled him awake and nearly sent him plummeting off his saddle. Regaining his balance at the last moment, he shook his head in an effort to wake up and peered bleary-eyed at the man beside him.

"Lucan." Hugh shook his head again, finding it hard to order his thoughts. A glance at the sun showed that he'd not slept long. Perhaps a matter of moments. It was still in the same position it had been in when his eyes had fluttered shut. Damn, he was getting too old for this nonsense. He was exhausted.

"What is that about?"

Hugh followed the other man's gesture to the body in the center of the clearing and grimaced. "He came rushing out of the woods just ere dawn this morning, sword raised in attack."

Lucan arched an eyebrow at this news. "That

does not look like a sword wound on his throat. Nor his face."

"Nay. Those beasts of Willa's did that."

Lucan whistled, his gaze moving to the dead man again.

Hugh peered at him too, then shifted uncomfortably and asked, "Did you bring anything for me to eat or drink? My throat is as dry as dust."

"Oh, aye." Lucan unhooked a sack from his saddle and handed it over, his gaze returning to the dead man as Hugh dug out the ale skin. "This could be a good thing. If we can convince Willa that 'twas you who killed the man, she may be grateful enough to agree to wed you."

Hugh shook his head as he tipped the ale skin up and gulped from it greedily. Pulling it away after several moments, he gasped, "No need. She has agreed to marry me. She is packing even as we speak. Still."

Lucan grinned. "Still?"

"Aye." Hugh grimaced. "They have been packing since dawn."

Lucan goggled at this news. "There cannot possibly be that much to pack! 'Tis a small cottage."

"Aye," Hugh agreed in mournful tones. "But there is also a stable, and her animal menagerie."

"Animal menagerie?"

"Do not ask," he said with a grimace, but Lucan did not have to ask. Baldulf chose that moment to bring the fully loaded cart out from behind the stable. It was piled high with junk. A crooked chair, animal cages, baskets and sacks of unidentifiable items.

Willa followed. She barely cast a glance their way before going into the cottage. Baldulf urged the horse to draw the cart forward until the back end stood a bare foot or two in front of the door, then followed her inside. They were both back a moment later, piling more baskets and bulging sacks on top of those already in the cart.

Lucan watched the goings on with wide eyes. "Are they just now getting to the cottage?"

"Aye." Hugh watched with resignation as the pair disappeared inside the small building again. "Willa started in the cottage, but then left Eada to finish the packing there while she went to aid Baldulf in emptying out the stable."

The two warriors watched silently as Willa and Baldulf came out with more baskets and sacks and dumped them in the cart.

"Maybe we should offer to help?" Lucan suggested as the pair headed back into the hovel.

Hugh shook his head. "I offered earlier. They said I would just be in the way. They wished to see to it themselves."

"Hmmm." Lucan looked uncomfortable with the idea of sitting about while Willa, Eada and Baldulf worked. "Well, what are your plans for *him*?"

Hugh followed his friend's gaze to the corpse still lying in the clearing and grimaced. "I thought I should have him taken to the village. Perhaps someone there will know who he is."

"He is a bit of a mess," his friend commented doubtfully. " 'Tis not very likely anyone would recognize him even did they know him."

"Aye." Hugh agreed, then shrugged. "Still, it cannot hurt to try."

"Hmm." Lucan nodded. "You are sure he was by himself?"

"Aye. At least I believe so. I am sure the wolves would have gone after others had there been any lurking in the woods after the first man attacked." Hugh glanced toward the cottage as Willa and Baldulf came out again with more junk to add to the cart. "Baldulf!"

The guard set down his burden, then walked over to stand before the two mounted men. Earlier Hugh had found it so difficult to mount that he was now reluctant to dismount. It wasn't his head that troubled him. That was a trifling injury, which Eada had admitted after poking and prodding at it until he was ready to bellow at her for her trouble. Nay, 'twas his derriere that pained him. The tenderness he'd noticed there earlier seemed to be increasing with every passing moment. It was bad enough just sitting on it, but the movement to climb in and out of the saddle agitated the tender spot until he had to bite his tongue to keep from groaning in pain. He was beginning to believe that it might be a saddle sore after all. Whatever it was, 'twas damned painful.

"Aye, m'lord?"

Baldulf's voice drew Hugh's attention away from his tender rump and he managed a smile that he suspected was closer to a grimace. "Is there going to be room on the cart for our friend there?"

Baldulf turned to peer from the corpse to the cart and back. "Nay," he decided, then added, "But

I'll fetch my horse from the stable. We can drape him over the animal and tie him hand and foot under the belly so he does not fall off."

Hugh was tempted to let Baldulf tend to the matter, but then decided with resignation that he must tackle it himself. He would have to dismount after all. "Bring the horse around. I shall see to the matter."

Nodding, the soldier moved off toward the stable. Hugh waited until he had disappeared from sight, then gritted his teeth, took a deep breath and quickly swung his leg up and over his saddle to dismount. Searing pain promptly screamed at him from behind, eliciting a grunt as he dropped to the ground. Fortunately, Lucan seemed not to notice.

Hugh found himself standing completely still, afraid to move. Trying to appear as if he was standing still simply because he wanted to, Hugh listened as Lucan informed him that the men he'd sent to Claymorgan had returned. They had not learned anything of use. They had asked absolutely everyone in the castle and its environs, but no one seemed to know anything.

Baldulf returned with the horse and a length of rope, and Hugh was forced to move again. He winced as the tenderness in his posterior increased with each step. The pain seemed to increase with movement. Sitting on it was uncomfortable, but only in a throbbing sort of way that could almost be ignored. Movement, however, made the pain excruciating.

With Lucan's help, it was a simple matter to heft

the body onto the horse and tie it down. Then Hugh was faced with the matter of remounting, which he knew from experience would be worse than simply moving. Resigned to the sudden increase of pain, Hugh gritted his teeth again and got the matter over with quickly. This time, however, he could not prevent a gasp of pain from slipping out and tried to disguise the sound with a quick curse.

"Something wrong?" Lucan eyed him curiously.

"Nay. Caught my finger on . . ." He let the sentence trail away and waved vaguely at his reins, too embarrassed to admit that he was developing a sore on his butt.

"M'lord?"

Hugh glanced down to find Baldulf at his side again. "Aye?"

"Everything is loaded."

Hugh glanced toward the cart. Eada was seated patiently on one side of the bench seat. Willa was nowhere in sight. "Where—?"

"Willa is just fetching her mount now," Baldulf explained.

"Jesu . . ."

Eyebrows rising at that awed comment, Hugh shifted on his horse and followed Lucan's gaze. Willa was riding her horse out of the stable, and she was an impressive sight. Her long golden tresses flowed around her shoulders. Her posture was upright, her grip on the reins secure, her thighs pressing firmly into either side of her mount. It was her position astride her horse that had drawn the awed Jesu from Lucan. She was also wearing men's braies and an oversized white blouse that billowed in the breeze as she slowed to a stop, then dismounted to check something on her mare's flank.

Hugh gaped at the way the braies lovingly hugged her shapely butt, his expression one of horror more than awe. He urged his mount forward with every intention of berating the wench for her unladylike behavior and insisting that she change and ride sidesaddle. Baldulf prevented him from doing so by calmly taking hold of his reins.

"When we first brought her here from Claymorgan we dressed her as a boy in an effort to keep her safe," the man announced.

Hugh stared at him.

"Disguised so, she had to ride as a boy. 'Twas necessary. She had to ride as a boy to be able to go to the fairs. 'Twas the only way for her to see his lordship at first."

"I thought he did not see her for the first five years," Lucan murmured. His attention on Willa's bent form was so fixed, he was completely oblivious to Hugh's mounting irritation.

"Aye. That is so. They could never actually meet and speak, and Willa never even knew that his lordship was there, but he could see her. Watch her enjoy the games and sweets and see for himself that she was well. 'Twas the most he allowed himself those first years. Of course, once she started to grow . . . er . . . womanly, we had to stop dressing her as a boy. Still, when he later did finally allow her to visit him, she went dressed as a boy but with a cape to help hide her figure. She never left the cottage on horseback in any guise but as a boy. 'Tis the only way she knows how to ride."

Hugh heard the entire explanation, but was too busy glaring at Lucan to acknowledge it. Becoming aware of Hugh's displeasure and of how rude he was being by ogling his friend's soon-to-be bride, Lucan cleared his throat and muttered something of an apology. He also shifted his gaze away from Willa as she remounted.

"A problem with Hilly's hoof?" Baldulf asked as she joined them.

When she did not answer, Hugh gave up scowling at her outfit and glanced up to find her concerned gaze on the white cloth Eada had wrapped around his forehead.

"You are bleeding through," she said with dismay.

"'Tis nothing," Hugh assured her.

"'Tis not nothing, my lord. A mere hour ago you were sure you were at death's door. I knew we should have left the packing of our things until after we got you back to Hillcrest and put you to bed."

Hugh felt himself flush as Lucan cast a sharp look his way. He'd not told his friend of his attempt to convince Willa to marry him by making her think he was dying. He had his pride.

"You are quite flushed," Willa fretted now. "Mayhap I should ride with you, just to be sure you do not fall off your mount and expire. You may hold onto me and save your strength that way."

Hugh opened his mouth to assure her again that he was fine, but did not get the chance. She'd already urged her horse next to his and was slipping from her mount to his own in a rather neat little maneuver. Settling against his chest, she then reached back to take his hands in her own and place them about her waist.

"Just hold on and rest against me," she instructed, taking control of the reins. "Save your strength."

Hugh had opened his mouth to protest that he was not weak and needed no coddling, but now snapped his mouth shut again. He was not feeling weak. At least not in the head. He couldn't say the same for the rest of his body.

The feel of her nestling against him was decidedly distracting. So distracting the pain in his posterior became something of a distant sensation. He forgot it entirely as he became conscious of her behind pressing against his groin and the bottoms of her breasts brushing the tops of his hands as she moved.

"Damn." Hugh wasn't aware he had breathed the word until Willa nearly unseated him by turning to ask if he was alright. Put off balance by her sudden shift, he grabbed wildly for something to hold onto and found himself cupping her sweet, soft breasts. Her eyes, bare inches in front of his own, dilated in shock even as Hugh's did.

"My lord?" The words came strangled from her sweet lips. "Are you well?"

"Aye," he said gruffly.

"Then mayhap you could hold onto something else?" she suggested, her voice rather breathless.

Hugh blinked at her words, slow to comprehend them until he became aware of the way she was blushing and heard a muffled chuckle from Lucan. Clearing his throat, he abruptly removed his hands and settled them at her hips. He held her firmly so he would not give in to the temptation of seeking out her breasts again. Hugh then took a moment to toss a repressive glance Lucan's way as Willa urged his mount into line behind the cart, which Baldulf was already heading out of the clearing.

Hugh was hard pressed not to reclaim the reins from her. He was not one to give up control easily. However, he managed to resist the urge. He was not as successful at keeping his thoughts in line. She was soft yet firm in all the right places. She smelled of lemons and sunlight and had agreed to be his wife. He would no longer need to worry about how he was going to feed his people. The worst of his concerns were over . . . or so he thought.

Hugh supposed that one of the men on the wall must have heralded their arrival. Wynekyn and Jollivet were waiting at the top of the stairs to the castle when they rode into the bailey. The older man rushed down the stairs as Willa drew his mount in at the base of the steps. Before Hugh realized what she was about, the chit had slipped from under his arms, and dropped to the ground.

"Uncle!" she called as she hurried forward.

"Child."

Hugh frowned as he watched the reunion. They greeted each other as if it had been years since their last meeting, when he knew it had been little more than a week. Oddly, he found himself disgruntled at the obvious and easy affection between the two.

"I thought you were her godfather, not a blood

relative," he grumbled irritably. Dismounting with care, he moved forward to take Willa's arm as their embrace ended.

"I was. I am," Wynekyn laughed.

"But godfather is such a long title and I used to muddle it when I was young." Willa grinned. "I called him God for short, which got quite confusing when Father Brennan taught me about religion."

"She thought I was Him," Wynekyn explained with a chuckle.

"Aye." She pulled away from Hugh to give the older man another impulsive hug. "I could not understand why—when he claimed to love me so much—he would not do the tiny little tasks I asked of him."

"What tasks?" Lucan asked curiously, dismounting to join them.

"Oh, little things, really," Wynekyn murmured dryly. "Every time I went to see her she made a different request. One was to make it so that her papa could see her again. Another was to bring her mother back from the dead so that she might be like other children. Then she wished me to make the days longer so that she could play more. And I believe during one visit she asked if she could not have a pony of her very own. Oh! And all the sweets in the world."

Willa wrinkled her nose slightly and explained, "Eada does not favor sweets."

"Finally, after I explained that I simply could not do some of the things she asked of me, she exclaimed *'But of course you can, you are God,'* and I understood her confusion. Eada and I tried to explain about godfathers to her, saying that they were rather like a surrogate father or an uncle, and she said, well, why did we not just call it uncle. I said that was fine, and she has called me uncle ever since."

"What a perfectly charming story!"

They all turned to Jollivet as he finished sashaying his way down the stairs. Walking directly to Willa, he caught her up in an exuberant embrace, then set her back down and grinned. "Hello, lovely. We have yet to be properly introduced. I am cousin Jollivet, your second choice for husband should this lummox here prove inadequate. All you need do is let me know and I shall make you a widow, then wed you myself."

Hugh was so taken aback to realize that Jollivet had somehow learned he was Willa's second option as a husband, it took him a moment to notice the awed expression on her face as she peered at his younger cousin. The moment he did, however, irritation and a touch of fear rose up within him. Fortunately, before he could make a fool of himself, she reached out to caress the sleeve of Jollivet's bright purple coat and exclaimed, "What a lovely material!"

Jollivet glanced down at himself and nodded. " 'Tis lovely, is it not? And 'twould look perfect on you. A lovely foil for your hair. Much nicer than the acoutrements you are wearing at the moment, my dear. If you do not mind my saying so, the lady of the manner should not arrive looking quite so destitute. You would have done better to emulate

Lady Godiva than to arrive dressed so. Certainly
your hair is long enough and full enough to be
a decent covering." He reached out to lift one of
the shimmering tresses that reached nearly to her
knees; Hugh slapped his hand away.

"Enough, Jollivet. Cousin or no, if you continue
to make a nuisance of yourself, I shall—"

"Who is Lady Godiva?" Willa interrupted curiously.

"A famous horsewoman," Wynekyn answered
quickly, a slight flush on his cheeks. Clearing his
throat, he went on, "Speaking of clothing, I have a
surprise for you."

"For me?" Willa turned to him, her eyes widening with excitement. "What is it?"

"Well, 'tis part of the reason I left so precipi-
tously after Hillcrest's death. I realize my leaving
so soon distressed you, my dear, but I did have to
find and inform Hugh, as well as King John, of
Richard's death. Then, too, I wished to be sure you
would be outfitted properly for your wedding."
He smiled suddenly. "I had a new gown made for
you to be married in."

"A new gown?"

"Aye. Come, I placed it in a room above stairs
and am eager to see if you like it." He took Willa's
arm to lead her inside the castle, then suddenly
paused and turned back. "Oh, Hugh, I almost forgot, I have spoken with the priest and he assured
me that the wedding can be held the moment the
two of you are ready." He glanced between Hugh
and Willa now. "I am assuming that all is well?

That you have settled matters and are ready to marry now?"

"Aye." Willa and Hugh gave the answer as one.

"Good, good, then perhaps you should send someone to fetch the priest. There is no sense delaying. Cook and the other servants have been working like mad these last three days to prepare. I think all is ready."

"I take it you have found the letter and resolved the problem of her name then?" Hugh said with a feeling of relief that faded when he saw Wynekyn's troubled expression. "You have not found the letter?"

"Damn me, nay." Wynekyn's shoulders slumped. "I was going through Richard's things again this morning when a servant hurried in to tell me you were riding for the castle with Willa. I was so excited I forgot—"

"What is the problem with my name?" Willa interrupted curiously.

Wynekyn forced a smile and patted her hand reassuringly. "Never fear, my dear. We shall find the letter, and then the wedding may be held. Hugh, perhaps you could—What is it, Willa?" he asked when she tapped on his arm to get his attention.

"Why do you need this letter?"

"We must have your last name to put on the contract, my dear. Richard promised he would leave a letter with your name in it for me, but there has been some difficulty finding it," he explained, patting her hand again. He then turned to Hugh to continue, "Perhaps you could assist me. I have searched his chamber several times already and— Yes, Willa, what is it?" he asked a little less patiently this time.

"I know my name."

"Of course you do, dear." He turned back to Hugh, opened his mouth, closed it, and jerked his head back around in amazement as her words sank in. "You do?"

"Well, of course, my lord."

"What is it?" Hugh asked when Wynekyn seemed stymied by this information.

"Willa Evelake."

"Evelake," Hugh murmured with a smile.

"Evelake," Wynekyn echoed, his forehead furrowing as if he were trying to place the name.

"Is everything alright then?" Willa asked anxiously. "The marriage may be performed?"

Wynekyn's expression brightened. "Aye! Aye, yes. Hugh—"

"I shall send someone to fetch the priest."

"Good, good. And perhaps—"

"I shall see to everything, Lord Wynekyn," he assured him patiently. "Why do you not take Willa above stairs and show her the gown you had made for her so that she may prepare herself.

"Yes, yes." Beaming now, the older man took Willa's arm and turned her toward the stairs again.

Chapter Eight

"I do hope you like the gown, my dear. I hired a woman to make it the moment I reached London. I knew 'twould take several days for my man to find Hugh and for him to ride to London. Of course, Hugh was swifter than I expected. He also left for here directly after meeting with Richard's solicitor, while I had to wait until later in the day for your gown to be finished before I could follow."

Willa made sympathetic noises as they entered the castle and crossed the hall to the stairs. She knew from experience that was the only response necessary. Lord Wynekyn was something of a talker.

" 'Twas quite a trial, I can tell you," he said with a laugh as they ascended the stairs. "I did not have you there for measurements, of course. Fortunately, the dressmaker's daughter appeared to me to be the same size as yourself, so she stood in for you. Then the woman wished to know in what style she should make it. As if I knew anything about ladies' fashions." He laughed at the very idea as they moved along the hall, then steered her through the open door of a bedchamber. "I simply told her to make it in the latest style, so I do hope it suits you."

The last was said as he gestured toward the bed, where a gown had been carefully laid out. Its arms were spread wide to show off the fine trim and wide sleeves, its skirts flared to best effect.

"The color of the cloth reminded me of your eyes," he said as Willa moved slowly forward, her fascinated gaze fixed on the soft blue-gray gown.

It was quite the most beautiful dress she'd ever seen. Willa could hardly believe it was hers. Pausing at the foot of the bed, she reached out tentatively and brushed one finger lightly over the cloth. A small breath slipped from her lips. "So soft."

Wynekyn moved forward at once, his expression terribly sad as he clasped her shoulders and peered down at the gown with her. "Aye. The softest material I could find. There will be no more coarse peasant cloth against your skin, Willa. That time is over. Hugh is a strong and able warrior. He will keep you safe without the need for subterfuge. Not that Richard was not a strong and able warrior, too," he rushed to add as if just realizing how his words might be interpreted. "He was. But—"

Willa hushed him by turning and placing one finger against his lips. A smile bloomed on her face despite the tears that now filled her eyes. "That part of my life is over now. I shall have a husband,

and children, and not need to hide. 'Tis a beautiful gown. Thank you, uncle."

She threw her arms around him in an exuberant hug of gratitude and simple happiness. Wynekyn cleared his throat and patted her back, then turned quickly away to move toward the door when she released him. She supposed the move was meant to hide the fact that he was wiping a suspicious wetness from his own cheeks even as Willa quickly brushed the silly tears from her own.

"Well, I shall remove myself so you may prepare," he said in bracing tones as he reached the door. "I shall have a bath ordered up and send Eada to help you dress."

"Oh nay!" Willa said quickly. "'Twas a long morning for Eada and she is not as young as she used to be. Let her rest. I can dress myself."

"Nonsense! You are a lady now. I shall see if I cannot find someone else to attend you." He smiled slightly. "Send for me when you are ready and I shall escort you below."

Willa returned his smile and nodded, then watched the door close behind him before turning to the bed again. She stared down at the lovely gown for one moment, then threw herself on top of it with a squeal. Gathering it in her arms, she rolled onto her back holding it close to her body. It was beautiful. Gorgeous. The most scrumptious gown ever made and it was all hers!

Realizing that her behavior might wrinkle the gown, she pushed herself quickly off the bed. Lifting the gown, she held it against the front of her body and peered down at herself, trying to see how it was going to look. She marveled at its beauty for several moments, wondering over its softness.

She was rubbing the petal-soft material against her cheek for the umpteenth time when there was a sudden throat-clearing from the door, followed by a tentative, "Wee Willa?"

Willa glanced toward the door with a start. It had been years since anyone had called her wee Willa. Not since Luvena. She peered at the older woman in the doorway. Several moments passed before Willa realized who she was. Luvena's mother. She and Luvena had been the only people to call her that name. The rest of the servants had addressed her as "m'lady," but Luvena, as her friend, had chosen the nickname and her mother used it, too. Willa had insisted on it.

"Alsneta." She breathed the name uncertainly as it came to mind. The woman looked like Luvena's mother. But the years had not been kind. Her once red-gold hair had turned mostly gray with just a few strands of color left to hint at its former glory. Her lovely laughing face was now too thin and lined with misery. She appeared a dried-up husk of the woman she'd been. Yet her face was transformed when she broke into a smile.

"You remember me." She sounded both surprised and pleased at the realization. The sudden smile softened her features, making her almost lovely again.

"Of course I do," Willa murmured. Letting the gown slip from her fingers to the bed, she moving impulsively forward to hug the woman. The cook was stiff at first, but then relaxed and hugged her back. Willa released her and said, "You helped raise me. You and Eada both had charge of me as a child until—" She ended the sentence abruptly and glanced away toward the bed, unwilling to bring up Luvena or her death. Spying the gown, she drew the woman forward by the hand. "Did you see the gown Lord Wynekyn brought me? I am to be married in it," she said quickly to change the subject.

When a moment passed in silence, Willa glanced uncertainly at the older woman, biting her lip when she saw the grief Alsneta struggled with. Knowing that her presence must be reawakening sad memories, Willa turned back to the gown, touching it gently. "I am sorry, Alsneta. I did not mean to—"

" 'Tis a lovely gown, is it not?" The older woman broke in with determined cheerfulness. " 'Twill look lovely on you." Reaching past Willa, she picked it up. "Lord Wynekyn asked me to send someone to help you dress. I have been quite busy with the preparations for the feast, but everything is ready now and I thought it might make you more comfortable to see a familiar face. My, is this cloth not soft?"

The aging servant continued to chatter with determined cheer as the bath was brought in and filled. She talked right through undressing Willa, helping her with the bath, drying her hair before the fire, and continued on as she helped Willa into the new gown. Most of what she said was just chatter; gossip about servants Willa had yet to meet,

tales of her sister who had died the year earlier, as
well as complaints of her nephew whom she was
sure had hurried the woman to her grave with
some of his antics. Willa let it drift over her head
as she enjoyed the extravagance of a bath. She
hadn't even realized she had missed the luxury.
She'd not bathed in anything but the river since
her tenth year. There was no tub in the cottage. It
had been the river in the summer and a pitcher of
water and basin for a hand bath in the winter.
Willa found it lovely to relax in fire-heated water.

Warm baths, soft gowns, and someone to fuss
over her and help her dress—it all seemed like a
little bit of heaven to her. Willa was almost sorry
when Alsneta pronounced her ready and hurried
out to find Lord Wynekyn.

"Well," Wynekyn said moments later, pausing
just inside the door Alsneta had left open. Then,
for the first time in all the years that Willa had
known him, he did not speak. He simply stared at
her, his face full of wonder.

Willa beamed back, feeling as beautiful as she
had ever felt in her life. "Is it not fine?" she asked,
running her hand over the blue-gray material of
the skirt. Nothing she had ever owned, even as a
pampered child, had equaled the beauty and comfort of this gown.

"Aye, well . . ." A slight frown now came to his
face. "Let us hope Hugh agrees. I had not realized
how snug a fit 'twould be. I was sure the dressmaker's daughter was your size. Obviously, I was
mistaken."

" 'Tis not snug. 'Tis a perfect fit, my lord," Willa

assured him. She ran her hands down over her hips with pleasure.

Wynekyn followed the gesture with some dismay. "You have become a woman! Odd, I always thought of you as a slender child. Willowy and graceful. But somehow, when I was not looking, you grew—" He cut himself off, but gestured vaguely to her breasts and hips where the cloth of the gown clung lovingly.

Willa gave a slightly embarrassed laugh at his bemused words, then frowned as she fingered one long sleeve. "You do not think that the sleeves may be a bit large, do you?"

Wynekyn shook his head. "Nay. Long hanging sleeves are the style just now, my dear." Clearing his throat, he held out a hand. "Well, come along then. We shall go below and see the deed done."

Willa gave up touching the gown with some reluctance. Managing a nervous smile, she slipped her fingers into his. He led her from the room.

"My . . . my . . . my—"

"God," Jollivet supplied dryly as he followed Lucan's wide eyes to see what had him stammering so. Willa was a vision descending the stairs on Wynekyn's trembling arm. "My God is what you are trying to say. Though goddess would suit the situation better, I think."

Hugh turned toward the stairs at that and immediately felt his mouth go as dry as ashes. Willa had been lovely in her course peasant sacks, but she was glorious in the gown Wynekyn had given her. A sigh from either side of him made Hugh glance at first one, then the other of the two men flanking him. He took in their awestruck gazes and had to wonder what the devil he was getting himself into. Even his effeminate cousin was drooling over the chit.

The wedding was held on the steps of the chapel. Father Brennan conducted the ceremony in a solemn tone while every servant and soldier of Hillcrest set down his work to witness it.

Afterward, they all sat down for a celebratory meal in the great hall. The air was fragrant with a mixture of spices and the smell of roasted meat. It was a long celebratory meal served in several courses. There were potages, tarts, bread, cheese, custard, mutton, venison, eel, figpeckers, pigeon pies, suckling pig, braised lettuces, gilded peacock, a festooned boar's head, oysters steamed in almond milk, goose in a sauce of grapes and garlic, a whole roast sheep with sour cherry sauce, pastries with pine nuts and sugar, frumenty and spiced mulled wine. There was even rosewater for the guests to clean their hands. Cook had truly outdone herself, especially given the short amount of time she had had to prepare.

Hugh sat through it all in a sort of daze, the combination of his cold and lack of sleep creeping up on him as he ate and drank. He was soon swaying wearily in his seat, his eyelids drooping and threatening to close on him. It was when he started awake nearly facedown in his trencher that Hugh realized he was in danger of passing out from exhaustion on his own wedding night. That possibility was unacceptable to Hugh. His gaze shifted around the room. He was pretty sure that they had reached the final course, but wasn't at all positive that the sotelty for this course had yet been presented. There had already been a large eagle after the first course, then an effigy of St. Andrew made of marzipan and dough after the second, and . . . no, that was it. The third and final sotelty had not yet been presented, he realized wearily. Then the kitchen doors opened and the cook strode out.

Alsneta was leading a parade of twelve men carrying a large platter bearing a six-foot square castle. It was an exact replica of Hillcrest, Hugh realized as she led the men to stand before him and Willa at the head table. And well done, too, he noted as everyone began to ooh and ahh over it. It appeared to be made of marzipan and colored dough. The detail was rather amazing. There were even little figures that resembled him and Willa standing on the top steps of the castle. It appeared he had a very talented cook here at Hillcrest, he realized with pride. He nodded his approval to the woman even as he wondered if it were an edible sotelty. Often such creations were not, but this one looked quite delicious. He got his answer when the cook led the castle-bearing men back to the kitchens and a small army of servants began hurrying out with wafers, fruit and a sweet called *vyn dowce*.

The castle could not be consumed. Not that it mattered . . . Hugh was quite stuffed to the gills. Everyone should be. He noticed that Willa was waving away any further food. Thank God, he

thought with relief as another fit of coughing over-
came him. He did not think he could sit at the
table another moment. Deciding he'd suffered long
enough, Hugh took a last sip of mulled wine to
help clear his throat. He forced a smile and tapped
Willa on the shoulder to draw her attention from
the conversation she was having with Wynekyn.

"Do you not think you should go above stairs
now?"

"Above stairs?" she asked with surprise. "But 'tis
early yet, my lord husband. I am not the least tired."

"Aye. Well, we would not wish you tired on this
night."

"Why? I will not sleep if I am not tired."

"Aye. But 'tis our *wedding* night," he said patiently, giving her a meaningful look. For a moment he feared she'd been left completely innocent
of what went on in the marriage bed; then her expression suddenly cleared.

"Oh! You wish to—" She cut herself off, blushing. Standing, she turned to Lord Wynekyn. Hugh
distinctly heard her say, "I apologize, my lord. I
must to bed now."

"So early?" Lord Wynekyn exclaimed in surprise, to which the sweet young bride said, "Aye, I
fear my husband wishes to bed me."

Wynekyn's startled gaze shot to Hugh. The old
man smiled wryly and said, "Of course he does."

Feeling color suffuse his face, Hugh stood impatiently and grasped Willa's arm. "Come."

"Nay." Wynekyn was on his feet at once. He
caught Hugh's arm. "This is not a race, Hugh. Allow her to prepare in privacy."

Hugh opened his mouth to protest, then spotted the hope on her face. His shoulders slumped in defeat. He'd already proven himself a bumbling oaf around her. He had no intention of continuing on that way.

"Very well," he agreed unhappily. "Go prepare."

Willa flashed a grateful smile at her new husband, then glanced around for Eada. But the woman was nowhere to be seen. Confusion filled her briefly, then she recalled that someone had approached the older woman at the start of the feast, asking if she would assist the village midwife in a difficult birth. It seemed Willa was on her own. That thought was rather dismaying and Willa found herself having to fight the urge to flee as she made her way toward the stairs.

This fear was a bit startling. Willa had never expected to feel such trepidation. After all, Eada had explained everything. She knew what to expect. There was no need for this cowardice. What was about to come did not sound very pleasant. Actually it sounded rather awkward, ungainly and unpleasant. Still, it must surely be more fun than it sounded, else people would not do it often, she assured herself. She started up the stairs, trying for a sedate pace.

She wasn't convinced.

Unfortunately, Eada had taken pains to stress that the first time might be unpleasant. She'd claimed there would be blood and pain the first time and that both proved the bride's innocence. Fortunately, the old woman also had taken some steps to help Willa with that unpleasantness. She'd prepared a decoction of herbs for her. The mixture was to help soothe Willa, to make the first time a more relaxed venture and perhaps ease some of the discomfort for her.

With the night ahead looming large in Willa's mind, it was not surprising that the herbs were the first thing she attended to on arriving in the room she and her husband were to share. Eada had pressed the small pouch of herbs into her hand ere leaving for the village earlier and Willa had hooked the laces of the pouch to her girdle so as not to forget it at the table. She unhooked the pouch now as her gaze settled with some relief on a pitcher and two mugs set on a chest by the fire. It seemed she need not send for a beverage. That was one bother out of the way.

Willa hurried to the chest, chose one of the mugs, opened the pouch and poured a goodly quantity of the mixture in. She then added some of the liquid from the pitcher, sniffing at it as she did. It smelled like meade, but with an unexpected nutty scent. She watched the herbs whirl around in her cup and wondered if she'd added enough.

Eada had told her to be sparing with them. But what exactly had she meant by sparing? Sparing as in a pinch? Or sparing as in no more than the pouch full? After all, there was only going to be one first night for her. She would never need the herbs again.

Aye, Willa decided. The full pouch should do it. She tipped the pouch into the mug and used a finger to stir the liquid. A grimace of distaste covered her face when she licked that finger afterward. Oh, this was going to be awful. The concoction was worse than vile. And she had to drink all of it? Perhaps suffering the bedding without it would be less painful, she thought, then nearly jumped out of her skin at the sound of footsteps approaching. When they continued on past the door, she relaxed with a sigh. Alright, she was obviously terribly tense, which Eada had said would only make the chore more difficult. A nice soothing potion might be for the best, after all.

Picking up the potion, she hesitated, then held her nose, tipped her head back and poured it straight down her throat. Oh! 'Twas truly vile. Disgusting! Ugh. Setting the mug back on the chest, she grabbed up the pitcher and began to drink straight from it, gulping at the fruity liquid in an effort to wash the taste and bits of herb from her mouth. She drained the pitcher dry trying to wash the vile potion away. The draught did manage to remove most of the taste from her mouth, but not all. She'd just decided she would have to put up with it when the bedchamber door opened.

Setting the empty pitcher back on the chest, she whirled toward the door. Surprised relief covered her face as she saw who was entering. "Eada! You are back!"

"Aye." The woman closed the door and bustled into the room. "And not a moment too soon, I see. Ye haven't even started to prepare."

"I just got up here," Willa explained.

"Oh. Well, let's get ye ready then. Where are the herbs I gave ye?"

"I already took them. I was just about to change for bed."

Eada's gaze turned sharp. "Were you sparing as I instructed?"

"Oh aye," Willa said, then to distract the old woman from further questions she asked about the birthing Eada had attended.

Hugh thought himself a most patient man. He'd watched his wife leave the table, then started to count to one hundred. He had decided that once he reached one hundred, he would be free to follow her. That seemed perfectly reasonable to him. After all, she only had a couple of items of clothing to remove and a bed to crawl into. Surely, that could not take much time. Aye, the count of one hundred was more than long enough for his bride to prepare herself.

He'd started out counting at a nice slow measured rate, but boredom had soon encouraged him to rush through several dozen numbers before he forced himself to pause and slow down again. Then Lucan had addressed a question to him about his new estates and Hugh had lost count as he paused to answer.

Irritated at himself for losing count, he'd arbitrarily picked ninety as the place to begin counting again. Hugh hastily counted off the last ten numbers and started to rise.

Wynekyn grabbed his arm. "You are not thinking of going above stairs already, are you?"

"Do you not think she will be ready?" Hugh asked uncertainly.

"Good Lord, nay!" Wynekyn pulled him back to sit on the bench. "She will barely have reached the room."

Hugh scowled and glanced toward the stairs. He supposed that might be true. She had not exactly been rushing up the stairs while he *had* been rather rushing the count to a hundred. She probably *had* just reached the room, he realized and stifled a yawn as he tried to imagine what she would be doing right now. Would she insist on a bath ere getting into bed? Nay, he decided, she had bathed before dressing for the wedding. So, at this moment she should be stripping off her clothes.

That thought helped to shake some of the sleep from his brain. Right that minute she was probably undoing the laces of her beautiful blue gown. She would let it slip off her shoulders and drop to the floor in a soft swish. She would step delicately out of the pool of cloth and move to the bowl of water in just her chemise. Her thin white chemise, so thin that when she stood there before the firelight, her legs would be visible through the cloth as she scooped water into her cupped hands and raised it to splash over her face. That water would drip down to dampen the cloth across her chest, making the material cling to her soft rounded breasts so that her hardening nipples—

"Do you not think so, Hugh?"

"Huh?" He blinked as the vision he'd been enjoying disappeared, then turned with some confusion to Wynekyn. "Do I not think what?"

"That the cook outdid herself? 'Tis something Richard always demanded. He considered Alsneta a master. She was training Luvena to follow in her footsteps—when the child wasn't off playing with Willa."

"Hmm." Hugh nodded absent agreement, then asked fretfully, "Do you not think she is ready by now?"

"Nay!" Wynekyn snapped, then gestured beyond him. "Look. Eada has returned from the village and is going up to assist her. No doubt she will come down to let you know when Willa is ready."

Hugh grunted at that. It was his considered opinion that Eada would only slow the process. It seemed to him that by this time Willa had probably finished with her ablutions and whatever else it was women did before retiring. She had no doubt already removed her thin chemise and slid naked beneath the linens.

He licked his lips at that thought, knowing that soon—in moments, he hoped—he would be taking her sylphlike body into his arms, feeling the soft brush of her nipples against the hair of his chest. His hands would slide down over her smooth back to cup the round cheeks of her bottom, then he would urge her legs apart with one knee, and ease his way inside her, planting his seed deep in her womb. Perhaps it would take right away and she would present him with a baby nine months hence.

Closing his eyes, Hugh imagined a small pink babe suckling at her breast, but the image was quickly replaced by himself suckling at her breast, her skin painted gold by the firelight, her shimmering hair winding and tangling around the two of them as they lay entwined, his hands on her hips, holding her in place as he drove himself into her—

"Enough!"

Wynekyn turned from his conversation with Lucan to peer at Hugh with surprise, startled by his outburst. "What is enough, my lord?"

Realizing that he'd spoken the word aloud, Hugh reached for his mug and downed a goodly quantity of ale. He had not meant to speak aloud, but . . . Damn, he'd waited long enough. Rising, he nodded determinedly at the men. "I am to bed."

He didn't wait to give Wynekyn the chance to protest again, or to suggest they follow any more traditions, such as a bedding ceremony. Hugh was damned if he was going to allow himself to be talked into that. Looking more like a man headed for battle than to bed, he strode to the stairs and jogged quickly up them. His expression dared anyone to interfere. He was ready for the bedding part of this marriage and he vowed no one was going to put him off. Hell, he'd been ready since the other day in the stable when the only thing that had stopped him was his inability to remove his armor. Why the devil did they make those things so bloody impossible for a man to remove alone, anyway? What about situations when there was no squire around to aid in the undressing?

He grimaced now at the thought. The first thing he'd done after Wynekyn had taken Willa above stairs was to send for his squire and a bath.

What a relief it had been to finally get out of that armor. Hugh was used to wearing it, but being stuck in it for three days and two nights straight had made him more than eager to shed it. Once the chain mail was off, he'd sent his squire away and had seen to the rest of his disrobing and the bath himself. He'd hoped to be able to get a look at whatever was causing him so much pain in the saddle. Unfortunately, its location had made that impossible. He still wasn't sure what the problem was, but the hot bath had seemed to ease the pain somewhat. That wasn't to say that he'd been comfortable sitting at the table for so long during the wedding celebration, but at least he'd managed to do so without grimacing or wincing in pain.

Chapter Nine

The murmur of voices made Hugh's steps slow as he neared the bedchamber he and his bride were to use that night. It took him but a moment to realize it was Eada's hoarse voice speaking.

"So never fear," she was saying. "I've read the future in the dregs of yer drink and ye'll be happy. Ye'll have much love and many children and live to a ripe old age. Now, I should go below and let yer new husband know ye're ready."

He heard shuffling footsteps move toward the door, and quickly backed up several steps as it opened. Eada stepped out into the hall and pulled the door closed.

"Is that true?" Hugh asked, uncaring that she would know he'd listened in on the conversation.

Eada turned from closing the door and arched an eyebrow at Hugh in question. "Is what true?"

"What you said," he explained, irritated with himself for giving the least credence to the woman's supposed visions. "About us being happy and having many children and living long. Was it true?"

"Aye. But I said *she* would. I don't recall mentioning you at all," the old woman snapped, then relented at his dismayed expression. "Ye'll come quickly to love her and, aye, ye'll give her many babes. In fact, ye'll give her twins the first time ye plant yerself in her."

"Twins?" Hugh peered at her in horror.

"Aye. And if ye untangle the riddle of her birth and remove the danger, ye may even live to see them nine months later."

"And if I do not?"

"Death awaits one of ye."

"Which one?"

The old woman shrugged. "Probably you. All I know for sure is that there are two possible endings. One is that the two of ye will live a long happy life together."

Hugh was just beginning to relax when she added, "Unless ye muddle things."

He stiffened. "Muddle things how?"

She shrugged again. "Don't know."

"You do not know? Did you not ask?"

Her glance turned irritated. "It's not like placing an order with the alewife, ye know. I see what I see, and what I see is that ye'll be perched on a precipice. If ye choose one way, all will be well. Do ye choose the other—" She shrugged. "Death."

"Where does the danger lie? Who would kill one of us?" She shrugged again and Hugh shifted impatiently. "Well, you must know something of use." When she merely stared at him solemnly, his eyes narrowed. "Know you who her parents were and who wished her dead as a child?"

"That is the riddle ye must solve." With those words, she moved passed him and walked away down the hall.

Hugh watched her go, then turned to the bedchamber door. His future lay beyond it. A future filled with the bliss he knew he would find in his bride's arms. He just wished he knew if it were a long or short future.

Realizing that he was giving credence to the old witch's visions, Hugh gave his head a shake. It must be exhaustion making him so muddleheaded, he decided. The hag could not tell the future. No one could. Feeling better, he opened the door and stepped into the bedchamber.

Willa had listened to the murmur of voices outside the door and had wondered what Eada and Hugh were discussing. She'd had no trouble recognizing the timber of their voices, though she could not quite make out what they were saying. She had wished they would hurry up, however, for she very much feared that it had been a mistake to disregard Eada's instructions and take the entire pouch of herbs. She was starting to feel quite unwell. So much so that she actually began to regret all the effort she'd put into distracting Eada so that she would not again ask about the pouch of herbs.

The potion was definitely helping her to relax. The problem was that she was starting to feel almost boneless, she was so relaxed. She was also quite lethargic and a touch queasy. And was the room really spinning, or was that the effect of the potion?

Hoping that sitting up would help the situation, she struggled upright in the bed, not even noticing that the linen dropped away to leave her bare from the waist up. Willa had felt funny about not wearing a shift to bed, but Eada had assured her there was no need for one as Hugh would no doubt just remove it anyway.

Slumping back against the bedpost she began breathing deeply in the hope that it would either clear her head a bit, or ease the queasiness building in her belly. It was then that Willa noticed the top half of the linen was pooled around her waist. She thought she'd best cover herself, but it seemed like too much effort. She'd definitely taken too much of the potion. Much too much.

The sound of the door opening and closing reached her ears and Willa managed to force her eyes open again. It was Hugh. He stood by the door, apparently arrested by the sight of her and she felt relief slide through her. No doubt he could tell by just looking that there was something terribly wrong with her. Which was a relief, for she did not even seem to have the energy to speak at the moment. But that would be unnecessary. He could see there was a problem. He would fetch Eada.

Hugh didn't know what he'd expected to find on entering the bedchamber. His bride all tucked up under the linens, a shy smile on her face, or perhaps even a nervous smile. Mayhap even no smile at all, but stark terror on her face. Who could know what to expect from a virgin? Hugh certainly couldn't. He'd never bedded one before. So finding her lounging in bed in a rather sexy, languid pose that left her beautiful breasts bared to him was not what he'd anticipated.

"Thank you, Uncle Richard," he breathed, marveling over the fact that he had at first actually protested marrying this woman. He must have been mad, he decided, his gazed fixed on the two sweet orbs he'd been fantasizing about below stairs. His imagination was coming up with many more things he could do with them now. Touching, suckling, nipping. . . .

Realizing that he was wasting time imagining these things when he actually could be doing them, Hugh moved forward, undressing as he went. His surcoat was off in two steps; his tunic hit the floor with his fourth; he undid the points of his breeches and began to shove them down. This brought him to an abrupt halt since he had yet to remove his boots and his braies were caught around his ankles.

Managing to drag his eyes from Willa's breasts, he pulled the breeches back up, lifted one foot to grasp his boot and began tugging it off, hopping awkwardly. It was quite a trick, but he managed it and quickly turned his attention to the other boot. With those out of the way, he let his breeches drop again, this time stepping out of them as they hit the floor.

Hugh peered at Willa's face to gauge her reaction to her first sight of his nakedness. He felt alarm

course through him at the pallor of her skin and
her rather sickly expression. He supposed he'd
hoped that she would be as impressed with his
muscular physique as he was with her own shapely
curves. It hadn't occurred to him that the very
size he took pride in might cause her some concern and distress. No doubt she was wondering
how they would ever fit together. For a moment
Hugh was at a loss as to how to reassure her; then
he took a deep breath, lifted the linen to ease into
bed beside her and said, "I am your husband. You
have nothing to fear from me. I shall ne'er harm
you. My duty now is to protect you and tend to
your wants and needs. You must trust me in this."

Her hand fluttered on the linens like a wounded
bird and her mouth opened and closed without
sound. She merely stared at him out of eyes full of
fear. Wondering what the hell Eada had said to
frighten the girl so, Hugh searched his mind for
the magic words that would ease her obvious terror about what was to come. Then he recalled the
passion they had shared in the stable and decided
that reawakening her desire was his best bet to
erase her virginal distress. To that end, he smiled
and scooted closer to her in the bed until his knee
touched her hip.

"We have no need of this." He flipped the linen
away from them both, his gaze immediately dropping to her body. She was beautiful. Full and cur-
vaceous and smooth-skinned. He was quite busy
devouring her with his eyes when a gasping sound
drew his gaze back to her face.

Willa was trying to speak, but was apparently

overcome by his own naked magnificence. Her mouth opened, then closed, her eyes jerking up and down, then side to side. She was obviously too shy to allow her eyes to study his male attributes for any length of time. Hugh felt himself soften and took one of her fluttering hands in his.

"'Tis alright, my lady. You may look at me. I will not think you forward." Her eyes seemed to roll then and he almost could have sworn she looked put out when they returned to him. He must be mistaken in that, he decided, but frowned as he saw what he was sure was panic and horror flash in her eyes. "What is it?"

He leaned forward, using her hand to pull her closer to him. She seemed to have some difficulty supporting herself, however, and slumped against his chest like a cloth doll.

"Willa?" he asked uncertainly, running his hand over her head. "Are you unwell? Do you wish to put off the bedding?"

He really hadn't wanted to ask that question, but Hugh was no animal. If she was unwell, the consummation would have to be put off. Dear God, please let her be well, he prayed. God wasn't in the mood to humor him. Nor was Willa. Her answer came in the form of a retching sound.

"A simple aye would have sufficed," Hugh whispered, then swallowed harshly as he felt his gorge rise. Dear God, the woman had just puked in his lap!

He sat unmoving, frozen to the spot by horror. Willa, however, hadn't finished making her opinions on the matter known. Her body shuddered as it was wracked with spasm after fierce spasm. Hugh peered down at her bent head where he still clasped her close to his chest, alarm beating his stomach into submission. Something was terribly wrong. She wasn't just ill, she was violently ill.

Afraid of his own stomach's response when he saw what she'd done, Hugh continued to hold her in place as his mind began frantically trying to figure out what had caused her nausea. It could not have been drink that had brought on this attack. He'd kept an eye on her throughout the meal and knew she had drunk very little. Was it something she'd eaten then? Nay, that could not be, he decided. They had shared the same trencher, eaten the same food, and his stomach felt fine. Well, it had before she'd spewed her meal on his thighs and . . . other parts.

Was it anxiety then that had brought this on? He had known a warrior once with a nervous stomach who vomited before every battle. Was that what she was suffering? Was she so frightened and nervous that she could not keep her food down? He'd heard of frightened virgins, but this was more than he'd expected. Or—Dear Lord! Had it been the very sight of him that had turned her stomach? That possibility was enough to make Hugh feel sick, himself.

Her retching increased in violence, stirring Hugh from his rather stunned state. Scrambling quickly away from her and off the bed, he paused to peer down at himself and had to swallow back the bile that now crept up his throat. This was . . . well, frankly it was disgusting, he decided and snatched the top linen off the bed to mop himself off. Having cleaned himself to the best of his abilities, he hurried around the bed to grab the basin of water there. He made a quick detour to toss the water out the window, then rushed back to the bed to shove the basin under Willa's face.

Hugh climbed onto the bed next to his new bride and held her shoulders, then patted her back helplessly as she continued to heave and retch. After several minutes of this, he began to feel a bit desperate. This was no nervous stomach. Something was terribly wrong. She needed someone more skilled to aid her. Eada was the first person who came to mind. She was considered a witch not just for her supposed ability to see the future, but also because of her healing abilities.

Unwilling to leave Willa alone, Hugh began bellowing from the bed. After three or four shouts, he admitted to himself that no one could hear him through the door. He would have to leave her briefly to fetch aid. Hugh wasn't even sure Willa heard his words, but he wasted several moments telling her where he was going. Then, he left her there on the bed and rushed out into the hall.

Of course there was no one about above stairs. Everyone was still in the great hall below. He rushed to the top of the steps, uncaring of his nakedness and began bellowing again. This time his shouts had a more gratifying effect. Despite the music and laughter and general noise, a few people heard him. Or perhaps it was simply that someone happened to look up and spy him. Whatever the case, there were gasps at the sight of the new lord standing naked at the top of the steps, bellowing at the top of his lungs. The great hall went quiet as everyone turned to stare at him.

"I need Eada," he roared into that sudden silence. "Willa is unwell."

The old crone was immediately on her feet and rushing for the stairs. Satisfied that she was on her way, Hugh turned and hurried back to the bedchamber. Willa was hanging weakly over the basin he'd set before her. This was an encouraging sight, he thought. At least she seemed more aware and not quite as weak as she'd been at first.

Hugh rushed to her side and sat on the edge of the bed. He brushed her hair off her face. "Willa?" he said gently, relieved when her dazed eyes opened and fixed on him. "You have been ill. Do you know what happened?"

She seemed to try to nod her head, then whispered, "Potion."

"Potion?" Hugh frowned, then left her lying there and moved off the bed to look around the room. He found the empty pitcher by the fire. Two mugs and an empty bag sat beside it. Examining the bag, he realized at once that it had held herbs of some sort or other not long ago. And judging by the weedy remains in the mug she'd used, there had been quite a bit of potion in the bag and all of it had been used.

Cursing, Hugh tossed the bag aside and hurried back to the bed. "Willa?" Grabbing her by the shoulders, he gave her a shake. "Willa? How much potion was there? What was it? What did you take?"

"Too much," she moaned miserably. Her head dropped back and her eyes closed. Hugh didn't know if she'd fallen asleep, fainted or passed out. He tried rousing her again by first shaking her, then patting her face, but nothing seemed to work. He was relieved when he glanced toward the door to see Eada rushing in . . . until he saw that she was followed by Wynekyn, Lucan and Jollivet. Hugh opened his mouth to order them out, but Wynekyn spotted Willa and stopped abruptly. He nearly tumbled forward onto his face as Lucan and Jollivet crashed into him from behind.

"Are you alright?" Lucan asked, managing to catch the older man before he fell.

"Oh my!" Jollivet breathed, though whether the exclamation was at the sight of Willa's nakedness, or the smell and mess in the room was hard to say. Hugh didn't care. Moving around the bed, he waved Eada toward Willa and strode grimly toward the three men, ready to remove them bodily if necessary. It wasn't necessary. The men blanched and retreated, their noses wrinkling, their gazes dropping to his decorated lap. He'd done a rather poor job of cleaning up but he'd been more concerned with Willa at the time.

"If you are hoping that will be the new fashion, I fear 'twill not take at all," Jollivet commented drolly, then turned sharply on his heel and exited the room as Hugh's face twisted with rage.

"We will wait in the hall," Lucan assured him and followed hard on the other man's heels.

"Er . . . yes." Wynekyn backed toward the door, his concerned gaze bouncing to Willa and away when she began to retch again. "Do let us know what is happening once you have—" he waved vaguely toward Hugh's groin—"cleaned up."

He pulled the door closed behind himself with a snap.

"What happened?" Eada asked. Hugh turned to find her examining the girl.

"She said she took too much potion." There was no denying the accusation in his tone or his eyes as he glared at the old woman. She ignored him as she worked. Hugh allowed her to disregard him, waiting impatiently as she lifted Willa's eyelids, poked at her skin, looked inside her mouth.

"She will not wake up," he said at last when his patience had about run out. "She took too much of your potion."

"The potion was to relax her," the old witch told him calmly. "'Twas to ease yer first night together."

"Aye. Well, as you can see, it worked. Too well. She is too relaxed."

"Nay," the witch said harshly. "She isn't relaxed. She's dying."

"What?" Hugh bellowed in shock. Ignoring him, Eada turned to peer about the room, then zeroed in on the pitcher and mugs by the fire. Hugh settled on the bed and half-lifted Willa to lean against him again as the crone crossed the room. He watched her pick up the used mug, sniff it briefly, then set it down and sniff the half empty pitcher. She stiffened then, her eyes shooting to him. "Did you drink any of this?"

"Nay. Why?"

" 'Tis poison."

"What?" His arms tightened convulsively around Willa. "She said she had taken too much of your potion."

"Aye." The witch picked up the empty pouch. " 'Tis probably what saved her. I told her to use it sparingly. A little would have relaxed her. The whole pouch is what made her purge the poison."

"Will she be alright?" Hugh asked, peering down at Willa's pale face with concern.

Eada's response was to set down the pouch, walk over to collect the empty chamber pot and carry it back to the bed.

"Lay her on her stomach with her head hanging off the bed," Eada instructed, removing the basin Hugh had fetched for her earlier. He shifted her around at once, then held Willa with one hand at her back, the other at her forehead to keep her head from falling forward. He watched curiously as the witch set the chamber pot on the floor beneath her and tugged a feather from a small bag she'd brought with her. She opened Willa's mouth and stuck the feather inside.

"What are you—" Hugh began, then cursed and tightened his hold on Willa as she began to shudder and convulse, tossing up some more of whatever mixture she had in her stomach. "Dear God, has she not suffered enough? Would you make her—"

"We have to make her purge all of the poison if she's to live," the witch interrupted calmly. She waited until Willa's fit ended then forced the feather down her throat to start another round of

retching. She did not stop until Willa was bringing nothing more up. Hugh winced as her body
spasmed over and over again without satisfaction.

"That should be enough," the witch announced.
He watched affection move across her features as
she looked at the limp woman he held; then her
expression closed and she stood abruptly. "She will
feel like death when she wakes up. Hungry, too, no
doubt, but she probably won't be able to keep anything down."

"Why did you not see this coming?" Hugh
couldn't keep his irritation out of his voice as he
eased his bride around to lie on her back. When
he glanced at the witch, however, she shrugged
with unconcern.

"I don't see everything," she said simply.

"So much for my twins." The witch actually
cracked a smile at his complaint as Hugh covered
Willa. He wasn't amused, however, and let her
know as much. "I do not see what is so funny. This
all just proves that you are an old fraud. You said
I would plant twins in her tonight. Somehow I do
not see that as much of a possibility. Do you?"

"I said ye would plant twins in her the first
time ye released yer seed. I never said 'twould be
tonight."

Hugh let the matter drop. He was too weary to
argue. Besides, he was beginning to see that there
was no sense in disputing the crone; she always
seemed to have an answer. But then, what woman
didn't? He watched her leave, then glanced down
at Willa. She was still pale, but not alarmingly
so as she'd been earlier. And even pale, she was

amazingly beautiful. He brushed some hair back from her face, his fingers caressing the petal soft skin of her cheek. She was such a lovely creature. Perhaps it wouldn't be so bad being married to her, even if he did have to deal with the hag.

That thought had barely entered his head when his sweet bride's eyes suddenly popped open. She lunged into a sitting position, threw up in his lap again, then promptly fell back on the bed, unconscious.

Chapter Ten

She was being roasted alive. Overwhelming heat awoke Willa. It forced her to rouse enough to strip away several of the furs causing her discomfort. By the time she'd removed all but one, she was wide awake and not pleased at the waking. She felt terrible. Horrendous. Her mouth was dry and filled with the most unpleasant taste. Her whole body seemed to ache. For the first several moments, Willa lay grimacing over her discomfort, then a grunt and a movement drew her head sharply around.

For a moment she stared blankly at the shifting mound of furs beside her; then Willa's memory kicked in. She was married now. The mass under the furs must be her husband. Last night had been her wedding night.

Of course, the rest of the memories quickly followed. Yesterday's ceremony. The feast. Hugh sending her above stairs to prepare for the bedding. That was where her memories got a bit fuzzy. Willa remembered mixing the herbs Eada had given her in the ale that had been set out. She remembered pinching her nose and downing the concoction. She remembered being suddenly dizzy and tired and realizing that she'd taken too much of the potion. She had a vague image of her husband leaning over her.

Willa glanced down at herself sharply. If Eada were right—and Willa had never known the woman to be wrong—he'd planted twins in her belly last night. Grimacing as she ran her hand over her stomach, Willa decided that was a good possibility. Her stomach was hard and cramping this morning. She'd never heard that planting babies hurt the woman's belly, but it was as good an explanation as any for her pain and discomfort. The consummation must have been quite energetic. Actually, considering the fact that she felt as though she'd been trampled by a horse, Willa decided that she was rather grateful she'd overdosed herself with Eada's potion. If this was how she felt afterwards, she wasn't all that eager to experience the act itself.

Grimacing at the thought, she slid carefully from the bed, doing her best not to jostle her new husband. Much to her relief, Hugh didn't even stir at her slight movements. Keeping one eye on him, Willa began to tiptoe around the room in search of clothes. There was no sign of the lovely gown she'd worn the day before. The only nice gown she had. She did come across the bed linens. That gave her pause. They were rolled up in a ball and lay in a corner of the room. Eada had told her that there was blood the first time, that the blood would prove her innocence. Now she stared at the wadded linens and thought with some horror that surely there had not been *so* much blood? But what other reason was there for her husband to have stripped the bed?

She turned away from the linens and found the small chest holding her belongings. The mourning gown Eada was making for her wasn't finished yet. The gown she'd worn yesterday was the only fine garment she possessed, but Willa had other ones, less fine, that she'd brought with her. She dragged one out, donned it, then made her way out of the room.

It had been a long time since Willa had lived in a castle, not since she was a child. But in her memories the castle had always been a busy, bustling place. At least Claymorgan had been. The silence that met her in the hallway was a bit disturbing. Ignoring the shakiness of her legs and the cramping in her stomach, she made her way to the top of the stairs. Her gaze slid around the great hall as she started down. One glance was enough to explain the unnaturally quiet castle. Most of the inhabitants were sprawled about the hall, snoring. No doubt the celebration had gone on well into the early hours of morning. The castle's inhabitants were still sleeping off their drink. She imagined most of them would be suffering the ale passion when they woke. Their sore heads would make them useless for the better part of the morning.

Willa was just stepping off the stairs when one

of the figures at the table shifted and stood. Willa smiled widely. "Good morn, Eada."

"Good morn." Eada patted her back gently as Willa embraced her, then studied her face. "How do you feel?"

"Horrid," Willa admitted with a groan and the old woman nodded.

"I expected as much. Come along. Some dry bread and fresh air will make you feel better." She led Willa through the sleeping servants to the kitchens.

While the rest of the castle almost appeared to be caught in the grip of a sleeping spell, the kitchens showed some life, though it was sluggish. Alsneta and several servants were stumbling about baking bread and other pastries. Eada ignored the fresh bread cooling on the table and sought out some day-old bread instead. Handing it to Willa, she moved off to find her something to drink. She rejoined Willa a moment later, with a mug of meade in hand, then herded her back out into the hall. She led her along the table to a clear spot where the two of them could sit. She then made Willa eat some of the bread and drink some of the meade, watching her closely the whole while.

Willa wasn't hungry, but dutifully she ate and drank, knowing that Eada would not be satisfied until she did. She was halfway through the small hunk of bread Eada had given her when the woman suddenly stood and moved off toward the kitchens again. Willa watched her go, then glanced around. Spying one of the castle dogs eyeing her hopefully, she broke off a good portion of the bread and

held it out to him. The animal was at her side at
once. Willa watched him gulp down the bread,
then glanced toward the kitchen and started to eat
the last of her bread as Eada returned. The old
woman glanced sharply from Willa to the dog and
back, but merely held out the small sack she carried.

"What is this?" Willa asked curiously, accepting the sack.

"For Wolfy and Fen. They must have followed
us to the castle yester morn. I heard them out baying at the moon last night. 'Twas a mournful sound.
They're missing ye. Besides, the fresh air and walk
will do ye good."

Concern filled Willa's eyes. "I did not hear them."

"Nay. Well, I'm not surprised. Ye were otherwise occupied."

Willa blushed slightly at those words, took a
sip of the meade, then stood. "I will go find them."

"Ye do that."

Hugh awoke with a groan. Most of the night had
been spent fretting over his wife. She had not slept
well. Even once she'd finished vomiting up the
poison, she'd tossed and turned fitfully for hours.
It was only once her struggles had ceased that
Hugh had allowed himself to doze off. That had
been near dawn.

His gaze slid to the bright sunlight slipping
around the covering in front of the window. By
his guess, he'd had only a couple of hours' sleep. It
hadn't been nearly enough. His chest felt as if a
great cow were sitting on it, his eyes were scratchy
and his head was splitting.

Ah, married life, he thought dryly. At this rate, the old witch's prediction that he would die ere the next full moon was likely to come true despite his crawling through the mud to Willa. A burst of coughing wracked his body and Hugh quickly covered his mouth, attempting to muffle the sound to keep from waking his wife. Willa would be weak and in need of much rest after last night's ordeal, he was sure.

That thought made him glance toward her, but she was buried under a mound of furs. Hugh sniffled and eased onto his side. He winced at the pain shooting through his derriere, a reminder of the sore he had there. All that rushing about and getting up and down last night to tend his wife had done his butt little good. He was exhausted and suffering a head cold and a pain in the arse. Aye, he was a mess, Hugh conceded as he began gently lifting aside the furs. He had perhaps overdone it with the furs, but winter was coming and the nights were cool. Now he lifted skin after skin away in search of his wife, only to discover that she was gone.

Hugh ignored his complaining backside and tossed aside the furs covering him. Willa had left the chamber. He couldn't believe she'd had the strength after the ordeal she'd been through. He couldn't believe she'd had the nerve after what she'd put *him* through. Hugh had seen a lot of blood and gore over the years. A man could not go to war and come back with innocent eyes, but dear God, he'd never seen the likes of last night. Give him blood and guts any day over a vomiting woman.

Cursing, he reached for the clothes he'd worn the night before, started to lift them from where they lay on the linens, then remembered why they were bundled there. They, along with Willa's gown and the linens, were soiled.

Tossing the soiled clothing aside, he gritted his teeth against the pain in his arse and stomped to the chest that held his things. He dug through it until he came up with some fresh braies and a tunic. Hugh donned the tunic as he walked to the door, then hopped from foot to foot as he pulled on the braies. Tugging the door open, he let it hit the wall with a satisfying crash, then continued to the stairs and down to the great hall. The crash of the bedchamber door had acted like a rooster's crow to those loafing in the hall. Most of them were awakened by it. Others were startled awake by the activity of their companions. They were all milling and stumbling about by the time Hugh reached the bottom step, but he ignored every last one of them. His gaze settled on the hag who sat, patiently waiting, at the table. He immediately started in her direction.

"Where is she?" he asked without preamble, pausing at her side.

"She went for a walk."

"Alone?" There was no mistaking the fury and fear mingled in his voice.

"She is safe enough," the hag assured him calmly. "She's safer with Wolfy and Fen than she is anywhere else in this world."

Hugh didn't miss the rebuke in her words. He'd allowed Willa to be poisoned. She'd been put in his care and he'd failed her. Cursing, he turned away, then paused and glanced back. "Is she on foot or on that horse of hers?"

"On foot. But she's been gone a while. Mayhap an hour," Eada told him.

Nodding, Hugh strode out of the castle. Willa had a head start and he had to find her quickly. Someone had tried to kill his wife before they had even consummated their marriage. Uncle Richard's worries and fears were already coming to pass. Willa's life was under threat, and Hugh didn't have any idea why.

His mouth tightening with displeasure, he headed for the stables. He would quickly hunt her down and bring her back to the castle. She obviously wasn't safe. And Hugh could hardly believe that the witch had let her wander off on her own, wolves or no wolves.

"My lord!"

Hugh slowed his step and glanced around at that call. Spotting Father Brennan rushing toward him, he stopped and tried not to appear as impatient as he felt at this delay. "Good morn, father."

Father Brennan was a little out of breath as he reached Hugh, but he was beaming. "Good morn, my lord. I am so glad to have come across you this morning. I fear yesterday was all so rushed, I did not fulfill my duties as I should have."

"Did you not?" Hugh asked politely, but his gaze was wandering toward the stables. He wished his squire was about so that he could send him ahead to ready his horse. Where was his squire anyway? He'd released the lad from duty at the feast yesterday, thinking he wished to be alone with his bride. He scowled as the memory of his wedding night rose up to plague him. Gad! Had ever a man been so beset by misfortune? A sore arse, a nasty cold, and a poisoned, puking bride.

"Nay. First you were off guarding Lady Willa. Then when the two of you arrived here, everything was so chaotic that I never managed the time to counsel you on the matter of the . . . er . . . bedding."

"The bedding?" Those words caught Hugh's attention and drew his wandering thoughts and gaze back to the priest's now slightly flushed face. "There was no bedding. My bride was poisoned."

"Aye. Lord Wynekyn informed me of the situation and I must say I see it as somewhat fortunate—not fortunate!" he amended when Hugh scowled down at him. "I did not mean fortunate, I meant . . . well, under the circumstances, since I had not counseled you—"

"Father," Hugh interrupted, no longer bothering to hide his impatience, "now is not the time. Willa has gone off on her own and I must find her and bring her back. She—"

"She is returned, my lord," Father Brennan blurted as Hugh started to turn away. He spun back at once.

"She is?"

"Aye. So you see, I brought this treatise." He held out a rolled up and beribboned scroll. When Hugh merely stared at it blankly, the priest undid the scroll and began to unroll it. " 'Tis *De secretis mulierum* and it gives advice on matters—"

"Father," Hugh interrupted again. This time

his impatience was gone, replaced by mild amusement. He knew Father Brennan had good intentions, but a priest was the last person whose advice he needed on bedding his bride. Not wishing to embarrass the fellow, Hugh managed a solemn expression and patted his shoulder. "I am not an innocent, father. I *have* been with women before. There is no need for counsel."

"Oh, certainly, certainly." The priest nodded his head, then shook it. "But Lady Willa is not some tavern doxy. She is a young, innocent bride. The consummation of your new relationship has been sanctified by the church. Your marriage bed is sacred. You cannot simply . . . er . . . give her a tumble like some pretty milk maid. If you see what I mean?"

"Well . . . ," Hugh paused, uncertainty creeping into his mind. He'd not considered the actual act. Well, alright, he'd considered it, but mostly from his own perspective. He had spent one brief moment wondering how she would greet his arrival in their chamber; then his thoughts had been rather full of the idea of finally sliding into her moist warmth. He hadn't considered the act from her point of view. Her pure, *virginal* point of view. Willa would not be a laughing tavern maid, dropping into his lap and grabbing his groin to let him know she was willing. She would be . . .

This new line of thought was giving him pains in his head. But Father Brennan was waiting patiently for an answer. What had the question been? Oh yes! "Nay. Of course not. I have never taken a woman's innocence."

"Just so. Which is why you are in need of counsel." He finished unrolling the scroll and moved closer, turning the parchment so that they could both read it. "*De secretis mulierum* is quite useful in providing instruction for marital ... er ... relations." A sudden squeak in his voice drew Hugh's glance from the scroll to the priest's now flushed face. The man was terribly embarrassed, but rushed gamely on, "It does advise preparing both the mind and body beforehand."

"Preparing the body?" Hugh echoed curiously. He didn't think he would have trouble with preparing his mind. His mind seemed more than ready. However, if there were special instructions on preparing the body, he would be interested in reading them. A bath perhaps ... that they could share. He had a brief picture of running a damp bit of linen over Willa's sweet breasts, her nipples coming to life, standing up and begging him to—

"Aye. Emptying the bowels and bladder is suggested, for instance."

Hugh's erotic imaginings died abruptly and he made a grimace of distaste. That *would* be the church's idea of preparing.

"It also gives *other* detailed instructions," Father Brennan said meaningfully, recapturing the earl's wandering attention. The bit about emptying the bowels had rather lost him, but his interest perked up a bit now.

"What sort of detailed instructions?" he asked, looking over the Latin script. When the holy man didn't answer right away, Hugh raised a questioning glance to find the priest cherry red and looking mortified.

"Well, they—" he squeaked, then cleared his throat and evaded Hugh's gaze as he tried again. "They suggest 'tis necessary to . . . er . . . fondle the wife's 'lower parts' to . . . er. . . . raise her body to the proper . . . er . . . heat—"

"Heat?" Hugh interrupted with surprise.

"Aye. You see women differ from men in that they are cold."

"They are?" Hugh asked with surprise. He had never noted women to be especially cold. Neither in behavior, nor to the touch.

"Aye, they are," Father Brennan assured him. "Men, by contrast, are hot."

"Really?" he asked with interest, recalling now a time or two when he'd been startled awake by a cold foot seeking his for warmth under the furs.

"Oh, aye!" Father Brennan exclaimed. "Heat is the male's essential quality. It . . . the man's heat creates the . . . excitement in the woman and through intercourse with a man, she gains that vital heat she is lacking."

"She does, does she?"

"Aye. So you see, the wife is thereby strengthened by the joining."

"Hmm," Hugh grunted, but his attention was on the treatise the priest still held open for him. He was looking for the section stating that there must be sufficient fondling of the "lower parts" to get the woman to the right temperature. He wasn't having much success. Scowling, he asked, "How do you know when she has reached the correct temperature?"

"Er . . . I believe it states . . . ," the priest ran his finger over the words, then nodded, his face flushing again. "Aye. Here 'tis. She will begin to 'speak as if she were babbling.' That is when you shall know to commence with the actual—" he waved a hand vaguely—"commencing."

Hugh nodded as he read the section the man was pointing to.

"Well. I am sure that you can read this on your own. I hope you find it useful."

Hugh nodded distractedly and murmured his thanks, sensing when the priest left.

"Speak as if she were babbling," he read aloud. "Hmm."

"Good morn, my lord husband."

Hugh glanced up with alarm at that greeting. It was his errant wife, of course. Who else would call him husband? Flushing guiltily, Hugh straightened and quickly hid the treatise behind his back. "Good morn."

"What is that you were reading?" she asked curiously, leaning to the side to glimpse the scroll he held.

" 'Tis nothing," he lied.

"Nothing?" She gave a soft laugh. "It does not look like nothing, my lord. It looks like parchment with writing on it."

"Nay, 'tis just something Father Brennan gave me to read. A treatise on . . . the church's instruction on . . . confession." He winced as he spoke, thinking that he would now have to confess this lie. But it was rather embarrassing to admit that he felt he needed instruction on such a personal matter.

"Oh." Much to his relief, she appeared to have lost interest in the matter. She straightened and offered him another smile. "Well, I should leave you to it then. Good day, my lord."

"Good day." He watched her go, his gaze dropping to the sway of her hips as she walked away.

Becoming aware that he still held the treatise *De secretis mulierum* behind his back, he relaxed and brought it around to glance over it. His original intention was to reroll it and put it through his belt to be read later, but his gaze caught on a line and, instead, he found himself caught up in reading it again.

"Good morn, Hugh."

Just as before, Hugh straightened abruptly at that greeting. He stashed the parchment guiltily behind his back as he turned to face his friend. "Lucan. Good morn."

"What have you there?" Lucan asked curiously.

" 'Tis nothing," Hugh answered, then grimaced. It was a ridiculous answer when he was hiding the parchment behind his back as if it were an erotic love letter. Relaxing his stance, he brought the parchment around between them and began to roll it back up as he said, " 'Tis a treatise Father Brennan gave me . . . on . . . marital relations."

"Ah. My father's priest gave my brother just such a treatise on the night before his wedding. 'Twas full of what you could not do and when you could not do it. Let me see, as I recall you were never to indulge in marital relations on holy days, Sundays, or feast days." Lucan shook his head. "I vow once you take out all the days you cannot bed a wife, there is one day a month left to do the deed." He put a hand on Hugh's shoulder as they began to walk, and advised, "I shouldn't pay attention to that, my friend, or you shall never see children. You shall also surely go insane."

Hugh grunted in response. He suspected Lucan was thinking of another treatise altogether, but in case he wasn't, Hugh would stick to reading only the instructions on the actual bedding itself. Surely a man couldn't go to purgatory for a sin if he did not know it was one, he reasoned. And there was no way he would restrict himself to bedding Willa only once a month. Dear God, he hadn't even managed to bed her once, yet already the church was trying to limit him.

"Have you decided what you intend to do about the poisoning attempt?" Lucan asked.

Hugh grimaced. "Aye. I intend to question everyone about the meade and discover who put it in the room. But first I am going to arrange for a food taster. Nothing shall pass Willa's lips that has not first been tasted by another."

Lucan nodded at that. "The cook?"

"Nay. Alsneta hasn't the time for that. But it should be someone she cares for. It will reduce the possibility of her getting distracted and allowing anyone near the food."

His friend nodded at the wisdom of that decision, then said, "Wynekyn mentioned that Alsneta has a nephew amongst the soldiers here. Gawain. He should do nicely."

"Aye. He will. Thank you."

"You are welcome." Lucan raised an eyebrow. "Did you plan to have Baldulf guard her again?"

"Aye. But I shall need others to guard her as well. I can hardly expect the man to watch her night and day here." Hugh shook his head. The soldiers at Hillcrest had all been his uncle's men. Hugh had none of his own, other than his squire. He didn't know which were trustworthy and skilled and which weren't. He would have to trust someone. Baldulf alone had been able to guard her at the cottage, but the castle was much bigger. "Aye. Baldulf during the day, and then two guards outside our door at night. I shall have to interview the men. See whom I can trust her with."

Lucan nodded as they walked. "Have you learned anything about her past?"

"We have a name now. Evelake." He murmured the name thoughtfully, sure he'd heard it before. He spent a moment trying to recall where he knew it from, then shook his head. "I thought I should send some men out to learn what they could about her family. Then I thought to look in Uncle Richard's room and see if I cannot find this mysterious missing letter."

"How were Wolfy and Fen?"

Willa smiled at Eada and bent to press a kiss on her withered cheek, then settled on the bench beside her before answering. "They are well enough.

I worry about them being so close to the castle and village though."

Willa had found the two wolves skulking on the edge of the woods that surrounded the castle. They were far too close for her comfort.

"Did Lord Hillcrest find ye?"

"Nay. I came upon him on my way back. Was he looking for me?"

"Aye." Eada grinned. "He was distressed that ye'd wandered off on yer own. I believe he intended to reprimand ye sternly and order ye never to do so again."

Willa stared at the woman with surprise. "Nay!"

"Aye."

She bit her lip. "Odd, he did not seem distressed when I came upon him. He was reading some treatise the priest gave him."

"Hmm." They both puzzled over that briefly, then the old woman examined her face. "The walk did ye good. Ye've more color to ye now, at least. How are ye feeling?"

Willa shrugged mildly, her hand going to her stomach. "My stomach is a touch tender, but no doubt that is due to his planting the twins there last night. Other than that I am well enough."

"Planting the twins?" Eada turned an amazed expression on her. "There was no planting of twins last night. Ye were far too sick for that."

"Sick?" Willa felt confusion well up in her. "What—?"

"Ye were poisoned, child," the woman told her. "Don't ye recall? Ye were sick the night through. The only thing Dulonget managed to plant was his palm on yer forehead as he held ye while ye tossed yer innards out."

"What?" Willa gaped at her in horror. "Nay!"

"Aye."

"But you said he would plant twins in me the—"

"I said the first time ye were together. Last night wasn't it."

Willa slumped where she sat, pondering this unwelcome news. She'd been so sure she was with child . . . well, with children. She grieved that loss briefly, then as Eada's other claim sank in, she straightened and confessed, "No one poisoned me. I took too much of that potion you gave me."

"Aye, ye did. And that's what saved yer life. It didn't sit well. Started ye purging before the poison could do much damage."

Willa frowned at this news. "You mean to say that someone truly did try to poison me?"

"Aye. 'Twas in the meade."

Willa grimaced as she recalled the bitter tasting meade mixed with Eada's herbs. It had not gone down well. She did recall feeling ill, then her stomach trying to fight its way up her throat, but everything else was rather fuzzy. Willa had assumed the nausea was caused by too much food and drink, nervousness, and Eada's herbs reacting badly together. Instead, it seemed someone was trying to kill her again. That was a depressing realization.

Willa had grown up knowing that someone hated her enough to wish her dead. That reality had affected her whole life. It had stolen loved ones and even her childhood. But there was nothing

she could do about it. She didn't even know who
or why someone wanted her dead. That was something Uncle had refused to explain to her, no matter
how she begged to know. The pitying expression
on his face made her suspect that learning who it
was would be unbearably painful to her. Which
had made her think it was someone who should
love her . . . like her father. This suspicion was only
increased by the fact that the subject of her father
was another one Uncle would not discuss.

All of it was terribly upsetting and frustrating.
The only way to cope was to put the matter from
her mind. Hugh was her husband now. He would
keep her safe. She had other problems to consider.
Like the fact that the marriage hadn't been consummated last night as she'd assumed. Now
she would have to get through another anxious
day and night of anticipating the act yet to come.
Bloody hell! Willa had thought herself an old hand
at it now—an ignorant old hand, but an old hand
just the same. Instead she was still an untried bride.
This was awful! She had yet to suffer the pain of
the first time.

Willa felt anxiety begin to swirl within her and
forced herself to take a deep breath. She let it out
on a sigh. They would consummate the marriage
tonight and be done with it. She would conceive
her twins, and he would . . . well, with luck he
would live to see them. Eada hadn't made any
promises in that respect. In fact, the old woman
had bluntly told her that the future was murky on
the matter. Hugh might live. Then again, he might
not. She had best get the twins off him tonight,

Willa thought. Just in case it worked out the "might not" way. Then she frowned and rubbed her stomach. She was still suffering from mild cramps.

"You are sure there was no consummation?" she asked hopefully.

"Nay. Ye were in no shape for that." Eada's lips curled with amusement at the disappointment on Willa's face. "Trust me, my girl. When it happens, ye'll recall. Ye won't be having to ask the next day."

"Oh. I suppose," Willa said doubtfully, then asked, "You are sure there is nothing I need know? Nothing I should do?"

"I told ye, child. He will know what he's about and tell ye what ye need to do. I have already told ye what to expect. There is nothing for ye to—"

"Well then, is there anything I should *not* do?" Willa asked.

Eada started to shake her head, then paused as Willa began to look fretful. "Very well. There may be something I can tell ye not to do."

Willa perked up, her expression becoming expectant. "Aye?"

"Ye know how ye like to talk? How ye tend to babble on endlessly about everything?"

Willa bit her lip to keep from laughing at this accusation. Many was the time she'd driven the old woman wild with her babbling over the years. But that had been due to loneliness. She'd had no one else to talk to. She hadn't yet shown that side of herself to Hugh. Willa supposed she wasn't completely comfortable with him yet. She didn't mention that to Eada though, but merely nodded.

"Well . . . don't!" Eada said firmly. "There's

nothin' a man hates more than a babbling bride in his bed. Just keep yer mouth shut. Say nary a word. That shall please him more than anything else ye could do, I'm sure."

"No babbling," Willa murmured and nodded. She could do that.

Chapter Eleven

Another coughing fit seized Hugh. He reached for his ale, grunting and nearly slopping the liquid everywhere as Jollivet began thumping enthusiastically on his back.

" 'Twould appear you are ailing, Hugh," his cousin commented cheerfully. "You would not be planning on dying, would you? If so, 'tis terribly kind of you to leave the field clear for me to marry Willa."

"Ha ha," Hugh growled, knocking the other man's arms away with his elbow so that he could soothe his throat with the ale. "Do that again, and you shall be the one in danger of dying." That comment was followed by another round of coughing. Hugh was gasping for breath by the time it ended.

"You really do not sound well, friend." Unlike Jollivet, Lucan actually sounded concerned. But Hugh was now feeling too miserable to appreciate it. He'd had a runny nose and hacking cough all day, but the coughs were growing deeper, stealing more of his breath with each onset. Perhaps some rest would help.

Hugh sighed at the thought of actually sleeping. How long had it been since he'd had a full night's rest?

"Perhaps Eada has something to ease that cough," Wynekyn suggested as Hugh was wracked with another bout of coughing.

Grimacing at the very thought of the old witch and her potions, Hugh shook his head and stood. "Sleep will set me to rights. Good night."

He went up the stairs without waiting for a response. Willa had retired several minutes earlier. Once again Hugh had waited so she would have a few moments alone to prepare. They were newly wed and hadn't yet enjoyed the intimacy of an actual wedding night. She would still be shy around him. Hugh had no desire to make her uncomfortable. It had been a long day. Hugh had personally questioned everyone with any reason to be near either the kitchens or his bedchamber. Unfortunately, no one had admitted to delivering the poison or even seeing it delivered.

He also had arranged for Alsneta's nephew, Gawain, to act as taster for Willa's food and had set Baldulf and two younger men to guard her. He'd sent men out to learn all they could about the name Evelake. He'd instructed them to find the family, learn its circumstances, and discover Willa's connection to it. They also were to discover what possible reason there could be for someone to wish her dead. He hoped these inquiries would be more successful than those about the poisoned meade.

Hugh also had planned to search his uncle's room, but had been distracted by pressing matters concerning the estate he'd inherited. He was coming to learn that there was more to running a castle than hiring skilled men to do it for you. There were several questions he'd needed to answer, decisions to be made, men to yell at. It had all been very satisfying, he thought with a smile as he reached the top of the stairs and started along the hall. Still, he really would have to search his uncle's room on the morrow. He had to get to the bottom of the mystery surrounding Willa's past. The longer the mystery remained unsolved, the longer her life would be in danger, and Hugh found he didn't like that at all. He might not have wished to marry her initially, but she was his now, and he'd be damned if anyone was going to take her from him!

Recalling the state she'd been in last night, he felt his teeth grind together. She'd been pale and trembling. He'd felt sure she would die. If she had, it would have been his fault. Willa deserved some happiness and he was just the man to give it to her. Of course, that would have to wait a bit. He knew she must be drained and exhausted, as he was. But just as soon as they were both rested, he would set to the business of making her happy. It was his job. He was her husband.

Nodding at the men standing guard outside his bedchamber, he opened the door and strode in. However, Hugh paused after taking a single step through the door. He had expected the room to be dark with perhaps a dim glow from the dying embers in the fireplace. It wasn't. The chamber was aglow with light, both from a roaring fire in the hearth, and a dozen candles placed about the chamber.

He would have to talk to Willa about waste, Hugh thought. Then his gaze landed on the bed. His wife sat upright, the linens resting at her waist, revealing the top of a thin chemise . . . a very thin chemise, he realized with dismay. He could see the aureolas of her nipples through the cloth. A rustle behind him reminded Hugh of the men in the hall and he promptly stepped forward and pushed the door closed.

He hesitated a moment then, trying to make his weary brain function and work out what the woman was up to. Hugh had been quite certain that she would be asleep on his arrival and found it difficult to understand why she wasn't. But then it struck him that she had probably thought he would wish to consummate the marriage. No doubt she had stayed awake to accommodate him as a good wife should. Hugh relaxed. She would probably be relieved that he didn't intend to bother her this night.

Offering a smile, he moved around the room, blowing out the candles one after the other. Once the last taper had been doused and the room was filled with only the fire's soft glow, he approached the bed and began to strip. Aware of her steady gaze on him, Hugh felt oddly self-conscious as he removed his clothes. Her gaze prompted him to move a little more swiftly than he normally would have; just moments later he slid into bed next to her. He hesitated, then offered a gruff "good sleep" before turning on his side away from her. Hugh settled down to sleep, sure that his wife would do the same ... until the bed shifted and he became aware of the patter of her feet crossing the floor. The sound returned a moment later and the bed shifted again. Then he felt her lean against his side and there was suddenly bright light shining through his closed eyelids. He lay still for a moment, but when she stayed where she was, Hugh opened one eye curiously.

She was leaning on him, as he'd thought, a candelabra held bare inches from his face. Hugh scowled at the sight of the lit candles.

"Wife?" he asked, keeping his tone pleasant.

"Aye?" came her equally pleasant response.

"What are you doing?"

"I am waiting for my husband to do his duty. What are you doing?"

"What?" Hugh rolled over abruptly, sending her flying backward. Catching Willa's arm before she could tumble off the bed, he snatched the candelabra she was waving wildly around. Maintaining his hold on her, he twisted to set the candleholder on the chest on his side of the bed, then turned back to glare at her.

"You cannot wish to consummate the marriage now!" he cried with disbelief.

"Well, of course I do not *wish* to!" When Hugh stiffened at the insult, she said, "Eada explained that 'tis going to be unpleasant and painful the

first time. Of course, I do not look forward to suffering pain. However, it must be done and I would
rather not spend another day agonizing over what
is to come. Two days of worry are quite enough.
So, if you would be so kind, do you think you
could plant the twins now?"

Hugh felt himself sag. It hadn't occurred to him
that she would be full of worry over the deed to
come. That had been rather shortsighted of him,
he realized. After all, even he had been suffering
some mild anxiety over his first time with a virgin, but at least he knew what was to come. It was
all a new and frightening experience for her. Of
course, she would be anxious. A huge yawn escaped him, ending in a cough, and he saw concern
enter her eyes. It seemed cruel to put her through
another day of anxiety. Weary as he was, he would
manage the task for her.

"Very well," he said with a long-suffering sigh.

"Oh, thank you, my lord," Willa breathed with
relief, then promptly fell back on the bed pulling
the linens up with her. She lay with her eyes
squeezed shut and the linens clutched tightly
to her throat, knuckles growing white with the
pressure of her hold. She was as taut as a bow-
string.

Hugh stared at her with pursed lips. She looked
as if she expected either to be beheaded or raped,
he thought with a sigh. Then she puckered her
lips as if having sucked on a lemon. He presumed
that was an invitation to kiss her. I really don't
have the energy for this, he thought miserably, but
merely cleared his throat.

Her eyes popped open at once, a question in their depths.

"The ... er ..." He gestured toward the linens she was so desperately clutching and she glanced down with seeming surprise.

"Oh!" She flushed. "I suppose we shan't need these." She tossed the linens aside, then hesitated and slid out of bed.

"What—?" Hugh began. The question died on his tongue as she bent to grab the hem of her shift and tugged it upward.

"Eada explained everything to me," she told him, continuing to draw the shift up to reveal legs, hips, belly. . . . "From what she said I suppose this will get in the way, too." She pulled the gown up over her head and shrugged her arms free. Her face was cherry red with embarrassment. She briefly used the material as a shield to cover herself from upper thighs to the tops of her nipples, then quickly scooped her hair before each shoulder with one hand and dropped the gown. As a cover, her hair was both effective and ineffective. It covered her breasts, flowing down over them from her shoulders and continuing down to the front of her legs. However, it left the outsides of her shoulders, the curve of her hips, and the juncture of her legs bare. Hugh had a moment to ogle her, then the golden tresses went swinging as she scrambled anxiously back into bed. She quickly tugged her hair to cover herself before settling, eyes squeezed shut again, and hands once more fisted at her sides. It took a moment for her to remember; then she puckered her lips, as well.

Hugh wanted to laugh, but found it hard to get the sound past the lump in his throat as he gazed at her beauty in the soft light. His gaze slid over her face, down her throat to her breasts. They were mostly covered by her hair, but the nipples were poking out like naughty children peering through bushes. He finally tore his eyes from the little red-brown pebbles to slide along her flat belly, down to the soft red-gold curls at the juncture of her thighs.

Oh, yes. He could do this, Hugh decided. His exhaustion was dropping away even as his manhood grew. He took a moment to enjoy the anticipation, his gaze skating over her shapely legs right down to her plump little toes. Then he eased onto his side, facing his wife. He propped his head on one upraised hand and leaned forward to press his lips to hers. She was stiff with tension, even her lips having no give. However, Hugh recalled the passion they had shared in the stable by the cottage and was patient.

He brushed her lips lightly with his own; once, twice, then a third time. Then he slid his tongue out to tease her puckered mouth. When that had little effect, he nuzzled her neck. She relaxed somewhat, a breathless laugh slipping from her lips as he tickled the sensitive flesh. Smiling, Hugh raised his head to find that the pucker was gone. He kissed her again, then let his tongue slip out to tease her full lower lip. She relaxed slowly, allowing her mouth to drift slightly open to him. Relieved that it had been so easy, he deepened the kiss, tilting his head and taking her mouth in a devouring caress.

He continued to kiss her for several moments until he thought she'd forgotten her fears, then he brushed the long strands of soft hair away from one breast and cupped it gently. Willa stiffened slightly, but showed no other response, so he fondled the breast, palming it, then catching the nipple between thumb and forefinger. Hugh enjoyed the feel of her soft flesh against his callused skin. She was kissing him back, which he took to be a good sign and he continued to touch her as he ran through the instructions from the treatise in his head. Preparations of the mind and body beforehand were out of the question now, but he didn't think that would matter. He didn't feel any burning desire to relieve himself. As for the rest. . . .

"You see, women differ from men in that they are cold. . . .'Tis necessary to . . . er . . . fondle the wife's 'lower parts' to . . . er . . . raise her body to the proper . . . er . . . heat—" Father Brennan's words rang in his ears.

"How do you know when she is the correct temperature?" He'd asked, and the man had answered, *". . . she will begin to 'speak as if she were babbling.' That is when you shall know to commence with the actual . . . commencing."*

Hugh hadn't had the chance to read all of *De secretis Mulierum*, but what he'd read had confirmed the priest's words. Breaking the kiss, he rubbed his thumb over her nipple, then bent to draw her flesh into his mouth. Willa didn't feel cold to him, but she wasn't babbling incoherently, either, now that her mouth was free. In fact, she wasn't making any sounds at all, he realized with a small frown. Not even the little moans and mewls of pleasure she'd made in the stable. She didn't even have her arms around him as she had then. They were lying—hands still fisted—at her sides.

Disconcerted by this realization, he wondered briefly if perhaps it might not be her position that was the problem. They had been standing in the stable; perhaps she was not as aroused lying down. He briefly considered urging her into an upright position, then decided against it. The treatise had said nothing about standing. It had said to fondle her lower regions until she babbled, so he would fondle her till she babbled. Continuing to suckle at her breast, he let his hand drift down over her belly, relief coursing through him as the muscles in her stomach quivered beneath his fingertips. Surely that was a good sign? Hugh slid them through the soft hair between her legs and dipped them in to find her core. His eyes slid closed when he found her warm and moist and welcoming. That had to be a good sign, too, he thought, straining to hear any babbling.

She wasn't babbling. But then, he'd just started, he reassured himself. She *would* babble. He intended to do this right.

Willa's head was about to explode like a rosebud bursting open at the kiss of sunlight. Hugh was driving her mad.

Eada's edict that she wasn't to say anything wasn't helping. Willa had the maddening need to move and groan and writhe and cry out. She was biting all of that back. Not that Eada had said she couldn't move, but she *had* said that he would tell her if she should, and he hadn't told her and she was afraid of doing something wrong. She wished to be a good wife. Besides, she was sure that if she arched and writhed as she wished to, she would be unable to keep herself from moaning.

Hugh's hand slid between her legs and Willa closed her eyes briefly, her fingernails digging into the palms of her hands as she fought her body. Oh this was . . . this was . . . oh dear God. She wanted to clasp him to her breast. She wanted to drag his head away from her breast and pull him up to kiss her again. She wanted to arch into his caresses and—

Cold air touched her wet nipple as he raised his head and Willa blinked her eyes open, managing what she hoped was a serene smile but suspected was more of a grimace as he glanced up at her. She noted the perplexity in his gaze and tried harder to smile, relieved when he bent his head to her other breast.

Dear God! Why wasn't she allowed to say anything? Eada had said, *"There's nothin' a man hates more than a babbling bride in his bed. Just keep your mouth shut. Say nary a word. That shall please him more than anything else ye could do, I'm sure."*

But, dear God, she was paying a heavy price for her silence.

Hugh raised his head again. Willa managed another grimacing smile. A bewildered expression passed over his face and he watched her closely. Then he left off his caressing and she felt him thrust one finger inside her. She bit the inside of her lip to keep from crying out, her expression twisting with the effort, her body as taut as could be to keep from riding his hand. This was becoming more painful than pleasurable.

Much to Willa's relief, Hugh shook his head slightly, and took his hand away. Finally, she thought. Finally, he would just get it over with. That was all she wished now. For him to mount her as Eada had said he would and plant the twins. She could not bear much more of this. She'd barely had that thought when she realized that he was not moving to mount her. He was moving down the bed to be sure, but he was—

"Ah!" The word slipped from her lips despite her best efforts when his head disappeared between her legs and she felt a caress like warm, wet velvet. The first touch sent pleasure through her like none she'd ever experienced. Her body seemed to contract under wave after wave of some release. Then Hugh raised his head, a hopeful expression on his face.

"Did you say something?"

"Nay," Willa lied on a breathy sigh. Hope entered her own expression. "Did you wish me to say something?"

He hesitated, frowning again, then shook his head in a bewildered way and again disappeared between her legs. Disappointed, Willa bit her lip as he set back to work on her sensitive flesh. His caress was almost too much to bear. She almost groaned aloud as the excitement began to build in her again. Oh, this was awful. She could not withstand another—She bit off a gasp, and strained not to move as he inserted a finger inside her while continuing his oral caresses. She could not bear . . . could not . . . she. . . . Even though her mouth was tightly closed, and her teeth were grinding together, she heard a high keening sound come from her as the waves of pleasure burst upon her again. She cut the sound off abruptly, hoping he'd not heard her as Hugh raised another hopeful gaze.

"I thought I heard something?"

She shook her head a bit frantically, aware that her breath was coming through her nose like that of a snorting bull. And was that more attractive than talking? she wondered a little resentfully. But perhaps he could not tell from his position.

"Hmm." He scratched his head, apparently greatly troubled by something. Then determination entered his eyes and he ducked out of sight again.

Willa felt tears gather in her eyes as he set to work again. This was awful! This was some form of hellish torment!

That was it, she realized quite suddenly. She'd died from the poisoning and gone to hell. She was to suffer through all eternity with this unbearable pleasure pounding at her as she tried to keep from moving or making a sound. Oh, the devil was a diabolical beast!

That was her last almost sensible thought before she was overwhelmed by pure sensation. Her body thrummed to the touch of the man who could only be the devil's assistant. She knew from the moment that the passion began to build in her

that this time it was going to kill her if she could
not react. Her eyes were tearing, her heart pounding, and her body trembling with the effort not to
speak or move. She would surely die. Then, just as
a hurricane-sized wave of pleasure was about to
overtake her, some friendly demon placed an idea
in her head. Willa clamped her thighs on either
side of Hugh's head to deafen him as she rose up
on the bed and screamed for all she was worth. It
was a magnificent scream. All those little grunts
and groans and moans and sighs that she'd been
forced to hold in, all the physical responses she'd
denied herself, all of this combined into one glorious earth-shattering shriek of pure pleasure. It was
most satisfying. Almost as satisfying as the pleasure that roared through her. She was so consumed
by her fulfillment, it took a moment to realize that
Hugh was clawing frantically at her legs, trying
to free himself.

Falling back limp on the linens, Willa let her legs
drop away and stared woozily at the top of the
draped bed. She felt quite intoxicated with pleasure. If this was hell, she was all for it.

Hugh came up gasping for air, which led to a
coughing fit of gigantic proportions. Willa was
strong. Once her legs had clamped around his
head, he'd been unable to remove them. His gaze
turned to her hopefully as his coughing ended.
He'd hoped that her closing her legs like that was
a good sign, that perhaps she'd started into her
babbling. Instead the woman looked dead bored.
She was lying as still as she had throughout, her

glazed eyes fixed on the drapings over the bed. She wasn't even tense anymore. Her fear obviously had been completely wiped away by the boredom she suffered. He was a complete failure.

Despondency overtaking him, he sank back on his haunches and glared at his lap. His manhood, of course, was not bored. He'd grown harder and stiffer with every moment as he'd attempted to pleasure her. She was so warm and soft. Just looking at her was pure enjoyment; tasting and touching her had excited him beyond anything he'd experienced before. Despite the fact that he had not raised her temperature as the treatise had instructed, he wanted her. Badly. Not only was he a failure, he was a despicable failure.

"Are you going to plant the twins now?"

Hugh glanced up sharply at that question. Her voice was euphoric; she sounded almost drunk. However, she still looked limp and bored. Perhaps it was his hearing at fault. She'd squeezed his head rather hard. He stuck a finger in one ear and jiggled it about briefly, then did the same to the other ear.

"My lord?"

He gave up on his ears and glanced at her still face. "Do you wish me to?"

"Oh aye," she breathed.

Well, he recalled now, the *De secretis mulierum* had said that a man's heat created the excitement in the woman and that she was strengthened by the joining. At least he knew he wouldn't be hurting her. But it would be a shame if she finally got excited only after he'd poured his heat and strength into her. He very much feared he wouldn't have the energy to do anything about her excitement once he was done. His exhaustion was creeping back up on him.

Shrugging, he moved between her legs.

Chapter Twelve

Willa was slow to wake up. Exhaustion seemed to cover her like a cloak and every muscle in her body ached. She felt horrible. Waking up really didn't seem a good idea. More sleep obviously was needed. Satisfied with that decision, she sniffled miserably, let her eyes droop closed and settled back into slumber again.

A groan sounded from the opposite side of the bed, and Willa scowled as she was drawn back to wakefulness again. The sound was familiar. She suspected it was that sound or one similar that had awakened her in the first place. Rather rude of her husband, she decided, since he'd kept her up half the night with his coughing. And that after falling asleep on her, she recalled, some of her irritation returning.

After torturing her with pleasure for what seemed like hours, the man had mounted her as Eada had said he would, and plunged into her, taking her innocence. That hadn't been painful at all. Well, not really. A twinge mostly. Not at all the agony she'd expected. Then he'd pumped himself in and out of her as Eada had also described, which had been merely interesting at first. Then his motion had started to stir some of her earlier excitement. She'd just started to tense up, her fingers curling into her palms again to keep from hugging him closer and urging him on, when he'd cried out and spilled his seed into her. No sooner had he completed the act than he'd collapsed atop her, remaining there without further movement.

At first, Willa had thought that he was simply recovering from his exertion and would resume his attentions and ease the tension that had built in her again. Then she'd heard what could only be a snore and had realized that he was sleeping on her! There would be no more sweet agony.

Irritated and disappointed, she'd pushed him off her in a fine huff, but he'd not awoken to appreciate it. Willa had rolled onto her side with her back to him and tried to go to sleep, but he'd kept her awake most of the night with his coughing. Her emotions had run the gamut through the night. Her irritation with him had given way to concern at the harsh, deep coughing, until she realized that he was sleeping right through it while she could not. Her irritation had promptly returned.

Now she was exhausted and grumpy and not at all happy to be awoken by his grunts and moans.

Another groan reached her ears and she turned to glare at him, only to see that he was trying to ease into a sitting position and having some trouble doing so. The grimace on his face could be mistaken for nothing but agony. Concern again replaced her anger.

"What is it? Is something wrong?" she asked with mounting alarm, turning on the bed and sitting up so that she could look at him.

He was off the bed in a trice, dragging the linen with him and quickly wrapping it around his hips as he turned away. "There is naught wrong. I am fine."

Hugh had managed to gain his feet without another groan, but Willa had seen the way his face paled at the action and she was not fooled. Frowning with concern, she watched him take one stiff step after another. He'd taken the linen right off the bed to cover himself, but the night before he hadn't been at all shy about being naked in front of her. He was hiding something. And that something was making him walk most gingerly.

Determined to find out what was wrong, Willa slid silently out of bed and walked around behind him to step on the edge of the linen trailing on the ground. Not expecting the action, Hugh was taken by surprise. The cloth slid from his fingers before he could snatch it back. Giving up on the linen, he whirled quickly to face her, covering the sore with his hand.

"What was that?" Willa asked sweetly as she tossed the linen on the bed.

Hugh eyed her warily. "What was what?"

"What was that on your arse?" she clarified,

then promptly ran around him to tug his hand away. She gaped in horror.

"What?" Hugh asked, the worry obvious in his voice. "What is it?"

"A great boil, my lord," Willa announced with awe as she examined the swollen and angry looking sore on his behind. Then she decided, "Nay, not a boil. A carbuncle. 'Tis too big to be a boil."

She glanced up at his face then. He was terribly red in the face and obviously embarrassed. Willa rolled her eyes and straightened. "Get back into bed."

"I am not getting back into bed." He straightened, gathering his tattered dignity about him once more now that she wasn't bent over peering at his sore bottom.

"Hugh, it must be tended. Get back on the bed," Willa insisted.

"I haven't the time to have it tended. I am a very busy man. I am an earl." He puffed up even as he said it and Willa's lips twisted.

"You are an earl with a carbuncle on your butt, my lord. Please let it be looked after." He deflated somewhat then and Willa pressed her advantage by adding, "One of these was what killed Ilbert."

That got his attention; he whirled back to face her with horror. "What? Ilbert, the third man sent to guard you at the cottage?"

Willa nodded solemnly. "Aye. He developed one near . . ." She gestured vaguely toward the groin area. "Where the leg joins the body. He became ill, feverish. It had poisoned the blood. He did not realize that was the source of the fever. By the time he brought the problem to Eada, there was little she could do about it."

"Dear God," Hugh breathed. "Death by a boil." He shuddered at the very thought of such an ignominious death, then turned and crawled back onto his stomach on the bed. "Very well. Tend to it."

Willa just shook her head and started to dress. She had her gown on and was gathering his clothes together before he finally glanced around to see what was taking her so long. She saw him frown when he took in her clothed state.

"Where are you going? I thought you were going to—"

"I am going to fetch Eada."

"Oh, nay!" He reared up onto his hands and knees on the bed. "I am not letting that witch near my arse!"

"You must, my lord," Willa said patiently. Raising one hand, she poked at the sore on his derriere. She wasn't at all surprised when he gave a grunt of pain and collapsed back onto his stomach. She could only wonder at how the boil had grown so big without his showing signs of it ere now.

"How long have you had this?" she asked. He mumbled something into his arms that she couldn't hear. "What was that, husband?"

"It started while I was standing guard at the cottage, but the bath I took before the wedding made it better. It hardly even bothered me until I awoke this morning. It seems ten times worse than it first was."

"Was your bathwater hot?"

"Aye. The servants were trying to impress me, I think."

Willa nodded. "The hot water probably softened it and allowed it to drain. It has refilled, however."

Hugh grunted at that unnecessary report. "Can you not tend it yourself?"

Willa glanced up at his face sympathetically. She didn't blame him. This was a terribly embarrassing ailment, and Eada would berate him for not admitting to it and having it tended sooner. "I fear not, my lord. Perhaps if you had let me know about it sooner, I could have taken care of it myself. Unfortunately, now it surpasses my skills. Eada is needed here."

She started for the door, then paused and collected his clothes from the floor, taking them with her in case he tried to make a bolt for it. Willa had not spent so many years stuck at the cottage with three men trailing her everywhere without learning that they could be the biggest babies at times.

Hugh watched morosely as his wife left the room. He had not missed the fact that she'd taken his clothes with her. He supposed that was to prevent his fleeing. As if he would. He wasn't afraid of the witch. Mind you, he didn't like the idea of her examining his derriere as Willa had just done. The very idea of her warty old hands poking at his tender flesh made him squirm. But, if it had to be tended, it had to be tended. He'd be damned if his epitaph was going to read, "Felled by a great carbuncle!"

Sighing, Hugh lowered his face into his folded arms. He felt like a fool. He lay there for a moment indulging in self-pity, then lifted his head, arched up on his arms and twisted about, trying to see the carbuncle. It wasn't possible, of course. The damn thing was not visible no matter how he contorted himself.

The door opened and Hugh scowled toward it as his wife and the old witch entered. His expression had absolutely no effect on either of them. They weren't even looking; they were conversing together as they closed the door and crossed the room to the bed. He let his head drop back into his folded arms, trying to pretend he wasn't there as they moved to the side of the bed and the witch bent to examine him.

A cold hand touched his derriere, there was much tsk tsking, then the old hag spoke, her voice moving away even as she did. "Ye should have come to me sooner. Dangerous, this. Lucky yer blood is not already poisoned."

He felt the mattress give and lifted his head to see that Willa had sat down on the edge. She took his hand in a soothing manner. Hugh met her sympathetic gaze, then peered over his shoulder to see that the witch had moved to the fire. He couldn't tell what she was doing and suspected he did not want to know.

"A grown man should know better than to behave so," the hag said as she moved back toward the bed.

Hugh scorched her with his eyes, then let his head fall back onto his arms. His neck was beginning to get a crick from the odd angle. But that didn't mean he was willing to take a lecture from that nasty old biddie. It was bad enough he had to subject himself to her treatment, he was damned if he would listen to her lecture, too. "Listen you gouty old harpy, just—arrgh!"

Hugh roared as searing pain shot through his butt cheek.

"My lord! What is about?" Baldulf's voice called out. Hugh hadn't heard the door open as the man entered in response to his yell. Unfortunately, he didn't have the breath to respond. He was gasping in pain.

"There is nothing amiss, Baldulf. Everything is fine," Willa said quickly. "Put that sword away."

"I think we would feel better if we heard that from Hugh," came another voice. It was enough to make Hugh regain his breath.

"God's teeth! Lucan, is that you?"

"Aye. I stopped to ask Baldulf if you were up yet and we heard you scream."

Hugh did groan now, humiliation eradicating his pain for a moment.

"Good God, what have you done to his arse!" Lucan's voice was closer now and Hugh could only surmise that he'd moved nearer to survey the matter.

"I bit it!" Eada snapped impatiently.

"She did nothing," Willa assured them. "Hugh did this on his own."

"I did not do anything to myself," Hugh growled. "'Twas sitting on that damned horse for days on end waiting for you to agree to be my wife that did it!"

" 'Tis a carbuncle," Eada interjected dryly. "He left it too long without telling anyone. 'Tis terribly infected."

"I'd say so," Baldulf's voice commented. "Dear God, I have never seen one that big before. It must be the size of my fist."

"Nasty," Lucan agreed.

"Aye, he should have told someone," Willa repeated.

"How ever did you sit on it?" Baldulf asked.

Hugh rolled his eyes at the question. "With great care."

"You would have been sitting comfortably long ago, had you bothered to mention it to anyone," Willa said.

"Oh well, as to that, I don't blame him," Lucan commented. "Damned embarrassing business, having a boil on your arse."

" 'Tis a carbuncle," Willa corrected.

"And not so embarrassing," Wynekyn said soothingly. "Every soldier has them at one time or another."

"Wynekyn!" Hugh shifted about on the bed, attempting to see how many people were in the room. But he couldn't see past Willa. "Is everyone here?"

"I knew a fellow once who had one that just would not go away," he heard Jollivet say. "It grew and grew and—"

"Jollivet! Is that you? That had better not be you! And you had best not be looking at my arse!"

"Never fear, cousin, 'tis a fine arse."

Hugh growled in his throat. Then a cry of pain was surprised from him as Eada squeezed his butt.

"What the hell are you doing back there?" He craned his head around, trying to see what she was up to.

"Draining it," she said shortly. "Have to get the infection out."

"She has to, son," Wynekyn said soothingly. "Just try to rest easy. It will be over soon."

"Rest easy! Rest easy? I will rest easy just as soon as everyone gets the hell out of here, by God! Begone! All of you! Begone!"

There was the shuffle of feet as they moved to obey, then Hugh yelled, "Wait! A word of this to anyone and I shall—"

"Oh now, my lord husband." Willa patted him on the head as if he were a grumpy child. "There's no need to threaten them. Who would they tell? Everyone is here."

Hugh glared up at her, but she was too busy sneezing to pay him any heed.

"There. 'Tis finished." Eada followed that comment with a light tap on his unmarred cheek. Hugh ignored her impertinence in his relief that the procedure was over. He started to rise. She stopped him with a hand on his butt and pushed downward. "Where do ye think ye're goin'? Ye're abed today."

"Aye," Willa agreed.

"But—"

"Ye risk blood poisoning do ye not take care of this properly," Eada said sternly. "Ye need to lie here and keep this poultice on it to drain out the infection. Yer on yer belly for the next day or so."

"Besides, sleep is the best thing for healing, husband," Willa said and sneezed again, then continued, "If you had just told us sooner—"

Hugh frowned as the sentence ended in yet another sneeze. "Are you sick? You are flushed and sneezing."

"Am not." The denial was ruined by another sneeze. "So, I am sneezing."

"And flushed," he insisted. "Have you a fever?" His glance slid to Eada and he ordered, "See if she has a fever."

Willa tried to avoid the hand the old which put out, but wasn't quick enough. "Aye. She has a fever."

"Well." Hugh suddenly looked more chipper. "Then you can keep me company in bed today. After all, sleep is the best thing for healing," he mimicked.

Willa's eyes narrowed on his face. "Sleeping with you is what gave me this, my lord. You gave me your cold. You made me sick!"

Hugh couldn't help grinning at the accusation. "Odd. Mine appears to be gone." He sniffled. "Well, almost."

"Aye. Because you gave it to me!"

"You are the one who insisted that I bed you last night," he pointed out with amusement.

"Well, you need not have—"

"Children!" Eada glared. "Get into bed, both of you! Now!"

Willa obeyed immediately. Hugh was already in the bed and he continued to grin as the old witch scowled at them both and ordered, "Try to get along. 'Twill help the healing." Then, gathering her things together, she shook her head and headed for the door. "I'll have Alsneta bring something up to break your fast."

"I am not hungry," Willa said petulantly.

"Have the taster, Gawain, bring it," Hugh ordered, ignoring his wife's childish pout. The old witch nodded as she closed the door. Hugh turned his gaze to Willa to find her still glaring at him. She was angry that he'd made her sick. He'd also done a lousy job of bedding her, he thought unhappily. He'd worked hard to bring about the babbling the treatise had mentioned. But to no avail. She'd lain silent and still, her glassy eyes a silent reproach. Then, he'd proceeded to fall asleep on her. At least, he suspected he had. The last thing he recalled was his incredible release, then sagging on top of her, too exhausted even to roll away. He was pretty sure that he'd not removed himself under his own power, though he had awoken on his belly on the bed beside her.

Hugh glanced at his wife again. Willa was asleep now. He scowled. He was glad she was getting her rest; she would need it to combat the cold he'd given her. However, that left him butt up on the bed with nothing to do and no one to talk to. He started to tap his fingers on the mattress, his brain a blank, then a soft snuffle from the other side of the bed drew his gaze and he grinned. She was snoring. Such a dainty little thing and she was snoring. Must be the cold, he decided, as she snored again.

His gaze drifted down over her body. Neither of them had bothered with the linens. They lay in a crumpled heap on the floor. She still wore the gown she'd donned to go fetch Eada. Willa had clambered back into bed without bothering to remove it in her scramble to obey the old witch. She couldn't be comfortable in her gown. His gaze moved over the ugly, overlarge garment. He must see to it that she had new dresses.

Willa moaned and shifted fretfully in her sleep, and Hugh was positive her discomfort must be due to her restrictive clothing. She would be more comfortable naked, he decided, his gaze moving over the soft mounds of her breasts hidden by the garment. Hugh licked his lips. Aye, definitely more comfortable out of the gown.

Ignoring the pain any movement caused in his backside, he shifted closer to her, eased onto his side and set to work at her lacings. Willa stirred as he worked but didn't wake until he was struggling to remove her gown. Blinking her eyes open, she muttered irritably and tried to brush his hand away. "What are you doing?"

"I am trying to undress you."

She came fully awake, her expression uncertain. "Did you wish to consummate again?"

"Nay. Of course not. You need your rest. I just thought you would be more comfortable unclothed. Sit up," he instructed.

Willa sat up and raised her arms dutifully as he lifted her gown over her head.

"We have to see you better dressed. A countess should wear jewels and fine silks."

"Silks," Willa repeated sleepily as he thrust the gown aside. She sank back on the bed, a frown coming to her face as she realized she was completely naked. "Where are the bed linens?"

"On the floor."

"Oh." She hesitated, then shrugged and turned on her side, apparently too tired to bother fetching them. The cold had knocked him out much the same way, Hugh recalled. The poultice Eada had placed on his backside had fallen off. He found it on the bed, lay down and slapped it in the general vicinity of the pain.

Willa murmured sleepily and shifted beside him. Hugh glanced over to see that she was asleep again. As he watched, she coughed in her sleep, sniffled, then rolled onto her back, her arm landing by her head. Hugh found his gaze going over her body. He suspected she would not be so open to his view again for a while. She'd been naked last night, but tense and stiff. Now she was relaxed and soft-looking, her breasts rising and falling with each breath. Rising and falling. Rising and falling.

Hugh licked his lips as he watched. Her breasts looked terribly lickable. Easing sideways until his arm brushed her side, he eyed her face, then leaned forward to lick one roseate nipple. It immediately sprang to life under the caress, standing at attention. Of course, one lick wasn't enough and he leaned down for another.

Willa shifted, arching upward into the caress and Hugh smiled as he suckled her breast. This was encouraging. He trailed a hand over her ribs, then across her belly, rubbing gently. She writhed and twitched at his touch. He let his hand drop to her hip, cupping the soft flesh there, and pressing against the bone. Willa twisted under his touch, murmuring incoherently as she pressed her hips upward under his hand. This was more movement and sound than he'd managed to elicit from her despite his best efforts last night.

"Damn," Hugh breathed against her wet nipple. Obviously, he hadn't relaxed her enough last night. She was responding now and murmuring incoherently, if not babbling. He let his hand slide between her legs and pressed against her as she gasped and arched into his palm.

It was the gasp that did it. The action ended in a coughing fit that brought her awake. Willa sat up abruptly, shuddering as her body was wracked by the deep cough.

Hugh released her nipple just in time to get out of the way. He removed his hand from between her legs and pounded her back, ignoring the pain the action caused in his behind. It was a bad fit. Willa wasn't able to catch her breath for some time. Concern and guilt filled Hugh as he tried to help her through it. If he hadn't been touching her while she slept, he was sure she wouldn't have coughed. It ended finally, and she dropped back weakly in bed.

Hugh promptly eased out of bed to fetch the linens and some furs. He covered Willa, then rolled several spare furs and arranged them behind her back, lifting her upright.

She murmured her gratitude, then sniffled miserably. Hugh tried not to wince with guilt. He was fully erect again and hoped she hadn't noticed. He would never bother her while she was ill. Well, alright, so he had, but he wouldn't again.

Chapter Thirteen

Willa did not feel at all well. She felt sure she was dying. Her husband had killed her with a cold. And why had Eada not foreseen this?

The man slumbering in bed beside her rumbled in his sleep as he shifted about. He was lying naked, with not even the linens on him, while she was buried under a mountain of furs and still freezing.

Pig, she thought with annoyance. He'd made her sick and now slept like the dead while her coughing had awoken her and would not let her rest. Her gaze dropped to his bare buttocks. The poultice had fallen off and now lay on the edge of the bed. Stupid man, how would he heal if he did not keep the poultice on? Willa pushed the furs aside and leaned over to snatch up the poultice. She slapped it back on his rear end.

The action had a most satisfying effect on Hugh. Even as Willa dropped back beneath the furs, his snores ended and he reared up on the bed with a bellowed, "Yow!"

"Bad dream, my lord?" she asked innocently as his bleary eyes found her.

Grunting, Hugh dropped back onto his stomach. Willa glared at him, then forced a smile when he glanced her way. He frowned. "You should be sleeping."

"Aye. I should," she agreed dutifully.

"Why are you not?"

"I cannot sleep. I do not feel well and I am cold."

Hugh's forehead wrinkled as he pondered her words, then he reached out one arm, hooked it around her waist and dragged her to his side. The next thing Willa knew, she was tucked up half beneath him with his leg cast over both of hers. He tugged the furs up to her neck and settled his arm on top of them so that it lay in front of her face.

"Your poultice," she squeaked against his forearm.

" 'Tis dried out now," he said on a yawn. Then he settled his head on her breast and brushed it back and forth atop the furs. He settled with a satisfied sigh.

Willa lay completely still, realizing he planned to warm her with his own body heat. He *was* warm, she realized as some of the chill left her. She relaxed a bit and peered at his face. His eyes were closed again, but she didn't think he slept.

"Thank you." She smiled shyly when he opened one eye to check on her.

"No thanks are needed. You are my wife. 'Tis my

job to warm you when you are cold. 'Tis my job to give you what you need. Do you need for anything, you must ask me." His eyes closed again, and Willa made a face at him. His words had somehow belittled his action. She lay still for a moment, then asked, "Lord Hillcrest was truly your uncle?"

Hugh blinked his eyes open, looking vaguely surprised at the question. "Aye."

He closed his eyes again, and Willa glanced over his arm at the room around them. No, there was nothing to entertain her there. She peered back at his face. "I do not recall that you ever visited us either here or at Claymorgan."

He opened his eyes again, but this time annoyance was the overriding expression on his face. "Nay."

"Why?"

He shifted, his leg moving restlessly across hers. "My uncle never really encouraged visitors. In fact, more often than not he discouraged it."

"That would be my fault," Willa said unhappily. "He was probably trying to protect me, as usual. Lord Wynekyn was the only visitor he allowed."

She saw Hugh scowl and turned her face away with remorse. He caught her chin and turned it back. " 'Twas not your fault. My father and uncle had a falling out," he said firmly, then released her chin again and closed his eyes once more.

"What sort of falling out?" Willa asked.

Hugh frowned but didn't open his eyes this time. He merely said, "You are ill and should rest."

"I am bored and you did say that 'twas your

duty to supply whatever I need," she wheedled. "I need information . . . to reassure me that I was not at fault for your not being able to visit Papa."

That brought his eyes open. "Was he your father?"

Willa flushed. "Nay. He said not, but I thought of him so. He was the only father I knew."

Hugh nodded slowly, then said, "You were not at fault. I do not think you were even born when they had their falling out. I was only nine or so at the time."

"What happened?"

For a moment she thought he would not answer, then he heaved a long-suffering sigh and explained, "My father was the second son. He used to run Claymorgan for Uncle Richard, but they argued over how he should run it. My father decided he would strike out and make his fortune as a knight. He failed. Sleep."

Willa blinked at the abrupt order at the end of the short explanation. He'd closed his eyes again. She glared at him briefly, then dragged one hand out from under the furs to poke his arm. "What happened then?" she asked the moment his eyes opened again.

"When?"

"Well, after you left Claymorgan?"

"I told you, my father tried to make his fortune as a knight. He failed."

"Why?"

He looked unhappy, then said, "He was a fine warrior, perhaps the best of his time, but he had

spent too many years running Claymorgan. He
was used to luxuries a knight cannot afford."

"Well, what of you?"

"What of me?"

"Where were you and—Do you have any broth-
ers and sisters?" Good Lord, she couldn't believe
she'd neglected to ask such things ere this.

"Nay. I was an only child. Mother called me her
miracle child. She was with child many times, but
I was the first and last to survive birth."

Willa accepted his words with a nod, then asked,
"Well, where were you and your mother while your
father was trying to earn his fortune as a knight?"

"We traveled with him."

Willa wasn't fooled by his matter-of-fact tone of
voice. She knew it must have been a hard, lonely
life. "Where are your mother and father now?"

"Dead." The word was hollow. "My father died
while I was fostering. Mother followed shortly
after."

"Then you are alone, like me."

Hugh glanced at her sharply, but merely nodded. "Aye."

"Except, of course, for Jollivet and Lucan," she
added and watched the grimace that flashed across
her husband's face. She'd noticed that he seemed
to react so every time his cousin was mentioned.

"Aye, well, Jollivet is the son of my father's sister.
His mother was a lady-in-waiting to the queen. He
has spent a great deal of time in London and around
court since earning his spurs. Much to his detri-
ment," he added under his breath.

"And Lucan?" Willa asked, her lips twitching at his comment. "He seems a very good friend to you."

"He is. We fostered together. He is like a brother to me. We both had poor prospects while growing up. He is a second son. I was the first born of a second son. If Uncle Richard had had children. . . ." He shrugged and fell silent.

"I am sorry you did not get to know Lord Hillcrest better. I know you are angry that he made you marry me, but he was a good man."

Hugh was silent for so long, Willa thought he wasn't going to respond. Then he said solemnly, "Aye. He was a good man. I did not think that he knew where I was or what I was doing, but the day I earned my spurs, a messenger arrived leading the most beautiful horse I have ever seen. The stallion bore the finest chain mail and sword that I could have dreamed of. There was a letter with it. He had been following my progress. I had done him proud. This was his gift to me."

Willa felt tears fill her eyes. "Aye. That sounds like Papa. He was terribly kind. He must have loved you a great deal."

"Aye." Hugh looked uncomfortable; then his expression became stern. "Now sleep."

He closed his eyes again. Willa considered asking another question; there were quite a few things she would like to know about him, but she'd already made him speak more in the past few moments than he had in all the days that she'd known him. She didn't wish to push her luck. Besides, she would no doubt have a couple of days to get those answers from him. She also was growing weary again.

Yawning, she noted Hugh's deep breathing. He appeared to have fallen back to sleep. However, he was not snoring anymore. Willa watched him sleep, her eyes growing weary and beginning to droop. Then she shifted to a more comfortable position and slid a hand out to move his arm lower. Though she enjoyed the warmth of his body, his arm felt like a great felled tree across her chest. The weight made it even harder to breathe than the stuffiness of her cold.

Hugh murmured in his sleep and tightened his hold on her waist. He pulled her even closer until her left breast was pressed against him. Willa peered at her husband's face in repose. He did not look nearly so fearsome in sleep. His face was almost endearing like this. Not that he wasn't attractive when he was awake, but it was a harsh handsomeness then. Dark and stern. Well, alright, grumpy. He looked young and sweet in sleep.

Smiling, she cuddled closer and shut her eyes to allow sleep to claim her.

"I am ill! You should let me win," Willa exclaimed as Hugh called check.

"Ha!" He laughed up at her from where he lay on his belly, surveying the chessboard. "You win often enough on your own without my letting you win. Who taught you to play?"

"Uncle." She grinned, pleased that he had noticed her skill. "I have beaten Baldulf, Howel and my uncle over the years. I like to win."

"Aye." His gaze became considering. "You have a competitive nature."

Willa opened her mouth to deny it, but then closed it. She wasn't sure why the description bothered her. It simply did not seem an admirable quality in a woman and the description sat awkwardly on her shoulders. Willa hadn't been raised to be competitive. She'd been raised to do as she was told. Knowing that those around her risked their lives to guard and care for her, she'd been as well-behaved and obedient as was possible.

"Tell me about your childhood," Hugh said suddenly and Willa glanced at him with amusement.

"I have already told you about my childhood, at length," she said. And it was true. They had spent the past three days getting to know each other as they recovered. Eada, Lucan and Gawain had been their only visitors. Eada checked on them twice a day, changing Hugh's poultice and dosing them both with various vile tasting herbs meant to help them heal. Gawain delivered the food, tasting it before Willa was allowed to eat. And Lucan had kindly stepped in to act as intermediary between Hugh and his responsibilities as lord while he was mending. He delivered messages from Howel and anyone else who wished his counsel, then carried away Hugh's decisions with him.

Other than that, they had spent their time playing chess, dice and talking. Willa had quite gotten over her shyness with her husband. That never-ending chattering that Eada had commented on had taken over and she'd told him almost everything there was to know about herself. In return, Willa had pestered him about his past and had found herself saddened to learn that his youth sounded as lonely as her own. She felt a kinship with him.

"Not everything."

Willa glanced up, feeling suddenly wary. "Aye. I have."

"You have told me all about your life since moving to the cottage here at Hillcrest," he agreed. "However, you have not even started on your time at Claymorgan."

Willa stared down at the chessboard and shook her head. "I was very young. I do not recall that time."

"Nay?" He took her hand and began to toy with it.

"Nay," Willa assured him, watching their hands. When he lifted them to press a kiss to the back of hers, she followed the action with her eyes. Then his tongue slid out to lick at the tender spot at the joining of her first and second fingers. Little tingles immediately ran up her hand and arm and made her toes curl.

"Not even Luvena?" he queried, licking the sensitive spot again.

Willa swallowed and shook her head. He licked between the second and third finger now. The tingling seemed to shoot further with each lick, and Willa found herself shifting as those tingles made it all the way to the apex of her thighs. It did not help that she clearly recalled the night they had consummated their union and the delectable things he'd done then.

Hugh drew her third finger into his mouth with his tongue and Willa bit her lip to keep from saying anything. He nipped it gently with his teeth, suckled the digit, then removed it. "Tell me about Luvena," he coaxed.

Willa shook her head and curled her fingers into a fist. Hugh was silent for a moment. At first she thought he was angry with her, but then he shifted to his knees and leaned forward to press his lips to hers. Willa opened to him at once, inviting the deep kisses she enjoyed most. The ones that made her hungry for more. She wanted to wrap her arms around him and press him close to her body, but Eada had said he would tell her what to do and he'd not said that was alright, so she forced her hands to remain at her sides and merely drank all the satisfaction and pleasure she could from his mouth.

Willa nearly spoke her gratitude into his mouth when he pressed her back on the bed and came down on top of her. She wanted to feel his body against hers. All of his naked body against hers. Unfortunately, while Hugh had remained unclothed the last three days, she had not. Except for when they slept, Willa was dressed. As she was now. Her clothes were between them and she didn't like it. It was a relief when he began to tug at the lacings of her gown. He hadn't even finished undoing the lacings, however, when the door opened without warning.

Willa and Hugh broke apart at once, both of them looking to see who had entered. It was Eada. She was late this morning. Or they had woken early. They had been playing chess while they awaited her arrival and that of Alsneta's nephew, Gawain, with food for them to break their fast.

"Well, ye must be feeling better if ye're up to that nonsense," Eada said dryly as she moved to the bed.

Hugh saw Willa flush with embarrassment at the acerbic comment, and scowled at the old witch for distressing her. He waited until he was sure the hag had seen his displeasure, then shifted to lie on his stomach to be examined. He grimaced and tried not to shudder as her cold hand clasped his arse. He could swear the old woman got her jollies examining him. She certainly seemed to like to touch him more than he felt was necessary.

"Hmm." He glanced over his shoulder to see her bent over, peering at his healing carbuncle. "Yer a fast healer, m'lord. 'Tis doing very well. Very well, indeed. Ye can get up. But try not to sweat and don't sit on it. I will be checking it tonight and if it has increased again rather than shrunk more, I shall have ye back on yer belly."

Hugh scowled at her stern words, but couldn't help noticing that Willa was beaming at this news. She was obviously pleased that he was healing well. As she should be. She was also looking quite expectant as the old woman walked around to her side. Getting off the bed, Hugh found his braies and began to drag them on as the witch examined his wife.

"How is yer cough?" the hag asked as he tied the string of his drawers.

"I hardly coughed at all last night," Willa told her promptly. "And only once or twice since awaking."

Hugh saw the crone reach out to feel Willa's forehead, then turned his attention to searching for his tunic.

"Hmm." That noncommittal sound drew his gaze around. The hag had her head bent to Willa's chest, listening to her breathe. As he watched, she straightened with a nod. "Very well then, ye can be up and about, too. And not a moment too soon. Those beasties of yers are drawing nearer the castle every day. They showed themselves in the clearing last night and scared the willies off the guards."

"Oh dear!" Willa scrambled off the bed and started for the door.

"Just a minute," Hugh said sharply, but he was overridden by Eada, who barked, "Yer shoes!"

Willa whirled at once to begin searching for her shoes. Though she'd dressed every day, she'd not bothered with footwear since taking her shoes off the night they had consummated their marriage. Hugh wasn't surprised they were not readily at hand. He saw her cast one quick glance around; then she dropped out of sight on the other side of the bed. Frowning, he walked around the bed, stopping abruptly at the sight of her derriere poking out from under it. She'd half-crawled under the bed in search of her shoes. Apparently, somehow, at some point, they had been kicked under the bed, because she released a victorious "ah ha," then backed out, and straightened, shoes in hand.

"Here they are!" She grinned at him and Eada, and began to pull them on.

Hugh opened his mouth to speak, but again, Eada beat him to it. "Good. Now, ye'd best run down to the kitchen and see if Alsneta has something ye can take to those beasties. And see if ye can't lure 'em back to the clearing by the cottage."

"I will," Willa called, hurrying for the door.

"Just a damn minute," Hugh bellowed as she opened the door. Finally, he had her attention. She paused in the open door and turned a surprised face back.

"Aye, my lord husband?"

"You are not going out alone to find those wolves of yours," he began. That was as far as he got. His pretty little wife laughed lightly and shook her head.

"Of course not, my lord. I shall take Baldulf with me." She rushed through the door and pulled it closed before he could comment further.

Cursing, Hugh started across the room after her. He couldn't let her leave the castle with just Baldulf. The soldier was fine as a guard here. However, Hugh wasn't about to let her out of the castle with only one man to accompany her.

"My lord!" Eada called.

"What?" Hugh paused at the door and turned back with irritation, just in time to have a ball of cloth slap him in the face as she tossed it from the other side of the bed. Hugh caught the material automatically and glanced down to find it was his missing tunic. He actually managed a thank you before whirling away to open the door. He donned his tunic as he rushed down the hall, chasing after his wife and Baldulf. He caught up to the pair on the stairs.

"Willa!" He sounded as impatient as he felt. Willa didn't seem overly concerned about his sour mood, however.

She smiled over her shoulder at him as she continued down the stairs. "Is it not lovely to be up and about again?"

Hugh grimaced at the question. Though he was grateful that his arse was improving and that she was recovering from her cold, he'd rather enjoyed their time in the sickbed together. She'd been a tad testy at first—obviously she did not take illness well—but then they had talked and laughed and played chess and dice.

Hugh had relaxed for the first time in a long time and Willa had relaxed enough to show a tendency to chatter. He'd enjoyed that, too. Her voice was as sweet in speech as it was in song and he'd enjoyed listening to her speak. Of course, he hadn't always been listening to exactly what she was saying. Sometimes, he had simply watched her lips move and allowed the musical highs and lows of her speech to drift over him, grunting once in a while to keep her babbling. He was almost sorry to see their time alone together end. He especially wouldn't have minded another hour to finish what he had started. He was sure he could have made her babble now that she was no longer nervous around him. His wife did not appear to be of the same opinion. She seemed to think it was wonderful to escape their enforced stay in the bedchamber. That was hardly flattering.

Becoming aware that she and Baldulf had continued on down the stairs without him, Hugh frowned and chased after them again. "Willa, Wilf and Fin—"

"Wolfy and Fen," she corrected with a laugh. "I can hardly wait to see them. It has been three days. They must be starved. And I really must try to urge them back to the clearing by the cottage. They will be much safer there."

"Aye. Nay. You need a proper guard—"

"I know, husband. Baldulf is coming with me." She smiled at the silent man descending the stairs at her side.

"Baldulf is not enough. I would have at least six men accompany you."

"Six?" That made her pause and turn on him with dismay. "Wolfy and Fen will hardly come around if I have half a dozen armed guards traipsing behind me!"

"Six," Hugh insisted, crossing his arms over his chest in a manner meant to convey that he would not be moved on this matter. Then he scowled, not at all certain that six men were enough. Perhaps he should send more, he thought, then became aware of the anger in her eyes. He watched with fascination as it built, then was suddenly doused by a smile.

"Very well, husband." Turning, she continued down the stairs. "I shall go to the kitchens to beg some scraps from Alsneta. Have the five men you wish to accompany Baldulf and myself meet us at the stables."

Hugh watched her go with narrowed eyes. Suspicion was rife within him. Willa had agreed too easily and far too pleasantly. In his experience with women, that meant she was up to something. Recalling how easily she had escaped his guard a time or two at the cottage, he let his shoulders droop with defeat. He couldn't trust her safety to even six men. He would have to accompany her himself. Hugh was scowling over that fact when it occurred to him that it meant his time alone with her was not yet over. He would get to spend at least part of another day with her.

Feeling more cheerful at this thought, he continued down the steps. A burst of laughter drew his eyes to his wife as she and Baldulf approached the kitchen doors. Now that he wasn't distracted by the need to see that she did not leave the castle with only Baldulf to guard her, he was free to watch the sway of her skirts as she walked. Unfortunately, there wasn't much sway to her skirts. The material was too coarse and the fit too large. Which reminded him that he simply had to get her some new gowns. She was now the wife of an earl and should be outfitted accordingly. He scowled over the matter briefly, then thought of his cousin. The poppinjay ought to be good for something. Hugh would have a word with his cousin ere he went to the stables, he decided.

Chapter Fourteen

Willa was watching a group of children play when the sound of an approaching horse made her turn. She found herself staring up at her mounted husband.

"My lord," she greeted, then glanced past him toward the stables, wondering what was taking Baldulf so long. He had suggested she wait outside while he saw to things in the stables. Willa expected to see the soldier come from the stables leading five mounted Hillcrest soldiers and a saddled horse for herself. She was completely surprised when Hugh rode up by himself and suddenly bent down to catch her about the waist. Willa gave a startled gasp as she found herself settled on the saddle before him, the sack of meat she carried banging against her leg.

"Hook the sack to the pommel," he ordered. He shifted her, rearranging his hold on his reins.

"Where is Baldulf? Why—?" Her questions

stopped abruptly as he took the sack from her and hooked it to the pommel himself.

"I gave him the morning off. I am accompanying you."

"But what of the six guards you insisted on?"

"I shall do." He cut off any further questions by urging the horse into a trot across the bailey.

Faced with the possibility of biting her tongue off, Willa refrained from asking anything more and grabbed at his arms to help keep her balance as they rode through the castle gate.

It was a beautiful day, made more so by the fact that they had been trapped in their room for three days. Willa had enjoyed getting to know her husband, but staring at the same four walls had quickly grown tiresome. She was used to being out of doors most of the time. Long walks, swimming in the river and just lazing at the river's edge with Wolfy and Fen had formed the pattern of her life for many years. Being locked inside did not sit well with her.

She leaned back against Hugh's chest and breathed in deeply of the fresh air, simply enjoying the sunshine on her face at first. But then she became aware of a lump at her back, nudging against her bottom, and she shifted to try to find a more comfortable spot. It did seem that Hugh had a most uncomfortable saddle. Willa was quite sure that if this were still the saddle Lord Hillcrest had purchased for him, then its lumpiness must be due to age. Or perhaps the old saddle had worn out and Hugh had replaced it with a much more inferior one. The man who had raised her certainly would have insisted on top quality, and the lumpiness of this saddle left much to be desired.

Willa had barely had that thought when she became aware that Hugh had shifted the reins to one hand and was holding her in place with the other. He'd splayed his hand flat against her stomach and was pressing her firmly back against his chest. Willa considered telling him he need not bother, that she was well-seated and would not fall, but she rather enjoyed the warm and safe feeling his touch gave her, so she held her tongue.

They were moving rather swiftly and the motion jostled his hand so that it drifted upward. Willa found herself holding her breath as it drew closer to the bottom of her breasts. When his fingers finally brushed their roundness, she let her breath out on a whoosh that pressed her breasts more firmly into his hand. Her nipples began to tingle under the unintentional caress and she bit her lip, wiggling against the hardness behind her.

Willa was terribly disappointed when he began to slow his mount and she realized that they were nearing the cottage.

"Where did you wish to go?" His voice was husky and Willa wondered if he weren't getting his cold back.

"The river," she said quietly.

"How do you know they will be there?"

"They will follow us. They have been following us ever since we left the castle," she told him. Glancing over her shoulder, she saw surprise cross his face, but he merely turned in the direction that would lead them to the river. They rode in silence again.

Moments later they broke out of the woods at the edge of the river and he slowed his mount. Willa slid from the saddle the moment he'd brought the animal to a halt, catching her breath as his hand unintentionally brushed her breasts while he helped her down. Leaving him to tie up the beast, she moved to the water's edge and opened the sack Alsneta had given her. She'd nearly finished dividing the meat scraps it contained into two even piles when he joined her.

Setting out the last of the meat, Willa straightened. She moved to the river's edge to wash her hands in the cool water, then sat back on her haunches to stare at the slow-moving water. She wanted to swim but was too shy to do so in front of her new husband. Which was silly, she supposed. He'd seen her completely naked. She glanced back at him uncertainly to find that he'd settled on the rock Baldulf usually occupied.

Catching her glance, he arched his eyebrows. "What?"

"I thought I might swim," she admitted shyly.

He opened his mouth in what she suspected would be a refusal to allow it. She was still recovering from a cold, after all, but then he paused, his gaze drifting down over her. He was looking at her as if she were a tender morsel and he a starving man, she thought with discomfort. Then he smiled. It was a rather wicked smile that sent shivers over her skin.

"Aye. You should swim."

Feeling suddenly uncertain, Willa debated the matter. In the end, she took her courage in hand and began to work on her lacings. She was slow at the chore, her discomfort making her clumsy as he watched her. Eventually she managed the task and shrugged out of the loose gown Eada had made her. Willa considered removing her shift, too. She usually kept it on if Baldulf were there, but Hugh had seen her naked and the pleasure of the water against her naked skin was tempting. Unfortunately her courage did not extend that far. Leaving the shift on, she shucked her shoes and started into the water. It had felt refreshingly cool on her hands, but it seemed colder on her feet and legs. Willa moved slowly, easing out an inch at a time. She was terribly aware of Hugh's eyes burning into her back.

Willa walked out to her waist like that, then she could no longer stand the strain of his gaze and dove under. She came up squealing at the shock of the cold water. Pushing her hair back, she hopped about, trying to adjust to the temperature.

The sound of chuckling from the shore drew her head around and she made a face at Hugh. He was still sitting on the rock, but was now laughing at her antics.

"You may laugh," she called out. "But I do not see you braving the water!"

He shook his head, his amusement fading into a grin. "I do not swim. 'Sides, I am standing guard."

"Ha! A likely excuse, my lord." She splashed water in his direction, falling far short of hitting him. "You should just admit that you are afraid you might catch a chill."

He continued to grin at her and shake his head; then his gaze lowered to her chest and paused. The grin faded. Willa followed his glance downward, blushing as she saw that she might as well have left the shift off. Wet, it was completely transparent. She dropped until the water covered her to the neck.

"Perhaps I *shall* join you." He began to rise.

"Nay! Do not move!" The urgency in her voice made him pause, his look becoming wary.

"What is it?"

"Wolfy and Fen," she breathed, but he heard her. Either that or he read her lips, for he relaxed back on the rock.

"Where are they?" he asked. Willa wasn't surprised at his curiosity. He really hadn't seen them up close in the light of day. This was the first time they had approached while he was present.

"They are coming out of the woods," she told him. "To your right."

He turned his head and they both watched the animals' cautious approach. They were normally more relaxed than this with her. Hugh's presence made them wary, she supposed. But then she was shocked that they would approach at all with him there.

"What do I do?" Hugh asked. He didn't sound frightened, just concerned that he might scare them off.

"Nothing. Just sit still and watch them. Are they not beautiful?"

Hugh nodded silently, his gaze moving from one to the other. The wolves were watching him too, eyeing him warily as they approached the food. Deciding that her own tension probably was not helping the matter, Willa forced herself to relax and began to splash about in the water. She swam a bit, floated some, then grew bored and decided to get out. Wolfy and Fen were just finishing their meal. Willa walked calmly out, pausing to stroke first Fen then Wolfy, before moving over to collect her gown and shoes.

"You will catch a chill if you don your gown over that wet shift."

Willa paused and turned at Hugh's quiet words. "I cannot return to the castle like this."

"Nay." He looked thoughtful for a moment, his gaze moving over the damp, clingy chemise. "We shall go to the cottage and start a fire. You can dry your shift and hair before it."

Willa nodded and glanced toward the wolves, but they were gone. Every scrap of meat had been eaten.

"They are quick and quiet," Hugh commented, standing now. "Why did they not stay?"

"They will not have gone far," Willa told him, folding her gown over her arm. "They will go find somewhere to sleep. They always sleep after eating."

He nodded at that, then untied his horse. They walked the short distance to the cottage in silence.

Her childhood home looked different somehow when they stepped into the clearing. It had always appeared warm and inviting to her. Now, however, it seemed forlorn and abandoned, Willa thought as she moved toward it.

Aware that Hugh was no longer at her side, she paused at the door and glanced around. He was leading his horse to the small building they had used as a stable. Leaving him to it, she opened the door and stepped inside, frowning at the musty scent. They had only left a few days ago, yet they could have been gone for months. Her gaze slid around the dim interior, landing on the table, then the cot, the only two furnishings left. The small cottage looked barren without the chairs, the linens, the flowers. . . .

She walked into the room and ran a hand lightly over the rough surface of the table that had been the heart of this home. Eada had sat there sewing a new gown or mending old ones. Baldulf had sat opposite her, polishing his armor or making Willa shoes. She'd eaten, done her lessons and grown up at this table.

"I meant to have this place burned down. I should have." Willa turned with a gasp at that comment from Hugh. He stood in the open door, frowning around the dim interior; then his gaze returned to her. " 'Tis making you sad."

"Nay," she said quickly. " 'Tis not the cottage. 'Tis just . . ." She shrugged helplessly as her gaze slid around the dim interior. It would never be home again. She'd lost that too. Willa promptly berated herself for such thoughts. After all, Hillcrest was her home now. Still . . .

She heard the door close, then felt Hugh's heat as he moved up behind her. He brushed the still damp hair away from her cheek and neck, and brushed a kiss across the sensitive skin below her ear.

"I will not have you sad." It sounded almost like an order, and Willa found herself smiling, then murmuring with pleasure as he kissed her neck again. Hearing the sound made her frown. She bit her lip against releasing another one as he continued to tease the skin of her neck. If she were to turn her head just a bit, she could find his lips with her own. She wanted to, but she wasn't sure if she should. Willa was grateful when Hugh removed that dilemma by turning her head for her with a finger at her chin. He claimed her mouth in a questing kiss and Willa kissed him back enthusiastically.

She did so enjoy his kisses, she thought vaguely, then stiffened as she felt his hands at the neckline of her shift. He tugged it down, baring her damp breasts to the chill air, then covered them with his callused hands, immediately warming them. Willa squeezed her eyes closed, some of the pleasure diminished as she concentrated on remaining silent and unmoving as Eada had instructed. It was terribly hard. He was cupping and squeezing her breasts, his thumbs rubbing excitingly across her nipples. She had the almost irresistible urged to arch into that caress and grind her bottom against him, but she managed to restrain herself.

Continuing to kiss her, Hugh turned her in his embrace, backing her up until her behind bumped against the table. Then he cupped her breasts again. Moments later, he broke the kiss to bend his head to claim one erect nipple. Willa stared down at his bent head and ached to run her hands through his hair, but forced herself to remain still. When she did not respond, he raised his head, a perplexed expression on his face.

"Do you not like when I do that?" he asked, his voice husky with passion.

Willa nodded silently but fervently, and his perplexity seemed to deepen. He pushed the chemise that had caught at her waist down over her hips until it dropped into a damp pile on the floor. His hand slid between her legs and he touched her intimately. Willa bit her lip and stiffened at the caress.

"Do you like that?" he asked uncertainly, and she nodded her head ardently again. He seemed all the more confused.

"Then why are you so quiet?" he asked at last. "Why do you not hold me or touch me back?"

Willa's eyes widened at the almost hurt confusion in his voice. "Eada," she croaked, then had to stop to clear her throat.

"Eada?" he prompted, a touch impatient.

Willa nodded. "She said that men did not like babbling women and that you would tell me if I should do anything."

Hugh went still at that, his eyes taking on a dangerous quality. "Do you mean to say that when we consummated the wedding you were so still and quiet because *Eada* said you should be?"

"Aye," she admitted, then babbled. "'Twas the most horrible experience I have ever had ... and the most glorious. I wished to scream and thrash and I wished to hold you close and—But I thought I had to await your instruction and remain still. I did not wish to displease you. Where are you going?" she added with concern as he groaned and suddenly turned away. He answered the question by moving to the door and banging his head against it several times. Willa bit her lip, then asked uncertainly, "My lord? Are you alright? Have I done something wrong and angered you?"

"Nay." Hugh stopped banging his head to give it a shake. Then he chuckled and turned to face her. His voice was very calm and clear as he said, "Eada was wrong."

"She was?" Willa asked uncertainly. "Are you sure? Eada is never wrong."

"Well, she is wrong in this case." Moving forward, he cupped her face in his hands and said, "I wish to hear your pleasure, wife. How else am I to know that I please you? And God! Please do not wait for me to instruct you. Touch me. Hold me. Claw me if you wish."

Willa jerked in shock. "I would never claw you, my lord. I would never hurt you."

A determined sparkle entered his eyes. "We shall see about that."

"My lord?" Willa asked, backing uncertainly away as he moved forward. "You sound almost as if you should like me to claw you?"

"'Twould be a high compliment," he assured her, and then Willa found her retreat ended as she bumped up against the table. The rough wood against her backside reminded her that her shift was gone and she was naked. Then Hugh swooped

down to kiss her again. This was no questing kiss.
This time his mouth seemed intent on devouring
hers. Willa was, at first, too stunned to respond,
but gradually she inched her hands up around his
neck. She heaved a gusty sigh into his mouth and
began to kiss him back.

It was so glorious to be able to hold him. Willa
squeezed her arms tight around him, then ran her
hands up into his hair, her fingers brushing against
his ears. Hugh's response was immediate. His own
hands dropped to cup her bottom, urging her forward as he thrust a knee between her legs. Willa
gasped into his mouth as the rough cloth of his
braies rubbed against the center of her. She could
feel his erection against the front of one thigh and
squirmed against him, gasping at the excitement
caused by the friction of his leg between hers.

Still pressing her lower body tight to him, he slid
his other hand between them to fondle one breast.
When he next tried to pull his mouth free, she
caught his head and held it in place. She knew he
was probably intending to seek out her breast to
suckle it, but the sensations he was causing between her legs were already too much and she desperately needed his kisses. She *needed* his tongue in
her mouth.

Willa felt his hand drop away from her breast,
but didn't really care until she felt it nudge its way
lower. She broke the kiss then, tossing her head
back and gasping for air as he touched her. He slid
his knee free and she promptly closed her thighs
around his hand, squeezing to increase her pleasure as she rode it.

She was groaning and moaning and grunting and didn't care. Hugh had said he wanted to hear her pleasure. She let him hear; she was begging incoherently for the release he could give her.

"Thank God! You are babbling." He sounded exhultant, though Willa didn't know why that pleased him so. Then he withdrew his pleasure-giving hand and suddenly lifted her to sit on the edge of the table. Willa had barely registered her disappointment when he slid into her.

Crying out, Willa arched and closed her legs around him as he cupped her bottom. She clawed at his shoulders and chanted, "Please, please, please," by his ear as he pounded into her. Cursing, he tugged her tighter to him with his hold on her bottom, grinding himself against her with each thrust until she stiffened and shrieked as she convulsed in his arms. Lost in a world of sensation, Willa was barely aware of his stiffening and shouting as he joined her in that release.

When next she became aware of her surroundings, it was to find herself still seated on the table, leaning limply against her husband's chest. She heard him groan; then he pulled back slightly and she felt him press a kiss to the top of her head. Lifting her head, she met his gaze briefly, then blushed as she recalled her abandon of moments ago. Willa started to duck her head, but he caught her chin and pressed a kiss to one flushed cheek.

"You pleased me," was all he said. It was enough. Still inside her, Hugh scooped her up off the table and turned to walk to the cot in the corner. She felt him move inside her and grow stiffer with each

step, and then he eased her onto the bed and slid
out of her as he straightened.

Willa watched in silence as he removed the
open braies hanging off his hips. He was fully
erect again, or so she thought until his manhood
grew even larger under her gaze. She found it
rather shocking that something so large had fit
inside her and felt good in the fitting. Then her
gaze moved up to admire the broad expanse of
his chest as he tugged his tunic off. Willa's hands
reached up of their own accord to smooth over his
torso as he joined her on the cot. She closed her
eyes and enjoyed the feel of him under the sensitive tips of her fingers as he lay half on top of her,
holding most of his weight with his arms. She allowed her hands to drift to his nipples, rubbing
her thumbs over them as he did to her. Her eyes
opened at a sound from him. Hugh was smiling.
He seemed to enjoy her touch, so she slid her hands
down across his stomach, then to his hips. She
caught him there and tried to pull him against
her, but he resisted, looking a bit vexed.

"What is it?" Willa asked.

"This cot is small; 'tis hard to find purchase. I
may crush you." He hesitated, then lay on his side.
He shifted until he lay on his back and had ma-
neuvered her on top of him. Willa lay there uncertainly for a moment, then pushed herself upright
until she straddled his hips. She felt him hard beneath her and blushed, then began to run her
hands curiously over his chest as her drying hair
slid down to curtain them.

Smiling, Hugh caught several strands and used

them to tug her down for a kiss. Willa sighed against his mouth as the movement rubbed her across the hard flesh of his erection. Then she kissed him eagerly as he let go of her hair to clasp her hips and draw her across his flesh in a deliberate caress. Enjoying the sensation, Willa took over the movement, sliding along his shaft as Hugh shifted his hands to cup her breasts between them. She was enjoying the sensation so much that she was almost disappointed when she angled herself too much and he slid into her. Willa hesitated, then sat up and clasped his hands over her breasts as she began to ride him. She was awkward at first, and uncertain, but she was also in control and quickly found just the right position and angle to gain the most pleasure.

Hugh pulled one hand away from her breast to grasp her hip, attempting to urge her to a faster motion, but Willa resisted, driving them both mad with her slow pace. As her excitement mounted, so did a frantic need to kiss him, but she was unable to reach his lips. Finally she grabbed the hand at her hip and drew it up to her mouth, licking, nipping and finally sucking on it in her urgency. This just seemed to make Hugh move more desperately beneath her.

This time it was he who begged in an incoherent plea, and he who first arched, raising his back up off the bed with a shout as he poured himself into her. Willa followed quickly, biting down on his finger and arching into her own release. Then she collapsed on top of him, feeling completely drained and thoroughly satisfied.

Hugh mumbled something that might have been a compliment or an endearment as he wrapped his arms around her to hold her close, but Willa was too exhausted to ask what he'd said. Snuggling close, she sniffled, frowning slightly at the scent of smoke in the air. It reminded her that Hugh had meant to light a fire for her, but they had forgotten. She didn't suppose she needed it anymore and drifted into sleep.

Chapter Fifteen

Hugh was dreaming. He stood in a thick fog, shouting for Willa. He knew she was there somewhere, but he couldn't find her in the swirling mist. Hugh stumbled forward through the haze, calling her name and begging her to answer. But the only response he received was the mournful howling of her wolves.

Hugh blinked his eyes open and, for a moment, thought he was still dreaming. The dim room was aswirl with fog and the concerted howls of Wolfy and Fen were still echoing in his ears. Then he realized that the sound wasn't an echo. Wolfy and Fen *were* howling. And the fog in the room wasn't fog at all, but smoke . . . from a fire . . . that he'd forgotten to light.

"Fire!" He sat up, unintentionally dislodging Willa and tumbling her to the floor. He leaned over to peer at her at once, but couldn't see her for the smoke. "Willa?"

"Hugh?" Her voice was pained and confused, but at least she was answering him. She hadn't in his dreams. Relief slid through him even as she began to cough. Then she asked, "What is happening?"

"The cottage is on fire." He got off the pallet, careful to avoid stepping on her and began a blind search for his clothes. Hugh found what he thought were his braies and started to drag them on, only to realize that he was trying to stick his feet into the arms of his tunic. Cursing, he pulled it on over his head.

"Nay. You forgot to light a fire," Willa said. Her words ended on another coughing fit.

Hugh knew the smoke must be irritating her already sore throat. He had to get her out of there. "Get up, Willa. Find your clothes."

Hugh found his braies and pulled them on as he stumbled in the direction of the door. The smoke was heavy in the room and he couldn't tell exactly where the fire was. He was hoping that opening the door would allow some of the smoke out and increase visibility. He could then help Willa find her gown and they could escape. Hugh would take her naked if he had to, but didn't wish to return her to Hillcrest in such an embarrassing state.

Fortunately, it was a small cottage and he had correctly recalled the direction of the door from the cot. Hugh released a breath of relief and pushed on it. A chill ran down the back of his neck when it did not budge. He pushed again. Nothing. It wasn't moving at all.

Hugh took a step back, then rammed himself against the door. It didn't budge. Stepping back, he tried to understand what was happening, but the sound of Willa coughing drew his attention. He glanced in her direction, but the smoke was thick. As it had been in his dream, he could not see her. Panic seized him briefly, but a coughing fit of his own brought him out of it. Leaving the door for the moment, he followed the sound of her coughs until he stumbled over her.

"Willa?" Bending, he grabbed the first thing that came to hand. Her derriere. She was on her hands and knees. However, she was also partially dressed. She had donned either her shift or her gown, Hugh wasn't sure which. Whatever it might be, it was enough. Shifting his hands to her arms, he dragged her to her feet. "We have to get out of here." He felt her nod against his chest as she coughed.

"The door is barred from the outside."

"There is no bar on the outside," she panted weakly as her coughing fit came to an end.

"Aye, well, there is now."

Wolfy and Fen howled in concert again, and he felt Willa stiffen. "The wolves."

"Aye. Their howling woke me." He stumbled toward the place where the table should be, relieved when his hand bumped against it. "Here, stay here. I am going to try to open the door."

"You said 'twas barred."

"Aye. Something is keeping it closed. Is this cottage of cob or wattle and daub?"

"Wattle and daub. Baldulf once said 'twas almost

twenty years old. The back wall has been damaged by rainstorms. He said 'twould have to be repaired or another cottage built soon. He—" She broke off to cough again and Hugh thumped her back a couple of times, then told her to remain where she was and moved to the back wall. Much to his relief it *was* wattle and daub. Cob would have been much harder to smash through. And Willa was right, it had suffered water damage. It was crumbling under his touch. It was also hot.

Hugh made his way back to the table, following the sound of Willa's coughing again. Finding her hand, he hooked it into the waist at the back of his braeis. "Hold on to me. I am going to break through the back wall. Do not let go of my braies," he ordered, then picked up the table and moved toward the back of the small cottage. The table hit the wall first and jarred against him. Hugh felt along the wall until he was sure he knew where the timbers were. He did not want to waste time on the frame of the building. Once assured he knew where to hit, he reached back to make sure that Willa was out of the way behind him. Hugh then used the table as a battering ram and smashed it through the panel of woven sticks with its cover of straw and cow dung. The table went pitching through on the first blow.

Releasing a sigh of relief, Hugh grabbed Willa's hand from the back of his braies and bent to charge through the splintered opening. He didn't stop running until he was sure they were well clear of the burning cottage. He paused and turned toward Willa then and cried out when he saw that the back of her gown was on fire. Throwing her to the ground, he used his hands and the untouched parts of her own gown to smother the fire. Hugh had just doused the last of it when Wolfy and Fen came charging around the cottage. For one moment, he thought that the beasts were going to attack . . . and they did. They leaped on Willa, licking her face with joy to see her alive and well.

Cursing, he pulled Willa up into a sitting position, then paused to survey the burning structure. The cottage was now nearly completely aflame. The thatch roof was one large torch; the walls had gone up like tinder.

"You said their howling woke you?"

Hugh glanced down at Willa and nodded. He frowned. "I wonder where they were when the fire was set?"

"Probably still sleeping after their meal," Willa said. Her eyes sharpened. "When the fire was set?"

"Hmm." Hugh helped her to her feet and started around the cottage toward the clearing. He wasn't really concerned that whoever had started it might still be present. Wolfy and Fen would have taken care of him if he were, but he wanted a look at the front door. He wished to see what had been barring it from opening.

It was a wooden plank. They barely got around front in time to see it before the roof collapsed into the cottage. The walls followed quickly, and the wolves immediately took flight and disappeared back into the surrounding woods. Hugh glanced at Willa to see that silent tears were running down her cheeks. This had been her home for ten years, he recalled, as he hugged her to his side. It would be hard for her to watch it fall like this. They stood in silence for several minutes watching it burn, then Hugh recalled his horse and led her to the stable. It was a relief to find the animal still there. Leaving Willa leaning against the door, Hugh walked inside and quickly checked the animal. Finding him uninjured, he saddled, then led him out of the stable. Hugh mounted, then lifted Willa up before him.

It was a silent return journey. Willa huddled before him in the saddle, careful not to touch him more than necessary. Her face was pale and drawn and Hugh could feel her tremble. What worried him most, however, was that her eyes seemed empty. It was like his dream, in a way. He felt as though he had lost some vital part of her in the smoky cottage and now could not find her. She had withdrawn from him, and he didn't like it.

Hugh rode his horse straight up to the castle stairs, and gently deposited his wife on her feet there. She stood there, looking lost, and Hugh noticed for the first time that her face was soot-streaked. The wolves had cleaned some of it away with their joyous greeting, but had missed much of it. He also saw, with some regret, that the bottom of her hair had been singed when her gown had been afire. It would have to be cut off a little above her waist.

"Go change. Order a bath to help remove the smoke and soot," he added as she started up the stairs. "I will send Baldulf up to wait outside our chamber for you. Do not leave until he arrives."

Willa didn't say anything, but he thought she nodded. Hugh watched her until she disappeared inside the castle, then turned his horse toward the stables. He wanted to leap off his horse and take her upstairs himself. He wanted to bathe away the signs of the fire from her body, then make love to her until he had also banished it from her mind. But he had to talk to the men. This was the third attempt on her life. He wanted the culprit caught before there was a fourth.

Willa made it all the way upstairs to the bedchamber she shared with Hugh without anyone stopping her. Once there, she didn't seem to have any idea what to do. She had a vague recollection of Hugh telling her to do something, but the memory was hazy. She stared around the room. Today had been a glorious day. Today had been hell. This morning her husband had taught her passion beyond anything Willa had dreamed of. This afternoon she had nearly lost him to death.

Of course, Willa had nearly died, too, but someone had been trying to kill her all her life. Every day she breathed was a gift. But the assassin had nearly killed Hugh today; as he had killed Luvena years ago. Her own mother had died giving Willa life. Ilbert had died while guarding her. The man who had raised her as his own child had died just days ago. . . .

Willa was terribly tired of losing those she loved. She dropped onto the edge of the bed with a moan. Her feelings for Hugh were new and confused. Willa had thought herself in love with the man before she'd ever met him. It was her duty to love her husband. But before these last few days, the thought of his dying would not have affected her as it now did. She was sure if he had died ere they had met, she would have felt sad regret. Nearly losing him today had caused terrible fear and wrenching pain. Willa didn't know if she could bear losing Hugh. She did know she couldn't bear it if she lost him to someone who was trying to kill her.

A thud drew Willa from her thoughts and she glanced toward the wall between this bedchamber and the master chamber that had been Richard Hillcrest's. As far as she knew, there was no one staying in that room. She heard a muffled scuffling sound and found herself on her feet and walking to the door. It was probably just Lord Wynekyn looking for the letter, but anything that distracted her from her thoughts was welcome.

She stepped out into the hall and found it empty.

Willa had a vague recollection of Hugh saying he would send Baldulf up. The guard hadn't yet arrived. The hallway was quiet and growing dark as the bedchamber door swung closed behind her. The rest of the doors leading off the hall were already shut, leaving the passage dark. Though it was not late, the torches should have been lit.

Willa was a little more than halfway to Lord Richard's room when it struck her that they must have been lit when she had come above stairs just moments ago or, surely, she would have noticed. A frown crossed her face. She couldn't really swear to that; she had been rather distressed at the time. She still was. Willa considered fetching a candle and glanced back toward the bedchamber she and Hugh were using. Then a cool draft drifted around her. It stirred her hair and made her toes curl inside her shoes. That explained the unlit torches, she decided. A breeze from one of the rooms had put them out.

A soft click drew her gaze down the hall. Willa was sure it had been Lord Richard's door closing. She stared into the inky blackness ahead, trying to make out whether anyone was there. "Lord Wynekyn?"

Willa moved cautiously forward, feeling along the wall until she touched the wood of the door. She paused there, her ears straining to make up for her lack of sight. She would swear she could hear someone else breathing. Another click made Willa pause and peer further along the hall. Another door had been softly closed. She listened for a moment, but could hear nothing above the sound of her slamming heart. It was only then that she realized her heart was racing violently. It was acting as if she had something to be frightened of.

"Silly," she reprimanded herself as she reached for the door. Lord Wynekyn would be inside with candlelight, searching Papa's chamber. She opened the door, but found herself hesitating on the threshold. Her gaze slid nervously around the interior. The chamber was cold and musty smelling, but there didn't appear to be anyone inside the room. That just made her more nervous. She was sure she had heard someone in here.

A clatter made her eyes jump nervously to the window. Willa gave a nervous chuckle as she saw that one side of the tapestry that had always hung over the shuttered window had fallen away. The shutters had also been unfastened, allowing sunlight and a cool breeze into the room as they clattered open and shut. That was probably the sound she had heard from next door.

Feeling foolish for jumping at shadows, Willa started across the room to pull the shutters closed.

"Willa girl! Where are you? Willa!" Baldulf's panicky call reached her and Willa wrinkled her nose. At least she was not the only one made nervous by recent events.

"In here, Baldulf!" she called as she reached the window and leaned out to grab the swinging shutters.

"What the devil are you doing in here? Hugh said he had ordered you to stay in your room until I—" His surly words ended on a grunt that made Willa turn toward the door. She caught a glimpse of someone slipping out of the room, but it was just a glimpse. Her dismayed gaze was focused on her friend as he crumpled to the floor.

"Baldulf!" She rushed to his side with alarm. "Baldulf?"

Kneeling at his side, she turned the old soldier onto his back. She examined his pale face with concern and whispered, "Oh, Baldulf," as she brushed the hair back from his forehead. He moaned in pain, but his eyes did not open.

Biting her lip, Willa lifted his head with one hand. She ran the fingers of her other hand carefully over the back of his head until she found where he had been hit. There was a bump and some blood.

"Willa? Yoohoo! Hello?"

"Jollivet?" Willa called uncertainly.

"Ah, I thought you were up here. I saw you return with Hugh and thought we might discuss the latest fashions to see what sort of gown you would prefer. He asked me to help you assemble a new wardrobe and—Whatever are the two of you doing on the floor?" he asked with amusement as he reached the door to the bedchamber. Then concern replaced his amusement and he rushed forward to kneel on the opposite side of the fallen guard. "Faith! Is Baldulf alright?"

"Someone hit him over the head. Can you fetch Eada for me?"

"Aye, of course." Letting the parchment he had been carrying slip to the floor, Jollivet launched himself to his feet and hurried from the room. He began shouting the moment he was out of sight.

"You did not see who set the fire?"

Hugh scowled at Lucan's question. He had left his horse at the stable and sought out Baldulf first. He'd taken the time to give the soldier a quick rundown of the situation so he would be aware that vigilance was needed. The moment the guard was on his way to Willa, Hugh had gone in search of Lucan and Lord Wynekyn. He had thought clearer heads than his were needed to sort out this mess.

Hugh was too furious to think clearly at the moment.

Having found Lucan and Lord Wynekyn in the great hall, he'd related all that had taken place at the cottage. Well, he had left out certain personal bits, but had explained about the fire. Then he had awaited their opinion on the matter. Wynekyn had been silent since Hugh had finished speaking. As for Lucan, he seemed more interested in asking stupid questions than in offering any wisdom on how to bring an end to these attacks.

"I told you we were sleeping," Hugh said with forced patience.

"In the cottage?" his friend asked with one raised eyebrow.

"Aye. In the cottage. We were sleeping. I did not see who set the fire," Hugh growled.

"You were sleeping in the cottage?"

"Did I not just say that?" he snapped.

"Aye. 'Tis just such an odd thing to do. Why would you go all the way down to the cottage to sleep on a tiny pallet that would barely fit you, alone, when you have a lovely large bed here in the castle?"

His friend's smile said he knew exactly why Hugh and Willa had been asleep on the pallet. He was just attempting to annoy him. It was working. Hugh was growling deep in his throat when Lord Wynekyn chose to intervene.

"I really do not think that is important, Lucan." He gave the man a reproving look, then added, "I believe it is more important to learn how whoever set the fire knew you were there."

Hugh stiffened at that remark. It had not occurred to him.

"Do you think the arsonist followed the two of you down to the cottage?" Lucan asked.

Hugh considered that, but shook his head. "Nay. I think the wolves would have been aware of that. They would have growled or something, as they did the night of the attack in the clearing."

"Then you do not think he was there the whole time?"

Hugh shook his head slowly, working it out for himself. He really didn't believe anyone could have followed them to the river. The wolves would have warned them somehow.

That meant the person had most likely come after the wolves had left.

"If he did not follow you, how did whoever set the fire know you would be there? Could it have been blind luck on his part?"

Hugh scowled at the question. He didn't believe in that kind of luck. Had he told anyone they were going to the cottage? Hugh considered the matter briefly, but knew he hadn't. Baldulf had known, though. The soldier had been on the stairs with Hugh and Willa when she had said that she must see if she could not coax the beasts to return and stay near the clearing by the cottage. Had anyone else been near enough to hear?

He was pondering the matter when shouting from above drew his attention. Turning toward the stairs, he saw Jollivet rushing down them. "Hugh! Eada! Where is Eada? Hugh!"

Hugh's first instinct was to roll his eyes at the

man's hysteria, but then he realized his cousin
was coming from above stairs, where Willa was.
And he was shouting for Eada. Hugh hurried to
meet his cousin at the bottom of the stairs. "What
is it? Is Willa hurt?"

"Nay. Baldulf. Someone hit him over the head
and—"

"Fetch Eada," Hugh interrupted and rushed
past him up the stairs. He went to his chamber
first, aware that Lucan and Wynekyn were on his
heels. They all paused in the doorway in confusion on finding the room empty. Hugh turned at
once, pushing past the other two men as he bellowed for his wife. "Willa!"

"Here!"

Following the sound of her voice, he hurried to
his uncle's chamber, only slightly relieved to find
her there. Sparing barely a glance for the man on
the floor, he hurried to her side. "Are you alright?"

"Aye. 'Twas Baldulf who was hit," she assured
him, then glanced to the door. Relief covered her
face. Following her gaze, Hugh saw Eada push past
the other two men.

"What happened?" Eada asked, kneeling to examine the fallen man.

Hugh glanced down at the fellow and scowled
at his pallor while Willa said, "I heard a noise in
here and thought Lord Wynekyn must be searching for the letter. I came to see, but the room was
empty." She gestured toward the window. "The
tapestry was down and the shutters were banging.
That was the noise I had heard. I was trying to

close them when Baldulf came in. He was speaking, and then he grunted. I turned, and he was falling. Someone had hit him over the head."

"Did you see who hit him?" Hugh asked.

"I—"

"The letter!"

Hugh glanced around at that exclamation from Lord Wynekyn. The man was holding a rolled scroll. Standing, Hugh moved to his side. "Where did you find it?"

" 'Twas right here on the bed." His troubled gaze lifted to Hugh. "I searched this room thoroughly— several times. 'Twas not here earlier."

Hugh's mouth tightened, but he merely took the scroll and slid it in his belt. Then he returned to stand behind Willa. She twisted where she sat, her gaze sliding curiously from the scroll to his face and back again. Baldulf groaned and she turned her attention back to the man who had guarded her life for so long.

"Baldulf?" She reached out to touch his cheek in an affectionate gesture that made Hugh oddly jealous. He forced the petty reaction away as the man clasped her hand and blinked his eyes open.

"Willa?" He appeared confused.

"Aye." She smiled. The expression was full of a love and tenderness Hugh would have given his title to receive. He silently vowed to himself that someday she would look at him just that way. He just hoped he wouldn't have to receive a kosh on the head to get it. Hugh grimaced over that thought as Willa asked the man, "How is your head?"

"Aching."

"Hmmm. That's good," Eada announced.

Baldulf turned his head to peer at her doubt-fully. " 'Tis?"

"Aye. Means ye're alive and well enough to complain."

Hugh had to work to keep from laughing at that comment. Baldulf's outraged expression did not help much. Clearing his throat, Hugh scowled at the woman. "Could you give the man something to ease the ache?"

"Oh, aye." She heaved a put-upon sigh and straightened. "If ye great men could stop standing about long enough to lug him to the bed, I shall fetch some meade and mix him a potion." When Hugh lifted an eyebrow at the order, she added, "The potion will make him sleepy. He can rest here while Willa and I see to cleaning this room. Now that the letter has been found, there is no reason not to move the two of ye here. An earl should sleep in the master's chamber."

Hugh glanced around as he considered her words. She was right. There was no reason now not to use this room. The delay had been due only to the fact that he and Lord Wynekyn had wished to search it for the letter ere moving things about too much. Now that the letter was found, there was no reason not to use it. It was much larger than the chamber he and Willa were presently in. Hugh nodded. "Aye."

"Get him in the bed then," the old woman or-dered as she straightened. She ignored Hugh's ir-ritation at being ordered about by one of his own servants and left the room in search of meade into which to mix her herbs.

Uncle Richard obviously had allowed the woman to get away with much during his time as earl. Deciding that it was probably too late to train her to behave more respectfully, Hugh urged Willa out of the way and knelt beside Baldulf. He'd just pulled the soldier's arm over his shoulder when Lucan rushed over to take the opposite side. Between the two of them, they got him into the bed.

Eada returned shortly afterward and dosed the man with something that made him grimace and curse. Having suffered the woman's potions himself, Hugh could sympathize. Still, although he wasn't sure whether it was the potion or Baldulf's disgust with the taste of it that did the trick, the man did have more color in his cheeks by the time Eada was finished with him. Deciding Baldulf appeared recovered enough for the questions he'd been waiting to ask, Hugh stepped up to the bedside. "Did you see who hit you?"

Baldulf shook his head apologetically. "Nay. I was hit from behind as I entered the room. I saw nothing but the floor coming up to meet me. Whoever it was must have been hiding behind the door."

Hugh scowled, his gaze moving to the door in question. He'd been hoping that Baldulf had seen something useful. Of course, life was never that easy. He nodded and stood. "Well, you rest here. We will find the culprit soon enough."

He started toward the door, aware that Lord

Wynekyn and Lucan were following while Jollivet hesitated by the bed.

"My lord?"

Willa's voice made him pause. Turning back, he
smiled at her wearily. "Aye, wife?"

"The letter?"

Hugh felt for the letter at his waist, relaxing
when his hand touched it. He'd forgotten he had
the letter, but the moment she'd mentioned it, he
had feared he'd dropped it. "Aye. I have it."

"Aye, husband. Did you plan on letting me
read it?"

Hugh knew his surprise showed. "Nay. There
is no need. I shall tend to it."

"I see."

Hugh felt wariness creep over him at the displeasure obvious in those two short words. "You
see what?"

"That you shall keep the secret from me as
well," she said quietly.

"There is no need for you to be upset by—"

" 'Tis about me, my lord. About who would see
me dead and why. Do you not think I have the
right to know its contents?"

Hugh hesitated. He would rather she didn't
know the letter's contents. At least not until he'd
read it himself. Perhaps not even then if it would
hurt her. But, peering at her face, he had the sneaking suspicion that if he did not allow her to read it
now, he could be in for some misery later. She
would probably refuse him her bed. That was a
woman's most effective weapon. He winced at the

mere thought. Aye, it was effective alright. His body was cringing at the very idea.

Cursing, he tugged the letter from his waist and handed it to her.

Chapter Sixteen

Willa stared down at the letter in her hand, almost afraid to read it. Her gaze slid to her husband. Hugh had moved to stand at the window overlooking the bailey. Lord Wynekyn shifted, drawing her gaze. He seemed both anxious and a touch impatient. She supposed he was wishing he'd read it before giving it to Hugh. They were all anxious to know what it said. But Willa was afraid, too.

Her gaze slid to Baldulf. The man was sitting up in the bed, reclining against furs someone had rolled and set behind him. When her old friend nodded, Willa took her courage in hand, settled on the edge of the bed and opened the scroll. The state of the parchment was somewhat surprising to her. It was obvious someone had opened and read it many times. She doubted if that had been Lord Hillcrest. The person who had hit Baldulf over the head must have read and reread it. There were smudges and water stains, as if some clear liquid had been dropped on it. Tears? she wondered.

"My dearest child, Willa," she read aloud, aware that Hugh was now turning from the window to look at her. She supposed he hadn't expected her to read aloud, but it seemed only fair. It also seemed more expedient than each of them taking turns reading the letter.

Willa cleared her throat and continued.

"First, I should like to say that I love you. I could not love you more had you been of my own seed. I love you as a daughter, and as such, it breaks my heart to tell you the sad tale to follow. Pray, forgive me for being too much a coward in life to hurt you with the telling. I am hoping that Hugh can somehow soften the blow to come. He is a good man, Willa. I have followed his progress through life. Give him the opportunity and I believe he could be the best of husbands."

Pausing, Willa glanced toward Hugh. His face was expressionless, carved in stern lines. She glanced back at the letter.

"Now, to the sad tale of how you ended up my daughter. Willa, the secret is in your name. I named you Willa because you were, in effect, willed to me. Your mother gave you to me with her dying breath and begged me to keep you safe. I told you that your name was Willa Evelake. Forgive me that lie. I will tell you your proper name later, but first,

your mother was Juliana Evelake. She was a beautiful woman. In all ways. You look very like her except for your coloring. Your mother had long chestnut tresses. Your fiery blonde coloring comes from your father.

"Juliana's parents sent her to my brother's wife to be trained. My brother, Pelles, and his wife, Margawse, were much in demand for training while at Claymorgan. Pelles was one of the best warriors England has ever produced and Margawse was as accomplished a wife as could be found anywhere. As I say, they were much in demand. I even sent my own son, Thomas, to train with Pelles and this is where Juliana and my son met.

"I do not know all the particulars of their friendship, but I do know that there was nothing in it to shame anyone. Their affection for each other was like that of a brother and sister. They were the dearest of friends for nearly ten years as Thomas trained to be a warrior and Juliana was trained to handle her wifely duties. Then, shortly after her sixteenth birthday, came her wedding day. The match had been arranged for years. Ten years. Her betrothed was Tristan D'Orland, a fierce and much lauded warrior. He was nearly twenty years older than she, and Juliana—Thomas later told me—had feared that she might find him an abhorrent old man. I smile even now at this memory. To the young, someone twenty years older often seems ancient. But Tristan was far from old. At five and thirty, he was in the prime of life, a strong and healthy specimen. He was a handsome, skilled warrior and carried himself with *confidence. I believe Juliana fell in love with him the moment she beheld him. 'Twas a very auspicious beginning. Everyone assumed they would do well together. Everyone but me."*

Willa paused to clear her throat, murmuring a thank you when Jollivet rushed to refill Baldulf's meade from the pitcher Eada had brought up, and handed it to her. She took a sip, then another. Then—aware that everyone was waiting most impatiently—she cleared her throat again and continued.

"You may not believe me when I say that I foresaw trouble ahead, but I did. I was there when Tristan arrived for the wedding. Juliana and Thomas had been walking together in the bailey and I had been seeking my son to ask him something. What 'twas I cannot even recall now, but it matters little. What matters is that I was standing perhaps a dozen feet away when Tristan D'Orland rode into the bailey. His traveling party was large, his banner unfurled and he led his party into the bailey as if charging an enemy. 'Twas obvious he was eager to claim his bride. He had waited ten years. Everyone paused to stare at the spectacle. Even I. I knew the exact moment when he spotted Juliana. Even from where I stood I could see his eyes light up. He knew her at once, so I can only assume that—though she had claimed never to have seen him—he had seen her over the years. But then a dark cloud of fury obliterated the light in his eyes and I glanced toward Juliana in

confusion. 'Twas then I saw that, in her nervousness, she had clasped Thomas's hand tightly in
her own. 'Twas a common occurrence, they were
very close, but that action was what had put the
scowl on the man's face. I think he would have
liked to strike Thomas to the ground right then.
But of course he could not. I joined my son and
Juliana as he rode to them and dismounted. Juliana, too, must have seen his displeasure, for she
was quick to introduce both Thomas and myself
and explain that Thomas was her best friend, the
brother she had never had. D'Orland seemed to
relax then and was pleasant to both my son and
myself. But I watched him closely during those
few days leading to the wedding and though he
hid it well, I could see the jealousy in him. He
loathed my son. He wished him gone from Juliana's side. I feared trouble ahead, and I was right.

"Oh, things went well enough at first. The
wedding went without a hitch and Juliana and
Tristan were very happy as they left for Orland
together. Thomas returned to Claymorgan to earn
his knight's spurs and I returned to Hillcrest, and
things trundled along. I had meant to talk to
Thomas, to warn him to be careful of his friendship with Juliana, that he might cause her trouble
did he not exercise caution. Had I done so, perhaps the tragedy that followed could have been
averted. However, I got caught up in arguments
and disagreements with my brother, Pelles, over
the running of Claymorgan and quite forgot the
matter, so Thomas became a frequent visitor to
Orland. Then came the trouble.

"I swear to you, dear child, there must have been something in the air that day. I rode to Claymorgan to have yet another argument with Pelles over the running of the estate. This time was not like all the others, however. This time I pushed Pelles too far. The disagreement blew up into a battle that ended with his gathering Margawse and Hugh and riding off in search of fortune as a warrior for hire. He would suffer no more because of my petty jealousy.

"I should like to confess now to Hugh—should he be reading this letter—that Pelles was right. There was no reason for these arguments other than jealousy on my part. I lost my wife to the birthing bed with Thomas and was envious of the comfort and happiness your father had found with his Margawse. He accused me of this at the time. I denied it then, but I confess it now. He was right. The faults I found with his running of Claymorgan were the result of petty jealousy. I drove him away, Hugh. I sent him on the quest that made yourself and your mother so miserable and I am sorry for it."

Willa paused in her reading to peek up at Hugh's face. He had turned away while she read and all she could see was his stiff back. She wished she could comfort him somehow, but Jollivet was pushing the cup of meade at her again, apparently hoping she would continue. She took a quick drink, handed the meade back and read on.

"Pelles had barely herded Hugh and Margawse out through Claymorgan's gates when Thomas rode in. I was angry and upset after my argument with Pelles, but it took little more than a glance to see that Thomas was more so. We retired to the great hall and he told me the tale.

"All was not well at D'Orland. I knew Thomas had been visiting Juliana and Tristan there, but I had not known just how frequent and prolonged those visits were. It seemed that Tristan's nephew, Garrod, was D'Orland's seneschal. He had befriended Thomas on his first visit and encouraged him to stay longer than he had planned and to return sooner than he would otherwise have dared. Thomas had thought himself and Garrod the best of friends. He had enjoyed his visits, but had begun to notice during the last of them that Juliana seemed a little less happy. She still obviously loved her husband, but she seemed anxious and nervous in Thomas's presence. They had often walked together, always in the open as was proper, but away from others so that they could speak privately. But Juliana was evading such talks. In fact, she evaded Thomas altogether, talking to him only when her husband or Garrod were present and then with a stiffness that left him bewildered.

" 'Twas not until he earned his knight's spurs and visited to share his success that he was able to corner her alone and ask what was wrong. That was when he learned how little a friend Garrod was to either Juliana or him. Garrod had learned of Tristan's jealousy. Rather than reassure Tristan, he had been exacerbating his fears. All the time that Garrod had been encouraging Thomas to stay longer and visit more often, he had been using those *frequent and prolonged visits to needle Tristan, fanning the flames of his jealousy. He was making Juliana's life hell.*

"Thomas left directly after that conversation and returned to Claymorgan. He was wretched over the misery Garrod was causing Juliana, but the only way he could think to aid her was to stay away and allow Tristan's jealousy to ease. He determined to join King Richard on crusade. The king and his men had assembled with King Philip and his soldiers in Vezelay in July. 'Twas September now, and the English were outside Messina in Sicily. The news was that they were expected to remain there for a while. King William II of Sicily had promised to provide a fleet for the crusades, but William had died in November and there was some dispute over the succession. Tancred of Lecce had placed Queen Joanna under house arrest and confiscated the treasure meant for the crusade.

"Thomas determined to sail for Sicily in the hope that the rumors were correct. He hoped to meet the crusaders before they set sail. I did not wish him to go, but he was a man now, and a knight. I could not stop him. My hope was that they would leave ere he arrived. As it turned out, luck was with him—or against him, as the case may be. Both the English and the French were forced to winter outside Messina. Thomas wintered there with them.

"The next eight months passed slowly. I had driven away my brother and his family, and my son had gone on crusade. I had found a new seneschal

for Claymorgan, but Pelles was impossible to replace. The new man needed constant attention.
My seneschal at Hillcrest had been with me for
years and did not need as much supervision. I
was spending most of my time at Claymorgan. So
it was that I was there when the messenger arrived with the news that my Thomas would not
return from the crusade. He had not even made it
to Acre. They had set sail from Messina April
tenth. His ship was one of two that were wrecked
off Cyprus.

"'Twas a crushing blow for me, Willa. I had
loved my son dearly. I sank into a pit of despair. It
seemed to me everything had been taken from me
at that point. I had lost all. For days I sat staring
at nothing, feeling nothing, concerned with nothing. Then one of my men rushed into the great
hall, where I had taken to sitting, staring into the
fire. He was shouting that a woman was approaching alone on horseback. A lady. This was
sufficiently unusual to stir me from my misery
long enough to go out to the bailey to see who 'twas.
I recognized Juliana. She was heavy with child
and in some distress. She was weeping copiously
and her first words were to ask where Thomas
was. When I said he was dead, she paled a more
frightful white, clutched her belly and whispered,
'Dear God, we are lost.' Then, she fell limp from
her mare.

"I had her moved inside and laid in Thomas's
room. I thought it a mere faint and that she would
recover soon enough, but she woke moments later,

*clutching her belly and screaming. She was in la-
bor and Lord knows how long she had been. She
should not have been riding in that state. I knew
no woman would choose to do so. I sent for Eada
and, the moment Juliana stopped screaming, asked
what had happened. She told me the tale between
gasping breaths. Thomas's absence had eased
Tristan's jealousy . . . until it became obvious that
your mother was with child. Tristan had at first
been joyful over the news, but then, quite suddenly, his feelings had changed. He had grown
morose and angry, his eyes following her with accusation and glaring at her belly with an unnatural loathing. Juliana suspected that Garrod was
behind this change as well, but was helpless to
understand. All she knew was that her husband
was drinking more each day and that her fear was
growing in conjunction with it. Then her maid
came to her in a panic. As she had feared, Garrod
was behind this latest problem. He had pointed out
that her getting with child coincided with Thomas's last visit and hinted that perhaps it wasn't
Tristan's child at all. The maid said that Garrod
encouraged him to drink, then whispered these
evil lies in his ear, turning him against his wife as
surely as he could. Juliana had felt indignation
and rage grow within her at her husband thinking
such a thing . . . Until the maid had asked uncertainly, 'They are lies, are they not, my lady?'*

"Only then did she realize how her innocent
friendship with Thomas had appeared to others.
Juliana had considered confronting her husband

when the maid told her that Tristan was even then soaked in ale and that Garrod was again whispering in his ear. Now he was encouraging Tristan to help his wife rid herself of Thomas's bastard. Did he wish the fruit of another man's seed inheriting all? Garrod was suggesting several ways to get rid of this child of uncertain paternity. Tristan could always get another on Juliana to replace it.

"Your mother was staggering under this news when she heard Tristan begin to roar in fury. When she realized he was climbing the stairs toward their chamber, she panicked and fled the room. Juliana hid in the chamber next door until he passed by in the hall. Then she slipped out and down the stairs. Garrod had still been seated at the trestle tables and yelled when she raced down the stairs and out the door, but hadn't given chase right away. Juliana supposed he had gone to fetch his lord. In the meantime, she ran for the stables, collected her mare and rode out of the bailey, forsaking a saddle for speed. She had ridden straight for Claymorgan in the hope that Thomas could keep her child safe.

"You were born moments after she finished telling this tale. Eada placed you in your mother's arms, then attempted to staunch her bleeding, but 'twas no use. Juliana quickly grew weak and, when she could no longer hold you, I took you from her. That was my downfall and my blessing. Even wrinkled and red-faced, you were a beautiful child. When your mother left you in my care and begged me to keep you safe and hide you from Tristan, I

could not refuse. You became my new purpose in life. My only purpose."

Willa paused and promptly found the meade shoved at her again. She waved it away, then sniffled and wiped away tears. Lord Wynekyn promptly stepped forward, producing a handkerchief to wipe her eyes. Willa murmured, "thank you," as he finished, then found the cloth over her nose.

"Blow," he instructed briskly.

Willa flushed, but dutifully blew into the handkerchief. Lord Wynekyn nodded his satisfaction and wiped at her nose, as if she were a child, before stepping back and nodding for her to continue.

"Little time passed after your birth and Juliana's death before Tristan rode into Claymorgan bailey with Garrod at his side and a hundred soldiers at his back. I hid you with Eada in my chamber and met them in the great hall. Tristan was angry and bold. When he demanded his wife, I led him to Thomas's room, where your mother still lay. I think he believed Juliana to be sleeping until I told him she had died giving birth to a stillborn child. I told him she should not have been riding in her condition and asked—as if I did not know—what had sent her fleeing Orland as if for her very life. His answer was a cry full of anguish I well knew. 'Twas the same pain I'd known at the deaths of my wife and Thomas. I almost felt pity for him at that moment, but his jealousy had killed Juliana and sent Thomas to his death and was still a threat to you. He never asked after your body, or said

another word. He lifted Juliana in his arms, held her to his chest and strode out of the room, looking much older than when he had arrived.

" 'Twas not until they were gone that I learned Garrod had followed us above stairs. He did not come into Thomas's room and I worried that he might have been poking around the other chambers. Eada did not see him, but I feared if he had got too near my room, he might have heard you cry. My fear was not eased when I began getting reports that someone of his description had been seen about the village and even once in the castle bailey.

"I had lost everyone else, my sweet girl. I was determined not to lose you, too. I decided that you were to remain in Thomas's room and never to leave there until I was sure you were safe. I brought a wet nurse in from the village and she and Eada looked after you. But then one day Luieus, Lord Wynekyn, visited. We have been friends since childhood, as you know, and I was too proud not to flaunt you before him. I ordered a servant to have the wet nurse bring you to us. She did, and I quite enjoyed showing you off; then she took you back to your room. I was about to explain who you were and your presence at Claymorgan when the wet nurse started screaming. Luieus and I rushed to the room to find her clasping you tightly while gaping in horror at her own child. She had lain the babe in your cradle to sleep while she brought you to me. Her child was now obviously dead, her face blue from lack of oxygen.

"Babies often die for no reason. 'Tis as if they

forget to breathe. Still, I felt a chill run down my neck as I looked on that child and thought it could have been you. These fears were not eased when I learned that a man fitting Garrod's description had been spotted descending the stairs and rushing out of the castle shortly before the death was discovered. I decided not to explain to Wynekyn and kept my own counsel on the matter. I was sure that the wet nurse's child had been smothered by Garrod. He must have mistaken her for you.

"I should have gone to the king then. But, of course, he was still on crusade and while John was running the country in his absence, I had no proof, merely suspicions. Perhaps I also feared your being taken from me—if not to be returned to your father, where I felt your life was in danger, then to court where royal nannies would raise you. I convinced myself that the best thing I could do was to remain quiet and keep you safe.

"You were just a babe, Willa. At first, 'twas easy to keep you a secret. I had you moved to the room next to mine and was more determined than ever to keep you above stairs. Eada and the wet nurse continued to tend you. I visited you daily.

"When you grew old enough to eat solid food and to find the bedchamber confining, I allowed you below. However, I instructed the servants that you were never to be mentioned outside the castle.

"The years passed and the time came when I should have explained these restrictions to you, but did not. I expected you to obey without question.

It never occurred to me that you might wish to play out of doors as any normal child would. You had Luvena as a friend and I thought that enough. As time passed without trouble, my vigilance slackened, and so 'twas that—unbeknownst to me—you and Luvena were able to slip out of the castle to play. What happened to Luvena was none of your fault. You were children, acting as children do. What harm could you imagine in playing outside in the sun?

"Nay. 'Twas not your fault. 'Twas mine.

" 'Twas May of 1199, and you were not quite nine years old. King Richard had died in April and John was to be coronated. As earl of Hillcrest I was expected to attend the coronation and pledge my fealty to him. I did not realize it then, but you had already slipped out of the castle on several jaunts with Luvena. The two of you had avoided the village, no doubt for fear of word getting back to me of your excursions. However, you had been seen on one or two occasions anyway and the word had spread that there was a child; a young girl in rich clothing, running the woods with cook's daughter. The coronation was accomplished, I pledged my fealty, concluded some other business I had to attend to and returned home. Wynekyn traveled with me. When we arrived at Claymorgan, you and Luvena were missing.

"The whole castle was in an uproar and I only added to it. I was furious that someone had not noticed you slipping away. I stomped about, yelling orders and taking out my frustrations on the servants. I questioned everyone. When one of the *things I learned was that a man fitting Garrod's description had been seen in the area again, my blood ran cold. He had been at court with Tristan when I first arrived, but I had not seen him during the two days after the coronation.*

"Then you were found. My relief was boundless . . . until I saw Luvena wearing your gown and lying pale and still in Baldulf's arms. She was dead.

"I know at first you thought she had fallen, but the bruising told the tale. 'Twas not an accident. The bruises formed very distinct fingerprints on her arms and throat. I was horrified, crushed and— God forgive me—so very grateful 'twas not your life that was lost.

"I know it confused and hurt you when I sent you away with Eada. But 'twas the best I could do at that time. I spread the news that you had died, had you moved to the cottage with guards, and refused to see you myself. Not seeing you was the hardest thing I have ever had to do. But I feared leading him to you. The absence of your sweet face was my punishment for the lack of vigilance that had caused Luvena's death and once more placed your life at such risk.

"Now, as you read this, I can no longer keep my promise to Juliana to keep you safe. All I can do is place you in the hands of someone I think strong enough to do so. This is why I arranged the marriage between you and Hugh. He is strong and smart, an excellent warrior. You will need him, Willa. The moment you marry, your existence will be known. The marriage will be reported to the

king. You shall have to accompany Hugh to pledge his fealty as the new earl. The news of your existence will travel through court like fire. Tristan will know you live and your life will again be at risk . . . from your own father, Tristan D'Orland.

"I can only think that he still believes you to be Thomas's child. He would know better if he had ever laid eyes on you. He could not fail to recognize himself in you. While everything else is Juliana's, you have Tristan's eyes and hair. Thomas was dark-haired, as your mother was. But I fear he will not wait to see whom you resemble, but send his nephew after you again. I pray to God that if he does, he will fail and Hugh will be able to keep you safe.

"Your loving Papa, Richard."

Willa let the scroll settle in her lap, and stared at it silently. She wasn't ready to face those standing so still around her. They all remained silent for a moment, then Lord Wynekyn cleared his throat and breathed, "Well . . . that clears things up."

"Aye," she heard Lucan agree quietly, then gave a start as something heavy settled on her shoulder. Turning her head, she peered at the large hand resting there, then followed it up to her husband's face. He was peering at her with silent sympathy. She quickly turned away, afraid she might cry otherwise.

"So," Jollivet gave a dramatic sigh. " 'Tis your cousin and father causing all this trouble."

Willa felt her mood lighten at once at his exasperated tone. She lifted a crooked smile to him and shrugged. "If my father is aware of Garrod's actions."

"Oh dear," Jollivet breathed, his expression becoming pitying. "Willa, you cannot believe the man could be unaware?"

Willa shrugged again and glanced down at the scroll in her lap to find that she was twisting it between her hands. She made herself stop at once and said, "He may not know. 'Tis possible."

She could practically feel the pitying gazes of everyone in the room, even Eada. They all thought her a fool. And perhaps she was. Perhaps 'twas just wishful thinking that she might have a parent who would care for her. Willa stood abruptly and moved toward the door.

"Where are you going?" Hugh barked.

"I think I should like to lie down," she said, and much to her relief, Hugh let her go. But she didn't go to her room to lie down. Not right away. First she had to speak to Alsneta.

She found the cook in her kitchen, tossing food about and shouting orders. Willa watched her from the door for a moment, then stepped into the room and crossed to her.

"Alsneta?" she said.

The woman turned to her with surprise, then smiled. "Hello dear. Did you come looking for a sweet treat?"

"Nay." Willa hesitated, then took a deep breath and said, "I came to ask why you wish me dead."

Chapter Seventeen

Hugh stared at the door his wife had just gone through, his mind filled with his last vision of her. Worry gnawed at him. Willa was obviously unready to accept that her own father wished her dead. Hugh knew she was hurting and he ached for her. He wished he'd thought of a way to prevent her from reading the letter. He wouldn't have her hurt this way.

"Hugh?" Lord Wynekyn's voice drew his attention.

"Aye?" he asked. His eyebrows rose when Wynekyn jerked his eyes between him and Baldulf several times, then began nodding his head in the soldier's direction.

When Hugh merely stared at him in confusion, his uncle's friend clucked his tongue impatiently. "Did you not have something you wished to ask Baldulf?" he asked meaningfully.

The question merely added to Hugh's bewilderment. "Did I?"

"About the cottage and whom he might have told—"

"Oh!" Hugh moved to the bed and scowled down at the man. "Did you tell anyone that Willa and I intended to go to the cottage?"

"Nay!" Baldulf appeared surprised at the very question; then his forehead wrinkled and he said, "Well, not really. I mean I did, but—" He glanced sharply at Hugh. "You are not thinking—Were you not followed to the cottage?"

"Nay," Hugh assured him. "The wolves did not act skittish or growl. They would have known had someone followed us would they not?"

"Aye." The soldier nodded slowly. "So whoever set the fire had to have come later. Which means they knew you were at the cottage."

Hugh nodded, his expression stern. "Whom did you tell?"

"Gawain and Alsneta," Baldulf answered promptly. "When the nooning hour came and you did not appear, Gawain apparently went to ask Alsneta if you were eating in your room today. She had no idea. She and Gawain came to ask me if I thought all was well and what they were to do about the meal. I told them that you and Willa had gone to the cottage and probably would not be back for a while."

"Gawain and Alsneta," Hugh murmured, mulling this over. Then he straightened and glanced at Eada. "Have a bath brought up for Willa. She needs

to wash away the soot ere she does anything else."
When Baldulf promptly began to struggle upright,
Hugh waved him back to a reclining position.
"Nay, Baldulf. Stay here. I shall watch over her.
When she is finished, I shall return her here for
you to guard while I talk to Alsneta and Gawain."

"Do you wish me to fetch Gawain and Alsneta
for you?" Lucan asked.

"Nay. Not yet. I may be a while with Willa, but
I should appreciate your finding them and keeping an eye on them in the meantime." Hugh waited
for Lucan's nod, then strode out of the room. His
thoughts were troubled as he hurried to his chamber. Willa had shown some affection for the cook.
That being the case, Hugh did not like any suspicion cast on the woman. He would have to see to
this matter quickly. Right after he saw to his wife's
bath and getting her to bed.

Hugh grinned to himself, then quickly banished the expression. This was a serious business:
Willa had endured a long and terrible day. As her
husband it was his *duty* to help her through this
troubled time. And he knew exactly how to do it.
He would relax her with a nice leisurely soaking,
helping her with the chore. Perhaps even joining
her in it. That thought made him smile again. It
had been little more than a few hours since he'd
bedded his wife at the cottage, but the very idea of
having her warm and wet in her bath was enough
to perk him up greatly.

Hugh's smile remained in place until he opened
his bedchamber door and strode in to find the room
empty. Stopping dead, he searched every corner

with his eyes, then opened his mouth and bellowed, "Willa!"

There was an immediate flurry of stomping feet from the hallway. Hugh turned to find Lucan, Jollivet and Lord Wynekyn standing in the doorway looking into the room with concern. Behind them, a swaying Baldulf was being held up by Eada. All of them had responded to his roar.

"Where is she?" Jollivet asked with alarm. "Where would she go?"

"She said she was going to lie down," Baldulf grumbled.

Hugh started to shake his head in frustrated bewilderment, then paused. "Willa did not answer my question," he realized suddenly.

"Which question was that, son?" Lord Wynekyn asked.

"When I asked her if she had seen who hit Baldulf. She started to answer, but then you discovered the letter and—Alsneta and Gawain," he breathed in sudden horror. "The kitchens."

Hugh nearly trampled the men in the doorway in his rush to get to his wife. He was positive she'd seen who had hit Baldulf. He was equally positive that she would not have told him who it was, not if it had been Alsneta. The mother of Luvena, the dear childhood friend who had died in her place. Uncle Richard could write that the child's death was not her fault, but Willa's very dislike of discussing the matter told Hugh the guilt weighed heavily upon her. She would not blame Alsneta for wishing her dead. Willa would empathize with her.

* * *

"I don't—I would never—" Alsneta floundered, then fell silent, guilt twisting her time-worn features.

"I saw you hit Baldulf, Alsneta," Willa told her solemnly. "And the scroll had the distinct scent of onions about it. I presume you have been hiding it in here somewhere?"

Alsneta's shoulders sagged.

Aware of the silence surrounding them, Willa glanced around the kitchen. Every last servant had stopped working and gone still as all strained to hear what was being said. Taking Alsneta's arm, Willa urged her to the door, leading out into the garden behind the kitchens. When she paused to face Alsneta then, the woman's eyes were awash with tears.

"I'm sorry," the cook blurted before Willa could speak again. "I never meant to harm you. I mean, of course I did at first. But I was just so angry. I had thought you—that day—they told me that both you and Luvena were dead. I had spent ten years grieving you both. You and Luvena were so much together, I had begun to think of you as my own. I lost my two babies that day." She turned and paced away, her hands twisting in her apron. "My babies."

"Alsneta." Willa followed and touched her arm sympathetically.

The cook turned, but shook her hand away. "Don't touch me. Don't be nice to me. I don't deserve it. And I won't be able to explain if you are kind and make me cry."

Willa withdrew her hand, her own eyes filling

with tears. The woman did not appear to know it, but she was already crying. Silent tears were streaming down her face. "Very well."

Alsneta nodded, then blurted, "I wanted you dead."

Willa flinched, but remained silent, allowing Alsneta to continue.

"That's not true," she countered herself, then appeared confused and shook her head. "Nay. Not at first. When I thought you dead, I grieved for you as much as for Luvena. I had nothing more to live for. Days passed like years. Life was interminable. I considered suicide, but the priest said I would go to hell and never be with my Luvena and you again. Then Lord Richard's health began to fail. I spent most of my time in the kitchens, but the servants began talking about a beautiful young woman visiting him in his chamber. I was curious, but had no idea 'twas you.

"I was the one who found him. I had been bringing his meals up to him in his chamber since his health had begun to fail. I took his breakfast that morning as usual. I walked into the room and set the tray on the chest next to his bed. When I turned to look at him, I knew at once he had passed. His face was gray and slack, empty. He was clutching a scroll, and the name Willa was written on the outside. This bewildered me. Why would he die clutching a letter to a child who had died ten years earlier? I could not resist reading it.

"I could not believe what I read in the letter. He was addressing you as if you still lived, yet I knew you were dead. He had told me so himself. Then I read what he said about that day, that my Luvena had died in your stead, and that he thanked God for it." Her bitterness was obvious, and Willa's heart ached for the woman. But Alsneta lifted her head and continued determinedly. "Another servant entered then and I hid the letter in my clothes. I told her that the lord was dead and to send for Lord Wynekyn. Then I collected the tray I had brought and left, taking the letter with me. I read it countless times. Over and over. And each time I read that she had died in your place and he was grateful for it, I—"

She paused and took a deep breath, then gave her head a shake as if to clear away her anger. "Lord Wynekyn left to inform Lord Dulonget that he was now earl. I meant to return the letter while he was gone, but could not seem to let it go. Then Dulonget arrived and Lord Wynekyn behind him. I was quite busy with the wedding preparations, and every time I had a moment to slip away and return the letter, Lord Wynekyn was up there searching the room for it. Then you came." Her hands clenched at her sides. "I wasn't sent to help you that day; one of the young maids was. But I set her to work in the kitchen and went in her place. I had much to do, but I had to see for myself that you lived. I thought perhaps the letter was merely the rambling of a sick and dying man."

Her eyes returned to Willa, filled with a mixture of anger, grief, regret and sadness. "You had grown up to be so lovely . . . and now you were to marry the earl. While my baby lay rotting in a cold grave. I—" Her voice choked and Willa could stand it no more. She stepped forward, reaching out to comfort her. Alsneta quickly backed away.

"I hated you at that moment," she confessed with shame. "You lived while my child had died. You were lovely and happy and about to marry. I wanted you dead beside my daughter where you belonged. Where I had thought you had been all those years while I grieved for you. 'Twas all I could do to keep from choking you with my bare hands as I helped you dress. I had to smile and admire your lovely gown and your lovely hair and your lovely good fortune while inside the bile was eating me alive. It ate at me through the wedding, and the first part of the celebration, until I could stand it no more. I—" Her voice broke.

"You filled a pitcher with meade and poison and set it in our bedchamber." Both women gave a start as Hugh said what Alsneta could not.

"Husband!" Willa cried in alarm, then managed to force a smile. "I—"

"You are supposed to be in your room."

Willa flinched at his sharp tone. He was most definitely displeased with her. "Aye, but I came down to—"

"Confront the very person who has been trying to kill you since your arrival," he finished harshly, then turned on the cook. "Who was the man who attacked me in the clearing? Your lover?"

"The man in the clearing?" Alsneta asked with bewilderment. "I do not—"

"And who was it who set the cottage on fire

today? Your lover was dead, so I presume it must have been you. Unless you have dragged your nephew into this mess?"

"Set the cottage on fire?" Alsneta gaped at him in horror for a moment, then drew herself up. "I know nothing of an attack in a clearing or setting a cottage on fire. I poisoned the meade that first night, aye. But . . ." She met Willa's eyes. "I regretted it the moment I saw you go above stairs."

"Not enough to rush up and keep her from drinking it," Hugh snapped.

Alsneta ignored him, her attention focused on Willa. "I nearly followed to confess all, but I was afraid. My only hope was that you would not be thirsty and would not drink it. I passed an awful night."

"Not as awful as mine," he muttered with disgust.

"I could not sleep, and what little sleep I got was haunted by Luvena berating me for harming someone she loved like a sister. I was glad when you came through alright, grateful it had not worked. I have not tried again to harm you, I promise. Though I could have. I have cooked every meal you have eaten here and could have seen you dead long ago had I wished it," she added in her own defense.

"Only it would have seen your nephew dead, since I made him the taster after the first poisoning," Hugh commented dryly.

Alsneta waved her hand in disgust at this suggestion. "Bah! Gawain. I have no affection for him. The possibility of his dying would hardly stop me had I wished Willa dead. He was an annoying little brat as a boy and is just as annoying as a young man. Gawain is spineless and greedy, a bad combination. He is always looking for the easy route, that one. I suggest you keep your eye on him. He would stab you in the back for a pair of shoes."

Hugh was silent for a moment, then said. "So you deny having anything to do with the fire at the cottage today, or the man in the clearing?"

"I started no fire. I would not even know my way to the cottage and clearing you speak of. I did not know the cottage existed." The cook drew herself up to face her misdeeds. "Nay. I had naught to do with either incident. But I am responsible for the poison. And taking the letter . . . and hitting Baldulf."

She looked chagrined and Willa asked, "Why did you hit Baldulf?"

Alsneta bit her lip. "I am sorry about that. I am sorry for everything. I shall have to apologize to Baldulf, as well. I did not mean to hit him so hard. I was just in such a panic. I had gone to the room to return the letter and finally found the chamber empty. I was attempting to find a spot to put it that Lord Wynekyn might not yet have looked. I had opened the shutters to see better, but they began flapping about, making a horrible clatter. I was rushing to close them when I heard you call out for Lord Wynekyn. I knew you must think him in the room and that you would come. I gave up on the shutters, tossed the letter on the bed and dashed to hide behind the door. I thought I was safe when you entered and headed straight for the shutters without spotting me. I was about to slip out of the room when I heard Baldulf calling your name. I feared I was lost, then. He would come in, the two of you would find the letter. One of you would see me." She shrugged. "I panicked. I grabbed a candle holder off the table beside me and the moment Baldulf was far enough into the room, I koshed him over the head and fled."

"Whom did you steal the letter for?" Hugh asked.

Willa glanced at her husband in surprise, then realized that he must have arrived after Alsneta had explained about the letter.

"I stole the letter for myself."

"Do not lie to me!" Hugh said harshly. "Whom did you steal it for? Is it Garrod you work for?"

Alsneta drew herself up stiffly. "I did not steal it. Certainly not for the man who killed my daughter. I took it to read myself."

Hugh was staring at the cook with uncertainty. Suspecting she knew the source of his confusion, Willa said, "Luvena was schooled with me when we were children. Papa Richard allowed it so I would have company. 'Tis how we became friends." Hugh looked at her questioningly. "She . . . we used to teach Alsneta what we learned each day while she fed us sweet treats in the kitchen. Alsneta can read."

"I see." His shoulders lost their tension. He rubbed wearily at his neck, then turned his gaze to Alsneta, his expression was grim. "So you did not steal the letter and try to kill my wife for Garrod?"

Willa winced at the anger she heard in his voice.

Stepping forward, she placed her hand on his arm, giving him a pleading look. "She was upset, my lord. Alsneta thought I had died with Luvena. The letter revealed that Luvena died in my stead. She was . . ." Willa gave a helpless shrug. "Alsneta was overcome by grief. Her thinking was unclear. She is sorry. No harm was done. You cannot punish her for—"

"No harm was done?" Hugh gaped at her. "She nearly *killed* you! You vomited all over my lap. We could not manage the bedding until the following night."

Willa rolled her eyes at these complaints. At least the last two. "Aye, my lord, I nearly died. But I *did not*. And—" She paused, then asked, "I vomited in your lap?"

"Aye." His grimace told her that it had been a most unpleasant experience and Willa felt herself blush with embarrassment. Then she shrugged such trifling concerns away and repeated, "She is sorry."

Hugh stared at her with bewilderment. "Willa, she—How can you forgive her so easily?"

Willa let her hand slip away from his arm and ducked her head, then said, "Because Luvena *did* die in my place. I was the one who wished to sneak out that day. It was a beautiful spring day. Luvena would only agree if she could wear the new gold gown Papa Richard had given me before he left for the coronation. She died in my place and I have borne the guilt of that for more than ten years. I have even, on occasion, wished I had been the one who died that day."

Hugh grabbed her hands in a painfully tight grip, drawing her gaze to his face. Willa managed a sad smile. "You heard the letter, my lord. Papa was grateful that it was Luvena and not me. How then could Luvena's mother not be bitter for the same reason? All these years she thought we had both died. She grieved for us. Then, quite suddenly, she learned that I lived, her daughter had died in my place, and I was to marry and be her mistress. How could she not wish me dead, too? If only for a moment?"

His hold on her eased and he let his breath out. Then he released her altogether. When he spoke, it was to Willa. "I am sorry. She tried to kill you. At the very least, I cannot allow her to continue to work here in the kitchens where she might poison us all. I shall have to replace her."

Willa nodded her head in resignation, knowing that he would not be dissuaded.

"I shall have to think on how else to punish her. I cannot allow her behavior to go by unpunished, Willa. You nearly died." He turned to Luvena's mother. "For now, you will stay away from the kitchens, and you are not to go above stairs. I want you nowhere near Willa or the food. But I want you to stay in the castle until I have decided what to do with you."

Alsneta nodded and removed her apron. Her movements were slow and weary. She seemed to have aged twenty years in fewer seconds. Willa felt pity stir in her. She watched sadly as the woman turned to walk back into the castle through the door by which they had exited. Then she paused and walked around the castle instead. Hugh had ordered her to stay out of the kitchens and she was taking him at his word.

Once Luvena's mother was out of sight, Willa glanced at her husband. She immediately wished she hadn't. He wasn't watching Alsneta, he was watching her, and his mouth was starting to turn down with displeasure again. Willa supposed he was recalling that she'd come below to the kitchens to confront Alsneta, when she'd said she was going to lie down.

Sighing, she awaited the lecture sure to come. She watched him open his mouth, and tried to prepare herself, but whatever he'd intended to say died on his lips as the castle door swung open.

"Oh, good, you found her," Lucan said from the kitchen door.

"Aye." Hugh hesitated, then said, "I should like to speak to you and Lord Wynekyn. I shall be along shortly."

Lucan nodded. "We will wait for you at the high table."

Hugh waited for the door to close, then took Willa's arm and marched her between the herb and vegetable gardens to the apple trees behind them. Once he'd taken her deep enough into the trees that no one could possibly overhear or interrupt their conversation, he turned her to face him and promptly began to shake his finger before her nose.

"You have disobeyed me three times today."

"Nay. I have not, my lord," Willa interrupted before he could say more.

"Aye. You did. I told you to go to our room when we returned to the castle."

"And so I did," she quickly pointed out.

"Aye. But I also said you were not to leave that room until Baldulf arrived."

"I did not intend to," she said apologetically. "But I heard a sound and thought only to investigate. I—"

"Left the room. Without waiting for Baldulf."

"Well," she agreed reluctantly. "I suppose I did, but—"

"And then you did not go lie down after reading the letter from your uncle, but came below," he went on.

"You did not tell me to lie down," Willa protested indignantly. "*I* am the one who said I was going to lie down."

"Ah ha! Then you lied to me. That is even worse!"

Willa grimaced, then heaved a deep sigh and Hugh's eyes immediately dropped to her chest. She noted with interest that some of his anger seemed displaced by a different heat. Curious, she took another deep breath and heaved it out too. Hugh's eyes watched her chest rise and lower with distracted interest. Willa found herself beginning to grin.

"You have every right to be angry with me, my lord," she began appeasingly. "I behaved very badly. I—Oh!" She paused abruptly to slap at her leg.

"What is it?" Hugh asked with concern.

"Something bit me," she lied, bending and beginning to tug her skirt up.

"Where?" Hugh was immediately on his haunches at her side. He helped her to lift the long skirt.

"A little higher, husband," she murmured when he paused with the skirt pushed up to her knee.

Hugh dutifully lifted the skirt higher, squinting at her pale leg and running one hand over it. "Here?"

"A little higher." Willa bit her lip and felt her toes curl as his splayed hand slid further up her leg, pushing the material of her gown before it.

"I do not see anything." His voice had that husky tone that Willa was learning to love, and she felt herself quiver in anticipation.

"Are you sure? 'Twas a definite sting."

"I thought you said 'twas a bite." He glanced up, his eyes meeting hers. Something in her expression made him pause; then the small sparks in his eyes burst into flame and his hand began to move again. "Perhaps I should kiss it better."

"Aye. Please. Kiss me better," Willa whispered, her own voice husky now, too.

Still watching her, he leaned forward and pressed his lips to the skin of her outer leg, then his tongue slid out and tasted the pale flesh.

"Better?" he asked.

"Oh, aye. Much better," Willa breathed.

"Good." He straightened so abruptly, Willa found herself quickly stepping back to avoid being knocked over. Hugh grabbed her arm to steady her and grinned. It was a rather evil smile, in Willa's opinion. "Now. If you had gone to our room as you had said you were going to, we could have indulged in what I can see you wish. I went to the room to join you with the same thoughts in mind, but then I discovered you had lied to me and were not where you should have been."

Willa grimaced; her first attempt to seduce her husband had ended in failure. She almost gave up the attempt to distract him, then reminded herself she was not one to give up so easily, and smiled apologetically. "I apologize, my lord. However, before you lecture me as I deserve, might I ask a question?"

Hugh's eyes narrowed suspiciously, but he gave a slight nod of acquiescence and Willa smiled sweetly. "I merely wondered . . . That thing you do to me, can it be done to you? And if so, would you enjoy it?"

"That thing?" He appeared uncertain.

"Aye. When you . . ." She hesitated and blushed, then pressed on, "Could I kiss you here?" She reached down to press her hand against his hardness. It surged against his braies in reaction, almost seeming to try to jump through the cloth and into her hand. Willa waited expectantly, watching with interest as expression after expression flew across his face. When his face settled into stern lines and he cleared his throat—presumably to try to return to his original topic—she squeezed experimentally. Then she rubbed her hand over him, because it was something that felt good when he did it to her.

The sternness left his face as he groaned; Hugh grabbed for her, but she dropped out of reach,

landing on her knees before him. He blinked down
at her in bemusement. "What are you—" The question died an abrupt death as Willa quickly removed his belt, letting his sword drop to the ground
with a clatter. She then began to untie the lacings
of his braies. When his hand suddenly covered
hers, she glanced up to see him peering wildly
about.

"Someone might see," he hissed worriedly.

Willa brushed his hand away so that she could
continue to undo his ties, and reassured him, "Nay.
You chose a good spot, husband. We will not be
seen."

Her words seemed to recall him to the reason
he'd dragged her out there, and he drew himself
up and gave her a steely look. "This is not going to
work, wife. You—Damn," he groaned as she finished with his ties, and his braies slid down his
legs, allowing his erection to pop out and wave
gaily at Willa. She stared at it uncertainly for a moment, unsure what to do, then decided there was
only one way to find out, and began to experiment.
She started out by grabbing it in one hand. When
Hugh gasped at that, sucking in great gulps of
air, she decided it was a good start. She wrapped
her other hand over the first so that she was holding him two fisted, with the tip sticking out. She
promptly began to press kisses to that tip.

"Jesu!" Hugh exclaimed with a pained half-
laugh. "Willa—"

"Tell me what to do," she said, pausing to look
up at him with wide, pleading eyes.

·

Hugh met that gaze for a moment, then let his breath out in defeat. "Touch it, kiss it, lick it, fondle it, take it in your mouth and—"

"All at once?" Willa interrupted with dismay.

"Nay. Just—God's teeth!"

Willa had slid her hands along the shaft, rubbing them over the tip, but looked up now at his curse. She wasn't sure, but she thought he liked that. His expression was pained, but he'd grasped at two branches of the apple tree and was holding on as if caught in a stiff wind. Willa was emboldened to try some of his other instructions . . . which had been rather vague, in her opinion. It would have helped if he'd explained just how she was supposed to touch him, and whether there was an order she need be concerned about. Did she touch first, then kiss, then lick, or was there another order to this business? Since he hadn't bothered to be precise, she decided to just do as she pleased. Since she enjoyed it so much when he put his mouth on her, that was what she tried next. Willa took him into her mouth. After a brief hesitation, she began to slide her mouth down his shaft. A groan from above her head told her that this was satisfactory and she began to move her mouth with enthusiasm. Remembering that he'd mentioned licking, she began to lave him with her tongue as she slid her mouth back and forth. She was most pleased with the grunts, groans and "arghs" her husband was issuing.

Willa had only been doing this for a few moments when she became aware that Hugh was moving upward. Or his staff was, and it was forcing her to crane her head to keep him in her mouth. Glancing upward, she saw with some exasperation that he was practically climbing the tree. If she were not doing this right, all he need do was say so and give her further instruction. There was no need to try to climb away from her, she thought, disappointed that she might not be doing as well as she'd thought.

Removing her mouth, she glared up at him. "Husband, pray stop climbing the tree. I cannot— Oh!" She was taken by surprise when he let go of the tree, dropped back flat on his feet and grabbed at her arms to haul her upward. The next moment, Willa found her back against the tree and her husband against her front as his mouth devoured hers. She did not try to protest this end to her experiment. His hands and mouth were everywhere, moving with lightning speed and stirring up all sorts of sensations that quickly erased her exasperation.

Willa was more than ready when he began tugging her skirt up. She was panting heavily, and slightly stunned as she glanced down to see that her gown was unlaced and hanging off her shoulders, leaving her breasts bare for his pleasure. She hadn't even been aware he'd done that, Willa thought a bit dazedly. Then she was distracted from this revelation by Hugh's hand grazing lightly up her inner thigh as he dragged her skirt above her waist. Anchoring her dress there with one hand, he dipped the other between her legs. She thought she heard him thank God when he found her wet and ready for him. Then he caught her behind the legs, pulled them up around his hips and slid into her. Willa cried out as he filled her. Hugh kissed her again as he withdrew, then drove himself into her again.

The tree was hard and ungiving at her back, but Willa hardly noticed; her body was filled to bursting with Hugh and the sensations he was causing in her. She could feel the tension building inside her. Her muscles were starting to clench and Willa knew she was about to find that blissful release she enjoyed so much. He thrust into her a third time, then suddenly stiffened and cried out.

Willa clutched at his shoulders, confusion reigning, as she felt him pour himself into her. It wasn't until he sagged against her, holding her up with his weight against the tree that she realized it was over. He'd finished and she . . . had not. Well that was bloody unfair, she decided. Just as Willa was trying to decide if she shouldn't punch him in the arm and demand that he fix this, Hugh released a contented sigh and eased her to ground. He then stepped back to peer at her.

"Did you—No, you didn't." He answered the question himself as he glimpsed her vexed expression. She brushed her skirt down, then tugged her top back into place, and he said, "I am sorry. You excited me so much, I—"

Willa did not stick around to listen. Sniffing her disgust, she started away, working on her lacings as she went.

"Willa! Wait I—Oomph!"

A glance over her shoulder showed him face down in the dirt, his braies tangled around his ankles. It served him right, she decided spitefully, then began to move more quickly as he started to struggle back to his feet. He would come after her, Willa knew, but she had no interest in talking to him. In fact, she had no interest in talking to anyone, she realized, as she neared the edge of the small grove of trees. She was suddenly in a foul mood. Her decision was made quickly. After a glance back to see that Hugh was busy trying to pull his braies back up, Willa ducked quickly to the right. She wove her way deeper into the trees in search of some much needed time alone. It had been an exhausting day. So much had happened.

"Willa?"

She glanced around at that call, and ducked behind a tree as she watched Hugh hurry toward the door into the kitchens. He was tying his braies as he went. She watched until he slipped inside, then began to wander through the trees again. She moved slowly back toward where they had been, thinking that the orchard would surely be the last place he would look for her.

Only a few minutes had passed when she heard the snap of a branch. The hair at the back of her neck prickling, Willa paused and turned in a slow circle, her gaze searching the trees. She didn't see anything, but suddenly felt uncomfortable. Deciding that perhaps she would return to the castle, after all, she started to turn in that direction, only to pause as she spied Hugh's sword lying on the ground ahead. It was in its sheath, attached to his belt, lying where she'd let it drop when she'd removed it earlier. He'd been in such a rush to chase after her, he'd apparently forgotten it. Tsking in exasperation, she moved quickly forward, intending to retrieve it for him.

Willa had almost reached the sword when the sound of another twig snapping underfoot reached her. It sounded closer, much closer. And this time she was afraid to look around. A shot of panic raced through her, and she ran the last few feet to the tree she and Hugh had used earlier. She glanced over her shoulder then, her panic turning cold in her belly as she spotted someone charging at her. Bending, she grabbed up Hugh's sword and started to turn to face her attacker, but the sword was much heavier than Willa had expected and lifting it as she turned put her off balance. She staggered against the tree, the sword half-raised as she found herself confronting Gawain.

Alsneta's nephew didn't say a word. His expression appeared slightly frantic as he raised his own sword. Willa felt her heart stop as she watched it come down toward her, then she heard a shout and was suddenly thrown out of the way of the falling sword. She landed on the ground on her stomach, but quickly rolled onto her back and stared at the tableau behind her. Gawain stood gaping, his sword lodged deep in his own aunt. It was Alsneta who had pushed her out of the way.

Gawain stood frozen for a moment, then seemed to regain himself. He pulled the sword from Alsneta, watched her slip to the ground, then turned again on Willa.

Chapter Eighteen

Willa was sure she was about to die. She glanced wildly around for Hugh's sword, her heart sinking when she saw it lying out of reach beside Alsneta's prone body. She was helpless to save herself.

Willa turned her gaze back to Gawain. He stood, legs braced, raising the sword he held. Willa tensed as he prepared to bring it down on her. When the sword began to swing down, she rolled quickly out of the way. Dirt and leaves flew up in her face as the sword slammed into the ground mere inches from her head.

Gritting her teeth, she shifted to her hands and knees. Willa started to scuttle away, but Gawain stepped on the hem of her gown, bringing her to an abrupt halt. She rose up then, and whirled to face him on her knees. If she could not escape her fate, she would face it. Willa would not die from a sword wound to the back. If Gawain wished her dead, it would be a frontal blow. She hoped her face haunted him through eternity.

Gawain hesitated the briefest second, and that was all it took to save her life. In the next moment a furious roar filled the air. Sure it was Hugh's voice she recognized, Willa sagged with relief as her would-be assassin turned to face the charging man. It was only then that she saw it wasn't Hugh who had issued that deep, feral growl. Much to her amazement, the man now battling Gawain was Jollivet.

She sat still, gaping at this turn of events. Shock held her in place as the clash of swords rang out; then a moan from Alsneta drew her attention. Still on her knees, Willa crawled the few feet that separated them.

"Alsneta?" she whispered. Her gaze moved over the cook's wound and Willa's heart lodged in her throat. The cook's shoulder had been cleaved midway between neck and arm. The slice went deep. Willa knew she would not live, but began trying to save her anyway.

"Willa?" Alsneta's eyes opened as Willa began applying pressure to the injury.

Willa tried to smile, but knew it was a miserable attempt. "Hush," she whispered, her voice cracking. "Do not speak. Save your strength."

"There is nothing to save it for," the woman breathed. "I am dying."

"Nay, you—"

"Aye. Leave off that. You are only hurting me and 'tis of no use."

Willa hesitated, then gave up trying to staunch

the flow of blood. It hadn't been working anyway; even using both hands, she hadn't been able to stop the blood from oozing out. When Alsneta's good hand fluttered weakly, Willa obeyed the silent demand and grasped it tightly in her own. "You saved me."

"Aye." It was a slow exhalation. "As I walked around the side of the castle, I glanced back and saw Gawain skulking on the edge of the apple trees. I knew he was up to no good. I thought I had best follow. At first, I thought he was just going to spy on the two of you. Which would have been bad enough," she said with disgust and shook her head. "I waited, intending to reprimand him once you two left and would not be embarrassed by his actions." She paused to take another breath, the air rattling in her chest. "But then he charged you and I knew he was the one behind all the trouble. He and that no-good friend of his, Uldrick."

"Uldrick?" Willa queried.

"Aye. He went missing about the same time as that man was killed by your wolves. I didn't recognize him with his face all chewed up, but he was about the right size and coloring. It must have been Uldrick. He and Gawain must have been working for Garrod. I couldn't let him kill you. That bastard had already taken my Luvvy." She let her breath out on a slow wheeze.

"Thank you for my life," Willa said. The words seemed paltry in comparison to Alsneta's sacrifice. She had given her life for Willa, a child she had loved, and a woman she had hated, however briefly.

"I wish—" Willa began, then winced as Alsneta squeezed her hand with sudden strength.

"Nay. Do not take my death on your shoulders, as well," she snapped. "You are not to blame. You were not to blame for Luvena, either. I was wrong. I was taken by surprise and mad in my reawakened grief."

"But if I had not wished to go out that day—" Willa began sorrowfully.

"Whose idea was it the first time? The very first time the two of you sneaked out?"

Willa blinked at the question, then reluctantly admitted, "Luvena's."

"Aye." Alsneta's clasp on Willa's hand eased again. "I thought as much. I knew my girl. You rarely challenged Lord Richard's authority, but my girl . . ." She released a shuddering breath. " 'Twas no more your fault than 'twas hers. 'Twas fate and that bastard father of yours."

"Oh, Alsneta." Willa bit her lip as the woman's eyes focused on her. A frown creased her face.

"Do not cry for me, child. I am going to be with my Luvena, my little Luvvy." She smiled wearily. Her voice was growing weaker as her life's blood slipped out. "And I am ready for it. A mother shouldn't live to see her child die. 'Tisn't right. It makes her bitter and old before her time."

Feeling the tears running down her face, Willa turned her head and lifted her arm to rub them away with the sleeve of her gown.

"Willa?"

She turned back to see a worried look on Alsneta's face. "Aye? What is it?"

"You do not think—Do you think God will forgive me for trying to poison you?"

Reading the sudden fear in her eyes, Willa was quick to reassure her. "Aye, Alsneta. You saved my life. Surely that makes up for it. God will forgive you. You will be with Luvena."

The woman released a breath of relief and her eyes began to wander, the light in them fading. "Aye. I have . . . missed her. She was . . . my little sun . . ."

"Sunshine," Willa finished for her on a sob, as the life slipped soundlessly from Alsneta's body. Sunshine. It was a phrase that echoed in her memory. *"You're my little Sunshine."* Alsneta often had said that to Luvena as she hugged her in greeting when the two girls had come into the kitchens in search of sweets. *"You're my little Sunshine, Luv."*

Willa sat holding her hand until it began to grow cool in her own, then laid it gently on Alsneta's unmoving chest. She sank back on her haunches, feeling suddenly limp. Something hard was pressing into her shins, but it took her a moment to investigate. Shifting to the side, she stared at Hugh's great sword.

God had left her a weapon, but Willa had been too weak to use it. Now Alsneta was dead. She grasped the handle and lifted the sword until it stood before her. It reached higher than she did on her knees. Grasping the handles, she used it to get to her feet.

"Damn me! He ruined my best doublet."

Willa turned at that exasperated comment to see that Jollivet had dispatched Gawain. He was now standing beside the taster's prone body, examining the tear in his doublet with irritation. Letting it go, he shrugged and smiled at her as he started forward. "Ah well, better the doublet than my hide. Can Alsneta walk or shall I go fetch Ead—Jesu!"

Jollivet stopped dead as he spotted the death blow that had felled the cook. He knelt quickly at her side, checking for signs of life that obviously weren't there.

"Hugh!" Lucan crossed the great hall toward him as Hugh jogged down the last of the steps leading to the upper chambers. He'd rushed back into the castle, chasing after Willa. He'd passed through the kitchens, then the great hall, ignoring Lucan's shout as he'd run up the stairs.

It had occurred to him that just moments ago he'd been the one angry and she the one in the wrong. The tables had turned, however. And all because he could not control his lust around her.

To be fair, Willa had not helped matters. In fact, she'd deliberately incited his passions, undoubtedly to distract him. And she'd done a damned fine job of it. Just the memory of her kneeling before him and taking his erection into his mouth was enough to reawaken the passion he'd just spent. Perhaps he could offer his wife more than apologies to ease her frustrations. Then he'd opened the bedchamber door to find their room empty. She'd not returned to their chamber as he'd assumed.

After a brief glance into his uncle's chamber to

see that she'd not returned there, he'd started back down the stairs. Now, as he reached the bottom step where Lucan awaited him, he forestalled whatever the man would have said by demanding, "Where is my wife?"

Lucan appeared surprised at the question. "She was outside with you, last I saw."

"Aye. But she came back in . . . did she not?" he asked with a little less certainty.

"Nay. She did not come through the great hall, and Lord Wynekyn and I have been sitting here since I found the two of you outside."

"God's teeth!" Hugh exploded with exasperation. The woman would drive him mad. She had no difficulty obeying Eada, or his uncle when he'd still lived. Why could she not obey him, just a little? From the first time they had met, she had seemed to be forever slipping out of his presence, or sneaking away from his guard.

"What happened?" Lucan asked.

"We had a . . . er . . . disagreement," Hugh told him evasively, starting for the doors to the kitchens. "She stalked off. I *thought* she had returned inside. Obviously I thought wrong. She must still be out in the garden."

"Oh." Lucan was following him. "What was the disagreement about?"

"None of your—"

"Damn business," Lucan finished with a laugh that grated on Hugh's nerves. "Never mind. I can guess."

Hugh grunted at that as he pushed through the kitchen door. "So you think."

"You think not?" Lucan asked with an amusement that made Hugh scowl. Then he asked, "Where is your sword belt?"

Hugh glanced down sharply, his hand reaching automatically for his waist. When he felt nothing but his untucked tunic, he stopped dead in the center of the kitchen and cursed more volubly. Lucan merely laughed and sauntered to the door leading out into the gardens. Pushing it open, he gestured with one hand for Hugh to lead the way. His friend had a far too confident smirk on his face, Hugh decided as he stormed past him.

He'd barely taken more than a half dozen steps when Jollivet came racing out of the trees. Hugh took one look at his cousin's face and rushed to meet him. "What is it? What has happened?"

Out of breath, Jollivet grabbed Hugh's arm with one hand, gesturing back the way he'd come with the other, and panted, "Gawain attacked Willa!"

Hugh didn't wait to hear more. Bursting into a run, he raced toward the trees. What he found made his heart stop. At first, all he saw was a woman lying in a pool of blood. Then he realized that the blonde hair that had spilled around the woman's head wasn't peppered with fiery red as Willa's was, but speckled with gray. "Alsneta."

"Aye," Jollivet wheezed, leaning weakly against the tree Hugh had earlier been trying to climb in his excitement.

"Where is Willa? Was she hurt?"

"Nay," Jollivet assured him quickly. "She is fine. Alsneta pushed Willa out of the way and took the blow meant for her. I was too far back to help Alsneta, but I arrived in time to dispatch Gawain before he could harm Willa."

"Too far back? How did you all come to be here?" Hugh asked with bewilderment.

Jollivet straightened away from the tree. "I noticed Gawain in the great hall when we came below. When you hurried into the kitchens in search of Willa, he slipped out into the bailey. He was acting—" Jollivet shrugged. "Odd. I was suspicious after having just heard that he and Alsneta were the only ones Baldulf had told of your whereabouts before the fire. So I followed him. I trailed him around the castle to the gardens behind. He slid into the apple orchard and watched you two talk to Alsneta. When Alsneta left and you led Willa deeper into the trees, he again followed. Then Alsneta spotted him and began to shadow him and I was forced to follow her."

"Dear God, you mean to say all three of you were there when—" He bit the end off the sentence, coloring with mortification. It had not been his finest hour. If they had had to witness him enjoying his wife, could they not have picked a time when he had pleasured her in return? Realizing how petty that thought was, he shook his head and gestured for Jollivet to continue.

The fop was looking more like his taunting self, but said. "I was not *there*, cousin. At least, I could not see anything. I was more concerned with watching both Alsneta and Gawain. Though I am sure Gawain could see from his vantage point," he added.

" 'Tis good he is dead, else I would have to kill

him myself," Hugh muttered, giving the dead man's leg a kick.

"Why? What happened?" Lucan asked, then raised his hands and laughed when Hugh turned on him. "Never mind. I know. 'Tis none of my damned business."

"Anyway," Jollivet said, drawing their attention back to him. "After the two of you finished . . . well, after *you* finished," he corrected himself.

Hugh's mouth thinned. "I thought you could not see?"

"Aye. I could hear most of it, though." He grinned, enjoying Hugh's discomfort, then went on, "Willa started toward the castle, then suddenly veered off into the trees. Once you got your braies untangled from around your ankles and gave chase—" Jollivet grinned as Lucan burst out laughing.

Hugh scowled and caught Jollivet by the shirt. Jerking the smaller man off his feet, he barked, "My wife?"

Jollivet cleared his throat when Hugh released him, then continued, "After you ran back into the castle, Willa walked back to where you had been together. Gawain started to move after her, Alsneta followed him and I trailed her. I was staying back a bit, trying not to give my presence away to Alsneta. I couldn't see what was happening ahead of her very well, but I knew it was trouble when she suddenly burst into a run. I gave up trying to move stealthily and hurried after her. When I got there, she had been struck down and Gawain had turned on Willa. I fought him and won." He shrugged. " 'Twasn't until then that I realized the extent of Alsneta's wound. I knelt to see if she was truly dead and while I did, Willa ran off."

"Ran off?" Hugh barked. "Why did you not say so at once?"

"Well, I assumed she ran inside . . ." His voice trailed away and he grimaced and added, "As you had when she first started back to the castle. I take it she did not return to the castle?"

"Nay." Hugh turned in a slow circle, searching the surrounding trees. When he didn't see any sign of his wife, he started back the way they had come.

"She may have gone back inside after we came out," Lucan suggested, falling in beside him.

Hugh grunted at the possibility, then stopped and suddenly turned back, nearly crashing into his cousin. Stepping around him, he let his gaze skate over the area around the tree. "Where is my sword?"

"She took it with her," Jollivet announced, then glanced down and smiled. "In fact, 'twas too heavy for her and she was dragging it."

Hugh followed Jollivet's gaze and relaxed when he saw the trail the end of the sword had left behind. The three men began to follow it.

"There you are!" Lord Wynekyn's call brought them to a halt as they emerged from the trees. All three men peered up from the trail to frown at the man. Lord Wynekyn blinked in surprise at their unanimous irritation. His expression turned wary as he said to Hugh and Lucan, "You rushed off through the kitchens without a word. I became worried that something was wrong."

"Gawain has killed Alsneta and attacked Willa," Jollivet told him. "I had to dispatch the fellow."

"You did?" Lord Wynekyn was clearly astonished.

"Despite being a fop, my cousin is—and always has been—quite handy with the great sword. He trained under my father," Hugh announced stoutly. It was true, of course, but he probably wouldn't have bothered defending the younger man if it were not for the fact that he'd just saved Willa's life. They'd been sparring all their lives . . . it was how they showed affection. Jollivet annoyed Hugh with taunts of his being an uncouth barbarian, and he responded with the dandy and fop comments. The two of them were very close.

"Oh." Lord Wynekyn sounded doubtful, but Hugh didn't have time to bother with the matter. Lowering his head, he found the trail and began to follow it again. Lucan and Jollivet immediately fell into step on either side of him.

"What are we doing?" Lord Wynekyn asked as they started around the corner of the castle and Hugh realized the man had fallen in line behind them.

"We are following Willa," Lucan told him.

"We are?" Lord Wynekyn again sounded doubtful. "Should we not be looking up then? It might be easier to find her that way."

"She was dragging Hugh's sword behind her," Jollivet explained. "We are following the trail to find Willa."

"She has Hugh's sword?" Lord Wynekyn asked. "If she had your sword, are you sure that 'twas

Jollivet who saved her and not the other way around?"

"*I am sure!*" Jollivet growled and stopped abruptly. "Damn me! Display a few manners, and speak courteously and everyone thinks you are a—"

He halted abruptly as Hugh turned in surprise at his outburst. After a brief struggle that showed on his face, he relaxed. His usual smirk came to the fore. "Ah well . . ."

Jollivet turned his attention back to the trail and continued following it. The other three men exchanged glances, then joined him. None of them had ever before seen Jollivet lose his temper over the fop business. They all kept casting him curious glances, but no one said anything as they followed the trail along the side of the keep wall.

"Damn!" Hugh cursed when they reached the bailey in front of the keep and the trail suddenly ended. It had been trampled under carts and footprints and horses' hooves.

"What is going on there?" Lucan asked. Hugh followed his gaze to find a large crowd of soldiers and peasants gathered around the practice area.

His expression grim, Hugh strode forward. He had a feeling that Willa would be somehow involved in whatever spectacle held everyone's attention. She did seem to be at the center of things whenever there was trouble.

Aware that the other men were following, he pushed his way through the growing crowd. Hugh paused, however, when he reached the inner circle and saw that it was, indeed, his wife who had drawn this crowd. Willa had dragged his sword to the practice area and was presently hacking at a quintain. Which would be fine, except it was one used for jousting practice. The bag of sand on one end was swinging around with every hit. Not that she seemed to notice. She was simply following the shield on the other end, hacking away as she walked in circles. She appeared to be monstrous angry. It was the only explanation for her surprising show of strength.

"What is she doing?" Lord Wynekyn asked with alarm.

"You can see what she is doing," Hugh pointed out.

"Aye. But why?"

Hugh didn't know the answer to that. However, as her husband, he supposed it was his duty to find out. Moving forward, he began to follow his wife around the turning quintain.

"Wife?"

Her response was a grunt. Since no one was close enough to hear, Hugh decided it was sufficient acknowledgment of his presence. "What are you doing?"

"I am practicing."

"Practicing?" he repeated with disbelief. "Why?"

Much to his amazement a growl slid from her throat. Then she snarled, "Because not another life shall be lost for mine. If I'd had Baldulf and the others train me these last ten years, I could have saved Alsneta. But *nay!*" Her blows came faster and harder. "I let everyone else care for me. I must learn to care for myself!"

Hugh felt his heart turn painfully in his chest. She was now blaming herself for Alsneta's death as well as the others'. It was the seat of her present rage, a rage that had probably grown over the years as she had helplessly witnessed the deaths of those she loved. Hugh understood the ache and anger she was suffering. He wasn't sure how to help her ease it, though.

He started out trying the *"Me warrior, you wife"* tactic. "Nay, Willa," he said firmly. "I will care for you. I am your husband. I will keep you safe."

"As you did in the orchard?"

Aye, that had been the wrong approach, he thought as her words burned him. Damn. Willa had aimed her words well. He already felt a great deal of guilt over not keeping her safe and her words pointed out that he had failed her again. First he'd allowed her to be poisoned, then he'd nearly seen her burned alive, and now he had almost lost her to Gawain's sword.

Hugh was indulging in a nice round of self-recrimination when a knock to the head sent him stumbling. Cursing, he turned to glare at the turning sandbag that had crashed into him and nearly got popped again. Stepping quickly out of the way, he hurried after his wife.

"Willa, I realize I have failed you—" That got her attention. She stopped abruptly and turned to gape at him.

"What? Nay, my lord! You have never failed me."

Hugh would have been more reassured if he didn't know it was a lie . . . and if she didn't have the sword upraised and wavering in her trembling hands. He watched it warily and opened his mouth to speak, but she wasn't finished.

"Why, you have saved my life many times. You killed the attacker in the clearing ere he could get into the cottage."

"The wolves killed him," he pointed out dryly.

"You slowed him down until the wolves could help you," she argued. "Then you saved my life when I was poisoned, too."

"Eada saved you with her potions. I merely held your head as you . . . purged."

"You let me purge in your lap, too," she said stoutly. They both grimaced at that, and she rushed on, "Then you saved my life today and got me out of that fire."

"I—" Hugh closed his mouth. He couldn't argue with that one. He'd finally done something right. Then his gaze moved over her soot-streaked face, and down over the singed ends of her hair to the scorched gown she still wore. She was beautiful.

"My lord husband." Willa let the sword fall. Hugh was forced to leap to the side to avoid being cleaved in half. Hardly seeming to notice, she stepped forward and touched his cheek in the same affectionate gesture he'd been jealous of Baldulf receiving earlier. Hugh felt warmth seep through him. Her expression held the same warmth he'd yearned for when she'd looked at the soldier.

"You are a strong and brave husband. You will keep me safe to the best of your abilities, I know. But there will be times when you are not near and I will have to rely on myself."

"I will have guards—"

"I do not wish to spend the rest of my life imprisoned by my own guards. Besides, Baldulf was guarding me today. All it took was a candle holder to the head to make him useless. Had she wished to kill me, Alsneta probably could have done so then. You cannot be with me at all times. I must learn to defend myself."

"She is right, Hugh."

He turned a startled glance to find that Lucan had joined them. As had Jollivet and Lord Wynekyn. The crowd had also pressed closer. Hugh's gaze moved back to his wife. He contemplated her for a moment, then gave in and stepped forward to take her hands and shift them on the sword.

"If you must do this, you shall do it right. This is how you hold a sword," he instructed and Willa cast him a smile that made his stomach roll.

"She is improving."

Hugh grunted at that approving comment from Jollivet as they watched Willa and Lucan spar. It had been a month since Alsneta had died saving Willa's life. The time had passed without incident and the days had taken on a pattern. The pattern was that Willa got up in the morning, grabbed a crust of bread, downed a mug of meade and harried Hugh out to the practice field. She then spent the whole day there until the evening meal.

Hugh grimaced. It had been worse when they had first started this routine. When Hugh had insisted on being the one to train her. That had proven to be the most frustrating chore he had ever taken

on. He still didn't understand why the activity had
chafed so much. Hugh was a good trainer of warriors. He'd learned from the best, his father, and
had proven himself the most patient of men over
the years. However, Willa had managed to drive
him mad several times before Lucan had suggested that he take over the chore.

As much as he hated to admit it, that arrangement had worked out much better. At least there
was less friction between Willa and himself. Now
he went about the daily business of running Hillcrest and Claymorgan, occasionally stopping to
watch as she worked in the practice field with
Lucan and, lately, Jollivet. His cousin had not gotten involved in the training at first. He'd devoted
himself to Hugh's request that he aid Willa with
her wardrobe. Jollivet had spent the first few weeks
overseeing Eada and several other women who
had proven themselves handy with a needle. It
was only this last week that Jollivet had decided
her wardrobe was moving along nicely and he
could turn his attention to other things. Since
then, he'd joined Lucan in training Willa. Now
Hugh and his cousin stood watching Willa slam
her sword against Lucan's and wince as her arm
vibrated with the impact. She was starting to look
weary.

Hugh glanced toward the sky, not surprised to
see that the sun was still high. It was not yet time
to lead his weary wife in to the evening meal. No
matter how much she hurt after her practice, Willa
would follow him to the table and suffer through
the meal in silence. Tiny winces were the only sign

of the aching muscles she suffered as she lifted the food and drink to her mouth.

Once she'd managed to swallow the last of her food, Willa would drag her exhausted body up to their chamber. Hugh would follow close on her heels to massage liniment into her sore muscles, taking liberties along the way. If she were not too tired, those liberties would arouse Willa, and they would make love. Hugh contemplated the chances of that happening tonight, but didn't think they were good. She looked more exhausted than he had seen her since the start of her training a month ago.

"Lucan must have worked her harder than usual," he commented.

Jollivet shook his head. "No more than customary. There is no need. She improves daily. 'Tis as if she were born to it. She should have been a man."

"Dear God, Jollivet," Hugh growled. "She is not a man. And she is mine. Stop looking at her like a leg of mutton. Why are you still here, anyway?"

"I have been asking myself that question much of late. Unfortunately, I promised to help outfit Willa." He pursed his lips with displeasure. "Equally unfortunate, your wife has more interest in fighting than in gowns lately. 'Tis terribly tough going. I can barely make her stand still long enough for a fitting. Other than that, she has left everything up to me." He brightened. "Of course, I have magnificent taste. And Eada and a couple of the other women around here are marvelous seamstresses. The wardrobe is coming along nicely. There are already several gowns done and more nearly finished."

"Then why has she not worn one of them?" Hugh asked with irritation.

"She says they will just get ruined at practice," Jollivet announced with disgust.

Hugh grunted at that.

"Have you heard back from Lackland?" Jollivet asked suddenly.

"King John, to you," Hugh said shortly, then shook his head. He'd sent a letter to the king the day after the attack in the orchard. He'd explained the contents of the letter from his uncle and the latest attempts on Willa's life. He'd stated that he should like to pledge his fealty as the new earl of Hillcrest at King John's earliest convenience, and would appreciate his aid in resolving this situation. Hugh would not have Willa's father and cousin continuing to try to kill her. Unfortunately, Jollivet had been forced to kill Gawain before Hugh could speak to him. Which meant he could not prove the man had been hired by Garrod or Lord D'Orland, but Hugh was hoping that just involving the king might end the attacks.

Perhaps it had, Hugh thought. There had been no further attacks on Willa since he'd sent the letter. But then Gawain, whom Hugh suspected had been paid off by Garrod to kill Willa, had been removed. Then, too, Hugh had stationed men at the gates to stop anyone who was not known to them from entering the bailey. He just wished the king would answer his missive. Surely enough time had passed for him to have received and responded to it?

The clash of metal against metal drew his gaze

back to the battling couple. Hugh watched his wife attack Lucan. She was very aggressive in her assault and he found himself watching with fascination. Her arms strengthened daily, her body becoming more supple. He'd noticed newly developed muscles in bed as he'd smoothed the liniment into her naked flesh. His hands would move over the hard muscles, first making them relax, then causing them to tense for a different reason. Hugh would allow his fingers to brush the sides of her breasts as he worked on her back, or glance against the core of her as he worked on her legs. Then he would turn her and allow his hands to close over and cup her breasts, his—

"Enough!" he barked suddenly. "'Tis time to stop."

Willa and Lucan turned to him with surprise, but it was Willa who spoke. "'Tis not! 'Tis hours 'til supper."

"You are tired," Hugh said firmly. Moving forward, he removed her sword and handed it to Lucan.

"Nay. I am not tired," Willa denied as he took her arm to urge her toward the keep.

"Then I am," Hugh said.

"What is that to do with me?" Willa bounded up the steps to the keep at his side.

"A good wife helps her husband relax," Hugh announced arrogantly. Before she could protest further, he paused and scooped her into his arms. Then he pressed a kiss to her lips. It started out a firm *"Be silent. I am the king of this castle"* kiss, but ended an *"I want you. I need you . . . now"* kiss.

Willa's protests died as her passions stirred. One afternoon off wasn't so much, she decided as she began to kiss Hugh back.

She felt herself jostled as he began to move again, but caught his head in her hands and refused to let him break the kiss when he tried. When Willa finally did let him lift his head away, they were inside and halfway across the great hall. Now that he could actually see where he was going, her husband began to move quickly again. He took the steps to the second floor at a jog and was soon kicking the bedchamber door closed behind them.

Willa glanced around the room that used to be Lord Richard's. She still wasn't used to thinking of it as theirs. They had only moved into the room the week before. Thanks to Willa's preoccupation with training, and Eada and the others being busy making her new gowns, it had taken longer than expected to clear out Lord Richard's things and move theirs in. Her attention was recaptured by Hugh when he set her on the floor and began tugging impatiently at her gown.

Laughing, Willa batted at his hands. "Husband, you will rip my gown."

Hugh paused to smile at her. "A brilliant idea, wife." In the next moment, he'd grasped the neckline of her gown and ripped it open to the waist. Willa sucked in a breath, then gaped at him.

"Jollivet has had several new gowns made for you." He reached out to touch one soft breast. "This ugly old one shall not be missed."

His head followed his hand and he latched on

to her nipple. Willa swallowed thickly. She felt sure she should reprimand him for ruining a perfectly good gown. But it *was* ugly, and he was doing such delightful things to her that she couldn't seem to muster the energy to berate him. Instead, she caught his head in her hands and drew his mouth up for a kiss. The moment he began to kiss her back, she let her hands drop to work on his clothes.

She attacked his belt first. The sword hanging from it made a loud clatter as it hit the floor. Willa then began tugging at his shirt, forcing him to break the kiss she'd initiated so that she could drag it over his head. She chuckled happily, and ran her hands over his chest. He had such a lovely, wide and strong chest. It was a pleasure to be free to touch it. Willa had learned a lot this last month, and not all of it had been on the practice field. She'd learned not to be shy of touching her husband and now knew various ways to pleasure him.

She let one hand slide down inside the front of his braies to clasp him and smiled when he groaned. Oh yes, a break was definitely a good idea, Willa thought, as he claimed her lips again. She slipped her hand back out and set to work on the ties of his braies, undoing them quickly and smiling her satisfaction against his mouth as the cloth dropped away.

Hugh growled deep in his throat as she returned to fondling him, then pushed the remains of her gown off her shoulders so that she was naked, as well. He started to urge her back toward the bed then, but paused and broke their kiss with a curse. Following his gaze down, Willa allowed a chuckle to slip from her lips. The braies had tangled round his legs, impeding forward movement.

Hugh raised one eyebrow at her amusement, then pushed her back onto the bed. Still chuckling, Willa watched him struggle to remove his boots and braies and opened her arms to him as he came down on top of her. Then they began to kiss in earnest. Willa scraped her nails over his back and buttocks, before finding his manhood. She clasped him as he kissed her neck and caressed her breasts. Tension building within her, she caught her free hand in his hair and dragged his head up, demanding a kiss. Then she twisted suddenly, catching him by surprise and tumbling him onto his back. She immediately slithered atop him, straddled his thighs, then sat up to smile triumphantly.

Willa had just taken his hardness into her when a knock sounded at the door. Both of them froze briefly, then irritation flickered on Hugh's face and he snapped, "Go away."

"Er . . .'tis Lord Wynekyn," came the announcement through the door.

Hugh rolled his eyes, then gritted his teeth as Willa shifted, taking him deeper into her. His voice was harsh when he asked, "What is it? Can it not wait?"

"Nay, well . . . nay. A messenger from the king has arrived."

Hugh cursed. Willa felt like joining him, but merely slid off to sit on the bed.

"I shall be right down," Hugh called and sat up

to kiss her. It was a quick, hard kiss; then he stood and began to dress.

Feeling chill without his heat to warm her, Willa slid under the furs and watched him don his braies and boots again. He then bent over the bed to give her another quick kiss and said, "Wait here. I shall be back directly. We can then continue this . . . discussion."

They shared a grin, and Hugh grabbed up his tunic. He donned it as he left the room.

Chapter Nineteen

Willa shifted on the furs and grimaced into the darkness of the tent. She had a terrible need to relieve herself . . . again. It was a frequent problem of late, though it had only become inconvenient since the beginning of this journey.

They were on their way to court. Willa had no idea what the king's messenger had said, but Hugh had returned to their room after meeting with him to announce that they were leaving for court the next day. He'd said they were going to pledge their fealty and resolve the matter of her father once and for all. Willa had felt a touch queasy ever since.

Her father. Lord Tristan D'Orland. The man who was trying to kill her. Or, at least, the man whose nephew was trying to kill her . . . presumably at his behest.

Her discomfort forced her back to the matter at hand and Willa scowled with displeasure. They'd had to stop often and repeatedly that day to allow her to tend to this very need. It was most annoying. It was also embarrassing, since everyone had to stop and wait on the path for Hugh to lead her off into the woods to find a handy bush. Of course, he *would* insist on accompanying her, which had only made the matter more embarrassing for Willa. She supposed it was odd after all the intimate things they had done, but she found it rather mortifying to relieve herself over a log while her husband stood guard inches away.

Willa rolled onto her side and peered at the dark shape of her husband. She wished she could hold it until morning. Unfortunately, her body wasn't cooperating.

Making a face, she considered slipping out on her own to tend to the matter, but knew that would infuriate Hugh. Besides, the idea of creeping about alone in the dark woods was rather daunting. Then, too, even if she'd found the courage to do so, there was a guard sitting by the fire in the center of the camp. She wasn't likely to slip past him undetected.

"Husband?" She gave him a gentle shake. Hugh snuffled in his sleep and rolled away from her. Willa shook him more vigorously. "Husband?"

He muttered something in his sleep and shrugged her hand away.

Willa scowled. She *really* had to go. She punched his arm. "Husband!"

"What? What!" He sat upright at once, taking the furs with him. Willa slid off the camp bed she and Eada had made earlier and felt around for her gown.

"Willa?" He hissed. "What is happening?"

"I am getting dressed, I have to go. . . ."

"Go?" She could hear the frown in his voice. "Go where?"

"I have to go . . . you know." She grimaced into the darkness as she found her gown and pulled it on, then added meaningfully, "Now."

"Again?" There was no mistaking the irritation in his voice. It sparked a responding irritation in Willa. It was not as if she wished to go. Nor was it her fault. She didn't know why she was so plagued by the need of late.

"You needn't exert yourself, husband. I can tend to the matter on my own. I simply did not wish you to get upset with me for wandering off alone." Forsaking her shoes, she sailed out of the tent in a fine snit.

"Willa!" Much cursing and rustling sounded inside the tent and she could imagine him bumping blindly about in search of his clothes. Willa offered an embarrassed smile to the guard when he glanced curiously her way, then began to tap her foot as she waited outside the tent flap. Hugh charged out a moment later in only his braies, nearly knocking her to the ground in his rush. He sighed his relief as he steadied her.

"I thought you had left without me," he explained.

Nodding, Willa turned and led the way into the woods. She hadn't gone far when her annoyance petered out under nervousness . . . and that embarrassed her, too. She'd grown up in an isolated cottage in the midst of the woods. She should not be so tense and anxious now. But she was.

"What is it?" Hugh asked in hushed tones when she paused.

"I cannot see where I am going," Willa lied. It *was* dark, but it was also a clear night and the stars were shining brightly. Her eyes had adjusted quickly and though she was not able to see as well as she could during daylight, she could make out trees and logs and things in her path as darker shadows. She simply wanted him to lead the way. Which he did. Taking her hand, Hugh stepped around her and began to lead her deeper into the trees.

It wasn't long before he stopped. Apparently he'd found a place he felt was appropriate. Willa peered at the dark spot he gestured to and grimaced. She was suddenly beset with a vast list of concerns. Snakes, poison ivy, insects and night creatures were among them.

"Well?" Hugh prompted.

Willa pushed her concerns aside and moved to tend to the matter. It was no less embarrassing a chore in the dark than it had been in daylight and she decided that traveling—something she'd done rarely in the past—was perhaps not for her. First off, Hugh would not let her ride astride. He'd not even been willing to consider it. No wife of his was going to wear braies and ride astride. Even after a whole day riding sidesaddle, she still found the position uncomfortable. Willa wasn't one to think of herself as needing coddling, but this traveling business was a damned nuisance all the way around.

"Are you done?" Hugh whispered and Willa rolled her eyes at the question. Surely he could hear that she wasn't done? To her, it sounded as loud as a downpour of rain in the silent night. It was on that thought that she suddenly realized how silent the forest was. The rustle of night creatures had died. The night was still. She knew this was a bad sign.

Finishing quickly, Willa straightened. She set her clothes back in order as she joined her husband. When she touched Hugh's arm, she found him hard with tension. He was almost humming with it. Willa let her gaze slide over the shadows surrounding them. None of them seemed out of place or alarming. There was a tree, another tree, another tree that moved. Willa's nails dug into Hugh's arm, but he'd apparently seen it as well, and was even then grabbing her arm and dragging her behind a tree. Willa listened to her thundering heart and watched the dark outline of her husband. She was trying to judge by his pose whether he thought they had been spotted.

After a few moments of tense silence, she moved her mouth to his ear and whispered, "The guard."

Calling out for the guard at camp to come aid them seemed a good idea to her, but Hugh shook his head. Willa settled in to wait, then nearly gasped aloud when Hugh's grip suddenly tightened on her arm and he drew her slowly backward through the trees. When he paused again after a few moments, she pressed her mouth to his ear again and asked, "Why do we not just call the guard?"

"Because 'twould pinpoint our position, and I left my sword behind in my rush to follow you," he hissed back. Then he added, "He is between us and camp. He may just be one of our men looking to relieve himself as well, but I cannot be sure, and without a sword I dare not—" His words died an abrupt death as something whistled past their heads. Then Hugh suddenly whirled her around and shouted. "Run!"

Willa broke into a sprint at once. Crashing blindly through the trees, she winced as branches slapped at her face and pulled at her hair. It was possible the guard at camp had heard Hugh's shout and might come to their aid, but it didn't seem prudent to wait for him with arrows flying past their heads—for that was what that whistle had been, an arrow sailing by. Whoever the shadow was, he obviously wasn't one of the men seeking to relieve himself.

Aware that Hugh was at her back, vulnerable to any future arrows the man might send their way, Willa ran as fast as her legs would carry her. She had no desire to lose Hugh now.

Her husband jerked on her arm, turning her to the right, and Willa continued in that direction without breaking stride. She managed to avoid colliding with a tree by doing a twisting turn that Lucan had shown her to avoid an oncoming blow from a sword. The action briefly broke Hugh's hold on her, but when it returned seconds later, she guessed that he'd avoided the tree as well.

After several moments, Hugh suddenly jerked her to the left, though not as sharply as the first turn. She again continued to run without faltering. Willa was sure that her training during the last month was the only reason she was able to run as far and fast as she did. She was just starting to tire when the trees suddenly fell away. That was enough to make her slow. Unprepared for this sudden action on her part, Hugh trod painfully on the back of her heel. Despite that, Willa was grateful for her caution when she realized the deeper darkness yawning ahead was the edge of a cliff. She stumbled to a halt at once, throwing her arms out to prevent Hugh from racing past her.

"What is it?" he asked, grabbing her to steady them both. Then he came to her side and peered over the cliff edge where she had halted. A curse slid from his lips as he gazed down at the water bubbling far below. He turned away at once and Willa could see his eyes frantically searching for a hiding place in the moonlight. Now that they were out of the trees, it was much lighter. Light enough to see features and expressions. Light enough to be a good target.

"The trees," he said at last and took her arm to drag her back the way they had come. "We will climb one and hope he does not see us."

"But what if he does?" Willa protested, dragging at his hold. "We shall be plump pigeons for him to shoot down with his arrows."

Hugh paused and turned to his wife, frustration boiling within him. He could hear their pursuer crashing closer through the woods. The man was not far behind them. This was no time for Willa to be questioning his decisions. Why could she not just obey him? "Wife—"

"Husband," she countered quickly. "The trees are the first place he will look. He will not expect you to make me jump with you. And look." She held her arms out, drawing his gaze to the white shift she wore. "I dressed in the dark. I thought I had donned my gown, but nay, 'tis my shift."

Hugh swallowed as he felt alarm crawl through him. Her white shift was very visible in the night.

"Let us jump," she urged. "I am a strong swimmer. I spent many summer days swimming once we moved to the cottage."

The sounds their pursuer made as he ran after them were becoming alarmingly close, but still Hugh hesitated. He considered their chances; hers, then his, then theirs. Finally, he nodded and urged her back to the cliff edge. He peered down and almost changed his mind again. It was an awfully long way down, the jump risky. Unfortunately it was too late to change his mind. He turned and pulled Willa against him for a quick kiss, then instructed, "Swim downriver as far as you dare. I would suggest you try to make your way back to the camp, but 'tis too risky. You might run into our pursuer. Instead, follow the river to the next castle and try to get help there."

Even in the night he could see her frown. "Are you not coming? Will you send me off on my own?"

Hugh's expression was tortured. "Willa . . . I do not swim."

"You told me that at the river, my lord. But do you not think this might be the time to make an exception?"

"Nay. You do not understand. I *do not swim.*"

"Do not?" She was silent for a moment, and then her eyes widened in comprehension. "Do you mean you cannot? You do not know how?"

Hugh winced. He preferred the "do not" to the "cannot." He'd always forsaken such frivolous pursuits as poetry writing and swimming for the more lauded skills of battle. The skills he'd chosen to hone had served him well. Until he'd encountered Willa. Only lately had these less lauded skills seemed almost necessary. Much to his relief, Willa did not force him to admit to this lack in his abilities. Instead, she asked, "What will you do?"

"I will climb a tree."

"You cannot!" she cried. "There is no time now. He is almost upon us."

"All the more reason for you to go. Now." He urged her closer to the edge.

"Husband. Prithee, come with me. I shall swim for both of us."

Hugh started to shake his head, but she caught his face with her hands. Her gaze burned into his in the darkness. "You must trust me, husband. I shall not let you drown. I love you."

Hugh froze at this revelation. This was the absolute worst time she could reveal such a thing, and the absolute best. But did he dare allow her to try to carry them both to safety? He believed he had no chance if he did not jump. He also believed he had no chance on his own in the water.

But Willa . . . Hugh was sure she had a chance on her own, but that he would be a burden that would much diminish her chances.

"Trust in me," Willa pleaded.

Torn, Hugh closed his eyes. Suddenly, the witch's words ran through his head as if she were whispering them in his ear. *"What I see is that you will be perched on a precipice. If you choose one way, all will be well. Do you choose the other . . . death."*

A rustling sound drew his attention and he opened his eyes to see that she'd removed her shift so it would not hamper her. Willa stepped naked before him and held out her hand.

Hugh hesitated briefly, then took it. In the next moment they had jumped and were sailing toward the water below.

Landing in the river was like leaping into a hill of snow. Willa gasped at the shock, then closed her mouth as the water covered her head. She shot downward and hit the river bottom with a jolt. Gritting her teeth against the pain, she pushed upward. Her hand tightened on her husband's, dragging him with her. Relief coursed through her as she broke the surface, but then Hugh began trying to free his hand. Gulping in air, she turned in the water; he didn't know how to stay afloat and was panicking. Willa quickly moved closer and wrapped her arm under his chin, pulling him back against her chest to keep his head above water.

"Do not fight," she panted, tightening her hold on him as he instinctively struggled. Fortunately, he ignored his instincts and obeyed almost at once.

Willa felt relief course through her again. They could do this. She could do this. Her gaze slid up the cliff and she spotted the dark shadow of a man standing there. He was surveying the river, but she didn't think he could see them. If he could, she was sure he would be pointing his bow at them. Still, Willa immediately stopped fighting the current, allowing it to carry them downriver and away from him.

They traveled a good distance like that before Willa judged that they had gone far enough; then she cut toward shore at a wide angle so she would waste as little energy as possible struggling against the current. It was still a wearying battle as she dragged him inch by inch toward the riverside. Hugh was trying to assist by kicking his legs, but he was less than helpful, especially since he was kicking her with every other move. She nearly ordered him to stop, but decided against it. This would be hard enough on him without taking away any small illusion he might have of aiding their escape. Willa was very aware that her husband felt he'd failed her several times since their marriage. His male pride needed no further battering.

"Are you alright? If you are tiring, let me go. Save yourself," Hugh said, and suddenly Willa realized that she *was* tiring. Her muscles were beginning to ache and she'd unconsciously slowed her efforts. She was not going to let him go, however.

Willa twisted her head around to see that they had covered perhaps half the distance to the riverside. They should have gotten farther than that, but then she realized that the current had grown swifter. The river must be shallower here. She let one foot drop, hoping to find the riverbed, but it hadn't gotten that shallow. Gritting her teeth, Willa renewed her efforts, grateful for the weeks of training that had strengthened her muscles and taught her to continue through the pain. She did the same thing she'd learned to do on the practice field; Willa ignored the pain and counted her strokes to distract herself. The trick worked. Still, when her heel suddenly brushed solid ground an eternity later, she could have sobbed with relief.

Willa immediately let both legs drop and floundered briefly as she tried to gain her footing. Apparently thinking her strength had given out, Hugh began to struggle, trying to catch at her and hold her above water even as he was sinking. Then his own feet hit the riverbed and she heard him mutter, "Thank God," as he stood and helped her to her feet in the water. The current was strong here and Willa was so exhausted, she needed his assistance in stumbling to shore.

The moment they were out of the grasping water, Willa collapsed to her knees on the ground. Hugh knelt beside her, concern on his face.

"Are you alright?" he asked, hugging her close as she began to shiver. She felt his hands begin to chafe her skin, trying to warm her. Hugh rubbed her arms vigorously, then her legs, then started on her back and sides. Willa's muscles began to relax and some of the chill left her. They were safe. They had escaped their pursuer and the river. Nothing else mattered. Not her exhaustion, not the cold, not her nakedness—

She pulled away from him and sat upright with a squawk.

"What is it?" Hugh asked, glancing swiftly around with alarm.

"I am naked!" Willa cried.

Hugh relaxed, a grin covering his face as his chafing slowed to a more caressing movement. "Aye. That you are, my lady wife. I rather like you this way."

Willa rolled her eyes and clucked her tongue impatiently as she struggled to her feet. Leave it to a man to see this calamity as a benefit. He was not the one who had to return to camp naked as the day he was born!

Hugh stood beside her, his lascivious expression fading to concern. "Mayhap you should rest awhile longer. You strained yourself to save us."

"*We* saved us," Willa told him firmly and struck out in the general direction she thought would lead them back to camp.

"*You* saved us," Hugh corrected, not sounding too pleased to say so.

"Nay," Willa insisted, batting at the branches that tried to scrape her tender flesh as she struggled through them. "We saved us. You saved us first, then I saved us. We saved us."

"How did I save us?" he asked with amazement, reaching past her to grab at a branch and push it out of her way.

"You saved us in the woods by detecting the

presence of our attacker and then shielding me with your body as we ran."

Hugh snorted at that and reached past her to remove another branch from her path. "That was hardly saving us. You could have run through the woods alone."

"But I did not. I did not even realize there was a problem and would not have on my own. I would have sat there all unsuspecting, like a fat pheasant for him to shoot." She grimaced at the idea. "I can imagine my epitaph now. 'Here lies Willa Dulonget, shot through the heart whilst draining the dragon.' Dear God, the mourners would be giggling into their sleeves."

She heard what sounded suspiciously like a snort of laughter from Hugh; then he cleared his throat and asked, "Er . . . where did you hear that term?"

"Baldulf," Willa told him, then cursed and paused to rub her foot. She'd stepped on something sharp. Releasing her foot as the pain eased, she started to walk again and explained, "He used it all the time. When I was young, I thought he was really going to drain a dragon, though I was not sure how you would drain one, and of what, exactly. I was curious to find out though, but Eada caught me sneaking out to try to see the dragon and had to explain that 'twas not what I thought."

"Hmm." He pushed another branch out of her way. "Apparently, she did not do a very good job in the explaining."

"What do you mean?" she asked indignantly.
"Of course she did."

"Nay. She didn't. Else you would not have just
used it."

Willa stopped walking to turn on him, hands
on hips. "Why?"

"You haven't a dragon to drain."

She blinked in confusion at his words, then her
gaze dropped to his braies and her eyes went
wide as she understood. "Oh."

"Aye. Oh." Hugh laughed then scooped her up
into his arms when she stepped on something
else and paused to rub her foot again. Willa began
to protest, but he merely shook his head. "Hush.
You got us out of the water. I shall get us back to
camp. Just rest."

After hesitating, Willa leaned her head against
his chest and gave in. She was warmer in his arms
and she did not have the trouble of stepping on
things. Why fuss?

They fell into a companionable silence as he
carried her. Willa would have spoken but did not
wish to tax him by making him talk while carting
her. Eventually, her eyes began to droop and she
yawned. Before she was even aware of it creeping
up on her, sleep had claimed her.

Willa wasn't sure how long she'd slept when
she next open her eyes. Hugh was still walking
with her in his arms, but the night seemed lighter.
Morning was coming.

"How far—" she began, but he hushed her and
suddenly slowed. Willa tensed in his arms.

After several moments of silence had passed, she could stand it no longer and asked in an anxious whisper, "What is it? Did you hear or see something?"

"Aye. I think the men are coming. The guard must have heard my shout. They have sent a search party." He frowned down at her, then around at the surrounding bushes. He started toward the bushes on their right, then paused. He was obviously hesitant to leave her there, but equally displeased by the idea of the men seeing her naked as she was.

"Cover yourself with your hair," he suggested at last. Willa immediately began pulling her damp hair around and arranging it over her breasts and stomach. Unfortunately, it wasn't as long as it used to be. The fire at the cottage had singed a good length of it and Eada had had to cut it off at waist level. It left her bare from the waist down, but Hugh shifted his hold so that his right arm was under her bottom. He tilted her up so that her front was toward him. All that would be seen was some of her derriere. That was mortifying enough.

"Could you not leave me here and fetch me back a gown?" she asked hopefully, but wasn't surprised when he shook his head.

"Our attacker failed. He has proven persistent. I will not leave you unprotected."

Willa's shoulders sagged with resignation. She buried her face against his chest as a call rang out through the trees and Hugh shouted back. There was an immediate flurry of activity and Willa

guessed the men had broken into a run. She then
heard what sounded like several people crashing
into the clearing. The men must have stopped
dead at the sight of them, for there was an abrupt
silence and Willa could almost feel several pairs
of eyes on her. She was suddenly grateful that it
wasn't full light, for she was sure she was blushing all the way down to her bare toes.

"Jesu!" She thought that was Lucan. The barely
breathed expletive seemed to act as a cue to everyone. Suddenly, there was rustling all around them,
and the snapping of twigs as the men drew near.

Willa felt warm cloth being draped over her
and blinked her eyes open. She turned to see that
it had indeed been Lucan she'd heard. He'd removed his doublet and was even now laying it
over her waist and hips. Even as she opened her
mouth to thank him, she saw that Jollivet was
there as well, and was shucking his own doublet.
He rushed forward to drape it over her upper
body. Baldulf was right behind him with his own
doublet. It went over her legs. Even as he stepped
away another man was stepping forward to add
to her covering.

Willa peered around in amazement. There were
at least six more men lining up to cover her nakedness. Of course, she wasn't naked anymore. In fact,
as garment after garment was piled on top of her,
Willa found herself with a new problem. She was
growing exceedingly warm, but found she did
not have the heart to reject a one of their offerings.
They all looked so solemn as they buried her under

the mountain of clothing, one would think she was dead. So Willa suffered the now uncomfortable heat and murmured her thanks, grateful when Hugh grunted and started forward again.

She listened idly as Lucan verified that the guard had heard his shout, roused the others and hurried out in search of them with torches. Lucan had found the arrow in the tree and Baldulf had found her gown on the cliff. They had deduced what had happened and started to follow the river in search of them.

As the men spoke, Willa had a sudden realization. Her husband spoke differently around the men than he did when alone with her. Around the men he mostly grunted and nodded and made short one- or two-word comments. When alone with her, he often spoke in full sentences. Hugh also tended to walk a little taller, brace his shoulders so they looked wider, and kept a much sterner expression around the men than he bothered with when they were alone.

She pondered these oddities all the way back to camp, and was still pondering them when Eada rushed forward to greet them.

"Are ye alright?" The woman asked anxiously, following Hugh as he carried Willa to their tent.

"Aye." Willa smiled at her over Hugh's shoulder. Then Hugh stepped into the tent.

"Let me see her," Eada ordered, waving him out of the way the moment he'd set her on their makeshift bed.

Willa cast her husband a sympathetic look as he

moved out of the way. His expression was disgruntled and she knew he found it hard to put up with Eada's bossiness at times.

" 'Tis a chill night for a swim," Eada commented as she stripped away doublet after doublet, handing each one to Hugh.

Willa merely grimaced, then released a breath of relief as the last of the garments came away. Eada began to examine her for injuries. "I am fine."

" 'Tis not you I am worried about," Eada said distractedly. " 'Tis the babes."

"Babes!" She and Hugh cried the word as one. Willa sat up abruptly on the furs, while Hugh dropped to sit on them, the doublets slipping from his hands. Eada rolled her eyes at their reaction.

"Well, I told ye he would plant twins in ye the first time he bedded ye," she said with exasperation.

"Oh . . . aye. You did . . . I had forgotten." Her gaze slid to Hugh and she saw that he'd quite forgotten, too. He looked about as stunned as she felt.

"I think they're alright." Eada straightened. "Ye must be more careful, though."

"She will be," Hugh said staunchly, and Willa immediately felt concern grip her. She had a feeling his idea of careful and hers might clash. He was looking rather stern again . . . and there wasn't a single man there to see it.

Willa opened her eyes and sat upright. After Eada had declared her alright, Hugh had suggested she rest. He'd then stood at the flap of the tent to give his orders to his men before returning inside.

Willa had just managed to make herself comfortable when he'd joined her in their makeshift bed and dragged her to his side. She'd been a tad annoyed as he arranged her like a rag doll half atop him, but had pushed the feeling away, deciding that his protectiveness was rather sweet, until he'd shoved her head against his chest and ordered, "Sleep."

"Sleep."

Willa shook her head, sure for a moment that she was imagining that voice. Her memory was playing tricks with her.

"Sleep," Hugh repeated, this time grabbing her arm to tug her back onto his chest. He pressed her head down as he had before and lay still.

Willa pursed her lips, irritation running through her. She started to say that she was not tired, then changed it to, "I need to drain the dragon that is not a dragon."

"Agai—" He cut the complaint off and sat up, taking her with him. "Of course. The babes are probably bouncing on your bladder."

Willa grimaced at this description and pulled away from him to search for her gown. She dressed, then stood to await Hugh as he donned his belt.

Once he was finished, he took her arm and led her out of the tent. Willa had expected him to lead her into the bushes right away, so she was surprised when he paused and barked out, "Rufus, Albin, Kerrich and Enion!"

The four guards rushed forward.

"Come," was all he said. Then he walked Willa into the woods, followed by the four men. After several moments, he stopped and turned to the men. "Rufus, you, stand there. Albin, over here. Enion—"

"Husband," Willa said, interrupting his arrangement of the men in a square around the tree. A horrible suspicion was coming over her.

"Aye?" He appeared irritated with her interruption.

"What are you doing?"

"Stationing the men," he explained. Then he turned back to point to the third man. "Enion, right here, and Kerrich there. What is it, Willa?" he added as she tugged at his tunic to get his attention.

"The men. What—I mean, why are they here?"

"To help me guard you, of course."

He said it as if she must be daft not to have realized this. She had realized it, but had hoped she was wrong. She wasn't.

"Go ahead," he prompted when she merely stared at him.

"Go ahead?" she asked weakly. "You expect me to—With them—I—"

"Oh." He smacked himself on the forehead with the palm of his hand, apparently just realizing the problem. Then he ordered the men, "Turn your backs."

He waited until the four men had all pivoted so that they stood with their backs to each other as well as to the spot Hugh intended her to use. Then he nodded his satisfaction and glanced at her expectantly.

Willa released a whimpering sound. This im-

mediately elicited an alarmed expression from
Hugh. "What is the matter? Are you not feeling
well?" Willa closed her eyes and immediately felt
his hands clamp onto her wrists. "Willa?"

Her eyes popped open. They were blazing. "I
cannot water the dragon with them here."

"Drain the dragon," he corrected with a frown.

"What does it matter?" she exploded. "I haven't
a dragon to drain, but you know what I mean."

He released a put-upon sigh, as if *she* were the
one being unreasonable. "Willa."

"Do not 'Willa' me!" she snapped. "I am not doing it with them here!"

"Why?"

"Why?" She stared at him, wondering how
she'd neglected to notice that her husband was a
complete clodpole.

"Aye. Why? They will not see you," he pointed
out reasonably. But he was looking even more
concerned over her outburst than he had at her
whimpering.

Willa supposed she shouldn't be surprised. She
did try to be a dutiful wife, but there were just
some limits to these things. Or perhaps she was
growing comfortable enough with him to allow
her true nature to reign. Trying for calm, she said,
"They will hear me."

"Hear you?" he asked with a disbelieving laugh,
and Willa glared at him.

"Aye. They will hear me. That is enough to make
it impossible."

They were silent for a moment, Willa glaring at

him, Hugh appearing to chew the matter over. Then he cleared his throat, turned to the men and ordered, "Sing."

There was a brief silence; then each of the men turned to peer uncertainly at Hugh. He scowled at their disbelieving looks. "Aye. You heard me. Sing."

The men now glanced at each other, then back. One of them—Willa believed it was the fellow named Kerrich—cleared his throat and asked, "What should we sing, my lord?"

"I do not care. Just sing," Hugh said with exasperation, then added, "As loudly as you can."

There was another moment of silence. Then Kerrich began to sing in a rusty baritone. Willa caught the first few words of what sounded like a rather ribald song, and then Rufus began something entirely different. Apparently, he didn't know that song. Enion and Albin were quick to follow, singing two entirely different songs from the first two. The woods were polluted with four different songs in four different keys, the noise becoming a horrible clashing clangor.

"There!" Hugh shouted with satisfaction. "Now they will not hear you."

Willa gaped at him briefly, then stomped around him and started back toward camp. Hugh grabbed her arm to stop her. "I thought you had to drain the dragon?"

"I do. But I refuse to do so with four men standing guard. 'Twas embarrassing enough with just you," she shouted.

He frowned at this announcement, then yelled

back, "Willa, I have heard that being with child makes women unreasonable, but surely you realize that I cannot send the guards away? Not after what happened last time. You cannot wish to risk your life as well as our babies' simply to save some embarrassment?"

That made her pause. She stared at his resolute face for a moment. It was obvious he would not be moved on this matter. It seemed to her that her options were either to relieve herself in the center of the singing men, or hold it until they reached court. It was a two-day journey to court. It could be the following evening before she could relieve herself. Willa was incapable of waiting that long for a privy. Deciding that someone was going to pay for this, she stomped to the center of her four-point guard. Pausing, Willa glanced around at the backs facing her, then at Hugh, who nodded encouragingly.

As the awful clashing noise carried on, Willa tended to business and wished she were dead.

Chapter Twenty

Willa paced the length of the room and kicked the bed. She then paced to the other end and kicked at one of the two chairs in front of the fire before repeating the sequence.

They had reached court early that morning . . . after *four* days traveling to make a two-day journey. Muttering under her breath, Willa kicked at the bed twice this time as she paused before it. As she'd feared, Hugh's idea of being careful did not mesh with hers. Much to Willa's mortification, the incident in the woods with her singing guard had been repeated many times during the last two and a half days. On top of that humiliation, Hugh had insisted on traveling at a much slower pace "so as not to unsettle the babes." Willa had spent this much slower journey in the back of a cart because he was sure that "riding could not be good for the babes." He'd also overseen her meals, insisting she eat plentifully to "help the babes grow strong in her belly." Worse than that, though, was how he'd taken to hovering over her like a mother over a sick child, until Willa thought she might pull her hair out . . . or his.

Nay, she decided as her pacing took her to the bed again, worst of all was the fact that he'd sworn off touching her in a sexual manner, for fear of "jostling the babes while they may be sleeping." Aye. She missed that most of all. If the man could not tell her he loved her, the least he could do was bed her.

This time rather than kick the chair by the fire, she dropped unhappily to sit in it. They had been at court for barely an hour and already Hugh had been called to see the king. She supposed at this very moment, he was showing King John the letter from Papa Richard and telling him how her father, Tristan, was trying to kill her.

Willa stared at the fire in the fireplace with dissatisfaction. Hugh had determined that her complaints at his smothering behavior and her singing guard were merely the result of her being with child. That reasoning made it easy for him to discount her complaints, and Willa could just throttle him for it.

Why hadn't he declared his love for her? Not that Willa had told him of her feelings expecting a declaration in return, but it did seem that his offering one would have been the polite thing to do. It would have been nice. She was carrying his children, after all. She was his wife. Eada had said he would love her. She wanted him to love her. Why didn't he love her?

Her cantankerous thoughts were interrupted when the chamber door opened and a young maid entered. Willa eyed her with annoyance. After four days without peace, Willa had wished only to be alone on arriving here. The moment Hugh had left to speak to the king, she'd urged Eada to visit the market to see if there weren't some things here she couldn't easily get at Hillcrest. The older woman had not needed much prodding to abandon her.

"I was sent to see if there was anything you wished for, my lady?" The maid sounded sweet-natured, which merely annoyed Willa all the more.

"Nay." She knew she sounded surly, but could not help it. Willa felt surly. Which was unusual. She generally had the sunniest of dispositions. Perhaps being with child was affecting her after all, she thought, then quickly pushed the thought away.

"Well, if you are sure?"

The girl had half turned toward the door when Willa suddenly sat up and asked, "Do you know if Lord D'Orland has arrived yet?"

"Aye. He has." The maid smiled, pleased to be of some assistance. "He arrived yester morn. Do you know him?"

"Nay," Willa admitted unhappily; then her gaze sharpened on the girl. "Do you?"

"Oh, aye." The girl's smile widened. "He is one of King John's finest warriors."

"Is?" Willa asked curiously. By her calculations, her father must be nigh on sixty, at least. "Surely, he does not still ride into battle?"

"Aye." The girl looked sad. "'Tis a broken heart that sends him constantly riding off to war."

"A broken heart?"

The maid nodded. "Everyone knows the tale. He loved his wife more than life itself, but she died with their child some twenty years ago. He has sought out battle after battle ever since. Some say he hopes to die and join them, but God has not taken him yet." She shook her head mournfully. "When not at war, he is here more often than at D'Orland. They say he cannot bear the memories that fill his castle. He is a very kind man. All the servants are happy to wait on him."

"I see," Willa murmured, but the girl wasn't finished.

"One of the footmen told me that his squire claims he rarely sleeps. He says that every time he does, Lord D'Orland is troubled by nightmares that leave him thrashing and crying out for his late wife. He begs her to forgive him, though the squire knows not what he has to be forgiven for."

Willa knew, but remained silent until the girl said, "Well, if there is nothing else?"

"There is," Willa stood abruptly. "I will need your dress."

The girl's eyes widened in shock and she began to back away, but a quarter hour later Willa had talked Joanne—as Willa had learned was her name—out of the gown and into helping her.

"'Tisn't going to work," Joanne said mournfully as she helped Willa stack the last of several folded gowns in her arms. They made a nice bit of wall to hide behind.

"Aye. It will," Willa assured her. "You just say what I told you to say and stay behind the door. Are you ready?"

The girl nodded, but still looked doubtful as she followed Willa across the room. When they reached the door, Willa paused and took a deep breath. She was about to attempt to escape her singing quartet of guards.

Hugh had told the four men that they were not to let her out of their sight . . . ever. They had taken him at his word and followed her everywhere since that first embarrassing trip into the woods. The only place they had not followed her was into their tent, and that was only because Hugh had told them to stand point around the tent instead. Once they had arrived at court, Hugh had stationed them outside her chamber and she knew they were still there now. She wished to lose them for a little bit.

Releasing her breath, she opened her mouth and called out loudly. "They need a good washing! They got muddy on the journey here!"

"Aye, m'lady!" Joanne answered equally as loudly when Willa turned an expectant gaze to her.

"Here, let me get the door for you!" Willa shouted at the door and nodded encouragingly at Joanne. She then ducked her head and lifted the stack of gowns in an effort to block her face as the girl moved forward. The moment the door was opened, Willa sailed through and scampered down the hall at a near run as she heard it close behind her. She didn't dare look back to see if the guards had noticed anything amiss, but turned the first corner she came to with a breath of relief. Stopping at the first niche she came across, Willa set the gowns down, then continued on her way.

Joanne had given her instructions on how to find Tristan D'Orland's chamber. Willa followed them now, her hand at her waist to settle her suddenly nervous stomach. She wasn't at all sure she was doing the right thing in going to meet her father. There was a possibility that the man wanted her dead. However, the tortured individual Joanne had described did not match the cold-blooded killer who had tried so often to end her life. Willa had to see for herself just what kind of man her father was.

Raucous laughter made Willa glance around as two men came out of a room and moved down the hall ahead of her. She slowed her steps so as not to catch up to them, then turned down the next corridor. This was where Tristan D'Orland's chamber was. Joanne had said it was the third door on the left. Willa counted them out. Stopping at the third door, she pressed an ear to it and listened. There was no sound from inside. She almost used that as an excuse to turn and walk away, but caught herself before she could. It was cowardice that was urging her to do so, and she knew it.

Taking a deep breath, she raised a hand to knock, then simply opened the door instead and slid into the room. At first, she thought the chamber was empty. There was no one in the chairs by the fire, nor on the bed. Then a movement drew her gaze to the window as the man standing there turned slowly to peer at her.

He wasn't what Willa had expected. Her father was about the same age as Lord Richard would have been had he still lived. But Lord Richard had spent the last decade leaving war to younger men. His body had reflected that, his muscles atrophying and a paunch developing. He'd looked his age. This man did not. Though his hair was pure white, without a hint of the fiery red-blond coloring he'd passed on to his daughter, Tristan D'Orland was as strong and fit as a man twenty years younger. He was tall, with broad shoulders and muscular arms. He had the posture and bearing of a warrior. His eyes were the same blue-gray as Willa's, sharp and startling in his tanned face. All in all, he looked like what he was: a warrior.

"I did not send for a maid. What—" He paused, his eyes sharpening on her. Several moments passed in silence as he examined her from head to toe. When he finally spoke, his voice had lost much of its strength. "What is your name, girl?"

"Willa." Several moments passed as she awaited some reaction. Then she recalled that the name would mean nothing to him. Lord Hillcrest had named her. She left the door open and stepped further into the room as she said, "The man who raised me named me that because I was willed to him. My mother asked him on her death bed to tend me and keep me safe. She feared my true father might kill me, did he know I lived."

"Your true father?" he echoed weakly.

"Aye." Willa could not bear to see the mingled

hope and fear on his face and turned, moving in the direction of the fire. "They say I took his coloring and have his eyes, but that I look most like my mother."

"Juliana," she heard him breathe.

Willa fought the urge to look at him and forced herself to continue toward the fireplace as she said, "They say he loved my mother dearly, but that he was terribly jealous. She had a dear friend who was like a brother to her, but my father feared there was something more to their friendship. His jealousy made him unbearable. He began to drink and that made things worse. Nothing she said could convince him that she loved only him and that there was nothing between her and her friend. They say—"

A crash made Willa glance toward him warily. He'd been holding his sword in his hand when she entered, as if he'd been polishing it and had carried it with him to look out the window. The sword now lay on the floor amongst a basketful of apples that had been sitting on a chest beside him. Either he'd moved and banged the chest, or he'd dropped the sword and it had toppled the fruit. Whatever the case, he now knelt trying to collect the spilled fruit. However, he could not seem to hold onto the red globes. Every time he picked up more than one, the first apple slid from his hand.

Willa hesitated, then moved to his side and knelt to help. They worked in silence, replacing the fruit in the basket, but she could feel his glance roving over her as they worked. Once all the apples had been gathered and returned to the basket, Willa picked it up and stood.

Lord D'Orland stood as well, grabbing at her hand when she turned to set the basket back on the chest. The move startled her and the basket tipped, sending the fruit back to the floor. Willa started to bend to again collect them, but he held her in place.

"Forget the apples. Tell me this man's name. The one who named and raised you and kept you from your father," he ordered harshly.

Willa met his gaze and said solemnly, "I think you know."

"Tell me," he insisted.

"Lord Richard Hill—"

"Hillcrest," he finished. It sounded like a curse. His eyes closed briefly in pain and Willa was alarmed to see him sway slightly. Then his eyes opened again. "The bastard stole you from me. All these years and he—"

"He saved me from you," Willa said quietly. "He knew you would kill me did you know of my existence."

"What kind of monster has he painted me to be!" Lord D'Orland cried. "I would never harm my own child. Nor anyone else's, for that matter."

"The night my mother fled you, were you not about to storm into your chamber to shake me loose from her belly because you thought me another man's child?"

"Nay! Dear God, no!"

Willa frowned at this denial, then asked uncertainly, "You *were* yelling and furious?"

"Aye. I was," he admitted. "Garrod had just told me that Juliana's maid had told him she planned to leave me to go to her Thomas. Aye, I bellowed. I was furious that she would think to leave me. I was going to stop her. But she had already sneaked out of our room when I got there." His face twisted with remorse. "I was too late. She had already fled to be with her lover. If I had just been a bit quicker, perhaps she would still live. Perhaps—"

"She did not flee you to be with Thomas. She did not love Thomas; she loved you. My mother fled because her maid had told her that you planned to rid her of me. That you felt 'twas better to be rid of me with my uncertain parentage, and beget another babe as heir."

"Nay!" He stumbled back a step, horror clear on his face. "I would never—Why would her maid—? How could Juliana believe that of me?"

"How could you believe she would be unfaithful to you?" Willa countered and he sank wearily to sit on the chest.

"I—she was beautiful." He shook his head helplessly. "Her laughter was like birdsong. Her smile made me heart-sore. I knew every man must love her on sight. Juliana, however, never seemed to notice the men chasing after her. Except for Thomas." His expression darkened with displeasure. "With Thomas she could talk and laugh for hours. They spoke of things that had happened long ere she and I had even spoken to each other. I felt unnecessary whenever he was around, like a fifth wheel on a cart. I tried not to let it bother me, but he came so often and always seemed to be there. He was like a constant canker on my arse."

Willa winced at his choice of words. They made her think of Hugh and how angry he was going to be when he found out about her slipping from her guard to visit the man he believed was trying to kill her.

Lord D'Orland shifted impatiently, drawing her attention again. "Garrod tried to soothe my suspicions. However, the very fact that he had noticed when I had not voiced my fears aloud told me that he found their friendship suspicious as well."

"Thomas told Papa—Lord Richard," Willa corrected quickly, a twinge of guilt singing through her when he winced at the loving term. "Thomas told his father that my mother loved you. Lord Richard said that Thomas and my mother were close from the time they both arrived at Claymorgan as children. He said there was nothing but friendship between them."

Lord D'Orland stared at her, his gaze moving over her features. There was deep pain in his eyes, and a bit of wonder, too. He stood and took a step toward her. He cupped her chin and he marveled, "You look so like her. If not for your coloring, I would think you were her ghost come to haunt me for being such a fool." His eyes met hers and he smiled faintly. "Do you know why I chose your mother to wed?"

Willa shook her head the tiniest bit.

"I saw your mother for the first time when she was but six. She accompanied her parents to a tourney in which I was participating. Juliana was a sweet little thing. Even then, she showed promise of being a beauty, but that was not what drew me to her. I had a page at the time, a skinny lad her own age. He was new and nervous, with the unfortunate habit of wetting himself whenever I yelled at him. She and her parents happened to be walking past my tent on one such occasion. I yelled, he wet himself as usual, and I fear I was less than sympathetic. I berated him for behaving like a babe. Your mother stopped. Her parents continued walking, unaware she was no longer with them. She simply stood there and glared at me until I took notice of her. When I finally scowled at her, she berated me for being so *mean*."

His face lit affectionately at the memory. "She was not the least bit afraid of me and berated me with a passion, championing my page. Then she patted the boy on the shoulder, told him not to be afraid and hurried off after her parents. She had such heart." His eyes filled with tears. "I was a fierce and powerful warrior. Grown men trembled in my presence, yet this little snippet of a lass had the mettle to stand up to me. I found myself watching her throughout the tourney. At every turn, I saw signs of the courageous, honorable and loving woman she would be. I approached her father about a match and agreed to claim her two weeks after her sixteenth birthday. And I did." His hand slipped away from Willa's chin. His voice was bitter when he said, "Then I destroyed her with my jealousy."

Willa felt her heart squeeze at his pain and self-recrimination. She knew he'd suffered them these twenty years. "I think, my lord, that you had aid in forgetting your honor. It seems to me 'twas encouraged."

"Mayhap. But 'tis no excuse," he said. His next words told her that he misunderstood the aid she was referring to. "I do not understand what her maid hoped to gain. Why did she lie to us both that day? Well . . . to Juliana and Garrod," he corrected.

Willa bit her lip, wondering how to explain that it had not been the maid she was referring to. Then her father suddenly brightened. "Garrod! I can hardly wait to tell him I have found you again. He shall be most pleased at this reunion."

"I somehow do not think so," Willa disagreed.

"Oh aye, he will," Tristan D'Orland assured her. "The day your mother died, all I could think of at first was tending to Juliana. But as we neared my keep I began to think that I should bury you with your mother. Then the fact that Hillcrest had not offered your body made me pause. I began to think that perhaps you were not dead as he'd claimed. When I spoke these thoughts aloud to Garrod, he volunteered to find out for sure one way or the other. He stayed near Claymorgan for weeks, asking questions and searching for news of your existence. Everything he learned, however, seemed to indicate that you were, indeed, dead. He returned quite distressed. I think he had imagined returning triumphant with you in his arms. He was quite distressed at your loss."

Willa turned away, hating to disillusion him. "About Garrod—"

"Is this not a touching scene?"

Willa turned sharply at those sarcastic words and found herself staring at a tall, red-haired man with a most unpleasant face. Her father confirmed his identity when he said, "There you are, Garrod. We were just talking about you."

"I am sure you were. I am sure little Willa could hardly wait to rush to your side to tell you tales." A cynical smile curved his lips. He closed the door and moved to the center of the room. "You have proven to be something of a thorn in my side all these years, Willa," he added, his cold eyes moving over her. "Aye. You are just as lovely as Juliana was. 'Tis obvious she was your mother. 'Tis equally obvious who your father is, of course."

Willa took a wary step closer to her father. She watched Garrod—a man she was sure had tried to kill her many times over—with the wariness and respect she would offer an adder.

"I was really hoping to kill you before you got here, thereby avoiding the necessity of murdering my own uncle," he announced, then gave an indifferent shrug. "However, perhaps this is for the best. Uncle Tristan has been taking his time about dying. I would have aided him in the endeavor but he never gave me the opportunity. If he was not off at war, he was here at court while I was stuck at the keep, running things. It made creating a believable accident difficult, I can tell you. I consoled myself with the thought that surely he would be killed in battle soon. From all accounts, he took plenty of foolhardy risks, but he has the damnedest luck. You appear to have inherited that, along with his coloring. You have managed to escape my every attempt."

"Garrod? What nonsense are you spewing?" her father asked in confusion. He was looking quite shaken.

"He is speaking of the fact that he has been trying to kill me ever since my birth," Willa told him quietly.

"What?" Tristan D'Orland turned to her with horror, and Willa nodded.

"Garrod did not return to Claymorgan to find proof of my existence, but to try to end it," she explained. "He lied when he said that everything he learned pointed to my having been born dead. He simply wished I had, and attempted to be sure I was before we could meet and you could see for yourself that I bore your coloring and was your daughter. When he was supposed to be seeking me out, he was actually sneaking into Claymorgan and smothering my wet-nurse's child. Ten years later, he broke the neck of my best friend, who had made the mistake of wearing my gown. Most recently, he has hired one man to kill me whom my husband dispatched, another whom his cousin dispatched, and then resorted to attempting the task himself. He chased my husband and me off a cliff into the river. Fortunately, we were able to make it ashore."

"Is this true?" Lord D'Orland asked his nephew sharply.

"Aye. 'Tis true. She has been a most troublesome wench. Is it not awful when women do not die as they should? Now her mother," he taunted,

"I did not even think of killing her. I merely wished her gone ere she could produce a squalling brat for you. I worked at rousing your jealousy to gain that end. Juliana, however, did me the great favor of dying. Your wife was truly a good woman, uncle. Your daughter, however, appears to have inherited your cussedly stubborn nature."

Lord D'Orland shook his head. "But you tried to convince me that Juliana was true to me. You were constantly reassuring me that you believed her faithful."

"And every time I did, it strengthened and encouraged your own doubts," Garrod pointed out with amusement. Then he took on an earnest expression and said, "I realize it looks bad, my lord. Thomas is ever here spending time alone with Juliana, but I am sure she would never dishonor you. They are close, 'tis true, but I am sure friendship is as far as it goes." His words ended on a masterfully doubtful note and Willa's father blanched as he recognized how he'd been manipulated.

"She was true to me," he said faintly.

"Of course she was," Garrod said mockingly. "Juliana loved you. Even I could see that. She cared for Thomas as a brother, nothing more. You were the only one she wished in her bed."

Garrod shook his head with disgust. "Dear Lord, I played you all like a brilliant game of chess. You were jealous, so I nurtured that jealousy. She was afraid of your jealous tempers, especially when you drank. I encouraged her fears with brilliant tales of the violence you were known to wreak while drinking. I made them up on the spot and amazed even myself with some of them." He laughed.

"I even manipulated Thomas. I befriended him and encouraged him to visit often and long. Then I frowned over the matter with you, commenting that he was taking advantage of your hospitality and I was sure it meant nothing that he spent so much time with Juliana." Garrod shook his head. "Then, that last night, I told Juliana's maid to tell her that you planned to force the babe from her belly. And I told *you* that her maid had warned me Juliana planned to leave you." He gave a short impressed whistle at his own brilliance. "It worked better than I had hoped. She fled, starting the early labor that led to her death at Claymorgan. Everything would have been perfect—" his gaze turned to Willa—"except that you lived."

Displeasure crossed his face. "I did try to rectify that one small flaw. Many times. But, like your father—who survives battle unscathed while all those about him are slaughtered—you appear to have the devil's own luck."

"Or perhaps you are simply inept," Willa suggested.

Garrod was bristling over that inflammatory comment when Lord D'Orland asked, "Why? After all I did for you, Garrod. Why?"

She glanced at her father and felt her pity stir at his hurt bewilderment.

"All you did for me?" Garrod sounded furious and Willa turned a wary gaze back to him. His hands were fisted with fury. "You have done nothing for me! Nothing! I am your steward. No better than a lackey! I have made your estate prosperous. I defend it, collect rents owed . . . and for what? A place to eat and sleep and a couple of coins! All those years while you earned your accolades on the battlefield, I worked for you. I had hopes, dreams of one day being master. And why not? You had not married and produced an heir. I thought surely you meant to leave me all on your death." His mouth tightened and he spoke through gritted teeth. "You never mentioned that you had made a match. Then, all of a sudden you returned and announced 'twas time to go claim your bride."

He struck an arrogant pose and mimicked her father. "Good day, Garrod. How are things? I am off to claim my bride now. I shall be staying here and raising a family."

Willa stiffened nervously as he withdrew his sword from its sheath in one furious jerk. Gripping it tightly in hand, he went on, "One day I was working hard, imagining the estate soon to be my own. The next you announced you were marrying and hoping to raise a son to take your place. I could have struck you dead on the spot! But I knew I would gain naught that way. I needed to be more clever. And I was."

"Not clever enough," Willa pointed out, aware that her father was inching slowly in front of her. He was preparing to protect her even though he was weaponless and she felt a stabbing pain in her heart at the thought of yet another person dying for her. Her gaze dropped to the floor. His sword still lay at their feet where he'd dropped it. If she could just reach it. . . .

"What do you intend to do now?" her father asked, inching another step in front of Willa. "You cannot think killing us will gain you anything."

"Of course it will, you stupid old man! It will keep my neck out of the noose. 'Twill also give me your estate."

"Do not be ridiculous, Garrod," Lord D'Orland snapped. "You cannot succeed at this madness."

Garrod suddenly went calm and smiled. Willa found that more frightening than his anger.

"Time will tell. I am thinking that perhaps just the sight of Willa enraged you," he suggested mildly. "Perhaps your hatred and jealousy were transferred from your poor dead wife to her. Perhaps in your senility, you even mistook her for your Juliana. You killed her. Then in your mad grief, you killed yourself." He nodded. "Aye. That should work. After all, I have already laid the groundwork by whispering to the king that you may not be quite right in the head. Now . . ." He raised his sword. "I will try to make this quick out of my past affection for you, uncle."

Everything happened in a blur after that. Lord D'Orland gave up his inching and lunged protectively in front of her as Garrod charged. Willa saw her father brace himself for the coming blow as she bent quickly to retrieve his fallen sword. She managed to straighten and rush around him, lifting the sword just in time to parry that blow. Garrod was strong, however. Willa cried out in pain

as her arms vibrated with the impact. She felt
them begin to give way, and the swords moved
toward her. Then her father's arms came around
her. His hands grabbed the hilt above her own,
adding his strength to the defense. The three of
them stood locked in combat for a moment, then
the door crashed open. A bellow filled the room.

Willa felt relief course through her as she
peered over Garrod's shoulder to see her husband
advancing toward them. He looked extremely angry and Willa felt a brief moment of pity for Garrod. Then Garrod tore his sword free and turned
to face a charging Hugh. He started to raise his
weapon, but was too slow. Hugh felled him before
his sword was fully raised.

Her husband glared down at the man whose
life blood was coloring the rushes, then turned
that glare on Willa and her father.

Willa had never been happier to see him. Even
if he hadn't declared his love for her. Releasing
the sword, she slid out from under her father's
arms and threw herself at Hugh.

"Husband!" she cried happily. Lifting herself on
tiptoe, she began to press kisses across his rigid
face. When he continued to stand still and stern-
faced, she pulled back to see that he was staring at
her father with wary uncertainty. "What is it? Oh,"
she said. "Hugh, this is my father. He had no idea
what Garrod was doing. He did not wish me dead.
Father, this is my husband, Hugh."

She beamed at the older man as he lowered the
weapon they had used to fend off Garrod's attack,

then tilted her head in question at his expression. Lord D'Orland was staring at her with a bemused expression.

"You saved my life," he said with awe.

Willa felt herself blush, but shook her head. "Nay. My husband saved us both."

"Aye. But you saved me first," her father insisted.

"Well, I did try, but he was quite strong." She frowned, then turned to Hugh. "I do believe that Lucan has not been using his full strength at practice. I was unable to parry Garrod's blow. Father had to save us by adding his strength."

"Nay, *you* saved *me,*" her father persisted.

"You saved me, too," Willa countered. "And Hugh saved us both."

"But you saved me first," he argued.

"But Hugh saved us *all* in the end."

"Dear God! Do stop arguing about who saved whom and shut up!"

Willa stiffened at that order and turned a scowl on the rude man who had spoken. He stood in the open door to the room, a crowd of gawking onlookers behind him. The man was dressed in the finest clothes she'd ever seen. Willa assumed this meant he held a high position at court. She decided his manners, however, did not reflect his position. She turned to Hugh and poked him in the stomach.

"Are you going to let this rude man speak to your wife this way?" she demanded.

Her husband's eyes widened in alarm. "Er . . . Willa . . . this is . . . er . . . King John."

"Oh." Her expression turned from outrage to

disgruntlement. "Well, I suppose he is allowed to be rude then, but really, 'tis not well done of him."

Hugh closed his eyes briefly as the king's narrowed on her. Drawing himself up, King John spoke with exaggerated patience. "You have obviously been through a harrowing experience, Lady Hillcrest, so I will forgive that impertinence. Hugh, see to your wife. Then I wish you and Lord D'Orland to come and explain this matter to me. I will have it resolved today."

"'Tis—" Hugh's hand over her mouth brought Willa's words to a halt. He smiled and nodded at King John. The royal's lips twitched with amusement; then he turned on his heel and left the room. The crowd of onlookers made way for him, then followed him away.

"I was only going to say that the matter *is* resolved," Willa explained when Hugh took his hand away.

Hugh gave a half laugh, then leaned his forehead against hers. "Wife?"

"Aye?" she asked warily.

"I love you."

Willa went still at that proclamation and pulled back so that she could see his face. "You do?"

"Aye. You drive me mad at times and are the most troublesome bundle I have ever come across, but—God save me—I love you."

"Oh, Hugh," Willa breathed, then beamed. "I love you, too."

Throwing her arms around him, she sought his mouth with her own in a kiss that soon turned passionate. Willa had just become aware of his hand drifting toward her breast when a throat clearing reminded her of her father's presence. Blushing furiously, she broke the kiss at once.

"Er . . . perhaps we should see Willa to your chamber and take ourselves off to meet with the king," he suggested to Hugh. "King John is not the most patient of men."

Chapter Twenty-one

"What are you doing? You cannot cross her legs like that. Uncross them. She must push now. Push, Willa," her father instructed. Tristan D'Orland's hair was a wild mass about his head and he wore only a robe.

Willa's father had visited Hillcrest often since their reunion at court. He and Hugh had become good friends, enjoying the hunt and sharing old war stories together. Willa had also grown close to him. She'd even begun to use the affectionate term Papa with him. Richard Hillcrest was still the father of her heart, but her heart had room for two papas.

"Do not push!" Hugh bellowed as Willa grunted and sat up in the bed. He'd taken the linen and furs with him on leaping out of bed, leaving her lying there in only her shift. Now he replaced the linen and ordered, "Wait for Eada. She will—"

"You cannot tell her to wait!" Lord D'Orland snapped. "The babe is ready to come now."

"Babies." Willa panted out the reminder and watched with exasperation as both men blanched.

The first pain had struck while she slept. She had woken with a scream. The sound had roused Hugh at once, and drawn her father from his bed. Lord D'Orland had rushed into the room before Hugh had even managed to find and don his braies. Now the two men were arguing over how things should proceed. Or at least they had been.

"Dear God. I forgot 'twas twins," Lord D'Orland breathed. "You did tell me but—Cross your legs, Willa, and wait for Eada," he ordered firmly. When she didn't move to do so, he stepped forward, clasped her ankles through the linen and crossed them for her. It seemed the great warrior, Tristan D'Orland, felt capable of managing the birth of one babe, but quailed at the thought of two.

Willa started to smile with amusement, but the expression died as her body cramped again. Closing her eyes tightly, she grimaced in agony.

"Does it hurt much?" Hugh asked with concern.

Willa's eyes popped open and her husband became the target of a pain-induced fury. "Aye, husband," she said through gritted teeth. "Shall I show you how it hurts?"

"Ah . . . no." Hugh moved warily out of reach as she reached toward his groin.

"Do not upset her, Hugh. You are upsetting her." Lord D'Orland frowned at his son-in-law, then managed an encouraging smile for his daughter. "Do try to relax, daughter. Eada should arrive shortly." He scowled toward the door fretfully. "Where *is* the woman?"

"Probably asleep in her bed since no one has bothered to fetch her," Willa pointed out.

Hugh and her father straightened at once, horror on their faces as they realized she was right.

"What the devil is all the racket in here?" Jollivet stumbled sleepily through the open door and found himself the cynosure of three pairs of eyes.

"Eada!" Willa's father barked. "We need Eada!"

That made Hugh's cousin pause, his sleepiness disappearing at once. "Is it the babes?"

"Aye, 'tis the babes," Hugh snapped. "Go fetch Eada!"

The man turned on his heel, nearly running into Lucan as he appeared in the hall behind him. Hugh's friend watched Jollivet rush off, then wandered into the room, stifling a yawn.

"Where is he off to in such a hurry?" Lucan asked.

"To fetch Eada. The babes are coming."

Lucan's mouth closed with a snap, his gaze shooting to Willa. *"Now?"* he asked with alarm. "'Tis the middle of the night!"

"They do not seem to care, my lord," Willa said wearily, sagging where she lay as the latest pain ended. Closing her eyes, she tried to think whose brilliant idea it had been for the men to have a hunting party. Oh yes. Hers. Hugh had been driving her mad with his anxious hovering around her and she'd hoped to divert his attention. Instead, she was now the center of almost everyone's attention.

Not almost. Everyone's, she corrected as a rustle from the doorway drew her hopeful gaze to see Baldulf rushing in with Lord Wynekyn on his heels.

"Jollivet said the babes were coming," Baldulf said.

Lord Wynekyn rushed around the guard as both Hugh and her father gave unhappy nods. Uncle Luieus also had come for the hunt. Lord Richard's oldest and dearest friend had even begun to develop a friendship with Willa's father. They were of an age, and now that the matter of Tristan's trying to kill Willa had been resolved, the two men got along like a cottage on fire.

"Why are her legs crossed?" Lord Wynekyn cried. "The babes cannot get out like that!"

Rushing to the bed, he grabbed her ankles through the linen and uncrossed them. Then he seemed to realize what he was doing and flushed bright red. Releasing her ankles, he leapt away from the bed.

"There, that is better." He looked terribly embarrassed, then stepped forward to pat her foot through the linen. "I believe you are supposed to push."

"Do not push!" Hugh and Willa's father shouted as one.

"Of course, she must push!" Eada hurried into the room with Jollivet on her heels. "Out! All of you. This is no place for men."

Willa did not miss the fact that every last man was quick to abandon her now that Eada was there. She heaved out a relieved breath as the door closed behind them. "Men!"

"Aye." Eada removed the linen with which Hugh had covered her. "But they love you."

"Aye." Willa smiled as she watched the other woman putter about. There was not a doubt in her mind that every last man who had just left the room, plus the woman now preparing to help bring her babies into the world, loved her. Willa had much love now. A family to make up for all she'd lost. These new loved ones couldn't replace those who had died, but their presence had eased the ache of loss. Sometimes their love filled her up so that it felt as though her heart might burst with joy.

"What has you smiling?"

Willa glanced toward the door in surprise as Hugh closed it behind him and moved to the bed. "I thought you were going below with the others?"

"I would not leave you to travail on your own. Now, what were you smiling about?"

The smile bloomed on her face again. "I was just thinking how lucky I am, and that Eada was right . . . as usual."

Hugh looked disgruntled, but nodded. "Aye. She told me I would quickly come to love you and that we would enjoy happiness, many babies and a long life. I have the love and happiness and we have started on the babies." His hand moved to cover her stomach. "I only hope that she was correct about the long life, for 'twill take a lifetime to show you all the love I have for you."

"Oh, Hugh." Tears filled her eyes and Willa squeezed the hand holding hers. "That is the longest, sweetest speech I have ever heard you utter. Jollivet is rubbing off on you."

He blanched at the very thought. "Dear God, I hope not!"

Willa chuckled at his horror, knowing it was feigned. Then she raised his hand to her lips and kissed it. "I love you husband."

Hugh retrieved his hand, taking hers with it to press a kiss to her knuckles. "And I love you, wife."

HIGHLAND ROMANCE FROM
NEW YORK TIMES BESTSELLING AUTHOR

Lynsay Sands

Devil of the Highlands

978-0-06-134477-0

Cullen, Laird of Donnachaidh, must find a wife to
bear his sons to ensure the future of the clan. Evelinde
has agreed to marry him despite his reputation, for the
Devil of the Highlands inspires a heat within her
unlike anything she has ever known.

Taming the Highland Bride

978-0-06-134478-7

Alexander d'Aumesbery is desperate to convince the
beautiful and brazen Merry Stewart that he's a well-
mannered gentleman who's nothing like the members
of her roguish clan. But beneath it all beats a heart as
intense and uncontrollable as hers.

The Hellion and the Highlander

978-0-06-134479-4

When the flame-haired Lady Averill Mortagne braves
an unexpected danger at Highland warrior Kade
Stewart's side, she proves that her heart is as fiery
as her hair. And he realizes that submitting to their
scorching passion would be heaven indeed.